Queer Metaphorosis

Queer Metaphorosis

speculative stories
by LGBTQIA+ authors

Metaphorosis Library Collection

edited by
B. Morris Allen

ISSN: 2573-136X (online)
ISBN: 978-1-64076-295-4 (e-book)
ISBN: 978-1-64076-296-1 (paperback)
ISBN: 978-1-64076-297-8 (hardcover)

from
Metaphorosis Publishing

Neskowin

Contents

From the Editor

The *Metaphorosis Library Collection* arose from a conversation with a Metaphorosis author who is also a librarian, and is initially intended to suit library needs. When a reader comes in and says, "Hey, do you have any SFF stories by this type of author?" here they are! But of course, the books are available to any reader.

The SFF community has become, over the years, and not always easily, a welcoming environment, accepting and in some ways even eager for diversity. Always at the forefront of new ideas, it has gradually opened its arms to the LGBTQIA+ community, and with that openness, produced more stories that reflect the lives of many of its readers.

This volume focuses on stories by **LGBTQIA+** authors, here gather loosely under the 'queer' label. This is one of the largest volumes in the *Library Collection*, which I take as a hopeful sign for the SFF community as a whole. Diversity of input can't help but be a benefit to us all. Plus, they're just great stories!

B. Morris Allen
1 July 2024

Cat Play

Mari Ness

When the girl moves almost next door — across the way in our apartment complex — I lose my breath. Literally. She's — well, gorgeous doesn't begin to cover it. Long, incredibly rich black hair that you know just from looking at will feel like silk, and extraordinary eyes that I've never seen before — large, green, tilted, kinda cat shaped, really. The eyes are the first thing you see in the face, which is incredible enough on its own, with the perfection I've seen on film, but never in real life. Not too thin, either — she's got cleavage that I'm trying to keep my eyes off, but failing. And young. Probably still in high school, maybe a bit older. A few years younger than me, but with looks like that, we can deal.

She's moving in boxes and furniture, and even in this heat, she's not sweating at all. I don't question that. Instead, I gulp. The right thing to do, of course, is to go and offer to help. To pretend, for a moment, that she might actually want to be my friend. She won't, of course, but I could have a few seconds of that before the word gets around, before she starts hearing about me and how I don't really have any friends. Not here, anyway. On the internet, and a few hours away, sure. But not here. Assuming she doesn't blow me off in the first place.

I watch her struggle in with a box. Oh, screw it. I'm just being chivalrous, that's all. Which automatically means she's going to put me into that "nice guy" category and we'll never be more than friends, but, you know, just being friends with someone that good looking is something, right?

Right.

So I head over. "Need help?"

She's so startled, she drops the box. I don't know if it's that she's unused to talking to people, or expects she won't get help, or what, but it lands, and the tape on it rips, and the stuff inside starts to slide out. Nothing much — I see what looks like towels and a few pots and pans. I bend down to help her stuff it back into the box, but she waves me away.

"Sorry about that," I mutter, although I wasn't the one that dropped the box.

"No, it's cool," she says, standing up after she's sort of repacked the box. I'm staring into her eyes, thinking that I've never seen eyes like that, and I really haven't — not anything that brilliant. Contacts, maybe? Man, I hope I don't say something stupid about them.

"I'm Javier," I say. "Almost a next door neighbor," I add, waving towards my apartment, so she won't totally think I'm just a freak who walks up and terrorizes women carrying boxes into their apartments.

"Oh," she says.

I wait to think of something brilliant to say, but I can't think of anything. *Come on,* I tell myself. You got past the introduction part. Now say something smart.

But I can't think of anything smart to say, so I just repeat my first question. "Need help?"

It's pretty obvious that no one else is helping her move things in, which suddenly strikes me as odd — usually, when people move in and out from these apartments they've got a few friends to help them out. I glance towards the parking lot and the rental truck sitting there. It's a bit difficult to see, but it does look as if she's got furniture inside.

"No, I'm ok," she says.

"Sure?" I ask. "I'm not doing anything."

She seems to consider for a moment, then holds out her hand. "Not sure," she says.

I take it, and surprisingly, even though it's August in Florida and she's been moving boxes, it's not sweaty or anything.

So we start unloading her truck. It doesn't take long, and I realize that she was probably right when she said she was OK. Everything, from the bed to the couch to the boxes, is remarkably, incredibly light, easy enough for one person to handle. My mom and I have moved our couch and chair enough so that I know. I want to ask her how she found such a lightweight couch.

"Thanks," she says, as we slam down the back of the truck. She wipes her hands on her jeans.

One of those awkward silences arises that I never know how to handle. I should say something, I know, but this is the part with girls that I always screw up, and knowing that is clamping my mouth shut. Luckily, after a few seconds that probably seem a lot longer than they really were, she says, "So, you live around here?"

I don't bother to point out that I've already pointed that out. "Yes," I say. "Over there," waving my hand. I don't mention my mother. For some reason, I don't want to let her know that I'm still living with my mom. It's just temporary, until I graduate from community college, but right now I only have one of those part time, sucky retail jobs, which isn't enough to pay the rent. The only good thing is that it lets me work around my school hours. And it's keeping me from ringing up the kind of debt some of my friends are getting from a full four year school. Sometimes I wish I'd just gone straight to a regular job, like Andy, but I can make more money with a community college or four year degree. Money. It's an important thing, money. You realize that when you haven't got any.

"Cool," she says, as I try to think of something hot to say. Something that will jump me out of the "friend" category and into the "interesting" category. It's hard, because I'm suddenly all too aware that I'm sweating, right through my T-shirt, even if she isn't. Luckily, before the silence gets too awkward, a large black cat saunters up, and sits near her, staring at me. It's a little unnerving, the way a really intense stare from a cat often is.

"Huh," I say. I remember reading something, somewhere, about how one way to get a girl to like you is to get her cat to like you. Of course, that depends on the cat. I kneel down and put out my hand. The cat just continues to stare. Feeling weird, I stand back up. "I'm not sure your cat likes me," I say.

"But she isn't my cat," says the girl smiling. "She's my sister. My twin."

Great.

I don't say this out loud, of course, because the girl's hot, and I'm not about to let her just put me on. "You have a twin sister," I say, trying my best to imitate Darth Vader's voice, and when that's clearly lost on her — she's probably not a Star Wars fan — "A biological miracle."

The girl smiles down at the cat. "Well. I don't know about biological."

The cat just continues to stare at me, in that unblinking way that cats have. The silence grows. But it's not an uncomfortable sort of silence, yet, the sort where you know you're just going to have to break it by saying something unbelievably stupid.

"So," I say. "Do girls with cat twins drink Starbucks?"

She grins at me. "You can try to find out."

●

The Starbucks is just a couple miles off. We go there. She doesn't say anything about my car, which is about one mishap from falling completely, but does have a kickass sound system, which I demonstrate for her. She grins. At Starbucks, I try to pay for us both, but she grins and hands over cash, and for some reason I don't feel like continuing to push. Oddly enough, she gets plain, straight black coffee, while I end up getting the chocolate raspberry latte with extra whipped cream. It doesn't seem, I don't know, overly masculine or whatever, but she doesn't say anything, and I like the thing.

And we talk. It's awesome. She's listening to me, Javier, and I'm not saying anything stupid, the way I usually do around anyone I don't know well, or most girls, for that matter. And she's laughing at my jokes. Not polite laughter when you realize that someone wants you to laugh, but really laughing. She's doubling over and pulling her feet up in the chair. She's got me telling more jokes and funny stories. I've never been this funny.

It's all going so well that I don't even realize the cat has followed us. I blink. I don't remember the cat even getting into the car, much less following us in. In my experience — not much of it, I admit — cats don't even like cars, or travelling, so how and why did this cat walk into the car in the first place? It must have been in the car; it's too long of a walk for even a cat to run here this quickly.

And why the hell is Starbucks not chasing the cat out? They've got signs on their doors saying that the only animals allowed in are service animals for the blind and deaf. Sure, I've seen a couple women sneak in anyway with those little toy dogs stuffed in a shoulder bag, but at least those dogs are up in bags, only their eyes blinking. This cat is walking around the furniture, slowly, looking for the best place to nap. She finds one, by the girl, and curls up in a ball. And nobody in the Starbucks says a word.

Maybe this Starbucks just has a lot of animal lovers. I don't know.

It's probably a couple hours — maybe a little more — when the girl stretches and says that she'd better go home. We aren't getting any looks from the place, but I offer to get more drinks anyway, just to stretch out my time with her. She shakes her head. She still has some unpacking to do, she says. And other things. We walk out and get into my car, still chatting. It's not until we're about a block away that I realize it.

"Crap," I say. "I think we left the cat back there."

The girl smiles a little. "Nah, she just wanted to stay a bit longer. Maybe pick up a guy later on, or something."

"Um," I say, not sure how I should respond to this.

"Don't worry," she says. "She can find her way back."

"It's three, five miles," I say. Not to mention, I think, but don't add, over a couple of busy roads that are not going to be too cat friendly. I make a U-Turn. "It's no big deal. I mean, other than having to admit that we own the cat —"

"Nobody owns her."

That shuts me up.

When we get back to Starbucks, the cat's just waiting outside, sitting on the curb calmly. As I pull up, it walks up to the car. I open the back seat, and the cat jumps in and curls into a ball on the back seat.

"Smart cat," I say, getting back in. "I'm almost tempted to ask it to put on a seat belt."

The girl doesn't answer that.

Once we get back, the girl and the cat head to her — well, I guess, their door. The girl turns to look at me. The cat doesn't. "Thanks," she said. "I had — it was a great time."

I'm grinning. That might not be cool, but I can't help it. "So did I."

There's a dead bird at our doorstep in the morning. *Gross,* I think. Already, a couple bugs are hovering over it, buzzing, along with the usual tiny moths in the air. I start cleaning the thing up.

When I look up, I see the cat staring at me. It — she — puts a paw up towards her mouth.

I find myself feeling a bit sick.

I'm even less happy when I find five dead lizards on the doorstep the next day. They're carefully fanned out, in a pattern that I guess is supposed to resemble a star or something, and I've gotta tell you, it's totally gross. *"Fuck,"* I say, out loud. I groan. I don't want to clean this, but I know damn well that once my mother wakes up, she'll make me clean it anyway, so I might as well get going.

While I'm scooping up the lizards, I look up, and see that cat watching me.

"Scram," I say.

The cat just stares.

I don't see the girl, or the cat, for another couple of weeks. When I do see the girl heading into her apartment in the afternoon, I hurry up. "Hey," I say.

She doesn't even answer me, or look in my direction, before slipping in. I see the cat at the window, looking out, but that's it.

Well.

You'd think I'd have gotten the message, but somehow, I keep trying to see her anyway.

Maybe it's because of all of those dead things that keep appearing at my doorstep — feathers, lizards, other things I really don't want to identify. I've heard that cats do this sort of thing to show affection, and even though this is beyond stupid — I mean, I've never even seen the cat leaving the dead things there, and certainly when I have seen the cat, it hasn't been particularly friendly — I'm letting myself hope.

It's early in the morning, not quite hot, and I'm cleaning up some lizards when I hear her voice again. "Hey there."

I cringe. Because as bad as it was to have a hot girl like that blowing me off, it's even worse to have her see me trying to pick up dead lizards from my doorstep. "Hi there," I say, trying to hide what I'm doing, which never works. "Just trying to clean something up," I finally say, lamely.

"Oh," she says.

"You're probably used to this kinda thing," I say. "Being a cat owner and all."

She grins. "I told you," she says. "I don't own a cat."

"Right. Right. Because the cat owns you and has convinced you you're twins."

She just grins.

I've got the remains of the lizards in a bag right now; I tie the bag and stand up, getting ready to throw it in the dumpster. She looks at the bag, and then looks at me, and something seems to darken her eyes. Disappointment, maybe, although it's not like I'm good enough with girls to tell. But maybe she's disappointed because she's expecting to hear something from me.

"Say," she asks. "Want lunch?"

I hesitate. "What is it?" I say, a little ungraciously.

"Tuna fish," she says, and she runs her tongue across her lips.

That does it. I immediately agree, and we head out to the little park right next to the complex. It's not much of a park — really small, and the playground equipment's all rusty, but it's got a couple of old picnic tables, and now, midweek, early afternoon before the schools let out, it's pretty much deserted. She hands over a tuna sandwich and a Coke, and grins.

And for some inexplicable reason, I start talking. Really talking. Telling her, really telling her, about everything. About wanting to be a musician, a really good one, only the only instruments I was able to practice on for years were the crappy ones at the school, and sometimes a friend's guitar or something. The way I'd first saved up money, bit by bit, for a guitar, a really good guitar, and the way I'd come home to find that my mom had taken the money, all of it. For rent, she'd said, but I'd seen the look in her eyes. It wasn't the rent. The way I'd snuck out to a second job at Subways, not telling her about it. They way she'd looked at me when Subways had called to see if I'd work another shift for them. What I felt when I'd finally gotten a guitar, started to play, terrified that I'd started too late, that all the other musicians were already ahead of me. And how, after all that, last year, Mom had bought me Guitar Hero for Christmas, and given it to me, expecting me to smile and be happy. The way the guitar felt.

She nods.

I don't know why I'm telling her any of this. I mean, it's only our second date. Or, hanging out.

But there's more to it. I swallow. This is as bad as not having an instrument, as not knowing how to get the tunes I hear in my head down on paper or on a computer, not knowing how to get the different sounds in a band to work together and sound *right,* knowing that I'm going to be taking all of these practical computer courses at Valencia instead of music classes because they're, well, practical. This isn't as bad; it's worse. It's the way I look. The way I am. The way —

She's been listening, up until then, but she cuts me off right there.

"Most musicians aren't good looking at all."

"You kidding me?" I say bitterly. "I mean, Tori Amos, the —"

"You think they honestly look like that? Or that they started looking like that? Come on. It's all Hollywood. All makeup and surgery and shit. It's not real. You wanna look like a rockstar, you can look like a rockstar."

"But —" I swallow. I don't want to say it.

"Sure," she says. "You're fat and ugly now." Well. That hurts. I've got tears in my eyes. Whatever people might say, honesty isn't always the best policy. "But that's changeable, I'm telling you. Surface shit. Nothing more. What's important is what's *there*." And she hits me in the forehead and on the chest.

"You been watching American Idol?"

"It's a really stupid show."

I can't exactly argue with her there, so I take another route. "Every person —"

"You telling me that American Idol is the only way to go?" she asks. "How bout just recording your stuff and putting it up on the net and seeing what happens?"

I have to admit, the thought makes me feel chilled.

"I don't have —"

"Oh, forget it," she says.

I don't know why that pisses me off, but it does. I forget that this is the first hot chick I've talked to, like, ever, forget that we're actually friends. "How the hell would you know what it's like?" I shout at her. "Being ugly and fat and all that. I mean, god, you stop people dead in your tracks. You haven't a fucking *clue* what it feels like."

Her face changes then. I can't exactly explain how, but it does, *shifting.* Suddenly, she looks a lot less perfect, a lot less pretty. Those eyes glow, even more than they usually do, and I could swear that they actually swirl, the way they sometimes do in a horror movie, or something.

"You think I was always like this?"

From nowhere, that cat pops up, and arches its back, hissing.

It's an absolutely gorgeous cat, as cats go.

"Yeah," I say. "Yeah. I do. You've always been pretty, ever since you were two or three years old. You've always had people come up to you and offer to do things for you, or give you candy, or pay attention to you just because you're pretty. You've had teachers smiling at you. You've had friends. You've had —"

It's all choking up in me. It's coming out, and yet I'm not really saying what I want to be saying.

"You've always had it," I manage, although that's still not really what I want to say. "You've always been gorgeous. You don't have a clue what it's like."

Those eyes can't possibly tilt up any more, but they do.

"You think so?"

Her hands extend out; for a second her nails look more like cat claws than anything else. She almost snarls.

"I wish," she says. "I *wish.*" And then she really does snarl. I can't explain how she does it, but it's exactly like the shriek of an angry cat. Even her hair is standing up.

"You don't know what we did to make ourselves look this way," she hisses. "But I'm telling you, it wasn't just Hollywood shit. That's the stuff you can do. We didn't have —"

But at that the cat is standing up, hissing. Well, more growling, and then it lets out a shriek, the sort you might hear from fighting cats, only this one is even worse than that, piercing, raw, actually painful. I slap my hands over my ears without thinking about it. The girl, too, seems startled. She opens her mouth, then shuts it again. The cat shrieks again. The girl nods. She looks back at me.

"Look, all I'm saying is you can change all that. Just — just don't go to extraordinary lengths to change it, ok? Nothing wrong with Hollywood stuff. Stick with that. Not what we -"

And then she's gone. Just like that.

It can't be just like that, of course. I must have put my head down for a second or something — more than a second — long enough for her and the cat to run off.

Or so I tell myself.

●

And that's it. I don't see her, except in the distance, again, and whenever I do see her, and wave, she never waves back. The dumb thing, the really dumb thing, is I don't have her number, or her email. Or even a name, to try finding her on Facebook or something. I have nothing except a couple of conversations, and her face. And knowing where she lives, and what her cat looks like. And hoping she'll come by again, just to talk to me.

But she doesn't.

Sometimes I see her on her porch, looking out. That's when I wave, only to be ignored. Once, just as the sun was almost slipping beneath the horizon, just at that moment when light plays tricks on you, I almost thought I saw two of her out there, both lightly leaning against the porch screen, fingers raised up against it, almost as if she — they — were trying to claw their way out. It's nonsense, of course. I wave again, but whether it's the light, or something else, she — they — don't wave back.

And then they're gone, just like that.

You can't always tell when an apartment is empty around here — most people keep their blinds down for privacy anyway, and behind closed doors, who knows? But I knew. I could sense it. Her apartment was empty.

"So, looks like those twins just hightailed out of here, huh?" It's another neighbor, looking at the door, an older guy I nod to on occasion. He's got a wife, or rather, had a wife, we think; we haven't seen her around for awhile.

"Twins?" I say, a little shakily.

"Yeah," says the neighbor, giving me a really odd look, as if I should know this, because I've supposedly been hanging out with the girl so much. Or, maybe, girls.

"I just knew one of them," I say.

"Well, I'll say that you didn't often see them together. Just early in the morning, or real early in the evening, sunset, you know. I guess they had really different schedules or something."

"Or something," I agree.

"Anyway, they were a lot quieter than the last group."

"Yes," I agree, although honestly I can't remember the last group.

She didn't even say good-bye. Or, I guess, they didn't say good-bye.

●

I don't sleep well that night. I keep thinking I see a cat at the window, or something, but every time I look up, nothing. I wake up really late the next morning, after some weird dreams about cats and guitars and some unrelated stuff I can't remember — pineapples, maybe. My mom's still passed out, so I move around pretty quietly, feeling like shit.

She could at least have said good-bye, or something.

I make some coffee, decide to throw away the trash, and open the door, clutching the trash bag in my hand, see a pile of black feathers on the doorstep.

Shit.

I head back inside, come back out with a small dustpan and some paper towels. I'm about to just start sweeping the whole thing up when I realize that the feathers are perfectly, completely dry, and something's under them.

It's a picture of two girls, identical twins. Maybe ten. Black haired.

Incredibly ugly. To the point that, if I'd passed them on the street, I might have averted my eyes. And yet — and this is the weird thing — even though they don't look anything like the girl, I can somehow tell that one of them is the girl, grown up. Maybe it's the nose or something.

Even if the girls in the picture have perfectly ordinary eyes.

I'm so involved in looking at the picture that I don't see what's below it for several seconds — minutes, really. When I do see it, I blink a little, and move the feathers that have drifted back on top of it away. I pick it up.

Sheet music.

Pages and pages of blank sheet music.

When I pick them up, I can actually hear music dancing in my mind. And — the most amazing part of all — I think I know how to write it.

Mari Ness' story "Cat Play" was originally published in Metaphorosis on Friday, 8 January 2016. See magazine.metaphorosis.com

About the author

Mari Ness spent much of her life wandering the world and reading. This, naturally, left her only able to eat chocolate, snark about popular culture, and occasionally write. She lives in central Florida, with a scraggly rose garden, large trees harboring demented squirrels, and two adorable cats.

Combustion

Kai Hudson

Jaxon has just finished doodling Captain Fiero's victory pose when the math teacher explodes.

Students scream as Mrs. Richardson flails back from the chalkboard, body suddenly alight. Her arms and legs make a bright windmill as she stumbles across the room, upsetting the fake plastic skeleton and catching the bookcase on fire. Jaxon shoots to his feet without thinking, grabs his jacket, and runs to her just as she collapses across Hannah's desk.

He's too late. Jaxon stands there staring as Mrs. Richardson's body jerks and twitches, the fire finishing its meal. The room fills with the stink of burnt hair and cooking flesh.

There's no time to mourn. With a high-pitched wail, Robyn catches fire across the room. Adrian rears back from her and turns to run—he lights before he gets two steps away. Order collapses. Children shriek and cry and dash for the exits, while the fire leaps from one tiny body to the next, Jaxon darting after it with his jacket flapping in futility. Smoke burns his eyes and clogs his throat, everywhere ash and heat and flame. Finally, he stumbles out of the classroom alone, coughing and retching as he scrubs flecks of classmates from his eyes.

Around him, the world burns.

He presses the jacket to his mouth and nose, staggers through thick smoke and lashing flames. A couple times he hears something like screams coming from a nearby room, but when he turns to run in—he'll save them, Captain Fiero would—all he sees is fire. Greedy orange tongues that speak in hisses and pops: *Come sit with us. Come here where it is warm.*

The school's front doorknob sears his palm. Jaxon yells and shoves forward, tumbling down the steps and into soft dirt.

He lies there and breathes, sucking in deep lungfuls of air that tingle and scratch on their way down. He keeps at it even though it hurts, because that's what Captain Fiero would do. Captain Fiero would breathe, and slowly push himself up to sitting, and go out to save the world.

When he sits up, the city is on fire.

Flames spew through broken-glass storefronts. Cars drift aimlessly into each other, their drivers on fire. Two blocks down, the old church lights the afternoon, huge flaming pillars punching out windows to grasp for the sky. Everywhere fire, everywhere death. What—what is going *on?*

A high-pitched scream, and he turns. A woman runs down the sidewalk, arms flailing. Smoke pours from her clothes and her whole head is aflame, a meteor with legs. She falls to the ground just as Jaxon reaches her and throws his jacket over her head, holding his breath to keep the smoke out as her body seizes and trembles beneath his. After a second he remembers to hit the jacket with his palms like the people do on TV, and the lady gives one last heave before going still. The parts of her arms and legs that aren't charred and crusting around bone are pale and scattered with freckles like only white folks have.

He holds the jacket down for a while longer, just in case the fire comes back. But though his palm still smarts from the hot doorknob, the heat seeping up through the thin cloth doesn't feel new. Jaxon takes a deep breath and lifts the jacket.

The fabric peels up with chunks of scalp, skull, and sooty hair stuck to it. Beneath, the lady's brain glistens grey and dead in the bright sunlight, like a new flavor of Jell-O Nana might serve for dessert.

Sickness punches up his throat. Jaxon turns and spews his lunch all over the asphalt. His hands shake as he drops the jacket.

Which is when something roars.

He looks up to see a monster approaching in the shape of a white van, flames shooting out its grill and from beneath the hood. It bears down on him, only feet away, and Jaxon stares. He wants to run but can't. He can only think stupidly, *This is gonna hurt.*

Then something hits him from the side. The world flips and he finds himself staring up at clear blue sky.

Strange, he thinks, that the smoke from a thousand burning souls can waft up into that great, endless unknown and simply disappear.

●

The man who saved him looks nothing like Captain Fiero. He doesn't wear a bright red cape with yellow flames at the bottom, or surf through the air on a fireball he makes from his hands. Arthur—"Call me Artie, son"—wears a shirt with sweat stains at the armpits, and thick jeans that look like they've been washed about a thousand times, the blue all sucked out of them.

He was in the Navy before, something called a coreman. Artie says that means he looked after people when they went out to sea or into the desert and got shot by the enemy. Jaxon wants to ask if Artie ever met Donte, if maybe he'd known Jaxon's brother before he got blown up in Iraq and came home in a flag-draped box. He can never seem to form the question, though. Donte's death is its own little hurt, like even now a part of Jaxon's heart is continuously burning sharp and acrid.

It's not the only thing still burning. Down below the mountain, the city continues to smolder, thin columns of smoke and ash drifting up from the charred husks of buildings. Two weeks have passed since everything went up in flames. The radio stations squawk nonstop, experts and analysts and counter-experts and counter-analysts all picking and pulling and voicing their theories, but to Jaxon their panicked conversations sound like water circling a clogged drain: motion without progress. They keep saying what a big tragedy this is and how everyone needs to work together to do something about it. Underneath it, though,

Jaxon only hears fear. Fear, and relief that it didn't happen to them.

There are conflicting reports about the spread of the destruction. Some stations describe whole countries consumed by fire, reduced to nothing but a wasteland of embers and ash like in the videogames Donte used to play. Others claim it's just a few cities here and there, Jaxon's included. No matter what the reports say, though, everyone agrees on two things. One: the fire keeps spreading, fast and unpredictable, a few people suddenly lighting up in the middle of the day for no reason and subsequently taking an entire city down with them. And two: no one knows why.

They could probably figure out that second one if everyone just came together, pooled their resources and ideas to try to find a solution to this. Isn't that what they did with the Ebola outbreak, and that MRSA thing a little later? But the fire is different, and Jaxon thinks he knows why. It's happening too fast and too close. It's not a bunch of poor dark-skinned people in a faraway country getting burnt up first, so folks can't just sit back and donate money with their credit cards and put those little stamps of solidarity on the corners of their profile pics on social media. No, the fire is *here*, it's come directly for them and exploded right in their faces. So they're doing what they do best: lockdown. Instead of *Let's all work on this together*, the message is *We must protect our own.*

"In the wake of this terrible tragedy, we in Chicago would like to announce that we are suspending travel in and out of the city indefinitely," says the tinny voice over the radio. "Those who attempt illegal entry will be turned away, using force if necessary. Of course, we expect this to be only a temporary safety measure, and our thoughts and prayers are with the residents of those areas that have burned—"

"Yeah, thanks for the support," Artie grumbles, and flicks the radio off.

A rumble of agreement rolls through the small crowd gathered around the campfire. Jaxon had shied away the first time they laid the rocks down and lit match to dry tinder, but Lawrence laughed and patted him on the shoulder. *Don't you worry, son. We know what we're doing.*

He wasn't lying. When Artie and Jaxon finally made it up the mountain, covered in dust and soot, with barely half a bottle of water between them, they'd found the campground already occupied by the employees of Fire Station 19; they'd been in the middle of their annual family retreat when the city went up. Lawrence is their leader, a real-life fire captain, which is pretty cool.

Jaxon doesn't know the others very well yet, even though they've been here a while. Everyone's friendly, but whenever Jaxon looks at them all he sees is his classmates burning up, or Mrs. Richardson, or the lady with her head on fire. Sometimes the thoughts get bad enough to make him sick again, so he tries to stay away from people in general.

The only person he's comfortable around is Artie. Jaxon doesn't have anyone else—Donte's in the ground, and they passed the blackened remains of the church on their way to the mountain, the church where Nana would've been in the middle of sorting old clothes and canned food, like she always did when Jaxon was at school. He left a note taped to the burnt wood of the church's front door just in case, but he's not so young as to hold out hope.

So here they are two weeks later, sleeping in tents while the city continues to burn down below. They talked about rescue the first few days, but that's dried up since the radio broadcasts made it clear: they're on their own. Which, to Jaxon, isn't actually new. Even before the fire and the worldwide swaths of death, he'd stopped believing in the government a long time ago. Nana probably said it best: *The world don't care about us, and we like it that way.* For the white folks in camp, it's probably a new thing, being abandoned. For people like Jaxon, it's really, really not.

Around the campfire, the conversation continues. "…igure it out," Lawrence is saying. "I mean, how does the fire pick who to burn?"

"Maybe it's not the people, it's the place," says one of the paramedics. "Did you hear the broadcast last night, about the fire that just died out in a hospital in Atlanta? It took a couple patients on one floor but that was it. The staff all came running for nothing."

"My cousin in Afghanistan says the same thing happened at his FOB," someone else adds. "Couple people went up at chow, everyone jumped on to put 'em out, and they all should've caught fire but none of 'em did."

"And then there's us," says a firefighter. "Those flaming cars came up the road the first few days, then nothing. No one here caught."

"Thank God for that."

"Maybe we were chosen for this, you know? The radio said there might be something special about—"

"Enough of that," Lawrence snaps. "Ain't no one here any more special or chosen or pretty-unique-snowflake than anybody else. You think like that and you might as well strike a match to yourself."

"Amen, brother."

Jaxon agrees. No one ever deserves to burn: not his classmates, not that lady on the street, not the millions already whose ash they breathe every day. That's why he didn't run away, two weeks ago when the fire started in the classroom. Nana didn't run when those angry men in white hoods tried to burn down the freedom bus she was riding on in '61. Donte didn't run when the bad guys were shooting at him in Iraq. It's just not in his blood, he supposes.

"You're thinking about him, aren't you?" Artie smiles down at him as the conversation around the campfire continues in the background, a soft, comforting buzz. "Your superhero."

He's not, but you never tell white folks they're wrong. Jaxon nods. "Yeah. Captain Fiero." He'd shown Artie the picture he drew when they first arrived in camp. He's not sure why, and he feels mostly embarrassed by it now. Captain Fiero seems so childish in the face of what they've seen.

"That's cool." Artie speaks around the granola bar he's eating; he always seems to have one sequestered somewhere on his person. "I've been meaning to ask you about how his powers work. Usually when you throw fire at fire, it just gets bigger. What makes Captain Fiero different?"

"Um." A strange mix of warmth and embarrassment gathers in Jaxon's stomach. He's pleased; no one's ever asked about Captain Fiero before, and all the other kids just laughed at his pictures and called him stupid. At the same time, what if he's wrong? About Captain Fiero's powers, about the good fire? What if Artie laughs at him too?

But Artie is just looking at him, chewing around an encouraging smile, and the man *did* save his life, so. "Well. Captain Fiero's fire isn't bad, not like the fire that burned everything up in town. His fire is good because it, um, it comes from his heart. It's made of his wanting to save people." It's sounding stupider and stupider by the moment. He ducks his head and mumbles the last few words. "So when his fire touches the bad fire, it puts it out."

"Oh." Jaxon's looking down at his feet so he doesn't see what kind of face Artie is making, but he doesn't sound like he's about to laugh or make sneering jokes. He just sounds curious. "So, back at your school...?"

"I had the good fire," Jaxon says, still not looking up. "I wanted to be like Captain Fiero, saving everyone, so I tried to put the other kids out because that's what he would've done. I think...I think maybe the bad fire sensed that, and that's why it skipped me. It didn't wanna mess with Captain Fiero."

"I see." It's hard to tell from his voice whether Artie actually does or not. He sounds distracted. Jaxon looks up and notices two things at once: one, Artie isn't watching him anymore, staring instead at the woods somewhere over Jaxon's shoulder.

Two, all movement in camp has stopped, everybody else staring in the same direction.

Very slowly, Jaxon turns.

The underbrush has birthed a man. Or at least, Jaxon thinks he's a man. It's hard to tell through all the smoke.

Because he's on fire.

Not *fire* fire, not like what happened in his classroom and then later through the entire city. But it's starting. The man stares at them with big, helpless eyes. Smoke pours from his clothes and his skin is a deep, angry red, like he spent too much time in the sun. He opens his mouth and croaks, "H-Help," and the word belches out around a fresh cloud of smoke.

Gasps all around. Several people back away as the man stumbles forward. Jaxon sees the fear in their eyes, the growing panic. A piece of the city, a clump of fiery infection suddenly invading their pristine haven. They should run. Bolt for the woods, hide away, save themselves. Let everyone else burn.

But that's not what Captain Fiero would do, is it?

"Help," the man begs again, just as something sparks and the top layer of his salt-and-pepper hair catches fire. Someone wails, and Jaxon can feel it in the air: the buzzing tension, the terror teetering on the brink of crumbling into chaos.

He doesn't even think about it, shooting to his feet and seizing his jacket. "Stop!"

He's not sure who he's talking to, but everyone obeys anyway. The man freezes, and all movement in camp halts. The couple of folks who had been edging toward the woods falter in their steps. All eyes go to him.

Jaxon lifts the jacket and steps toward the burning man. Tiny flames crown his hair and his breaths come high and panicked as he stares at Jaxon, but he doesn't move.

"*Son*," Lawrence hisses somewhere in the background, but Jaxon barely hears. He stops in front of the man, and they regard each other for a moment. The man's eyes are still full of panic, wide and near-crazy with it, and it would be so easy, Jaxon knows, to give in. He can feel it even now, the fear hovering on the edges of his consciousness. The bad fire is here, and it wants him to run.

But it didn't count on Captain Fiero, who has never said real words or breathed real air, but who lives in Jaxon nevertheless.

He looks up at the man, and it's surprisingly easy to smile. "I'm gonna put you out now," he says. Then he does just that: lifts up on his toes, throws his jacket over the man's smoking head, and pulls.

The man trips and falls to his knees with the momentum. Jaxon rolls with it, both of them tumbling to the dirt. Artie calls his name, but he ignores it as he quickly pats the jacket with his palms, just like he did back in the city two weeks ago. Except this time will be different. This time, he's not too late.

The man's body jerks beneath him, just like the lady's did before, and then goes still. The smell of something charred fills the air. Jaxon stares at the lump beneath his jacket, suddenly unsure. What if he's wrong? What if he lifts it up, and there's just more grey brains underneath?

Crunching footsteps, and Artie squats down next to him. His hand lands heavy on Jaxon's shoulder, but he doesn't say anything as he pinches a corner of the jacket and slowly lifts it up.

A few wisps of smoke and a pair of bright eyes greet them. The man coughs and shakes his head. Bits of burnt hair drift to the ground with the movement, and his scalp is all blotchy and pink and gross-looking, but he's alive.

He's alive.

Noise erupts all through camp. A million conversations get going at once, questions and exclamations and not a few prayers. Artie whistles. "Holy *shit*," he says, and before Jaxon can tell him that's a bad word, he gets a hearty clap to the shoulder. "Why didn't you run?" Artie asks.

And Jaxon can't really articulate it, not in the refined, sophisticated way it'll spread through the world over the next few days. He's only eight years old, after all, so he doesn't know fancy words like *valor* and *fortitude*. Right now, he only knows to look at Artie and say, "Because that's what the bad fire wants."

He sees it the moment Artie understands. His friend stands up and hurries over to the rest of the campers. Jaxon catches only bits and pieces of the conversation that follows, although one thing stands out above all: *spread the word*. People talk about putting a broadcast out on the radio, of putting an expedition together to head down to the city and tell everyone, tell the world. Start a new sort of sweeping conflagration.

They don't ask Jaxon to come, and he doesn't volunteer. He'll stay here a little while longer. He likes the quiet in these woods.

Something brushes his hand. Jaxon turns and it's the man he saved, reaching out with long, calloused fingers to wrap them around his own. The patches of skin that were burning before are now starting to blister, and he winces in pain with every movement, but when he squeezes Jaxon's hand, there is only softness in his eyes. "Thank you," he whispers.

Jaxon grins. He may not have a long red cape, or be able to make fireballs from his hands. He may not be tall, or handsome, or have lots of money or a big house or a pretty girlfriend, but right now, in his heart, he has the good fire.

Kai Hudson's story "Combustion" was originally published in Metaphorosis on Friday, 28 September 2018. See magazine.metaphorosis.com

About the author

Kai Hudson is a writer of speculative fiction who apparently writes better stories than she does author bios. Her work has appeared in *Clarkesworld*, *PodCastle*, *Interzone*, and other fine places.

The Guardian of Werifest Park

Carly Racklin

The train car reeked of cigarettes and rumbled like a storm. Loud enough to drown out the voice of every passenger crammed inside it, but still Inez's heartbeat rattled between her ears. It had started when she stuffed her backpack with clothes in the dark, and only boomed louder as she'd slipped out past her mother's wheezy, sleeping form on the couch, thirty-six or so hours earlier.

It had followed her through the cracked streets, then onto the bus, and all five trains after that. Or was it six, now? She hadn't slept a wink since the drumming started. She'd begun to think nothing would ever be quiet again.

The bruise on her cheek had faded enough now to be mistaken for a shadow on dusky skin, though it throbbed faintly in time with her pulse. No one had even spared her a passing glance when she boarded the train.

Inez had wedged herself into a far, windowless crevice of a seat, clutched her backpack hard against her chest, and waited for the dread to loosen its grip.

No luck yet. So onward it was.

Once her current train clanked into the station, she shuffled onto the platform and took a deep breath, only to taste even more bitterness in it. She reached into her pocket and drew out less than a dollar in change.

"Shit."

Strangers shoved past her and onto their trains. The longer she stood staring at those coins, the louder the dread rumbled in her skull. She needed to keep moving.

She drifted across the sprawl of washed-out tile, out of the paths of others who searched the flickering TV screens beseechingly. Everyone she passed was going in the opposite direction from her.

Inez stepped out into the stale summer air and walked. She walked until the afternoon bled into dusk and the day wasted away under the heels of her second-hand sneakers. She wove through gray streets flanked by gray buildings wearing more gray smoke like scarves. The hollow chill thickened in her gut with each step against the hard sidewalk, but she slogged on.

There had to be *something*. Something, not anything. No shelters—she wasn't a stray. A church could work. Hell, she'd take a bench at this point. Anything would do, so long as it wasn't that house.

Unlike her mother, Inez knew when to quit. When to give a place over to the vermin wasting it. The situation turned out to be comically simple, really. In the end, it all boiled down to a choice. Get out, or get wiped out.

Inez kept walking. Her stomach kept roaring, and her heart drummed on and on and on.

Then, the trees.

So many trees, all soft edges and swaying and green. An ocean of trees stretched to the sky and down the block and farther, farther than bleary eyes could measure. The first real trees she'd seen in days, wearing a collar of what was probably the sorriest excuse for a fence in the entire world. Inez jogged across the street and approached a large, slightly crooked sign.

TRESPASSERS WILL BE PROSECUTED.

The words were printed in bold black type and hung against a background that at some point must have been white.

PARK HOURS: 7AM-7PM.

The last dregs of sunset fell yellow and molten over the skin of her neck and the heavy padlock on the gate. Inez glanced over her shoulder to the city. Just looking at it made her itch to take a puff of her inhaler she knew she couldn't spare. No telling when she'd be able to refill her prescription again.

Despite the heat, Inez shivered, and a whisper from somewhere deep and dark in her chest asked, *What were you thinking?*

Behind her, the street was miraculously clear of cars. For one floating, dream-still moment, the only things breathing were her and those trees. Rustling, watching. Waiting to see what she would do.

She ignored the voice and climbed the fence.

Her feet hit the earth with a soft thud. She tore off her shoes and stuffed them into her backpack, sighing as grass eased the concrete's ache from her soles. Another sign accosted her a few strides in, this one so eroded it seemed ancient, hanging around the trunk of a tree like an amulet: a thirty-one point list of the park's prohibited activities. Vines and moss skirted its edges, entwined in the gaps of the chain that held it aloft.

No smoking, no hunting, no trapping, no littering, no fishing in the pond, no carving the trees, no, no, no. They would have saved a lot of paint if they'd just written KEEP YOUR DAMN HANDS TO YOURSELF. Inez wondered if there were security cameras in the park, but that would involve breaking about four of their own rules.

She ambled on until the fence disappeared from view. There weren't even any real footpaths, just vague stretches of faded grass, mostly concealed by the shells of parched leaves. *No digging. No vehicles.* Sounds of the city beyond waned with every step until they were barely memories. The dulcet crooning of unseen birds replaced the din of construction, of razing machinery. No sign of the skyscrapers, no sign of a single gray thing.

Huckleberries dotted the dark brush. Inez plucked them up in clusters as she walked, barely chewing, her relief turning even the most unripe clumps nectarous and intoxicating.

The path curved, and around the bend stood an enormous weeping willow. Under it: a bench. For the first time in weeks, maybe months, Inez laughed.

She sat down, shucked off her backpack, and took deep, even breaths. The air tasted sweeter than the berries.

But her clothes still smelled of her mother's cigarettes. So did the backpack, and the short dark coils of her hair. Now, though, in this park, the bitter smell seemed to have dissipated a little. Like the fresh air was washing her clean from the inside out.

Dusk elapsed in minutes; night draped the trees in obsidian. With the dark and stillness and her newly full stomach came syrupy fatigue. It colored everything—even the dingy bench was transformed into the softest and warmest bed she had known in years. For a long time, the only thing she did was breathe, letting herself sink further into the summer air, and it into her.

With every inhale, she imagined it purifying the black secondhand-smoke stains in her lungs, then sneaking into her veins and her brain, erasing every ugly thing that lived there, every memory molding in every dark corner and inside every wall.

Yes, she was alone in a city she didn't know the name of, broke and bedding down on a park bench. And there was a stubborn weight in her chest that she couldn't ignore, and bruises still clinging to her skin. But there were wild berries too, and trees tall enough to blot out the sky, and she didn't have to think of her mother ever again. For now, that would have to be enough.

The willow leaves rustled loudly above her, though the air was still. Inez couldn't bring herself to open her eyes again once they fell closed. So she just listened, and after a while, the rustling ceased.

She couldn't remember the last time she'd slept in air this clean, or the last time she'd lain in the night without listening to her mother slinking in the door with her latest fix. It was a different world entirely, a world made only of crisp, bright things. Balmy green things her mother's smoke could never spoil.

Inez slept like the dead, and dreamt of nothing at all. Until a sharp rattling cut through the gloom and jolted her awake into a dry early dawn.

For a moment the world reeled and her head spun, full of dizzy white flickers. She was stuck between spinning and floating, half numb still from the previous day's exhaustion. The rattling continued, and Inez jerked up from the bench when she recognized it as the sound of the metal fence.

The sun had just barely begun to light the park, like the first translucent strokes of an underpainting. What could it be, six in the morning? No way anyone was opening that gate right now.

But she hadn't needed to open the gate to get in.

The heavy crunch of footsteps sounded from nearby.

"Shit!" Inez hissed, and in a frantic blur, snatched up her backpack and dove for cover behind the thick trunk of the willow tree.

The footsteps lurched slowly nearer, down the same path she'd taken to the bench, and on. When they passed the tree, Inez held her breath, and leaned just slightly out into the open to regard her fellow trespasser.

Square shoulders, baggy jeans, dusty combat boots. The man plodding past couldn't have been much older than her, judging by his height and clothes. He stomped listlessly through the grass, clutching an aluminum can. Drunk.

He stopped walking a few feet past the bench. A lit cigarette teetered between the fingers of his free hand. He took a swig from the can, then a puff from the cigarette. The cloud of gray smoke he breathed into the air caused a queasy flutter in Inez's chest. Moments later, the scent hit her, and despite how hard she tried to fight it off, she couldn't breathe.

She hadn't smelled such strong cigarettes since her mother last lit one. That night could have been a lifetime ago, for how far away it felt. Ever since she was a little girl, any fresh whiff of that bitter smoke, and she was gasping, looking for fire, looking for ruin. She'd woken from nightmares of her mother turned to nothing but a heap of char on that ratty couch too many times to count.

When she was fourteen, the doctor had diagnosed her with asthma and recommended nicotine gum to her mother. And every night since for three whole years, Inez had slept with her window open and door shut.

Just when she thought she'd found the one place on earth where that smell couldn't follow her.

The man took another drag, his head lolling back with the inhale. Then he flicked the cigarette away, and it fell to the earth. The ashy end of it sputtered against the brittle foliage. Inez knew what came next, but when the orange flickers caught and burst outwards, she gasped as if she were the one burned.

The stranger whirled about. His glazed-over eyes met hers. Inez trembled and flinched, dropping back from her haunches into the dirt. Smoke drifted up from the ground in a thin curl.

A splitting thrum cut through the air. It sent a stabbing pain through the base of her skull, so loud it could have been coming from inside the bone. Like the whole forest had just trembled with her.

The willow tree above her shook violently again, without even a whisper of a breeze. The drunk man was not looking at her anymore, but up at the tree.

She followed his gaze to the branches. They weren't where she remembered them being.

The boughs bent to the ground, splayed apart wide like fingers. Inez took a breath that froze in her throat. Then the trunk of the willow tree uprooted from the earth.

It was much quieter than she would have ever guessed —to hear a tree tear itself out of the ground. For a moment, there was only a hum. Then a sharp crackle rippled through the stillness, and the trunk split in two. The halves met the ground, looking like the lean brown legs of a Titan. On either side of the tree, the remaining branches twisted into coils. Green vines dangled in a tight, roundish cluster at the willow's crest: a faceless head glistening with dew.

Inez had barely heaved in a new breath when the tree-thing angled its colossal semblance of a body toward the drunk man. At his feet, the cigarette still sputtered, glowing like a shrunken sun but giving no life. It would drain the green from anything it touched.

A yowl, like the groaning of a twig right before it snaps, sounded from the bundle of leaves atop the tree. It stuck in Inez's ears, in her teeth, in her ribs. It clashed with the piercing blare that the lit cigarette had conjured and for all she knew they were the same thing. Maybe that was what everything sounded like when you were going to die.

Inez's body moved separate from her mind. She crawled toward the cigarette on her hands and knees, and the willow moved too, overtaking her in one heaving stride. The drunk man had already started to run.

The whole world was rattling and that cigarette was still burning in the grass, like her mother, poisoning everything, and she couldn't breathe. She had to make it stop. In her peripheral vision the tree creature continued to move, its gnarled limbs cleaving through the air.

Inez mirrored it, throwing out her arm and smothering the cigarette against her hand. Ahead of her the creature halted, one of its branches seizing up mid-swing. The man disappeared into the brush and out of sight. When the metal fence jangled sharply in the distance not long after, the creature lowered its arm.

Inez's vision blurred. Panic pounded in her skull, almost loud enough to drown out the giant's gait as it turned back and thumped toward her.

Her chest burned with emptiness. She fumbled in her pocket for her inhaler. Blackness choked every thought in her head except the ones steering her hands.

Nothing left to exhale. *Click. Hiss.* Breathe in—hold—breathe out.

It took three puffs for the vise around her lungs to loosen. The world came slowly back into focus with every heave, centering on an ugly red burn glaring up from the center of her palm.

A tall shadow crashed over her. Inez looked up, breath thin again.

The creature had no eyes to meet but its stare still pierced. It stood rigid, a monument of bristled greenery. Tears welled up in Inez's eyes. Either from fear or pain, she wasn't sure. It didn't really matter, because she was going to die any second now. The creature craned its verdant body downward as if in confirmation.

Inez snapped her head down, closed her eyes, and waited to be crushed. Waited like she had those nights ago, back pressed to her bedroom door as it rattled with the force of her mother's fists, the air bloated with cigarette smoke and a voice screaming out for her blood.

She'd thought her mother was still sleeping off her latest bender when she flushed the pills. But her hands just wouldn't stop shaking, and everything had clattered to the floor, and she'd only gotten a few handfuls down the pipes when fingers had twisted into her hair and wrenched her back. A hand had crashed against her cheekbone, knocking her into the wall. Her ears rang and her mother had slipped on the tile, so Inez ran. She'd locked herself in her room and wept until long after her mother had given up on threatening to strangle her.

She'd made her decision before the latch even clicked. The next time she ran would be the last.

Curled in on herself in the dirt, Inez let the tears fall. Choked whimpers leaked through her teeth, clenched tight against the smoke. It could have been her mother there, all smoldering ash. Geared to snuff her out like an ember into a cracked tray.

Inez waited to die.

And waited. And waited.

Something soft brushed down her cheek. She gasped and the aroma of damp foliage flooded her mouth.

Rustling surrounded her. A faint creaking joined it, lurking just beneath the steady hum of leaves. Alike in timbre to what had sounded in the chaos, but with none of the venom—the same voice, a different tone. She blinked the tears out of her eyes. The green mop of vines hung just a few inches from her face, the rest of the creature bent in an awkward, jointless attempt at kneeling.

It didn't crush her. Instead, it raised one of the branches from its side and took her gingerly by the wrist of her burned hand. The long sprigs of leaves drew open her fist. This time, the noise that rose from the creature's unseen mouth was nearly a chirp, the pitch of it leaping, like a question. Shrill with curiosity, maybe even concern.

Before she could dwell on how pathetic that thought was, the giant punctuated its remark with a tilt of its massive leafy head, and sparks stirred in Inez's skull.

It was *talking* to her.

She searched for any hint of eyes behind those vines. "I . . . um, I don't understand," she muttered, unsteady with the new weight of this wonder. But it was true: she was still alive, and a beast dressed in forestry had really just materialized because someone burned the grass.

She looked to the gray smudge between the two of them, where the extinguished cigarette lay, then at her palm, cradled by the willow's wispy fingers. "It burned you too."

The vines around her hand drew upwards a fraction, and a thin stream of clear water trickled out from a fissure in the branch and washed over her ash-dotted palm. She flinched and hissed at the sting.

The willow made a cooing noise that sounded an awful lot like the calming hums other people's mothers made to their fussy children. Had it learned that from observation? Or did nature have its own language of tenderness?

"Thank you," Inez said, brushing her fingers over the bark.

Again that rustling echoed around them, and the giant let her go. It rose with a chorus of creaks and trod heavily back toward the patch of ragged earth behind the bench.

Sunlight broke through the canopy and gilded the grass so fiercely Inez had to squint. Soundlessly, the earth began to knit itself back together once the rooted feet of the willow settled into the hollow they'd created. Time seemed to move in reverse as its limbs unwound and stretched to their original shape. By the time she blinked the brightness away, the bench and willow tree stood perfectly undisturbed, the burn in her palm the only indicator that any of it had ever happened.

Inez pushed herself up on two wobbly legs and teetered over to the tree, a small grin fighting its way across her face. She hitched her toppled backpack onto her shoulder; it weighed practically nothing now. One errant breeze and she might just float away like a petal, sheer and light enough to never touch the ground again.

That didn't sound so bad.

When she was just a little girl, 'never' had been the scariest word in the world. A cage that would suffocate her if she got too close. But now, 'never' was more secure than anywhere. Not a cage, but armor. She could lie down inside it and it would keep her safe.

Never was a survivor's word.

She'd whispered it in the din of every train, to the dread each time it returned and choked the breath from her chest—*never, never, never.* She was never going back.

And the dread was quieter now, like she'd finally gone far enough.

Inez rubbed her fingertips gratefully over the knobs and valleys in the willow's bark.

Someone would be opening that gate soon. If she were careful, she could get out before anyone knew she'd entered at all. She would be anonymous again.

Anonymous, but not free. Not free of the dread, or the smoke, or the exhaustion of searching for hope in a colorless city.

At least this place had rules. Rules meant care, and she'd seen precious little of that for a long, long time.

Inez pressed her ear to the willow. She didn't know what she expected to hear, but when it was silent, she couldn't stop her heart from sinking.

"Hello?" she mumbled, and rapped against the wood lightly with her knuckles. "Are you still there? I, um, didn't realize this park was already occupied." Her chuckle came out crumpled like the leaves dappling the undergrowth. No reaction. Maybe it was sleeping. Maybe it just wanted her to shut up and leave it alone. Or maybe it didn't care about her at all, so long as she didn't break any of the rules.

Leaving it be seemed like the safest bet. She didn't want to test the limits of its hospitality, not after what she'd just witnessed.

Feeling childish and yet vaguely like she was being watched, Inez started off in a new direction, away from the pseudo-footpath she'd first followed and into the brush. The noisy layers of expired leaves crackled like tinder with each stride.

By late morning, the air swelled with heat. She downed one of the water bottles she'd had the good sense to buy during her train-hopping, and had half-stuffed the empty plastic shell into her backpack when the sound of real running water hit her, muffled a little by distance. She followed it until her bare feet pushed through a hedge and slipped into blessedly cool mud.

A thin stream wound through the clearing. On its bank, hundreds of yellow flowers gleamed from spray cast off the rocks. Inez propped her backpack up against a tree, sat down on the edge of the brook and dipped her legs into the cool, glossy water. She splashed a handful over her face and scrubbed the scum of the last few days away.

Sighing, she shut her eyes and lay back against the bed of flowers. Her fingers carded through their velvety leaves, tight and tangled like her own curls. Her head went woozy with the blossoms' sweet scent.

She listened for any sounds of the city, knowing it lurked on all sides of the park. Still nothing. If the skyscrapers were teeth, then this forest sat in the middle of a wide-open jaw, surrounded on all sides but never devoured.

Something was different here—she'd noticed it before, but not realized how deep the sensation ran. It wasn't just the air, or the trees, or the ground. It was everything.

Her thoughts drifted again to that list of rules. It hung in her mind in the same looming way it hung on its tree, fixed in place even by the foliage. Different from everything else, but not unwelcome.

Inez opened her eyes, and swallowed a yelp. A figure hovered over her, though that was all she could really call it. Its vaguely human-shaped body was comprised entirely of clustered leaves and budded flowers. It seemed to watch her, though the closest thing to eyes it possessed were two blossoms just slightly larger than the rest, fixed at the middle of its lumpy crown.

She sat up and turned around to face the thing. Its maybe-head followed her. It looked like some kind of artsy hedge trimming from a magazine. Like someone had tried to haphazardly sculpt a person out of foliage, someone who didn't know for sure, or didn't care to know, exactly what people looked like.

"Oh, there are more of you," Inez blurted, heart still racing. Rustling filled her head. She held up her burnt hand and gave a short wave.

The leaves on the creature shook slightly, back and forth.

Inez worked her bottom lip between her teeth. "No? You're . . . just one?" She gestured over her shoulder back toward the general direction of the willow.

Another hum, then all the flower buds on the creature's body bloomed into striking tiny suns. The blossoms skirting the stream repeated the display, petals flaring out in a long wave. Warmth so far from the summer's unflinching aridity saturated the air; she breathed in and felt it in her chest, searching for soil to take root in.

Inez smiled, and caressed the leaves below her again. The little red dot glared up from her palm beneath the vegetation, a reminder of the damage already done, how they'd both been burned. A handful of soft gestures wouldn't erase that.

But it was better than nothing. Or so she hoped.

Inez watched the creature watching her, and wondered if it felt her touch like it had felt the cigarette. Maybe it felt everything the forest did, every inch of every acre. Like veins, connecting each life to the next, tying blade of grass to sprawling tree to sunning flower, each to each to each. A system, and its heart. What a thing to share a wound with.

"Those rules back there are yours, aren't they? They were written for you," she said.

Thirty-one rules was nothing compared to all the ways a thing could be hurt. All the ways a life could be snuffed out. No death too small to grieve. Like it ignored no offense, no wrong. Carrying a memory as old as earth.

Inez saw it all again: the cigarette, and the man, and the creature's arm raised knifelike in the air. A threat, and a response. She'd only seen it respond like that once, but judging by that sign, she guessed it had happened before, and often, who knew how long ago. How many small wars had the creature waged before someone had taken pity on it and written the restrictions that hung over the place?

Too many, of course. It was always too many.

The sun retreated and plunged the bank into shadow. She looked up, but found her vision swimming. The creature was closer now, an unreadable blur of gold and green. Inez shuddered under its unyielding stare. Her smile grew heavy on her face, and fell away without a sound.

She peeled her limbs away from the flowerbed and stood. Papery yellow petals came away with her, stuck with sweat to her skin. The moments of her life from before then unspooled behind her eyes, faded by time but still clinging like old stains to the fabric of her memory. She didn't want them.

Her heart pounded. "Do you want me to leave?" Inez asked in a small voice.

The creature gave no response. The warmth in her chest turned sour.

"Do you?" she said, louder now, though a shameful crack in her voice split the word. Dread wormed a cold trail through her. She didn't need an answer to know it was true, but the miserable reality of it hollowed out her chest. She swallowed down a sob.

The creature's form shrank back at the accusation, all of its flowers returned to buds.

It wouldn't have been the first thing to want her gone. Wouldn't have been the first place better off without her.

Inez knew pity when she saw it. It looked just like disdain, but with a prettier face.

She stumbled back a step, then another, until the hedge she'd first emerged from brushed her ankles.

She really hadn't learned anything, had she?

"I'm sorry," she mumbled. Her feet scrabbled for purchase on uneven ground. "I just wanted—I just—"

Inez turned and ran. The tears finally fell as she lurched through the bushes, over brittle grass and twigs that jabbed like needles. Each one another twist of the knife, a reminder of what she had known before ever climbing that fence but had refused to admit.

She didn't belong here.

But it was worse than that, and she knew it. She didn't belong anywhere.

A root smacked her ankle, and Inez tumbled into the dirt with a weak yelp of pain. Every heaving of her breath scorched like swallowing a red-hot sword. She pushed herself up on limp arms. Stinging outside and in, she clambered backwards until she hit a tree's gnarled trunk, decked in winding dark leaves. Then she hugged her knees to her chest and wept into her hands.

She wished the earth would just swallow her up. If she could just bury all her deluded fantasies and dissolve into the soil, maybe something good and useful would finally grow out of her, something that deserved to be there in that fence, a part of that system.

Loved. Or worth loving, anyway.

And that was just it.

The nameless weight beneath Inez's ribs swelled and flooded her chest with a gloom blacker than her mother's lungs.

She couldn't breathe, again. She fished out her inhaler from her pocket and took a puff, barely able hold it steady. The last time she'd triggered an attack from crying had been the night she flushed the drugs. She could almost smell the smoke again. Could still feel the grain of her bedroom door grate against her shuddering back.

Her breath returned in gasps, a thousand aches with it.

Just barely, on the edge of the forest's din, Inez heard rustling. The foliage beneath her shook.

A whorl of vines crept away from trunk and curled around her, covered in enormous scarlet roses. The mass encircled her in moments, overflowing with the balmy scent of petals. She gasped, and a rose-dappled vine reached out and swept over her bruised cheek, wiping away the last tear still inching down through the grime.

Something had grabbed hold of her lungs again, and her heart too, and held them with such puzzling fortitude and tenderness that Inez thought she would weep again.

The mass of vines and roses embraced her. Softly and resolutely. Tenderly and fiercely. The way her mother used to, before everything went wrong. She'd forgotten what it felt like.

She exhaled and sank into the creature's arms. Links of thornless blooming vine cradled her, stroking her hair in the same smooth motions her hands had used in the patch of flowers back by the stream.

"Why are you doing this?" she whispered. "I'm just the same as them."

A low hum reverberated from deep in the petals, but Inez couldn't decipher its meaning. The creature only held her tighter when she made no reply.

Inez breathed until the pain in her throat subsided to a faint prickling numbness. She wanted to lie down until she remembered nothing of her mother or the gray-stained house she'd run from. But the memories clung to her bones like weeds. She wondered if she would ever be able to uproot them without also uprooting herself. If she would ever be as green and blooming and free as the things that held her inside the fence.

Hesitantly, Inez reached into the leaves and returned the embrace.

The creature's silken-edged form stiffened, then recoiled. The climbing roses and vines receded, slumping limp against the trunk.

By the time she'd gasped and called out brokenly after it, the creature was already gone. Inez stood. Confusion struck her first, then cold terror. Something was wrong. Goosebumps mottled her bare arms and legs. She stared hollowly into the horizon for a long time.

When a breeze blew, she tasted smoke on it.

Not the bitter tobacco, lung-rotting stuff. Worse. The kind that swallowed houses and skin. The kind that cooked.

Inez went rigid. All the green around her swayed as one vast wall, revealing almost nothing. No more than a few slivers of sky to search, and no sign of the stench's source.

"Move, just *move*," she spat at her quaking knees. "Where are you?" she cried up at the trees.

No answer.

Then, voices. Men's voices, the words turned garbled and staticky by distance. The murmurs became yelling, and by the time Inez had turned in their direction, three men careened out of the trunks' thick barricade.

They nearly barreled into her, but the one leading the charge skidded to a stop just inches in front of Inez. His scuffed combat boots kicked up a small cloud of dirt.

A flock of birds scattered noisily from the treetops.

"Holy shit," he whispered. Inez flinched at the rancid booze on his breath. "It's you."

Two others crowded at his back. They could have been triplets, for their shared tawny hair and pasty white faces. A lopsided tattoo of a tiger stared directly at her from one's bare shoulder.

Inez blinked, unable to call any words to her tongue.

"I told you someone else was there," Combat Boots said over his shoulder with a laugh. He stepped toward her, and she stumbled back in turn. Her pulse boomed in her ears.

"Who cares, dude? Let's get the hell out of here," interjected one of the others, grasping his friend by the shoulder and giving it a good shake. Shaggy hair obscured most of his face, except for a lip ring that glinted in the sun.

Combat Boots laughed louder. His right hand clutched an open lighter, the flame thrashing.

All the warmth drained out of Inez.

"I was right. All along—about everything, I was right. What do you think of that, assholes?" he howled, turning on his heels. Inez barely ducked out of the lighter's arc.

Tiger Tattoo stepped aside. "You're out of your damn mind!" he scoffed. "I'm not about to die here."

The smell of the smoke was stronger now. Past the undulating trees, Inez thought she glimpsed a smudge of gray. "What did you do?" she muttered, slack-jawed.

She took another step back, but Combat Boots swung around and seized her wrist. She yelped; his bony fingers held deceptively strong.

"Let go of me." She tugged hard, but he clamped down harder. "*Ow*—stop! Let *go!*"

A tremor traveled up her legs from the ground.

Lip Ring and Tiger Tattoo glanced at each other, then broke out running, following their original course into the treeline.

Another tremor, then another. Softly, in the back of her skull, a familiar hum sounded.

"You know I'm right. You were right there with me," Combat Boots ranted, pressing his pale, pocked face in close.

Inez had readied a leg to kick him where it would hurt, when thundering footsteps broke in. The air smelled like death.

The treeline shattered open.

Inez barely recognized the willow. Swirling fire engulfed its extremities, each wispy vine a wick. Dark billows rose thickly from its upper half. It looked hasty, incomplete, the trunk barely divided enough for movement. It limped forward, and each ungainly step filled the air with a cacophony of dreadful cracks. Behind it, a trail of red and black cut into the park as far as Inez could see.

The air was kindling.

She wanted to scream, but her lips formed useless shapes around nothing and made no sound. Combat Boots' grin melted away. He released her arm and ran.

The willow screeched, heaving after him. One leg splintered apart as soon as it met earth, and the whole creature teetered, then came crumpling thunderously down. Breathless, she couldn't call out for it.

Embers flew, swallowing the brittle foliage in a flood of char. The willow craned the blackened remains of its head down and made a high, broken sound, then collapsed in a tide of cinders.

Tears and smoke burned Inez's eyes. She whipped around and around, but couldn't find the trees, or the sky, or the creature. Ash coated her tongue and crept down her throat no matter how she coughed. She fell to her knees and wheezed helplessly.

Everything was falling apart again.

Nowhere to run. The air was red, her sweat was red, her thoughts were red.

There was a choice, a choice. What was it?

Inez reached for her inhaler.

Get out—

But it was gone.

—or get wiped out.

Darkness descended. It swallowed her whole and washed away the scorched clearing. A rough and solid slab slipped under her legs and hoisted her up, and up, and up from the ground. She scrabbled for balance, gasping weakly. Her fingertips scraped bark.

Cracks of light revealed the mass shielding her: a thick canopy of leaves.

Inez reached out to touch them, and her inhaler fell into her palm with a muted thump. She took two doses. On her first good breath she tasted foliage, then hacked out black dust.

The tree lurched into motion. The branch beneath her shifted and nestled her against the upper part of the trunk. She heard the distant crackle of fire, and vaguely smelled the smoke. More than anything she felt the rocking of the tree, of the giant as it walked, cradling her against its bulk.

Lost for words, she took deep, grateful breaths of the mossy bark. Tears streamed through the dust on her face, over her cracked lips, and onto the tree.

She was alive.

Seconds or minutes or hours passed before the creature creaked to a halt, and Inez's forehead lightly smacked its rough flesh. The limb that held her curled up and drew her away from the trunk.

Air crashed over her. The shield of leaves unraveled and bared her to the sunlight. She blinked, and saw the chugging smoke leaking from the center of the park, how glowing fire split the trees with crimson light. For a moment she soared, weightless, against the bleeding sky. Then the branch that bore her stretched and tilted. She slipped from bark to concrete.

Sidewalk chilled her feet. A shape heaved through the air and smacked the pavement: her backpack.

The creature pulled away, back toward the burning forest.

Inez howled with every last shard of herself, "*No!*" She shot forward, fingers grasping the rusted fence.

The creature's limbs groaned as it withdrew, unheeding. Fear thundered in her skull. She hauled herself halfway up the fence in an instant, until the tree turned back to her in a creaking blur. Bark met her shoulders, leaves pried her fingers open. Together they pushed her, struggling, back down to the pavement.

Sirens resounded from the verging streets.

"Don't go back in there." she rasped, fresh tears stinging in her eyes.

This couldn't be happening. It couldn't save her just to disappear again. She was so tired of being left, of being alone.

"It's too late. You'll burn."

The creature replied something just as broken. Still, it pushed her to the sidewalk.

"Don't, please. Stay with me," she cried, clutching the branch and tugging it closer. Leaves caressed her face.

The giant murmured quietly and pressed itself into her hands for just a moment, then pulled away. Behind the fence, the creature turned and stomped back into the forest as fire engines pulled up on the street, and Inez wept, drowned out by the sirens.

When figures began to pour from the trucks, she scrambled across the street and deposited herself on a bench beside a dried-up fountain. Flocks of chattering onlookers crowded at the fence as the minutes drew on and smoke stole the color from the sky. None spoke to her, and she didn't speak to them.

Once she turned her back to the park, and the fire, and all the clamor of the scene, she didn't look back. She wouldn't.

It was what she'd done when she left her mother. She made her choice and knew not to turn around, but not because she'd go back if she did. She couldn't look back and move forward at the same time. She had to choose. So she chose running. She chose a future, just like she'd done before.

Dread and shame roiled together in her chest. She'd had no right to beg a guardian to abandon its duty, its home, for her. She was nobody.

She'd been so naïve, thinking that running away was the same as escaping. The same as healing. But distance had nothing to do with it. There was no escaping the past, just learning to carry it.

Her mother, that house, they were just memories. Soon the park would be too. There were so many hollow places in her now; she had more than enough room to keep them safe. She could carry them forever.

Inez sat quietly for a long time. Then she put on her shoes and walked to the train station.

Inside, the building was even colder than before, with polished floors that squeaked with every footfall. She passed at least ten TVs, their screens all flashing red, alternating headlines reading, FIRE IN OLD LANDMARK WERIFEST PARK. AUTHORITIES RESPONDING TO REPORTS OF UNIDENTIFIED FIGURE SEEN WITHIN.

Groups huddled beneath the television sets, their eyes squinted, gesturing emphatically at the footage of the fire, but Inez was too far away to see what captivated them. They paid no mind to her or her ash-caked clothes.

She washed herself clean in a bleached white bathroom. The soap smelled harsh and fruity, and it erased the must of scorched earth from her skin. When at last she scrubbed at the tracks her tears had left in the dirt on her face, the door squealed across the tile, and a woman walked in.

Contorted over the sink, Inez froze, and the stranger did too. She was blonde, with ivory skin, and wore a red pantsuit. Her eyes examined Inez with scalpel sharpness for only a second, then softened to glimmering amber.

Droplets of lukewarm water ran down Inez's chin and puddled on the floor. The woman's hands flexed around the handle of her purse. In a saccharine voice that could only belong to a teacher of small children, she asked, "Are you all right, dear?"

"Yeah," Inez said.

"Are you sure?"

She wiped her chin. "Yeah."

The woman's lipstick was the color of freshly bloomed roses. "Do you . . . need anything? Is there anything I can do for you?"

"Yeah."

The woman bought her a ticket for the train. When asked where she wanted to go, all Inez could think to say was, "Somewhere green, with no fences." No more skyscrapers, no more smoke, and no more living things in cages. She was sick of suffocating.

They stood together on the platform afterward, and Inez thanked her, clutching her ticket. The woman just smiled, nodded, and pressed her hand on Inez's shoulder briefly. She watched the slight jerk of the woman's eyes as they flickered between her face and the news still playing on the TV behind her.

She expected some kind of warning. A *"be careful out there"* or, *"take care of yourself."* But all she said was, "The world is a very big place, you know. It's easy to get lost in."

But it's not, Inez wanted to say. *It's not. It's very small. And everything burns just the same everywhere. Burns again, and again, and again. The only thing that changes is who gets blamed.*

No words came. The woman smiled blankly, then turned and left, and so did Inez.

Practically deserted, the train started off with a metallic screech the moment Inez sat down. She let her backpack slide off her shoulders. A tunnel swallowed the car in darkness, and sleep stole her away before the light returned.

When she woke, the train was still moving, but the city was long gone. The woman had slipped her some extra cash before leaving, which she'd spent on a ridiculously expensive sandwich at the nearest food cart to her track. She scarfed the whole thing down in huge, graceless bites. Her stomach soured and ached after that, so she pulled her knees to her chest and stared out the long, scuffed window at the landscape whistling by.

The train passed sun-bleached hills dotted with sparse, squat houses, though for the most part, the land was sprawling and desolate. The weights in her chest shifted and settled and scratched at her like a bundle of needles. The train car was gray and the upholstery smelled just faintly of cigarettes.

Inez put her head into her hands. A soft rustling sound stirred between her ears.

She jerked up, and found bright flickers dancing in her peripheral vision. She turned to the window.

A swarm of golden petals floated astride the train, undulating like a murmuration. Inez gasped, then keened, and pressed her burnt palm to the glass.

A cluster of petals pressed back, vaguely in the shape of a hand.

Carly Racklin's story "The Guardian of Werifest Park" was originally published in Metaphorosis on Friday, 27 September 2019. See magazine.metaphorosis.com

About the author

Carly Racklin (she/they) is a queer writer, editor, and vulture enthusiast with a passion for the fantastical and visceral. Her work has appeared in *The NoSleep Podcast, Haven Spec Magazine, Frozen Wavelets*, and more. She can be found at carlyracklin.com and on most socials @willowylungs.

Sturm und Clang

Sara Kate Ellis

"Just use your homespun innocence, Sam. Those townies will trust you."

"Homespun, Barry? Really?" Sam says. "It's more like Pottersville from *It's a Wonderful Life*. Only without the fun."

Barry's her editor at *Pitch Magazine*, the West Coast's foremost—which means surviving—music magazine, but for an editor, he's surprisingly averse to details. She stares out the Lyft window at the dry, sunlit malaise of Felder's Pike, sees a nail salon and a boarded-up tax office, probably once a thriving brick-and-mortar. On the corner, a payday loan shop hides the thinly painted-over logo of a Starbucks that must have ducked in and out of the town within a season, and Hoagie's Diner, where her favorite band *The Waffle Irons* used to hang out after shows. Now it's a tavern with tinted windows and an entrance scattered with cigarette butts.

"Well, then, push the dying Americana angle," Barry says. "Get a feel for what was there. The sweetness. A look back at an America when it was okay to be aspirational."

He says it like it never was okay to be aspirational, but now that the danger's passed, he's willing to indulge the idea a little. Sam reaches into her handbag, brushing her fingers against her Tic Tac container of edibles for reassurance. Barry's never liked *The Waffle Irons*, just like most people don't like *The Waffle Irons*, but with the death of Mapes Higgins, the band's last living member, his hand has been forced. And Sam, much to her surprise, has just touched down to write a three-thousand-word feature, her biggest for the magazine yet.

She glances at the file she's brought with her, printed out so she doesn't have to squint at her phone. A photocopy of the old liner notes to a reissue of their album sneers up from the page.

'Wherefore art My Roameo' evinces the loneliness and confusion experienced by those average girls, unwillingly thrust into the music business and their strange brand of stardom. They were an amalgam of the everygirl. Not too pretty, but not homely either. Plump in that charming way of girls in farming communities, with the unambitious dreams of homemaking and boys.

Ugh.

"A nice memorial," Barry says. "We'll throw in some copy about Niles Deep."

There it is. The real reason Sam's here. Niles Deep, an algorithm in the guise of a soulfully bland white boy, just namedropped the song in his latest hit, 'Cool Run Deep'.

Wherefore art my Roameo
I'm here yo! I'm here yo!

Sam's not thrilled her chance to write about her favorite band has been generated by a bot-thario, but she'll take it. She's twenty-eight, still paying off loans in a rent-controlled apartment, and her mother is telling her to take up teaching. Poor man's Pottersville or not, she's come to find redemption or a recharge. Or something.

"A nice hometown memorial," Barry says. "Have it to me by Monday."

•

The first time Sam heard the *Irons*, she laughed like everyone else, played the LP once more out of disbelief, and then—telling herself it was for kicks—listened repeatedly until each song became an earworm. Either the girls—Mapes, Amy, and Edith — were geniuses, or they were the worst band in the world. Most critics bent toward the latter, describing their sound as "a nasal cacophony whose key changed like the Dow during a meltdown... a nonsensical mishmash of teenage melodrama mixed with plain Jane reserve." They were the garage band that never quite made it out of the garage, so bad they were brilliant. This was why Gen X women loved them. This is why Sam, a Millennial or a Zennial—that window keeps changing—loves them, too.

Her first stop is Felder's Pike High, the girls' erstwhile, not-quite alma mater. Ingrid Bevan, former Mapes classmate now school counselor, is giving her the grand tour.

"Not a lot of folks around here care for their music much, to be honest," she says. She leads her to a display case in the double-load corridor, her expression somewhat apologetic. "But we're proud of them all the same."

A few ribbons and photographs are pinned haphazardly to a felt board. There's an old black and white of *The Waffle Irons* jammed in between one of a winning golf team and someone taking a second-place award in a national speech contest.

"What was it like?" Sam asks. "On their last day?"

The story goes that their father Ward, a government contractor, cracked after tanking his portfolio. His solution? A get-rich-quick scheme involving a truckload of cheap instruments and pulling Mapes, Edith, and Amy out of school. From then until his death in the Bechlan asylum three years later, the girls spent their days isolated, practicing instruments and holding concerts at birthday parties and the Runyon Community Center. Preparing for a big break that never happened. The girls released one album with a print run of two thousand copies. It got little to no airplay and they never released a second, although they were working on it. Sam's got a few pages of the sheet music copied from the U.C.L.A. archive, scrawled by hand in a million different colors, and despite Barry's trivialization of the assignment, she harbors a secret hope she may unearth the rest.

Bevan shrugs. "They were pretty circumspect, but that was how those girls were. Honestly, I think Mapes was happy about it. She didn't get along with the teachers here."

"Really?" Sam's eyes drift over the photo: the girls hunched up on the stage, their instruments surrounding them like oversized luggage. They don't look much like rebels. Ward even boasted something to that effect in the liner notes, how they were 'counter to the counter culture'.

"Mapes was too smart." Bevan says. She glares at a pair of boys as they scurry past her down the corridor, late for class. "All three of them were. Mapes and Edith were already taking classes at the local college."

"College?" Sam turns back to her, blinking in surprise. "And Ward allowed it?"

Bevan waves her off like it's obvious. "Of course. He talked the college into letting them attend."

Sam takes this in as Bevan directs her to a set of carpeted stairs at the end of the hall.

"Do you know what they were studying?"

She expects to hear something like Intro to Accounting or Home Management, but Bevan smiles a little wryly, as if Sam's response was predictable.

"Advanced calculus, linear algebra, that kind of stuff. Mapes used to really tick off our math teacher, Mr. Dredley. She was way ahead of him." She stops before a set of heavy doors. "Here we are."

Sam shakes off her confusion. Nearly everything she's read about the band alludes to their averageness. Their being torn from school itself was never treated as a squelching of their potential, but the deprivation of what middling observers might refer to as a 'normal life'. She reminds herself to ask Bevin more questions later, but right now she's got to focus. The shop class is part of *Irons* lore. It's where the girls played their last show, unbeknownst to their father, returning on the day that, had they stayed enrolled, would have been Amy's last as a senior. Sam's got a lone, grainy black-and-white from the event. In it, the girls stand next to a boxy metal sculpture adorned with vacuum tubes and wires. Their instruments and amplifiers flank the trio like lumpish rooks.

"I wasn't there," Bevan sighs. "But the girls came in during the final class period, locked the room, set up, and started playing. Principal Mosier chewed them out and kept their equipment impounded for a couple of weeks, but not much else. Didn't tell their Dad on them."

"Nice of him," Sam says.

Bevan shrugs, a mix of sour and sad puckering her features. "He knew what they were dealing with at home."

The concert was just a few days before Ward checked into the asylum. Did the sisters sense a weakness and act on it?

She takes in a breath, readying herself for her *Abbey Road* moment, but the room Bevan opens up on lies strictly in the present. Bright halogen spills over row upon row of kids with anime hairstyles, all clacking away at their laptops. A clash of midis and dub beats and vocoder outbursts pings around the room like cannon fire. It's music, or a semblance of it, but it scrapes against Sam's eardrums like a saw blade. She's been on her share of music pilgrimages, The Motown Museum, Hendrix's grave, and the old Satyricon club in Portland, but she doesn't think she's ever been more disappointed. It's as if Niles Deep and his algorithms have usurped this part of the *Irons'* story too.

"Kind of like stepping onto the Tardis, I imagine," Bevan says, a hint of pride in her voice. "It's a computer lab now."

Sam's about to press her hands to her ears, but she stops herself as she takes in the equally confused gaze of the instructor, a dark-haired, bespectacled woman who slaps her laptop shut as if they've caught her running a search on homemade explosives.

"What is this, Ingrid?" She's clearly not happy about the intrusion.

Bevan plants a palm across her forehead. "Oh, my word, I forgot to tell you. Florence, this is—"

Sam crosses between them, offering her hand. "Sam Taber from *Pitch* magazine."

The woman bends over her desk to take it, her grip hard and a mild scowl tugging at her lips. She's buttoned-up yet effortless, in a denim shirt and dockers, a cross between a schoolmarm and a Silicon Valley hopeful. Sam suspects she must have seven exact copies of that outfit in her closet.

"Flo Nagourney." Her eyes drop to Sam's Tee with its bright orange logo reading *Gabba Gabba Hey!*

"This is where *The Waffle Irons* used to hang out," Bevan says. She's already backing toward the door. "I thought I'd—"

"Them?" Flo says. She trains her gaze at some kids in the back of the classroom. "I hear Fortnite, Georgi!" She glares. "And Davis! Update your fic later. I want those loops coded before the bell." She rolls her shoulders back and turns to face Sam. "That's fine, but my kids are up to their ears in Sonic Pi, so it would be great if you could make this quick."

"Not a problem," Sam says.

In fact, she's more than happy to oblige.

Bevan coughs out a quick excuse, ducking out as the din starts up again. Flo doesn't move, however. She's still staring at Sam like an object that doesn't sit right on the mantel.

"Guess this isn't what you came for," she says.

"Not... really," Sam says, a little disconcerted by the sudden awkwardness between them.

"Well..." Flo gestures to a pair of large sockets in the corner. "It's still got the wiring from the old days. I'll give it that. You could power an ENIAC in here."

"A what?"

Flo smiles, as if she shouldn't have expected Sam to get it. "An old mainframe." She looks back, somewhat ruffled. "So the *Irons*, huh?"

"Yeah."

"And someone's paying you for this?"

Flo eyes Sam's shirt again, and Sam can practically hear the calculations in her head. T-shirt plus age plus cheap sneakers equals eking out a freelancer's income at thirty.

"Take all the time you need," Flo says. "Got to get back to the real work."

She turns and leaves Sam in the corner with her face on fire.

●

Real Work.

She's still fuming in the Lyft to her next stop. Those are the same words her mother used, still uses to freeze her insides, dragging her back from that stubborn insistence—very lonely, very stubborn—that she has as much right to pursue a passion as the more privileged kids do. But she does get where this Flo person is coming from. In fact, what stuns her most about Ward's plan is less its ludicrousness than its relative viability. That in the late 1960s-early 1970s, the idea of getting rich off music was only moderately bonkers as opposed to downright delusional.

Imagine having a parent push you to be a musician. An artist, of any kind.

Just imagine.

Dave Blankenship, a former neighbor, still lives next door to the Higgins' old Victorian. It stands fenced in on the lot, sagging and condemned, but he's agreed to let Sam view it from his adjacent backyard.

There's been little upkeep. New battens and sarking boards have been patched in to keep out rain. The gabled roofs and spiny turrets have been dulled to nubs by time and neglect. But she can almost hear the clash of guitars against basement acoustics—Amy's drumbeats and the atonal chorus of 'Wherefore Art My Roameo'. He's one of the most enduring mysteries of the sisters' non-stardom. Roameo suspects have ranged anywhere from innocent crushes to older paramours and even a stray cat. The girls denied every theory.

"We already had a cat," Edith said. "And did you think we had time for boys?"

Blankenship has the look of an astronaut gone-to-seed, blotchy skin once pink with health, a belly pushing out the bright orange frond on the front of a Hawaiian shirt. He points through an opening in the fence between their properties where the boards have split off. "Mapes held on to the old place," he says. "Now she's gone, some upstart's gonna flip it."

Sam guesses that the properties in this town aren't that flippable, but she keeps that to herself. Ward Higgins was admitted to the Bechlan Asylum in the summer of 1969, and died there a year later. Edith and Amy went to live with an aunt on the other side of the country, while

Mapes hitchhiked to the East Coast. She reappeared Heathcliff-like in the mid-1980s, rich off some investment, and moved a few things into the house, but didn't stay. It makes sense and no sense at the same time, Sam thinks, like some sad secret Mapes couldn't quite let go of.

"I used to sneak cigarettes to Mapes," Blankenship says. "She'd stand on a footstool and smoke them by the window and blame me when Ward asked about the smell." He chuckles at the memory. Sam's eyes follow the uneven concrete around the yard, now cracked with age and dandelions.

"Were you close?"

"Good friends," Blankenship says.

"Must have been friction, with all the noise."

He shrugs. "Most of the neighbors weren't so wound up about the music. There were lots of kids trying to be *The Beatles* back then. It was the other stuff."

"Other stuff?"

He squints up at the sky, frowns as if he senses rain. "Lots of banging around in the basement."

"Drums?" Sam's almost checked out on this guy, but there's a note in his voice that transcends bloviating.

"Nah." He shakes his head, almost bitterly, like the kid who was never asked to play. "They were working on something."

She squints at him, then stoops to peer through the fence again. "New material?" She knows this is not what he means.

He pauses and then leans in a little. "If you ask me, nothing good or the Feds wouldn't have taken Ward away. Searched the house too."

Sam steps back, a clipped bark of laughter escaping her. "Really?"

Blankenship could have spouted this story to any of the other journos who've come to cover the *Irons*, journos, who from their previous coverage would no doubt have added some condescending marginalia to their lore. But he's kept this one, waited until Mapes' death.

"Never saw what it was," Blankenship says. "Ward wouldn't let any of their friends get past the front door, but I will say this," he pauses, his Coke bottle lenses glinting with a kooky certainty. "The funny farm doesn't usually show up in suits and sedans."

●

Blankenship's likely just an attention seeker or a sincere oddball, but she does another search for Ward Higgins. The Bechlan Asylum shut its doors in the early '80s and was demolished in '87. But there's a name in an old article in a now defunct local paper, Shepley Labs. It was the last company Ward contracted with before he threw everything into the girls' music career, notable for a series of domestic computing flops, including a cooking computer and an early home playmate called My Buddy. She pulls up a page on dead technology, double-taking on an ad featuring a boxy thing with lightbulb eyes and a grille for a mouth.

A companion more faithful than Rover.

He stays here, while you go there.

The ad copy is close enough to the Irons' lyrics to give her pause.

Not one sold, the website says, but she wonders if it wasn't one of Ward's designs, a preview of failures to come. Or maybe he brought home a prototype. She looks at her watch, regrets not having asked Blankenship more questions. But it's late now, and her mind is churning and there's another place she needs to visit.

Hoagie's is what she expected from the outside, dim and grimy and reeking of snuck cigarettes, but after the weirdness with Blankenship, she's more than pleased with the obscurity. She takes a seat at the far end of the counter and orders a beer. Niles Deep's 'Cool Run Deep' dribbles from a candied-up retro jukebox in the corner, the *Irons'* lyrics followed by his dumbshit rejoinder.

While you Roam

I'm at home

I stay here, You go there

No car, no bike, no feet, no wind

Wherefore art my Roameo

I'm here-yo!

I'm here-yo!

Thief.

The bartender brings her a Pabst. It's flat, but she downs half of it, her shoulders loosening with the buzz. She's about to order a shot when she hears a throat clear and turns to see Flo watching her from a darkened booth nestled behind her.

What's next? she wonders. Her mother walking through the door with a circled ad for entry-level daycare?

They stare at each other for a cold minute. Then Sam lets out a breath and tries, if not a smile, then a conciliatory nod. "Didn't seem like the type for this kind of place." She gestures to the stack of neglected worksheets next to Flo's beer glass. "I mean, with all that real work and all."

Flo shoots her a 'you got me' look and shrugs. "Here's to ladies loitering in ice cream parlors." She lifts her glass and gestures for Sam to join her.

Sam regards her suspiciously for another second. This has a strong whiff of all those times she ran into the cool kids outside of high school and they were inexplicably nice until Monday rolled around. But she grabs her bag and her beer and the gratis basket of popcorn and sits down with Flo in the booth.

"Bad day?"

Flo snorts. "You get warned about a lot of things before you become a teacher, but not that people have mistaken acronyms for algorithms. They really think that kids memorizing their ESLERS and IPFs means they'll automatically know how to conjugate French verbs or enter a Python value." She takes another long pull of her beer. "Even algorithms need content to work with."

"Even that?" Sam nods up at the speakers. Niles Deep's voice is oozing out of them like soft cream.

Flo shrugs, takes another sip of her beer. "Especially that. The formula's been built on thousands of previous successes."

Her tone is more philosophical than argumentative, but Sam's had enough of numbers and success metrics. "Not everything needs a formula."

"The *Irons* could have used one."

Sam doesn't deign to answer that. She senses Flo's eyes on her, feels her deciding in that minute to dial things down.

Flo leans forward, her weight on her elbows. "Honest question, and I don't mean reply guy honest. How can you stand them? The noise? Those listless voices?"

When people ask, Sam usually goes on the defensive. She'll talk about their lack of hipster disaffection, argue that they've got a genuine it-is-what-it-is quality that outshines the grandiose white dude pronouncements of songs like 'Let it Be' or 'Do You Realize'—the latter being the most cloying demand to smile she's ever heard. But from the beginning, their music tugged at something else inside her, an assurance that it was okay to be bad. That it was okay to make the wrong moves, because if you kept going, you might just land on the right ones. And if you didn't? At least they were yours.

"They…" she wraps her fingers around her glass. "I guess they're proof it's not too late, that you can suck by other people's standards and still stumble onto something beautiful."

Flo gives a half-smile, thoughtful but unconvinced. "Sounds like flailing."

"Flailing, huh?" Sam reaches for her backpack, pulls out that file she's been carrying around with her like a complex. "How about I show you something?"

She rifles through the mess until she finds what she's looking for: the photocopies of Mapes' sheet music. They're hand-written and color-coded, with so many looping scrawls across the page, you can barely see where the music starts and stops. "One of the greatest misconceptions about the *Irons*…" She wipes the condensation from the table before resting the pages on its surface. "… is that they were clueless kids banging out random notes. But Mapes and Edith wrote all the music out first. They wrote and rewrote it until it was just the way they wanted it. They weren't flailing. But they weren't imitating or running on some soulless program either. That's the difference."

She nudges the pages in front of her, a chaos of slashes and looping notations, and watches as Flo goes quiet. Her expression is humoring at first, and then that smile disappears.

"You sure?" she says, not dismissively this time, but like she's working out a problem.

"About what?" Sam says.

Flo runs her finger down to a series of slashes and numbers at the bottom of the page. She's staring at it with a mix of bemusement and fascination. "This kind of looks like score."

"That's what I mean," Sam says. "They compos—"

"No, I mean SCORE," Flo says. "A musical notation program. The first." She pushes up her glasses, and lifts the page for a closer look. "It started in '67, but it sure as hell wasn't *this* far along then. When did they write this?"

Sam hesitates, not ready for this sudden show of interest. "Late '69 or '70. Why?"

Flo doesn't answer and Sam doesn't press her. She's experiencing that vertigo when you realize you've gotten someone wrong. Flo's looking at her with the same expression.

"Mind if I copy these?" Flo asks.

"Sure," Sam says. "What for?"

Flo takes a long slug from a tepid water glass she's been ignoring.

"I'm not sure yet," she says.

●

Sam wants to think she's impressed her, that some part of Florence Nagourney caught a glimpse of the *Irons'* genius. In her room, she runs a search for SCORE and finds Flo isn't far off at all. SCORE got its start at Stanford in '67, two years before Ward pulled the girls out of school. Sam doesn't get coding, but the notations from the early incarnations seem rudimentary compared to the ornate chaos of Mapes' sheet music. Was the music part of a program? Was Ward teaching them programming language in addition to the music? Sam paces in the cramped space between the bed and the radiator. Wishes she'd gone right past Blankenship into the house.

Her phone buzzes, loud. She picks it up, her heart stalling as she hears Barry on the other end. He rarely bothers her during a story unless it's bad news.

He gets right to the point, too. "We're going to have to cut your piece down." He sounds exhausted, like this is the last among hundreds of similar calls.

"How much?"

"A thousand words. I'll throw in an extra ten cents per word. I didn't want to do this, Sam. Niles Deep has an album about to drop with 'Cool Run Deep'. Nothing confirmed yet, but I've got to be ready for it."

She doesn't protest. No buts. There's no arguing with Barry. She just asks another question.

"Did you know the girls were smart?"

"Ha. Funny."

"I mean like brilliant smart. Ward wasn't homeschooling them. Not really. They were going to college and—"

He laughs again, as if this time, she's gotten him. "Who've you been talking to? Look, we're not looking for Jim Morrison here. Just a nice, sweet story about some girls with stars in their eyes, okay? I'll see you Monday."

The next question dies in her throat.

●

The Runyon Community Center is one of the only *Irons* performance venues still standing. She's got more than enough material to cover the meager word count Barry's affording her—she's much more worried about affording rent—but she'll be damned if she misses this, for if there's anything remaining of the *Irons'* dissonant spirit, it's here. The stage is rickety, the floorboards sunken and listing toward the exit. For a few minutes, she thumbs in her earbuds and revels in the lopsidedness of it all.

Who you are, where you come from
Who really can care
When you've got
The family that's there?

For a few minutes, the Caligari angles fulfill their promise. She's back amid the jeers and the sweat, the tossed soda cans and doomed-to-fail expectations of nearly every teenage rite of passage. Maybe it's the old school smell of wood and scuffed sneakers, or the growing darkness blurring the edges of past and present, but she catches that ineffability, the flicker not so much of promise, but of the possibility that comes from the decision just to try.

Sam still wants to try. She's close to finding something that's hers; it's the world that keeps giving up on her. This time when her phone rings, she doesn't answer.

She only notices Flo's message after she's played the album all the way through.

[Mind coming by the school? I'd like you to hear something].

●

It's a long weekend with no kids around, and when the security guard leads her to the lab, it feels portentous, not at all like the dry disappointment of the other day. She can already hear a clip of 'My Confidant' playing on a loop, Amy's stroppy drumbeats warring with Mapes' and Edith's oscillating chord progressions.

On the stairs,
Under the chair,
You're there
Even in my hair

Flo turns down the volume and gestures for her to come in. "Sorry for calling you out of the blue like that," she says. "I worried you'd leave town."

There's an agitation in her movements that wasn't there yesterday, like a movie where an old curmudgeon switches bodies with a hip teen. She puts a hand on the back of her chair, swivels it absently back and forth, like she's deliberating. "Their music. It's interesting."

Sam coughs out a laugh. "Is that so?"

"I didn't say 'good'," Flo says, pulling into herself again. "But..." She turns up the volume, lets the rest of 'My Confidant' blare, messy and discordant. "Beginners make predictable music. Same three chords. Same harmonies. But hear that? That quick rise over the dominant chord as it slides up again and then back down for no apparent reason?"

"Ah," Sam says. "So you've got scientific proof that they suck?"

Flo waves off her remark, winces at feedback screech. "No. I mean, maybe. Ever hear of a Markov chain?"

"Not really," Sam says.

"It's a process that lays out a sequence of possibilities, with the probabilities always based on the event before it. They use it for weather, traffic flow, and to replicate the style of a composer. I input the *Irons* music to a program I've been tweaking. You'd better sit down for this."

What comes next is a revelation. It's a version of their music: the chaos, those wildly fluctuating sequences are still there, but each variation mingles perfect harmony with perfect discord, a balance where none should be. Sam's always heard this in their music and struggled to explain it, but here that euphony jumps out, a clear pattern running through the drumbeats and the melody, steady and endless and unforeseeable.

"I expected something roughshod," Flo says, lowering the volume. "Simple and predictable, but with this... every deviation evokes a myriad of other departures." She draws back, face drawn; her dark eyes are brimming with excitement. "I didn't mean to make things sound so soulless the other night. I was feeling pretty soulless myself, to be honest, but this is something special, Sam."

Sam feels a flutter of something roll through her, a faint reverberation of the music.

"Do you..." she says. "Do you maybe want to break into a house?"

●

At night, the Higgins' Victorian looks a little more forbidding; the paint is faded and chipping, blending into the overcast sky as if a shift in the clouds might cause it to flicker from view. They creep through Blankenship's driveway, squeezing safely through the hole in the fence without incident. Sam starts for the front of the house, but Flo gestures toward the same basement window through which Blankenship passed his contraband soda and cigarettes. If they keep it quiet, they should be able to carry this off.

Flo fishes a flathead screwdriver from the pocket of her denim jacket. "I jump motherboards with these all the time," she whispers, slipping the tip under the window beading. Rot has set in the wood, leaving only a thin line like black mold on caulk that gives easily. She slips the screwdriver beneath the glass and nudges it from the weather-damaged frame.

"You want to go first?" she says.

Sam doesn't mind if she does.

The basement is a showroom of her expectations: a time capsule of wood paneling, low-ceilings, and yellow carpet muted into blood orange by the darkness. This is where it happened, where Ward exiled his daughters, and where they practiced their instruments until their fingers bled.

Flo tracks the flashlight along the walls, across the pencil marks marking their heights in a doorframe, that long series of befores. The paneling's been stripped from the back wall along with a large block of carpet, revealing an expanse of pocked concrete and exposed wiring.

"They were powering something bigger than a few guitars," Flo says, nodding at a series of cupholder-sized outlets, their mouths worn and blackened from use. In the corner, obscured by a tangle of hippy beads, is a large, blocky shadow.

Sam freezes, afraid this will be nothing, another grandiose overture that flops into a limping coda, but Flo's fingers find hers, tugging her forward as she casts her beam over a surface of dark chrome. It's a cabinet, the interior a hybrid from a mad scientist movie and some old timey player piano. Row upon row of bulbs and buttons peer from inside like some primordial, eye-studded creature. Vacuum tubes sag from its sides like limp appendages. She flashes back to that shop class photo, that strange, cumbersome thing near the amplifiers. There's a resemblance to the *My*

Buddy model, but this is a bigger, far more complicated beast.

Bevan's and Blankenship's words come back to her.

Mosier kept their equipment impounded for a couple of weeks…didn't tell their Dad on them. Mapes was too smart.

They were building something.

"While you roam, I'm at home," she whispers. "They must have known those men were coming for Ward. They hid it at the school because they knew Mosier wouldn't contact him. And what self-respecting G-Man would suspect a trio of dopey girls capable of creating—" The words stop in her throat. She doesn't have them. Not yet.

Flo lets out a low whistle in accompaniment as she reaches over, her fingers trailing under a dusty cylinder of paper marked up in Mapes' chaotic hand.

No car, no bike, no feet, no wind.

"It was them," Sam says.

"Who?" Flo's gaze follows hers down to a faint scrawl at the bottom of the page.

Your Roameos,
Mapes, Edith, and Amy.

It's not a *My Buddy*, but a much larger version of it, more eyes, a larger grille for a mouth regarding them without judgment. Like it's been waiting for them all along.

●

On the drive back, they park the car at the edge of Goddard Lake.

The moon's out and the air has just enough chill to add a bite to their exuberance. They stay close to the car, not daring to risk the moldering treasure in the trunk; the books and papers, and the old and very heavy Disc Pack Flo jimmied out with her screwdriver. It's what they could carry away safely, but already Flo is talking about going back, even about putting down an offer on the house if she can scrape together the money. She's pacing back and forth as she talks.

"Hear of Alan Turing?" Flo turns to her, her voice shaky. They could both use a drink.

"Saw the movie."

"The good one with Derek Jacobi?"

"The lousy one with Benedict Cumberbatch."

She laughs, but something unspoken passes between them, an acknowledgement of what already feels steady, a routine. Flo is rigid and methodical, and much more in control of her life, but to Sam, she's a much-needed constraint in her algorithm.

"He built this monstrosity called the Aural Artefact," she says. "Programmed in the British National Anthem and Glenn Miller and..." She leans back against the hood of the car. "It was the first recording of computer-generated music, and it sounded awful, like a pipe blowing a raspberry." She slips her hands into her pockets. "But it reminded me of the *Irons*... There's a lassitude there, like the machine just wasn't in the mood." She takes in a breath, her dark eyes now deep with possibility.

"Look," Flo says. "I am not even close to understanding this, only that there's a lot more to this than a trio of girls and a failed music career, and..." She raises her hand, her smile flat as if she's growing impatient with herself. "I don't mean it that way. It's just that if you want someone to help you uncover the rest... I mean, I—I'd like to. Very much."

Sam feels the warmth travel to her cheeks. "Like maybe uncovering the shocking revelation that Roameo wasn't a boy?"

"Or a cat," Flo says.

"You've done your homework."

"I'm a teacher," Flo says. "I lead by example."

They grin at each other, bodies loosening as they meet in the middle. Sam doesn't worry about her mother or the thousand words she's got to plunk out by Monday. Barry will get what he wants: a phoned-in cutesy retrospective on three hapless, dopey girl musicians. And sure, Sam might even have to work in retail for a spell, but failure's just another disguise when they don't know what's coming.

She's got a real story now, about three girls in isolation; three lonely geniuses who built a friend and a collaborator, creating music into which the four of them could pour their loneliness. Art out of circumstances. It's a much better story than the one even the *Irons'* well-intentioned champions assigned to them; much better than the one she's assigned to herself.

And on the drive back, when Niles Deep's 'Cool Run Deep' drips from the radio, she finds herself singing along.

Sara Kate Ellis's story "Sturm und Clang" was originally published in Metaphorosis on Friday, 29 April 2022. See magazine.metaphorosis.com

About the author

Sara Kate Ellis is a Lambda Emerging Writers Fellow and attended the Milford Science Fiction Workshop in 2017 and 2022. Her stories have appeared in *Analog, Fusion Fragment, Shoreline of Infinity*, and forthcoming in *The Magazine of Fantasy and Science Fiction*. She is currently an assistant professor at Meiji University in Tokyo, where she lives with her partner and two ornery street cats. She occasionally writes academic-ish things about American comics and manga. Her first novel *If the Stars Are Lit* is forthcoming in 2005 from Luna Press.

Socials: BlueSky: Skateellis.bsky.social; Twitter: @skellis13; Instagram: sarakatellis

The Friendly Ghost

Ashley R. Carlson

A Year Before

Conversations with you were never dull (it was one of the main reasons I wanted to marry you), but that night things had taken a random turn from flirty innuendos and our cat's sudden-onset sneezing attacks to more macabre fare.

You'd just told me about a dangerous incident that happened on the work site, and that if things had been left running a *little* while longer, you could've lost a limb or worse from exploding shrapnel.

I'm probably not gonna make it past sixty, you texted, before insisting that 'when' you died before I did, I had to remain in lifelong mourning and embrace celibacy wholeheartedly. I told you that was ridiculous—on numerous counts—because our parents were older than that already, spry in that middle-class, Boomer way that propelled them haughtily on through retirement, golfing and brunching and perpetually driving five miles under the speed limit wherever they went.

Well if I die first, I'm going to haunt you, I joked. The text exchange was one of thousands we'd shared during our year-long marriage and two years of dating before that. They were a godsend to me, those (usually) cheerful blue bubbles coming in spurts (interspersed with the occasional NSFW Snapchat pic), to offer a comforting, digital tether for the two weeks of every month when work took you out of state.

Don't even say that.

It could happen, Dan! Don't live in denial! And I'm nice, because I want you to get remarried and everything.

It better not, and I wouldn't. But fine, I guess you can haunt me. Just promise you'll be a friendly ghost.

What, exactly, is a 'friendly' ghost? I munched on a Milano cookie as I typed, pausing my reality show on the flat-screen—a show you unwaveringly refused to watch because of the cast members' 'arguments about a chihuahua named Lucy Lucy Apple Juice' that comprised most of the season's overarching plotline. I had this sudden craving to know what sort of ghost you'd deem 'tolerable,' and added another message to our text stream—the ghost emoji, draped in white with its tongue stuck out, arms raised in mid-scare. *Boo! I see you. Do you see me?* it implied, a lighthearted caricature of the real thing for kids and still-honeymoon-phasing couples to send one another on Halloween.

One who helps the person they haunt.

What, like in the movie Ghost, *with Patrick Swayze? For justice and all that?* I texted, digging in the bag for another Milano and coming up empty with a disgruntled sigh; reality shows always made me ravenous. They were a modern-day, gluttonous feast of drama and intrigue, except that the fighters in the arena had been replaced by diamond-draped, viper-tongued housewives.

No, not like that, you replied. I could almost hear you utter it aloud, the threat of sorrow deepening the tenor of your voice, one normally so animated with jest. The topic had edged into depressing territory, especially when we were a thousand miles apart.

Then what? I typed, still acutely curious of your definition, for this was a page as-yet-unturned in the book that was your thoughts and feelings. *What kind of ghost would you like me to be?*

Maybe you'd been called away from your phone to tend to an issue on the construction site, or a manager had come into the office and scowled to find the team's star supervisor engrossed in his phone at the start of another nightshift—but you didn't respond for a while, and by then I'd finished my show, tucked the cat in, and lay curled under the covers of the king-size bed we shared only part time.

I promise, baby, I texted to conclude the discussion, for I knew you well, and while you were the epitome of showy masculine verve—you lived to lift weights at the gym, used gag-inducing "bro"-ish terms too often for me to count, and could grill up a perfectly smoked brisket in your sleep—you were the more sensitive of the two of us; your center was ooey-gooey, and I had to be careful not to jostle your insides while you were away. *I'd be a friendly ghost*, I asserted via text, and that was it, followed by a quick *goodnight, I love you so much!!!!* with lots of exclamation points because you liked them. Tomorrow we'd resume our conversation on those benign issues between newly married couples—paycheck amounts and which bills were coming up next, small health concerns centered around bowel regularity that kept us laughing and did much to close the gap of physical space between us in one perfectly timed poop emoji.

I'm happy to say that all these months later, I've kept my promise.

A Week After

It's my funeral today, but goddamn if it doesn't look like yours.

It's awful to see you like this—eyes as bruised underneath as over-ripe plums, thick dark hair gelled to one side by the budget-salon stylist you visited this morning at the request of your mother (and I'm thankful she insisted, because you haven't washed it yourself in nearly a week). I've only ever seen you looking this haggard once before, following our first and only separation eight months into the relationship, when I still wasn't sure we were right for each other. I'd showed up right after a long, expletive-and-tear-filled post-breakup phone call, because I missed you and it stung to hear you so distraught. As I walked up that narrow sidewalk to find you in the suffocating heat of midsummer twilight, the way your wilted stance against the doorway made me ache was evidence enough that regardless of our differences, I was deeply in love and never wanted to let you go again.

This hurts too—worse, because back then I'd chosen to separate from you, something I could (and swiftly did) remedy. These circumstances are unequivocally more permanent.

Your eulogy is nice, if a little short, and you don't cry. You haven't much, and it's concerning, but not because I'm worried you don't care. There's a place inside that I think you've gone to, burrowed deep, deep down to hide, even deeper than that time I ended it and you said on the phone you hadn't been able to sleep or eat properly in weeks, and didn't really see the point in changing that. You need someone to coax you from that insidious, inviting darkness before it seeps in and poisons you to the bone—and I'm not going anywhere until I lead you out.

I promised.

Two Weeks After

I'm still learning the rules of being a ghost.

You shiver if I touch you, but that's about it. You only seem to hear me at night while you're sleeping, and every time I've whispered "I love you" and "I'm going to help you through this," you've just moaned or whimpered, as if the mere lilt of my voice is a minor but still very present kind of torture.

I wander the house once you're asleep—wary of the glowing doorway that appears in the corner of every room I enter, softly lit along the edges of the closed door and inviting me to approach, but never demanding it.

I visit with the cat instead, who can definitely still see me based on the way his protuberant eyes follow me in the dark, wary and appraising, as if he's forgotten I was his beloved caretaker mere weeks ago. Maybe I look different; maybe my ghostly form has retained the gruesome injuries sustained during my death, and they frighten him. For all I know, an array of lacerations still spider-webs across my forehead, a bit of exposed gristle hanging where the truck burst through the driver's side to split the lower part of my face in half. There's no reflection in the mirror to confirm this, but when I run my fingertip across my chin, its journey is reassuringly smooth.

I don't need sleep or sustenance, but I'm able to perch on furniture well enough, and can even turn the TV on if I slam my hand against the remote enough times. It took me more than an hour to get the damn thing to work playing the latest episode of my favorite show—you haven't dismantled the DVR preferences yet, though when I was alive you bemoaned the fact that our limited recording space was always full of bullshit squabbles in fancy restaurants and phony attempts at finding the 'one'. These shows give me comfort in the silent hours of the night when you finally find rest—what I hope to be *true* rest, not the hours spent catatonic in bed until your mom or mine shows up and forces you to eat some of their homemade empanadas and pozole, before busying themselves with gathering up the growing, untouched pile of dirty laundry strewn about the house and momentarily freezing when they find a pair of my socks or underwear in the fray, before hurriedly tossing them in the washer with the rest.

It's not long before the cat joins me on the couch for our nightly viewings, moving between you in the bedroom and me on the sofa to purr and knead the thick, wooly blanket we used to nestle under for *Game of Thrones* marathons—a child in the midst of two parents separated by far more than divorce.

One Month After

You are acting strange.

I notice it first when you call your boss and quit out of the blue, even though they've been exceptionally understanding about it all, offering three months' worth of paid leave following the funeral.

It's when you try to give the cat to your parents that I realize my nightly stream of encouragements beside you in bed haven't ameliorated your grief in the least.

"I don't want him anymore," you slur on the phone, a full tumbler of whiskey in hand. You've been drinking all day, unaware of my reprimands to at least *eat* something between aggressively thrown-back shots of liquor. "He was hers. I don't fucking *want* him! I HATE THIS FUCKING CAT AND I DON'T WANT TO CLEAN UP HIS SHIT ANYMORE!" you bellow into the receiver.

That's a complete lie—I know it, you know it, for god's sakes, the cat knows it. He's scowling at you right now, having just left you another smelly gift in his litterbox.

Whatever your mom says on the other end sets you off. You shout again and throw the phone at the wall hard enough to shatter the screen, before storming into the hallway toward the medicine cabinet.

"What are you doing?" I cry as I follow you, watching as you rummage through the bottles of ibuprofen and Midol and Sudafed with trembling fingers.

You pivot and stride through me to return to the kitchen. Reach for a glass from the cabinet and fill it with water from the sink.

"What the fuck are you *doing*?!" I repeat as you fumble with the childproof lid on the bottle. "Hey! Stop it right now! *Stop!*"

I slam into you and it's like fighting against wind, like passing my hands through a cloud of smoke for all the difference it makes. You've got a palmful of round orange pills now, at least three dozen, and you're bringing them to your lips with a hand that's suddenly steadier than I've seen in weeks. I scream so loud and shrilly that it frightens the cat and he's off like a shot under the couch, but you're undeterred, they're in your mouth now, you're about to chase them down with water—

"DANIEL HERNANDEZ, YOU STOP IT *RIGHT FUCKING NOW!*"

My shriek shatters a nearby trio of glass bottles full of seashells we gathered on a Puerto Rican trip to celebrate our first wedding anniversary, splinters of blue-green glass and shells exploding across the kitchen table in all directions.

It also breaks the glass in your hand.

You stand there, stunned, bare feet strewn with fragmented glass, bottom lip split and bleeding from an errant slice. You bend over the sink and spit the pills out, a hunk of saliva-slicked half-white, half-orange rounds, and back away to survey the mess.

Your brown eyes are wary, wide.

You say my name—*mouth* it, soundlessly. Like a prayer.

You finally start to cry, torso-shattering sobs that bring you to the kitchen floor. I bend to take you in my arms, forgetting for a moment you can't feel a thing.

Eleven Months After

You've just returned to your new apartment from the gym, sipping on a protein shake. You've been lifting at this new gym a lot recently, and it shows in the supple sinews of your back and arms, the renewed vibrancy of your light brown skin.

It's all new, as if scouring me from your surroundings will also scour me from your memories: apartment, city, job, furniture, clothes. You sold the house, donated our stuff to charity, got a new position in another state—but you kept the cat. I encouraged each step, talking to you day and night about why you should stay alive, how much more there was for you to do. A fresh start was what you needed and what you got, but all that newness didn't mean I was ready to leave. You were still alone (the cat didn't count), and I'd decided that in order to *really* make it better—to live up to my promise—you deserved a full life with someone new.

I was concerned about a forced disconnection before my goal was achieved; perhaps I was bound to the *house* and not you, and when you drove off I'd have to say goodbye for good and finally go through the doorway I'd staunchly been avoiding for nearly a year.

On the day you packed your few remaining belongings and set off with the cat for the big city and the new job, I waited in front of the house, watching until your car's red brake lights were only an echo, a smeared corona when I shut my eyes; a ghost of what had once been concrete, been *there*. I paced the driveway, ignoring that damned glowing doorway ever-present in the corner of my vision.

"I'm not ready yet! *He's* not ready yet! Fuck off!" I finally hollered at the door, and it shrank and shrank, to the size of a doggie door and then a mousehole and then a pinprick, until it winked out completely for the first time since the car crash.

I paced that driveway in your absence, searching my memory for how I'd gotten from that fluorescent-bathed hospital room to the funeral and back to the house, but I truly couldn't recall.

It wasn't too long before I *did* end up where you and the cat were, suddenly going all misty like vapor passing between someone's lips on a cold night, only to come together again in your new apartment just in time to see you shuffling inside with the cat carrier and a suitcase.

"So I do haunt *you*, then," I said, thoroughly relieved. I still had a lot left to do.

A Year and Nine Months After

You're checking yourself out in the bathroom mirror, and I laugh.

"I *told* you you'd start losing your hair one day," I say as you gather a bit of gel in your palm and attempt to wrestle your brown strands into a coif that somewhat hides the thinning at your temples and crown. You've got a date tonight, the first since I died, and I'm not trying to be a brat, but she looks a bit...*basic*. That's my jealousy talking, I know—I was the one who prompted you about this online dating stuff anyway, murmuring in your ear night after night to make sure you heard me. But then you went and matched with some Basic Blonde who looks nothing like me and wore a goddamn bathing suit in every single one of her pictures (if you can call a strip of fabric up your ass-crack a suit), so your selection has me questioning whether this was all a huge mistake.

While you're gone I putter around the apartment, tidying up in ways I know from experience you won't notice. I'm watching the latest housewife mayhem when you start to unlock the front door, and I manage to turn the TV off just in time to see you tripping over the apartment's threshold with the Basic Blonde in tow.

"Christ, you're drunk," I mutter as you fumble for the light switch and quickly give up on finding it. "Better not have driven home—" I stop myself there; you've done a few questionable things since my death, but committing the very same act my killer did isn't one of them.

Without preamble, BB yanks you toward your bedroom. You leave the room's door open—no one lives here but you and the cat, right?—so I'm forced to listen to what happens next, glancing every so often at the ethereal doorway to my right with a sneer (it reappeared a few weeks back, just as incandescent and pleasant-looking as ever).

"This isn't *exactly* what I meant when I said you should start dating again," I chide, watching the cat vacillate between licking his butt and peering sympathetically in my direction.

When it's over, the blonde has the audacity to think it's time to talk. I waltz into the bedroom and lean against the wall—this is too rich a conversation to miss.

"So," she begins, spread-eagled on the mattress beside you. She's pretty (if generic) in person, and this irritates me to an unexpected degree. I snarl in her direction, and the drapes nearby ripple. "Am I the first?"

"What?" you say, breathless, but already sobering up, by the sound of it.

"Am I the first since...you know."

"Oh, Jesus Christ," I snort, crossing my arms like I'm hugging myself, but it's really because I'm filling up with rage—a rage I've never felt before, a *poltergeist* level of rage. "You *told* her? This chick? Really?"

You squint in disbelief. It must be the alcohol that's loosened your tongue, because you actually respond to her moronic inquiry. "Y-yeah. You are."

"Nice." She says it as if she's won a prize, and I mean yes, you *are*, but the fact she's made it her mission to be the first to bed a handsome widower makes me want to hurl. Just as I'm preparing to gather all of my ghostly powers and attack this girl any way I can—shit, I might even be able to throw a knife from that fancy block in her direction if I try hard enough—you kick her out yourself. It's glorious to watch, really, how you tell her with such authority to 'get your shit and get out'. The way her Juvederm-plumped donut lips fall open in shock is one of the favorite things I've witnessed all year.

When she's gone—in a tornado of slamming doors, incensed cursing, and half-donned clothing—you lock the front door behind her, bare-assed, brown-skinned, and Adonis-like in a swatch of moonlight through the foyer window. You break the thick midnight silence with a word: my name.

For a moment I'm weak-kneed, convinced somehow you know I'm here. The prospect frightens me—I've done this detached dance of communication with you for so long —that it feels strange to imagine interacting directly *with* you.

And so I hug the shadows and admire your familiar form, one I used to embrace from behind as you cooked us dinner, or cling to at the airport before you left for another two weeks away from home. I'm no longer able to do either of those things, but I'm still your friendly ghost—your first love, your wife—and one who's determined not to be your last.

Two Years and Eight Months After

"I have a good feeling about this one," I say as you stand before the closet and dress for the evening in a navy-blue suitcoat, slacks, and tan leather lace-ups. It's a getup you wouldn't have been caught *dead* (har, har) wearing when we were married, but you're a fancy executive now, and this girl is special. Your date tonight sort of looks like me, too— shoulder-length, wavy brown hair; petite; attractive in a composed, Type-A kind of way—which I take as a compliment, if a bit masochistic-leaning on your part.

She's another online match, a lawyer who seems too smart for you (although we thought that about me too). Her first message was polite and personalized, asking about your favorite food. You'd actually seemed to heed my suggestions as I told you each night how best to communicate with her during that pivotal introductory period—not too infrequently, not too often, always with proper grammar and punctuation, laying the wit and self-deprecating humor on thick—and you'd arranged a date at an upscale Brazilian steakhouse in downtown by the third day of chatting.

You've got a spring in your step now as you pour some more kibble in the cat's bowl, adding a spritz of cologne to that naked patch of skin above your collarbone I used to nuzzle on sleepy weekend mornings.

"Have fun," I call out in your wake, but you're already through the door—and if I'm not mistaken, you're whistling.

Four Years and Three Months After

The wedding was understated, chic, and an altogether classy affair I would've approved of myself. The reception was nice too, and there was dancing and music and cake-smashing in each other's faces, and you looked so goddamned happy baby, *so* happy, happier than I could remember you looking on *our* wedding day. I cried about that, but only for a little while.

Once you two leave for your honeymoon, I materialize back in the apartment. The cat's at your parents' place for a week, so it's lonely here now; your laugh and her laugh and your shared inside jokes and frequent lovemaking sounds have become a somber kind of music to me, a melancholic soundtrack that hurts to listen to but that I'm still not ready to turn off.

I watch a reality show as a distraction (she likes them too, and records my favorites), but it doesn't diminish the swirling, unsettled sensation where my stomach used to be.

"Is it time?" I say aloud to the silver-haired TV show host on the screen. You're married now, I've been replaced; my plan, for all intents and purposes, is complete. Yet I'm still not ready to go.

I recline on the sofa and ignore the silvery doorway in my periphery, checking every so often to make sure it's still there.

Five Years After

Normally I'd avoid going to another hospital, but today's a special occasion.

Your new wife's a champion, I'll give her that; I never wanted kids and so you said you didn't either, but based on the way you've doted on her for the past nine months, rubbing coconut butter on the stretched skin of her belly while murmuring in baby-speak to the little life growing beneath your hand, I've been convinced otherwise.

When the labor's over and a high-pitched squeal reaches everyone's ears, *your* expression is the one I look at as the baby comes into view—and it answers the question I've been asking since the day I died.

Later in the recovery room, all is quiet and still, the low, beige-pink lighting of the room far less invasive than it was during my visit years back. The baby is at your wife's breast, periodically eating and falling asleep, and your wife's drifting off too. You sit in the rocking chair to their left, studying them with a slight frown.

"It's scary, isn't it," I muse from the other side of your wife's hospital bed. "So much to take care of. So much to protect; that's why I didn't want one."

You wipe some tears from those beautiful brown eyes, and I know what you're thinking.

"Don't do that," I warn, more forcefully than I've spoken to you in a long time. "Stop it *right now*. That day wasn't your fault or mine, and there's nothing you could've done. You can't worry each day you might lose them too, okay? You can't." I round the hospital bed to kneel in front of you, and you stare right through me as usual. "I kept my promise, and now *you* need to keep one—you need to be free, Dan. You need to *live*. Because you've got so much to live for."

You wipe at your cheeks, at the wetness gathering in the patchy dark stubble along your jawline.

You smile.

Five Years and One Day After

She's one cute baby; takes after you the most, I think, but I'm biased. You've always been the best-looking person I've ever met.

The nurses are taken with her, remarking on what a good baby she is, so mild-mannered and sweet and *smiley*. You and your family are all ready to go; everything's packed, and the baby's received the health check go-ahead to send everyone home.

There's a shimmering doorway here in the hospital too —I've already seen several people go through it during our last two days here. I tried to peek around them to what awaited there, to read by their body language whether it was good or terrible, but I didn't really need to—it leads somewhere nice, and I think I've always known that.

The doctor just said it's time to go. Everyone is ready; the baby's wrapped up tight in a cream-colored onesie, and your wife's all settled in the wheelchair.

"What's her name?" the doctor asks, grinning down at the sleeping baby in the crook of your wife's arm. I expect you to respond the way you have been this entire time—that you both want to spend a few days with her first, to see what feels right.

But you don't say that.

Instead, you say "Eva," and I go rigid where I've been standing in the corner of the room.

"Her name is Eva," you say again, but you're not looking down at the baby, or at the doctor, or at your wife. You're looking at me.

"Eva," the doctor says, surveying your daughter with a smile. "I like that."

Your wife looks a little taken aback, but not for long. "I like it too," she replies, removing one arm from the swaddled baby to reach out and squeeze your hand. She knows who I am, obviously, and as far as I can tell this decision was never settled on—it was always, "Let's just wait and see."

"I've always liked you," I say to your wife as she cradles the baby close, cooing the girl's newly christened name a few times. "Keep taking care of him, okay?"

The doctor leaves, followed by the nurse wheeling your wife and daughter down the hall toward the parking lot. You stay here though, and so do I.

"Goodbye," you whisper, eyes unfocused and roving around the small hospital room. We were in a place like this once, for a much more heartrending reason than this. It's time we were both freed of it.

"Goodbye," I reply, and you dip your chin down, an infinitesimal nod, an acknowledgement. A letting go of that which is already gone.

When you walk out and down the hall the way your family went, I don't follow. Instead, I turn toward the doorway, which grows in size as I approach it, getting brighter around the edges, humming lowly, like the distant crash of waves while napping on the sand in bright sunshine, or that wondrous rumble of imaginary surf accessible at any time if one just cups a seashell to their ear. I grasp the door handle and it's warm in my palm; the first real, identifiable sensation I've had in years.

It feels wonderful.

And I go through.

Ashley R. Carlson's story "The Friendly Ghost" was originally published in Metaphorosis on Friday, 3 July 2020. See magazine.metaphorosis.com

About the author

Ashley is an award-winning author and freelance editor in Phoenix, Arizona. When she's not writing or editing, Ashley enjoys traveling (oftentimes internationally), playing Scrabble with her fiancé (to whom she loses a lot more often than she likes to), and fostering kittens through Arizona Animal Welfare League.

www.ashleyrcarlson.com, @AshleyRCarlson1

Hope on the Vine

R.E. Dukalsky

It was early August and hope was withering on the vine.

It had withered every year so far for the last eleven, so Nima was disappointed rather than surprised. Disappointed, frustrated, demoralized. She really thought she'd gotten the balance right this time.

She knelt in front of the raised mound of earth that should have been nourishing the hope vine's roots, her dirty boots poking out behind her and the sun glinting gently off her greying curls. By this point in the season, the vine should be about three feet tall, with multiple spurs twining eight to ten feet in every direction. Heavy buds the size of the first knuckle of her thumb should be swelling between pairs of reniform leaves gleaming a lustrous dark jade. She should be out here looking eagerly for the first open blossom, a rich yellow stellate flower the size of her hand, shading to the orange of glowing embers in the center. She hadn't seen one for many years.

Instead, she stared disconsolately at a meager vine supporting a few anemic yellow-green spurs. The remaining leaves, with two notable exceptions, were the same undernourished shade, their ribs showing more starkly every day, while their edges turned brown and flaked away. Only one spur, the one that twisted around the rail of the fence, showed any semblance of health, and Nima was as baffled by its continued vitality as she was by the parent vine suddenly giving up on life. It had seemed to be growing on schedule — perhaps a little undersized but a good color

— but instead of progressing to the next stage of growth and putting out buds, it had drooped, retreated, withered. Just like its ten predecessors — those that had even bothered to sprout.

Eleven long years on this struggling piece of earth, trying to tease a hope vine from seed to fruit. So far, this was the closest she had come to success. One fruit was all one could expect from such a young vine, but one was all she needed: proof she could send to her Arbiter that this vine would thrive. Then, at last, she could move on. On to the next impoverished, war-scarred town and the next desiccated, abandoned farm, where the potential for hope or fortitude or patience lay dormant under years of neglect and acres of weeds.

The next, and the next, and the next. One by one until the tired land put the years of war and sorrow behind it for good and all.

But there wouldn't be a next and a next if she couldn't bring this vine back to life. Nima doubted she'd live to see the land restored, but leaving here would be its own reward. She dreaded another roasting summer and dreary winter in the small blue house behind her. Another year of being ignored by her neighbors, loathing them in return, and never forgetting no one wanted her here.

Maybe she hadn't fertilized enough? But no; she'd been side-dressing the vine with the recommended half-cup of the special expensive blend that came from the Wizard's Herbarium, and she marked each application on her calendar so she knew she hadn't missed any. Was the mix itself wrong? They said it was guaranteed, but you never knew what that meant with the wizards you got these days. In her time, guarantees had come with blood, not a letter under shiny gilt seal.

If the mix was good, was water the issue? Possible, but hope vines were notoriously flexible in their water needs. In theory, they could take root and grow anywhere, with minimal tending. That was why they, along with fortitude trees and hedges of patience, were among the first recommended plants for war restoration project sites. Even someone who'd never set finger to a garden should be able to grow one — and once a hope vine established itself, every living thing in the area would flourish as well.

Probably she hadn't figured out the right tending regimen. This was where hope vines could be tricky, according to both her own vague memories and the instructions she received each year with the new seed. Fortitude trees could be watered with either sweat or blood (both of which she had in abundance, particularly in the summer). A hedge of patience would grow well with tears, sighs or, in a pinch, prayers. Hope vines demanded fiddly, intangible things: dreams recounted, promises exchanged, plans laid. But wizards didn't dream, she had no one to make promises to, and under the circumstances plans were not hers to lay. She'd tried making promises to the old farmhouse, to the wasted land around it, to the rickety fence and the empty road, but she wasn't sure they counted. If she were honest, the only promise she meant to keep was the one about leaving.

She'd walk out the gate now and never come back if she hadn't given her word, and not with some fancy seal, but in the old way, with consequences for breaking her oath. She'd promised to stay until she could prove she'd restored local resilience to an acceptable baseline — in plainspeak, until the hope vine was able (or willing?) to reproduce. No one back in the capital knew, or really cared, how long it took or what it asked of the grower. The point was to have wizards scattered across the land, repairing the scars of war where everyone could see them doing it. So here she was until she could cultivate her release.

Nima stroked a finger across one of the limp leaves. "If you stay alive, I leave and you never have to see me again. So save us both some pain and just *grow*," she whispered, putting all the force of her will into it. No effect, of course, except a dull burn up her right arm to complement her aching knees.

"What's wrong with your plant?"

The voice was high-pitched and unfamiliar. Nima looked up to see a girl of about twelve years draped across the fence near the gate ten feet away. Just about where the questing ends of the vine ought to be right now, Nima thought sourly. She'd never seen the girl before, though she had the look of a local: a short, wide body, tawny skin, a blunt nose, and straight, thick black hair cut short above her shoulders. Her eyes were close-set, small, and twinkling with curiosity.

"It isn't growing," Nima said shortly. She was sick to death of these suspicious locals. "Did you need something?"

"I'm Yun," the girl said, completely ignoring the pointed question. "Did you forget to water it?"

"No," Nima replied, trying to rein in her temper. It wouldn't improve her relationship with the locals if she started yelling at children. On the other hand, she didn't care that much about having a relationship with the locals. She turned back to the hope vine, scratching gently in the dirt around the main stalk to see if there was something preying on its roots.

"What about fertilizing? Did you feed it?" Yun asked.

"Yes," Nima said without looking up.

"Did you put it in the right kind of soil?"

"*Yes.*"

"Does it get enough sun?"

Exasperated, Nima gestured at the open sky. Her back twinged, and she looked up with an even more unfriendly expression than she'd intended.

"Hm. Maybe it's getting *too* much sun," Yun mused, unfazed. "Or maybe this isn't a good place for it to grow."

Nima clenched her jaw and bent back down. Maybe the irritating child would get bored and wander away. After a few seconds she heard soft footsteps against the dust and dared to hope. But no luck.

"But I don't know," Yun said, from much nearer, almost right in front of Nima. "It *feels* like it wants to grow here." A brown hand appeared at the corner of Nima's vision, stroking the leaves of the one remaining spur.

Nima looked up sharply. "Don't touch it," she snapped.

Yun whipped her hand away and looked, for the first time, as if she were picking up on Nima's unwelcoming demeanor. "Why not?"

"Because it's *my* vine," Nima replied, hearing how ridiculous she sounded even as the words came out of her mouth. "What I mean is, it's fragile and it isn't polite to touch other people's crops."

This was evidently a new concept to Yun. "I help Aunt Lio with her beans all the time and she says—"

But Nima was done with this conversation she hadn't wanted in the first place. She didn't want what passed for local agricultural expertise, especially from a child, and needed peace and quiet to think about what to try next. "Then I'm sure she would appreciate your help now," she interrupted, then stood up and stalked away, pushing through the stiffness in her knees. "Don't touch my plants," she called over her shoulder without looking back.

●

Working on a half-baked theory that her bad mood was somehow hampering the vine's growth, Nima stayed away from it for the next few days. She kept a sharp eye on the fence, but the girl had vanished back to whatever ramshackle farmhouse she'd come from. Nima saw her traipsing by once on the road, but the girl showed no inclination to stop or pester the vine.

After a week, Nima woke up having slept well, and decided she'd waited enough time to test her theory. If her mood did somehow affect the vine, she'd given it time to recover and should be able to see the effects. She filled her big watering can, sprinkled in the special water-soluble fertilizer and lugged it out to the fence.

The vine looked exactly the same: anemic stalk and spurs, withered yellow leaves slowly crumbling off their ribs... and one perfectly healthy spur climbing slowly around the fence rail along the road. The good spur had even put out another two leaves while the rest of the plant died.

"What...?" Nima stood there, hands hanging down open at her sides. She had learned to grow things; the profusely healthy vegetable garden behind the house attested to that. She glared at the vine, disregarding the theory she'd been testing. "What do you *want* from me?" There was no reason this should be so hard, no reason this spur should thrive while the parent plant died, no reason the one plant that mattered should wither while the rest of the garden flourished.

A sharp trill pierced her despair. Yun was tromping down the road in heavy boots several sizes too big for her, swinging two empty beaten metal buckets, whistling like the cloudy morning had been made for her alone. There was something odd about the buckets; they were the wrong shape somehow, too rounded on the bottom, with asymmetric sides. Nima squinted at them and realized they were infantry helmets, inexpertly beaten into a slightly more bucket-like shape by a *very* amateur blacksmith.

"Did you figure out how to fix your plant?" Yun asked. She must have taken Nima's attempt to parse the helmets-turned-buckets as an invitation to stop and chat.

"No," Nima said, trying to think of a task that would take her away from the fence but allow her to keep an eye on the girl.

"It looks better, though," Yun said, waving one of the buckets at the flourishing spur. At least she wasn't trying to touch it. She wrinkled her nose. "That part, at least."

Nima picked up her watering can and began dribbling the water gently around the roots of the vine. Yun didn't take the hint. She tromped a few steps closer, set the buckets down with a dusty *thump*, and squatted on her haunches in front of the vine. "I think it's happier on this side of the fence."

"Plants don't feel happy or sad," Nima said repressively. She saw Yun shrug out of the corner of her eye.

"Aunt Lio says they do." Aunt Lio was evidently the arbiter of reality. She leaned closer. "What kind of plant is this anyway?"

"A hope vine," Nima said shortly, then surprised herself by continuing, "at least, it's supposed to be."

"I never saw one of those before," Yun said, scrunching up her nose and peering at the plant with renewed interest.

"They aren't very common after the war," Nima found herself explaining.

"Ah," Yun said sagely, although she wasn't old enough to remember even the final years of the war and couldn't possibly understand what lay behind the disappearance of the country's native resilient vegetation. "What's it for?"

For giving you and all your ungrateful kin a future worth growing into, Nima thought but did not say. The last thing she wanted was this girl's irate aunt descending to put the wizard in her place. "If it grows," she said, biting off each word, "it will reinforce the local ecosystem — that means the soil, the water, other plants, the animals that eat those plants, and people who rely on the plants and animals," she added, confident that the local school, if one even existed, did not cover the ecology of resilience.

"We have been having some problems," Yun agreed thoughtfully, just as if she were a grizzled veteran farmer. She leaned even closer to the vine, body rolling at such an angle that Nima feared she would pitch face first into the plant — and the railing.

"Be careful," she said, more harshly than she had intended.

Yun straightened up, but didn't look abashed. "I think maybe this part of the plant isn't bothered by something that's messing with the rest of it," she said. "Or maybe it just likes that I talk to it."

Yun's comment niggled at the back of Nima's brain. Maybe there *was* something affecting the roots or the leaves on the parent vine that hadn't spread to the healthy spur yet — or maybe the spur had some kind of natural resistance...

"I have to go restake the beans," Yun was saying in the background, but Nima was no longer paying attention. She didn't even notice the girl stretching out a stealthy hand to give the new leaves a friendly tap. "I'll be back tomorrow."

●

Yun kept turning up after that. Sometimes for an hour, sometimes for ten minutes, sometimes carrying her ridiculous repurposed buckets, sometimes hauling a feed sack on a little wagon, frequently with her arms full of hollow reeds as wide as her wrist and as tall as she was. She never seemed to be in a hurry or fear that whoever sent her on these tasks would be impatient at her dawdling.

Aunt Lio either ran a slipshod operation or didn't particularly care what this niece was up to. Yun never mentioned her parents, so maybe she was a war orphan dumped on her only known relative. Maybe Lio had so much help on her farm that one lolly-gagging child made no difference. Or maybe they were just relieved to get a break from her questions.

"Do they have hope vines where you come from?" she asked one time.

"No," Nima said.

"Then how do you know how to grow one?"

I don't, Nima thought. "Resilient plants need the same things as any other plants—"

"Where *do* you come from anyway?" Yun interrupted.

"Not here," Nima said, picking up her rake and walking away.

●

"I know this isn't your farm," Yun said another time.

Nima was pruning back the dead leaves on the spurs closest to the healthy one, in case the problem was some kind of spore or mildew. Her shears jumped and nearly clipped a healthy leaf. "What is that supposed to mean?" she demanded.

"Everyone knows you aren't from here, even though you've lived here forever," Yun said with a limber shrug. "When are the people who belong to this farm coming back?"

"They aren't," Nima snapped.

"Maybe this would grow better if they did," Yun said, bumping the vine with grimy knuckles.

"Don't touch," Nima said, but she'd long since given up on the idea that Yun would listen.

"Don't worry, *I'm* not going away," Yun said, more to the vine than to Nima. "Hey look, there's a new grabby bit here!"

●

"How does a hope vine help the... ecosystem?" Yun asked after she'd been coming by regularly for almost a month.

"Different ways," Nima said distractedly, her words punctuated by the *thonk-crunch* of her trowel. She was digging some small trenches to drain excess water away from the hope vine's mound just in case the roots were becoming waterlogged. "Other things... grow better... near a hope vine. Fewer diseases... more abundant production. Roots... stop erosion and make dead soil fertile again. You can live... off a single fruit... for a long time. Healing tea or tincture from the leaves. And just being around the flowers..." she sat back on her heels and wiped her forehead, "I really can't explain what that feels like, you have to experience it for yourself."

"We could really use one of those," Yun said. "Aunt Lio says the beans need a miracle."

"Hope vines aren't miracles, they're applied magic," Nima said sternly. "And you shouldn't expect either to do your work for you."

"I am doing the work," Yun said, but without heat. "But there's a bug that came and it eats the buds before they can bloom." She reached a finger out toward the vine, then pulled it back again.

●

"What's it like?" Yun asked on one unreasonably hot day.

"What's what like?" Nima replied, only half listening as she teased a tendril gently through a gap in the climbing frame.

"Being a bad wizard."

Nima froze with the tendril balanced on one finger. "What do you mean by that?" she asked carefully. Sweat trickled between her shoulder blades.

"Everyone knows," Yun said without noticeable concern. "You're a bad wizard who made all the bad stuff happen in the war."

Nima snatched her hand away from the vine so she wouldn't transmit her feelings through the tender shoots. "That's a gross exaggeration."

"Also, I saw your thing," Yun pointed at Nima's right arm, where the geas runes constraining Nima's magic and her free movement crawled with slow abandon. She'd probably spotted it the first time they met, but Nima found herself tugging her sleeve down anyway, angry at her own shame. She hated any reminder that she was permanently separated from her magic, even though she'd accepted the geas binding to avoid lifetime imprisonment.

"Aunt Lio says getting a nice farm to run isn't a real punishment," Yun persisted. She reached out and casually flicked the vine. Nima winced, but the vine held firm. In fact, it flexed a tendril toward the sun.

Nima picked up her trowel, hefted it, set it down. She didn't like the idea of Yun and her aunt discussing her sentence as if were just moderately interesting village gossip. "Your Aunt Lio doesn't know everything. It's not a punishment. It's a collective obligation."

"Hah!" Nima wasn't sure whether Yun's hard, fierce laugh was meant to dismiss the possibility that Aunt Lio could be wrong or the official line that felt flat even to the wizard herself. "Then why do you have that?" Yun jabbed a finger at the geas runes.

"Yes, fine, technically it's a punishment," Nima said sharply, "but I *cooperated*. I *agreed* to community service. I could have just done my time, but I entered the program voluntarily to try to make amends for what happened. Nobody forced me to wear this." She shook her right arm at the girl. "Nobody forced me to be here."

"Then why don't you leave?" Yun asked in genuine curiosity.

In all the years she'd endured in this place, no one had ever asked Nima what she thought about her situation. It was humiliating to be grateful for a child's fickle attention, but her life was nothing but humiliations now.

"Because what the wizards did was wrong," Nima said, striving for patience. Not native to this farm and not native to her either. "We had the right — we had good intentions. But we did things that had consequences far beyond what we intended, beyond what we could have imagined when we started."

"What were you trying to do?" Yun asked. "Aunt Lio says all you wizards just wanted to keep your power and when the war happened you decided to burn the country down instead of sharing even one good thing with regular people."

There had been a time where Nima would have drowned in their own sweat anyone who dared speak so harshly, so honestly. "How fortunate that a bean farmer knows the absolute truth!" she snapped, then reined herself in. "Look, the war was complicated and you're too young to understand most of what happened."

Yun crossed her arms, stubborn. "Aunt Lio says the wizards hoarded all the best food and medicine and magic in their towers," she persisted. "She says the headwomen of all the villages went to the towers and asked for the wizards to share, but the wizards said they had nothing valuable to trade. So the villages stopped sending tithes to the towers and then the wizards came out of their towers and ruined everything. And Tonji says the wizards never loved anything but themselves and that's why they could do what they did to the land and the rivers and everything."

Nima had no idea who Tonji was and she didn't like their assessment of the war. "That's not an accurate picture," she said stiffly, although it was, if boiled down to its essence and told through the eyes of the victors. "There was... more to it." In the back of her mind she heard, was always hearing, the soul-shattering crack of her tower's foundations.

"Like what?" Yun asked pugnaciously.

Nima thought of her tower, its dimensions aligned precisely with the planes and angles of her interior self. Like a phantom limb, she could feel vast power seeping from the land into her tower's stones, and from its stones into her. Power that extended the reach of her hand as far as thought could take it, that honed her vision, peering keen-edged with magic into any secret she desired. When her tower stood, she was the secret composer of the song beneath everything... and then they had pulled her tower down and she was nothing. Keeper of a withered garden in a mutilated land. Bitterness welled up in her.

"I couldn't possibly explain it to you in a way you could comprehend," she said, aiming for austere, but coming no higher than cruel.

Yun gave her a very straight look then shrugged deliberately. "Well, it's not like you know the first thing about growing beans," she replied.

It toppled Nima like she was a tower herself. Yun hadn't spoken in pettiness, but rather with the world-weary familiarity of someone who often had to defend her own worth. Maybe she'd heard her aunt use the line and seen the seed of truth it held. Yun didn't know what it was like to wield power that could make and unmake the world. Nima didn't know how to grow beans. Once, the difference between them would have been too vast to comprehend. Now, it meant that between the two of them, Nima was merely the less capable subsistence farmer.

Nima was used to wrapping prickly defensiveness around herself like armor, but she suddenly couldn't reach it. They just sat there looking at each other, black eyes to brown. "I never had any reason to grow beans before," Nima said, conceding.

The silence stretched for several more minutes while Nima pretended to rearrange the dirt at the base of the vine's main stalk. "Wizards cared for the land a long time," she continued at last. "People couldn't see what we did. For generations we kept the soil fertile, managed the weather, sustained the forests...we didn't intend to destroy so much, not when the rebellion started and not after. We were just desperate to make the war stop."

Yun tilted her head skeptically. "If you wanted the war to stop, you could have just given the headwomen what they asked for. You didn't have to do all that bad stuff," she said.

Nima had used a lot of noble sentences and fine words to get her through the dark nights of doubt, but none of them volunteered to stand up against that unflinching logic. "You're right," she said, after a long minute. "But we did do it. I. I did it. All I can do now is try to repair what I can."

Yun glanced away as if the subject had never really been that interesting in the first place. "So why is this vine so important?"

Nima scrubbed her hands over her face. "This land, one of the things it has — had —" she paused. Started again. "A long time ago, wizards found a way to cultivate resilience. *Yes, wizards,*" she snarled at the skeptical look on Yun's face. "They taught seeds to grow hope, patience, and fortitude. They infused rivers with trust and stocked lakes with solidarity. They showed the land how to produce the things that would sustain it, no matter what came." She pressed her lips together and bit down hard on the sour feeling twisting her belly. "But the hope vines and trees of fortitude and all the rest of it didn't survive the war."

"Because of you," Yun interrupted. "You wizards, I mean. Right?"

"It wasn't just—" But it was. They had stretched out their hands and stripped the land of everything their forebears had grafted into it. She was out here trying to make amends for her role in that enormous crime, so what was the point of spinning a sweeter-sounding version of the truth to this child who wasn't buying it anyway? "Yes. Wizards weren't responsible for all the bad things that happened in the war, but they — we — did destroy the resiliency ecosystem. We did that."

"Why?" Yun asked.

A simple, deadly question. Nima had answers she'd given herself, answers she'd given her colleagues who doubted their course of action, answers she'd given the court that sentenced her.

Only we have the knowledge and experience to guide this country to its better future. Our better future requires peace and peace requires order, and order can only come when the villages bow to our authority.

These rebel armies are destroying the land — perhaps if they see harsh consequences they will surrender before we have to kill them all.

Some of the Wizard's Consortium chose to cross that final line and the rest of us let ourselves get pulled across.

So many answers. But none of them sufficient, in the end, to justify stripping the land of everything that held it together and helped it thrive. Not when you boiled it down to a young girl and an old wizard crouched on opposite sides of a fence in a dusty nowhere trying to understand why nothing good could grow.

"Because we forgot that wizards first built towers to serve and protect the land," she said at last. She suddenly became aware of how stiff and heavy her legs had become. "We thought of the land as something under our rule, not under our care. So when the rebels — when the war came, it was easy to use the land as a weapon."

Nima remembered standing atop her tower filled with grim righteousness as she stretched out her hands and drained the Ko River into the bedrock. She remembered the sense of urgency that filled her heart when she walked in the fortitude groves, blighting the ancient trees to strip the rebels of their will to fight. She remembered having those feelings, but she couldn't reproduce them. Now, all she could feel was shame and despair at the enormity of what they had done. How could she ever have thought that growing one stupid hope vine would mean anything in the face of their atrocities? Even if she lived to be the oldest wizard in history and grew a new vine or tree every year, it would be a pitiful drop in the desert their crimes had created.

"And now wizards must undo what wizards did," Yun chanted the first line of the decree that doomed all surviving wizards to a lifetime of penal restitution — out here in the backlands, it was probably the only part of the decree she'd ever heard. She bopped one of the withered leaves unceremoniously. "You're not very good at it, huh?"

Nima lurched forward to cup the leaf, jerked herself back, then stared at it as it seemed to stretch out luxuriously. Was a deeper green flushing outward from the central rib, or were her eyes lying to her? "This work is much harder than I expected," she admitted.

Yun nodded sagely. "I bet it's hard to make this place hopeful when you aren't." Then her head shot up as if hearing a voice calling her. "Whoops, gotta go," she said. She hopped to her feet, scooped up her buckets, and took off at a steady trot down the road.

Nima watched her go, rolling her last words around and around. *It's hard to make this place hopeful when you aren't.* That could be the problem. Perhaps the hope vine couldn't grow if its tender had no hope of her own to share.

But then — Nima leaned over the leaf Yun had bopped, without touching it herself. It was noticeably greener and drooped less. And then — she peered down where Yun had been flicking her careless fingers, and there was one, no two! new tendrils peeking out. Nima thought about all the times she'd scolded Yun for touching the vine. Was it a coincidence that the healthy spur was the one closest to the road, the easiest one for Yun to reach? Was the vine nourishing itself off her innate hope for the future, a future Yun expected to be part of in exactly the way Nima didn't?

Nima brooded on it all night.

●

Yun came back the next day, and the next, chattering about the problem with Aunt Lio's bean crop. Nima made noncommittal noises or gave answers she forgot even as they came out of her mouth. The beans weren't her problem. She was watching Yun and the vine, trying to learn the secret of how she made it grow.

The girl didn't appear to be doing anything special. She didn't even seem to be paying attention to the vine most of the time, although she always crouched by it when she stopped, even though it meant she had to perch in the ditch on the side of the road. She would bump or stroke or tap the leaves or tendrils to emphasize a point or sometimes as if it were agreeing with her, but she might have done the same thing with her buckets or the wagon. She certainly didn't treat the vine with the care or deference that Nima herself did. Nima couldn't see any one thing that set Yun's interactions with the hope vine above her own — except, of course, that the vine grew where Yun touched it and withered everywhere she did not.

And 'grow' was a bit of an understatement. On Nima's side of the fence, the other spurs had desiccated into dry, spindly stalks, their leaves long since crumbled into the dirt. On Yun's side, seven feet of rich jade green sprouted leaves the size of Nima's palm, twisted tendrils around every surface of the climbing frame and the fence rails, and were sending out new spurs in two places. There was even one tiny green nub that, given time, would become a bud.

Nima never, ever touched the healthy spur. She even stood on the dead side of the plant to water and dress it, hoping not to poison it with indirect contact. She didn't encourage Yun to touch it either, superstitiously worried that the vine would pick up on her desperation and stop responding to Yun's presence. She just held herself in nervous stasis, waiting for the bloom.

●

Maybe it was the empty rattling of the sledge that drew Nima's attention, or maybe it was how Yun's feet dragged in the dusty road as she approached. Whatever it was, Nima looked up one day to see a new expression on Yun's face: despair.

The girl squatted in her usual place on the other side of the fence, her hands flopped over her knees and her black hair sticking to her sweaty temples. She didn't touch the vine.

"What's wrong with you?" Nima said, more harshly than she'd intended. But then, she'd never been a gentle person.

"The bean crop failed," Yun said, looking burdened in a way Nima had never seen her. "Aunt Lio says there's no way to save it now, even though we built reed irrigation all the way from the river and I pick off all the bugs I can find."

"I guess you'll have to eat something other than beans this winter," Nima said, trying to remember if beans had some sort of local cultural significance. "Variety is good for you."

Yun looked at her like Nima had just suggested they try to eat the sun. "We don't eat beans, we sell them," she said. Then, in a cadence that sounded like something she'd heard from someone else many times, "No beans, no money. No money, no winter stores, no shoes, no seeds for spring."

"Oh," Nima said. Of course Yun's entire livelihood hung on those stupid beans. "That's...bad."

Yun sighed heavily and gave the swollen bud close to her face the gentlest of caresses. Nima sucked in her breath, but Yun didn't notice and the vine didn't show any immediate negative effects. "Do you know any way to fix the beans?" she asked suddenly, looking a little nervous for the first time Nima could remember. "I mean…I know you said we shouldn't expect magic to fix our problems, but you also said wizards used to take care of the land…"

"Not with this," Nima said, jerking her right arm in a sharp motion so the geas runes caught the light.

"Oh, right," Yun said, subsiding back despondently. She sighed again. "We sure could use one of these hope vines right now." Nima suddenly recognized the line as something she'd heard Yun saying a lot lately.

That night, Nima found herself thinking of Yun's beans instead of the hope vine. There wasn't any reason to be thinking about either one — all she could do for the vine was what she'd done, and Yun was someone else's problem — but she kept coming back to it like a piece of food stuck between her molars. It wasn't just the girl's despair; Nima hadn't spent a century as a powerful wizard with a tower of her own because she was susceptible to sad peasant children. But what if the bean crop's failure forced Yun and her family to leave the farm? What if they starved? What would happen to the hope vine if Yun suddenly stopped coming by, telling her cheerful stories and helping pass the long weary days with impertinent questions?

And more than that — Yun's intervention, however unintentional, had resuscitated Nima's own hope of escaping this pastoral prison. Which, in a way, put her in Yun's debt.

And that was the nub of the problem, Nima realized as she dried her dinner dishes. She felt indebted to Yun, who had helped her while enduring Nima's constant unwelcoming attitude. And there was a way to repay her. But it would cost Nima the one thing she valued: the opportunity to leave.

On the other hand, if she didn't pay this debt, Nima would be proving Aunt Lio and Tonji right: that wizards would rather let the land and everyone who depended on it suffer than share even one good thing. And even more than she hated being in debt, more than she hated being here, Nima found she hated the idea that Lio and her ilk could be right about her after all. If they were, then Yun would keep believing they were right about the war, would keep thinking wizards were bad people who embraced destruction to feed their own selfishness.

"Damn and damn!" she swore, looking down to discover she'd worried her washing cloth into threads.

She couldn't repair the land. She couldn't undo the systemic destruction they'd wrought, not even in a wizard's lifetime.

She could save one bean farm. She could persuade one girl — maybe one family — that wizards could help as well as harm. Not just for show, or to win release, but because she wanted Yun to welcome a future with wizards in it as enthusiastically as she welcomed everything else. It would cost at least a year of her life; there was no guarantee that this hope vine would fruit two years in a row. But after eleven years of loneliness and failure, was one more really such a sacrifice?

"Yes it *is*," Nima snarled to the empty room, to herself. "But wizards must undo what wizards did." Then she picked up her lamp and stomped out of the house.

Hope vines thrived on promises, after all.

Nima waited with characteristic impatience for Yun to arrive the next morning, but the girl didn't appear until mid-afternoon, trudging along in her too-big boots and carrying her mangled helmet buckets. She flashed Nima a wan smile as she crouched down by the vine, petting it as if seeking comfort from the silky leaves.

"How are the beans?" Nima asked awkwardly after a minute. She hadn't thought about this part, not once she'd made her decision. And, she realized, she'd never started one of their conversations before today. It was always Yun, interrupting her work with a question or observation.

"Still bad," Yun said. "Aunt Lio says we'll be lucky to get a quarter of the crop."

"Well, look," Nima said, her eyes fixed on the hope vine while her hands fiddled anxiously in the dirt. "This thing is about to flower. If it fruits, I could — you could have it. You could plant it near your beans. I'm sure it would grow for you."

Yun looked up, her eyes shining in a way Nima had never seen. It was like all the dust had washed right out of her world. "You mean it? We could have a hope vine of our own?"

"It won't make your bean plants come back," Nima warned. "Probably."

"But it means they'll grow good next year!" Yun said with an enormous grin. "That's right, isn't it? Everything grows better where a hope vine grows?"

"That's the theory," Nima agreed. She felt surprisingly guilty giving the girl hope when she wasn't sure the vine was capable of producing a fruit this late in the season. But then, hope was all she had to offer, from beginning to end.

"But... wait." Yun crinkled up her face around her nose. "Don't you have to send that fruit to your Arbiter? So they send you on to your next place?"

"There will be another fruit, in another year," Nima said with forced calm, giving the vine an affectionate little stroke with the back of her hand. And to her utter astonishment, a tiny bright green tendril unfurled from beneath her knuckles.

●

The vine bloomed four days later, opening like a star and drawing the eye from anywhere in the garden. Nima found herself staring at it for uncounted time, just tracing its silky depths with her eyes. She could see, if she looked closely in the way wizards were trained to do, runes tracing and retracing themselves deep within the flower's genetic structure. But mostly she just stood beside the vine, falling into its radiance.

Two days after the bloom, Nima came out early to gaze at the flower. It was a habit she'd fallen into immediately, getting in close to the luminous petals, tracing the dew that beaded gently on their surface, filling her lungs with the flower's scent before facing the tasks of the day. It made the whole day seem more bearable; no, it made tomorrow seem so promising it was worth today's labor.

At the cottage door she gasped in horror; even from that distance she could see the blossom was withered, almost completely gone after only two days. What would she tell Yun? How had she killed the flower so quickly even when everything seemed to be going well?

But when she drew close, crouching down and parting the leaves with trembling hands, she saw the flower had died a purely natural death. Hope blossomed fleetingly, it seemed, or perhaps her decision had hurried it along. There, glowing greeny-golden as a brand-new promise, a small orb poked up from the heart of the crumpled petals.

The vine's first fruit.

R.E. Dukalsky's story "Hope on the Vine" was originally published in Metaphorosis on Friday, 4 March 2022. See magazine.metaphorosis.com

About the author

R.E. Dukalsky is a bisexual writer of speculative fiction about memory, change, conflict and what happens afterward. She has been told that she has School House Rock charm and that she would make an excellent rebel leader, among other dubious accolades. Her stories have appeared in *Beneath Ceaseless Skies, The Fabulist, Metaphorosis* and other publications. She lives in the Pacific Northwest with her pun-loving wife and a disturbingly intelligent dog.

Packing List for Oblivion

Cameron Bertron

The statue was nothing like Enefai remembered. Before, it had been buried to its stomach, with both hands reaching forward to rest almost perfectly, palms up, on the hungry earth. Age had softened the statue's face, which crawled with orange lichen, to a shroud. Its open mouth was turned up to the sky and overflowing with dust. Enefai had watched, for a long time, as the wind spilled grit from the corner of its lips like an hourglass. Now, suspended in holographic color in the center of the council chamber, it looked sanitized and frail. Enefai appraised it for the last time, knowing the outcome before the first votes flickered in. The piece was not particularly innovative; it was not of historic value. It was not vital, it was only beautiful. It would be left behind.

Enefai fixed her eyes on the statue as she cast her vote against it. No councilor volunteered to speak on the piece, so the judgement was swift. The holograph blinked and was replaced by a new sculpture, but the previous image stayed on in Enefai's mind. The decisions were getting harder. At its start, the council had been a mess of overdrawn debates and personal attacks. But Enefai would rather deal with the chaos of those early days than the current, brutal pace of their decisions. It had taken several years, but time had run out for ego and guilt. Enefai was reminded every moment, by the defeated silence of the council and the packing crates in her own home, that the world was ending this year.

The news had broken slowly, then all at once. Before the first dispatch shuddered their calm, Enefai's partner Moore had read the signs in the planet around her. For months, she had come home from the fields with her mouth twisted to one side, calloused fingers thrumming against her leg. She had tried to explain to Enefai about the sourness in the soil and the odd patterns of the rain. Enefai understood little beyond the alarm in her voice, but they both dared to hope that the change was peculiar to their region. It was not. The planet Kenlanli's terraformation was reversing. It had happened on a string of other planets. Now the societies of Kenlanli, so recently settled, were packing back up into the finite space of stations to await the terraformation of a new home planet.

Moore had volunteered immediately to work in the countryside, spending long months collecting soil samples to assess the rate of decay and assisting frontier families in their preparations to leave. The crisis had unwrapped something in her. She swung into action as though she had been preparing for it her whole life. Enefai had done her duty as well, accepting the summons to serve on the council for cultural preservation. She had also received requests for consent to send in her own collection for consideration. She left the requests to collect dust, with everything else in her studio.

Another sculpture was on display. Its superb craftsmanship was doomed by the choice of material. Marble was shipped in from off planet, and the piece would be judged insufficiently Kenlanliin. Enefai hoped that it would be taken in by another planet or station. In the far future, perhaps it could find its way back to Kenlanli's people wherever they might be. It was one of the few thoughts that still offered consolation.

The marble statue was the last of the day. When the session closed, Enefai brushed her way out of the chamber and through the honeycomb halls, exchanging a few nods and sympathetic words with her fellow councilors. Everyone's voice was low, their exchanges quick but sincere. They also had homes to pack. Enefai stepped outside to a sky bruised with evening and stretched her legs as she waded through the city's shallow outskirts into the countryside. The long path home took her past one of her own sculptures. She did not slow as she passed.

She had carved it the same year that she met Moore. As they rattled through the countryside in the back of a transport vehicle, Enefai had felt something tipping over inside her the longer she spoke with this sprawling woman in muddied boots. Probably it was the apocalypse playing tricks on her, but all the memories from that time felt warm. Enefai missed the weightless quiet between them. She missed the long evenings in her studio they spent tinkering at her worktable, Enefai with her designs and Moore with her tools or sketches. These days, the ice cracked beneath their every conversation. When Moore was not working in the countryside, she was brimming with hard choices. Enefai dodged conversations about the space station. She wanted to preserve at least the bubble of their home from the world outside as it ransacked itself. But Moore kept opening the door.

In her head, Moore was already living on the station. Sometimes, it even seemed to Enefai that she was excited about it. Moore planned ceaselessly, scrambling to assure Enefai that they would have everything they needed. But it wasn't their future that weighed heaviest on Enefai, even as it seemed to consume Moore, it was their life on Kenlanli. It was the slide of sand under her boots and the way that sunrise tangled in Moore's hair. In her birth province, at midday the desert's horizon disappeared with a shiver into the pale sky. How to forget that? How to remember?

Her back was slick with sweat when she saw the welcoming round roof of their home. As she stepped inside, the peace earned from her evening walk was dissipated by the boxes crowding the floor. Moore was out for the week, but due back any day. She had left Enefai a list of requests to help with the packing process. Enefai did not need to look at it. Everything was done except one item. She needed to pack her studio.

She quickly ate dinner and prepared a cup of tea. She kept herself moving, knowing that if she paused in her momentum, she would not do any packing tonight. Mechanically, she entered the studio and evaluated the single crate reserved for her belongings against the gentle mess of her studio. The floor and work benches were cluttered with models, sketches, and photos. Only her tools stood in perfect order, hanging on the walls and from the ceiling. The darkness outside converted the studio's large windows to mirrors and Enefai kept catching sight of her own movement as she worked. She tried to summon nostalgia as she packed, but her memories felt glossy and distant. Each tool slid into the crate only left her feeling heavier.

By the time she stopped for a break, her studio was decimated and her tea was cold. Enefai sat down heavily on the floor, her legs splayed in front of her and her back against a slab. Its porous rasp felt reassuring on the back of her arms. Years ago, she had brought the stone from her home province for a design she planned. The rock was unique to her home, stark white and ribboned with pale orange and crimson. As a kid, she used to find patterns in the traces of color, pulling shapes out of the cliffsides. She wondered bitterly what abstractions she would be able to find in the expressionless plaster they would use on station.

She slid away from the stone and regarded it from her place on the floor. She had seen more statues in the last few years than in all her life. She imagined their shapes in the slab and marveled at what had been accomplished with a piece of rock, a set of tools. But it hadn't saved them, extinguished in a flash of holographic light. With time, their craftsmanship, her craftsmanship, would be weathered back to featureless slabs like the one which stood before her. She felt powerless against that future, against her unreasoning anger at Moore's resilience, against her love for Kenlanli. She felt small beneath the slab that stretched above her. Hardening her gaze, she stared into the stone to calm her mind and began to slowly trace the fiery streaks in the rock from top to bottom.

She remembered the design she had planned for this slab when she picked it all those years ago. She could see now that it was all wrong. The arch of a spine was already in the slab's contour, thinly submerged. Veins of color netted together in the side. They would run over an open palm like sunlight. She could only catch the shape in pieces, barely coherent, but it was enough. The night hours were re-aligning. The studio's gravity bent around the work. Moore's expression when she inspected her crops, when she lifted a long shoot with the tip of her thumb, was already in the stone. Enefai reached for it. She smoothed the memorized lips and rounded the jaw. She crinkled the eyes that would watch, unflinching, as their planet's atmosphere slumped to reclaim the horizon. She followed only that instinct which had first searched out shapes in the mountainsides. She followed it until the sunrise dripped dirty pink into her studio.

When it was done, she would face it towards the window, pack her tools away, and leave this room forever. But for now, she closed her grainy eyes and pressed her forehead against the statue's unhewn base. Through her headphones she could not hear Moore's clattering entrance. The world was quiet as arms encircled her. Quiet as a kiss was buried on her neck. She would take it to the stars.

Cameron Bertron's story "Packing List for Oblivion" was originally published in Metaphorosis on Friday, 6 January 2023. See magazine.metaphorosis.com

About the author

Cameron Bertron currently lives in Erdenet, Mongolia where she works as an English teacher. She has been a volunteer firefighter and a student of Slavic literature, but her most memorable work was as an almond milkman in her hometown Tampa, Florida.

Flann Brónach and the King's Champion

Allison Wall

Once, there was an ancient forest that had always been growing, as long as there had been plants to grow and dirt to grow them in. Its trees were as tall as mountains and so wide that ten deer could hide behind a single trunk. Flann Brónach, a spirit of the air, protected it and everything inside it.

The heart of the forest was a wide, still lake. The sun cast rays of golden light through the branches of the trees, and the water sparkled like diamonds. Flann Brónach swam on the lake as a red-throated loon.

One morning, as she moved through the water, in and out of the sunlight, ripples flashing in her wake, a cloud of songbirds met her. She raised her head and listened. In a flurry of wings and chirps they said men had invaded the forest, shouting, breaking branches, collapsing burrows, smashing nests. Eggs might even now be smashed.

Flann rose up from the lake, her head thrust forward. She soon found three knights of the king, hacking their way through foliage with drawn swords. She landed in their path and shed her loon form. Her eyes were crimson and she stood tall, dressed in gray and white linen.

"You may go no further," she said.

The men pulled back a few paces.

The youngest knight bowed. "We're here on the king's orders, looking for someone who disappeared into these woods."

"Who?"

"A knight, like us."

Her red eyes flashed. "Does the king order the desecration of sacred ground for every errant knight?"

The men glanced at one another but did not answer.

"There are no knights like you in this forest," said the spirit. "Follow your tracks of destruction, and there will be no knights at all."

The young knight bowed deeply. "We are careless from worry. The knight is our friend. We offer our apologies, but we can't leave without him."

The second knight lifted his sword. "We will not leave without him."

"After what you have done, you will be fortunate to leave at all."

With ropes of the north wind, she gathered the knights. She swung them high above the trees and flung them down outside the forest.

All day, the spirit followed the knights' trail, raising up tendrils of honeysuckle and blades of grass, restoring moss and lichen. She set broken branches, repaired burrows and nests, and put mushrooms aright. By the time the sun touched the western horizon, there were no signs any knights had passed through the forest at all.

But she was not satisfied. She didn't know whether a knight had truly crossed the forest's borders, or whether the story had been made up as an excuse to assault the forest. She needed to find out.

*

A stream ran through a tangled part of the eastern forest. Green willows hung over its banks, and birds called to one another from rocks in its midst. Nearby, a man was repairing a hut. He whistled as he bent and shaped the branches, weaving them together.

Across the stream, a loon fluttered to the ground, and Flann Brónach took on her human form. "You don't look like a knight," she said. "No sword, no armor, no horse."

The man had frozen, his lips still rounded, his hand gripping a bouquet of willow branches.

She blinked her red eyes. "Three knights came into the forest. I spent a morning getting rid of them and an afternoon undoing their destruction. They thought another one in here was in need of finding. Was that you?"

The man leaned his forehead against the heel of his hand. "Yes."

"What's your name?"

"I don't have one. It was taken."

She stared at him for a long time. Scars on the man's hands and arms swirled in concentric circles and knots. The patterns shone palely in the evening light.

"That's a nasty enchantment. No wonder they're looking for you."

The man's head snapped up. He extended his arm. "You can read it?"

"And taste it. Like blood and sulfur in the air." She tilted her head. "I can't undo it, if that's why you're here. It's cast in fire."

The man said, "I hoped for nothing more than a hiding place."

A finch let loose a long, warbling song.

"You've taken many lives," the spirit observed.

"I didn't want to."

She nodded. "Live now by the rule of the forest. If you take life, yours will be forfeit."

The man smiled bitterly. "Out there, my life is already forfeit."

"Then consider this a respite." Flann flapped into the sky, a loon disappearing into the west.

The man's hands began to shake. The branches and brush around him seemed an ever-tightening snare. They were looking for him. They might even now be searching. The sun set, but the man did not light a fire.

Screams on battlefields with moonless skies echoed in his dreams. Alone in his hut, he woke choking. Chipmunks snored, curled in their nests. One cricket played for the stars. Deeper in the forest, frogs laughed to each other from green bulrushes in the shadows. Nothing more.

The three knights flung down by magic in the north marsh had been separated and lost. The youngest knight found his way to the castle first, after midnight. Filthy and soaking wet as he was, he entered the throne room and told the king what had happened, about the woman who could turn herself into a bird and call on the elements of the earth.

The other knights returned in the same condition and told the same story.

"What *is* this?" the king hissed at his tall, bony advisor.

"Sire, it sounds remarkably like Flann Brónach."

"Cowards! Three of them together couldn't find him, convince him, or overpower him, so they blame their failure on a spirit."

The advisor twisted his fingers together. "She may very well be interfering, sire."

"To what end?"

"I couldn't say. Who knows what these spirits want?"

"I should have sent the entire army after him."

"Sire, you know it's best if the truth about the Champion is confined to as few people as possible."

The king grunted and waved his hand. "I have half a mind to leave him to his forest vacation and enchant another one. One with less of a conscience."

"And leave the Champion unchecked? Think of the havoc he could wreak. What if he fights for the enemy?"

The king ground his teeth. "Then I'll recover him myself. He won't be able to disobey if I'm there in the flesh."

The king whirled to the three dripping knights. He clasped his hands behind his back. "This witch has entrapped our Champion. He must be rescued and recovered. We ride on the forest at first light. Pray that it is not too late. He may already be enchanted to attack us."

The three knights bowed and left. Their mail-booted feet clipped and echoed in the stone hallways. A distance from the throne room, the youngest knight pulled the other two into a dark corner.

"Do you believe the king?" he whispered.

"Of course not," said the second knight. "We fought alongside his Champion during the Invasion, same as you."

The mustached knight grunted. "If he fights us, it won't be because of some witch's spell. He has incentive enough for desertion without another enchantment."

"I don't think she is a witch," said the youngest knight.

"It doesn't matter what you think," the mustached knight said, and shoved his way out of the corner. "The king has spoken."

●

A thunderstorm rolled over the forest, and the sun rose behind a gray veil. Rain whispered against the earth, dripped from branches, gathered in wide-rimmed leaves. The surface of the lake dissolved into rippled circles.

A group of wet-furred animals gathered among the brown cattails. Badger, chipmunks, rabbits, foxes, skunks, deer, and hedgehogs should all have been tucked safely away from the rain, or at least quarreling. They waited at the edge of the lake, soaked and quiet. Flann Brónach paddled through the reeds and climbed ashore.

The striped badger spoke for the animals. Fifty knights were headed for the forest, led by the king. All armed for battle and on horseback.

The spirit met the approaching army near the forest's edge. The trees grew far apart, and rain fell unhindered, plinking against fifty sets of armor.

"Didn't your knights tell you?" she said.

The king reined in his horse and held up his arm for a halt. He shook his wet hair aside and put on a smile. "Tell me what, lady?" he said.

"Murderers and death bringers may not enter."

The king's smile withered. "One of my knights fled into these trees. Show us where he is, that he may be brought home."

"Leave now, while you still can."

The king drew his sword. The spirit caught the blade in a vice of air. She flung it into the wet earth and it was swallowed, hilt and all.

The knights drew their swords. With rain-lashed wind, she collected the knights, their horses, the king's horse, and scattered them beyond the forest like dry leaves. Alone and abruptly unhorsed, the king fell to one knee in the mud.

Flann stood over him. "The forest is under my protection, and as such is beyond your reach. Do not cross its boundaries again."

She wrapped wind all about the king and threw him as far away as she could.

At the outermost forest tree, the spirit collected her fading energy. She gathered a skein of north wind and one of the south and knit them together. Then, as a loon, she flew around edge of the forest, wrapping it all inside the woven wind. She knotted the ends and stitched them together. A fork of silver lightning raced across the sky and sealed the forest with a roar of thunder.

●

Flann Brónach used the last of her power to fly to the Champion's home. Rain drummed against curtains of willow, and the rising stream rushed over its rocks onto grassy banks. She was too tired shed her loon form, so she waited, small and gray in the underbrush, for her strength to return.

A sparrow had become trapped in a thorn bush. The Champion sat cross-legged in the mud, leaning over the bird. He spoke to it in a quiet voice. It lay still, panting. Bit by bit, he pulled away the sharp spines and tangled stems, making a tunnel to the bird. Once it was big enough, he put his hand in among the thorns. The bird did not flinch. He took it gently and, protecting it from the thorns with his fingers, drew it out. He opened his hand, and the sparrow darted away, cheeping.

With effort, Flann shed her loon form. She leaned against a willow tree, her face pale.

He jumped to his feet. "Are you all right?"

She held up a hand. "The king and fifty knights came to the forest. They're gone. I have set protections in place that will not easily be overcome."

He said nothing.

The spirit closed her eyes. "I fear his anger will tear the world apart. He will not stop until he has won." Her voice ached with weariness.

He looked at his hands, where the sparrow's heart had vibrated against his palm. Thorns had gouged his skin more than once, but left no blood and no mark. "He'll stop if I'm dead."

Her eyes snapped open.

"I can't do it myself. I've tried. The enchantment stops me. But you have magic. You could do it."

"Taking your life helps nothing."

He stepped nearer to the stream. "I ask you to take it."

The spirit's eyes blazed. "If I used my power for death, I would become a demon, and the forest would be left without a guardian. Is that what you want?"

"No."

Her eyes closed again. "Even if I wanted to, there's no getting around the enchantment. Even for me."

Rain fell hard and fast, then settled into a soft patter. "It's hurting you, though, isn't it? Protecting a coward who can't die? I can't ask you to do that. I won't."

Flann smiled. "Not your decision to make." Her wings beat against the air and she flew into the rain.

He was alone.

The king had been in the forest. Rain still pattered overhead, but he could not hear it. His heart pounded at the walls of his chest, trapped within his own body. He opened and closed his hands, watching his fingers, checking for any sign of hesitation. They obeyed him every time.

He tried to sleep, but whenever he nodded off, his body leapt awake. He checked for control, flexed his toes, bent his knees, turned his head. Once, he slept long enough to dream that he was watching his hands rip apart sinew and bone. They wouldn't stop. He woke shaking. He held his hands in front of his face. Opened and closed them, one finger at a time. Open, shut. Open, shut. Still in control, for now.

The king had found himself half sunk in the north marsh, twenty miles from his castle. After hiking all day in rusting armor, he was muddy, furious, and coming down with a cold. He sat before a blazing fire and raged against the spirit of the air who had defied him.

"Does she think she can sit in that forest and keep my Champion from me? We'll burn it the ground, and her inside it!"

"Sire," his advisor said, "Is it reasonable to declare war on a spirit who can displace so many armed knights at once?"

The king flung the sheepskin rug from his shoulders. "What if she's lifted the enchantment?"

"I don't think that's possible."

"Why else would he go to her?"

"Cináed said—"

The king's face flushed and his voice went flat. "That sorcerer. This is all his fault. Cináed! Spirit of fire! Face me, you traitorous coward."

Orange embers showered upward. From beneath the burning logs, a salamander emerged, glowing red. It crawled over the grate and onto the rug. The king's advisor backed into a shadowed corner of the room.

The king glared down at the salamander. "When you swore to protect this crown, were you already planning to betray it?"

Cináed shed his salamander form and stood on two feet before the king, tall, skin smoking. "I only have power in the service of your protection," the spirit of fire said in a voice like gravel. "Why would I give that power up?"

"Power," the king scoffed. "Your enchantment failed."

"The enchantment holds."

"Then explain how he's able to walk free in the forest."

"The forest."

"Yes, yes, the forest, the forest, blast and burn it all to ash! A spirit of the air is harboring him there."

Cináed looked into the fire. "Flann Brónach."

The king snarled, "If I hear that name one more time, I will chop off the lips that pronounced it and shove them down the throat that uttered it. How was he able to get that far away in the first place?"

"Fire binds the Champion to your commands."

"And I commanded him to stay at his post."

"With your own voice?"

The king swore. "Is he to sleep in my bed with me at night?"

"The strength of the enchantment is in your voice. If you did not give the command to him, he is not bound to it."

"It is too late for admonishments, spirit. Keep your oath. Fix this."

⬤

Flann Brónach woke in the dark. A dull glow lit the western horizon. Smoke hung in the air. She gathered all creatures to the center of the forest, to the lake, where any fire could be quenched. The Champion was there already.

"This is dragon fire," he said. "I know the smell."

Flann turned away. She stretched her arms through her exhaustion for the strength to fly.

"Wait," he said. "What are you going to do?"

"Protect the forest."

"Against a dragon?"

She looked at him over her shoulder. Her eyes were dim, her lips pale. "If I don't, the forest will burn."

"You're going alone?"

She straightened her back. "I am a spirit of the air."

"And I'm sure normally, a spirit of the air like you could handle ten dragons without breaking a sweat. But the last days haven't been normal."

She raised her eyebrows.

He held his ground. "Do you have the strength?"

"I have no choice." She fell into her loon form and flapped up, scarcely clearing the tree line.

He clenched his jaw, and ran in the direction of the fire.

At the western rim of the forest, a dragon, red hot and smoking, reared on its hind legs. Fire poured from its mouth in a steady stream, breaking against the woven wall of wind. In many places the wall had cracked and splintered, boiled away to scorched charcoal. Leaves on near trees smoldered black.

Flann called, "Cináed!"

The dragon tasted the air with his forked tongue, lashing his head from side to side. He roared wordlessly.

She shouted, "Look at what you have become, guardian, what shape your master's hatred bent you to." She held a still air over the wall, and the flames grew less. "The king would have you attack another spirit and kill a sacred forest. Your magic is only as pure as what you have sworn to protect with it. The king is corrupt. Serving him has poisoned your power."

"Yet it is stronger than yours." Cináed raised his neck. He expanded upward six feet. A crown of spikes blossomed around his head.

The Champion burst from the underbrush, panting. He stared through the wall at the growing dragon.

Flann said, "Anger and hatred will swallow you whole. You'll never be able to put aside that monstrous skin."

The spirit of fire laughed. "Anger and hatred will burn your forest, and you will have nothing left to defend yourself with. I will consume you." Fire splashed against the wall. Tree branches swayed and groaned in the heat.

The air over the wall slipped. Flann steadied it, stilled it.

"What do we do?" the Champion asked.

She did not turn to answer. "I will hold the wall as long as I can."

"Then what?"

"Then nothing. If the wall burns, the forest burns. I only have the power of what I protect. Without the forest, I can do nothing."

"You die?"

Flann Brónach raised her arms to grasp for a strong north wind. It sliced through her fingers and knocked her to the ground.

He watched her rise. Before the spirit could stop him, and before he could stop himself, he sprinted at the forest wall. It opened around him, and closed shut tight behind.

He stood between Cináed and the wall. Fire billowed and engulfed the Champion. He passed through it unscathed. The dragon backed away, shoulder blades rippling with scales and spikes.

He advanced on the dragon. "You forgot what you made me, when you tore me apart and put me back together."

The dragon's tongue flicked in and out.

"I am indestructible. I am invincible. I slew tens of thousands, went without water or food or rest for weeks. An always-victorious slave of my master's will." He held out his arms. "But my master isn't here."

Cináed turned to flee. Faster, the Champion blocked the dragon. "You can't outrun me."

The dragon tucked his head low to the ground. "If you take a spirit's life, you'll be cursed."

"More cursed than I already am? I will never be free of what I've done. And neither will you." The Champion gripped the dragon by its collar of horns to break its neck. The adrenaline of an imminent kill bubbled beneath his skin.

"Wait." The dragon's head bobbed. "Let me live. I'll renounce the king. Give up the oath I swore. I'll diminish, play in fire pits, a powerless salamander. The enchantment will fail! There will be nothing to bind you with."

He looked into the dragon's eyes. He didn't want to kill it, he realized. He didn't want to kill anything, but had never been allowed to show mercy. "Do it."

The dragon blinked, swallowed. "I forfeit the oath to protect the king and willingly relinquish all the power of protection."

The dragon shrank. Rough scales smoothed, claws retracted, tail shortened. A black and yellow salamander scurried through the grass trampled flat by dragon feet.

"Stand ready," shouted the king.

The Champion's body locked at attention, waiting for orders. Despair crowded his mind in a mist. The enchantment held. Had Cináed lied to him?

Three men on horses waited at the edge of the clearing. A fourth, the king, rode forward and dismounted. He brought his boot down on the salamander, crushing it.

"Well," the king said. "I meant him to destroy the spirit in the forest so I could get to you, but this is better. Tidier." He scraped the salamander from his shoe, and approached.

Fear ran along the Champion's limbs, but they didn't shake. He was caught in the enchantment's vice.

The king sniffed. "Impressive. Not even dragons and spirits match you. I must have been too easy on you before. I won't make that mistake again."

He fought against his numb lips.

"Something you want to say? Go ahead. Speak."

"I won't go back."

The king spat to one side. "Oh, you're going back. I'm curious, though. What did you think would happen if you ran away? That I'd just let you disappear?"

Something shifted in the Champion, like earth beginning to erode. "I gave you ten years of slaughter." The king hadn't commanded him to talk, but his lips had loosened. Was the enchantment fading?

The king surveyed the forest. He didn't seem to notice the Champion spoke out of turn. "Were you hoping for something that would kill you? That witch, maybe?"

Anger flared through his fear. "She's not a witch."

The king glared. "Be silent."

His mouth tightened, but the command ebbed. He pushed at the enchantment's limits. "She is a spirit of the air. More noble than you'll ever be."

The king's face twitched. "Enough. You have acted treasonously against this crown. Return, fight for me, and all will be forgiven."

The order pulled his legs, but he maintained his footing.

"Come!"

His knee jerked forward, but again he stood.

The third time the king called, his body didn't respond at all. The impulse to obey flowed through him like water, but washed away. "No," he said.

The king's face blanched white. "You can't say that to me," he snarled. He drew his sword and advanced.

The Champion blocked the king's swing. He wrenched the sword away by its blade and threw it as hard as he could. It flashed end over end in the sunlight and disappeared into the distance.

The king looked wildly after it.

The Champion's hands bled freely. He held them out. "Look. It's over. The enchantment is gone."

"It can't be," the king said. "You're bound to my words. Stand ready!"

He turned his back to the king and walked toward the forest.

The king drew a dagger. He flung himself at his lost Champion, wrapped an arm around his throat to cut it.

The Champion ducked forward and pulled the king over his head. The king landed hard, his dagger caught beneath him. The silver tip protruded from his abdomen. His eyes stared, frozen in an expression of fury and hate.

The once Champion and the three knights talked for a long time. A pair of yellow butterflies flitted among the wildflowers at their feet. Together, they buried the body of their king. They covered the place with grass and did not mark it. The three knights rode away.

The nameless man and the king's horse approached the forest's edge, but did not enter. Fireflies glittered among the dark tree trunks. Flann Brónach stood in shadow.

"You're free," she said. "How does it feel?"

"Like a dream." The man breathed in the night air, sweet with grass and dew. "I came to say goodbye."

"Oh?"

"The knights will say the king was ambushed by enemy soldiers. It won't hold up for long, but it'll give me a head start. They'll hunt for me."

She did not answer him.

"I wish I could do something to repay you."

Fireflies danced green and gold in the roots of the trees. He thought she had gone, but her voice whispered on the breeze. "If you return, you will be welcome."

A flutter of wings disturbed leaves and underbrush. Over the canopy of the forest silvered in moonlight, a loon called.

●

Allison Wall's story "Flann Brónach and the King's Champion" was originally published in Metaphorosis on Friday, 30 September 2016. See magazine.metaphorosis.com

About the author

Allison is a Kansas-based writer. She teaches, and has taught many things, including but not limited to piano, second grade, and creative writing, and can usually be found in the vicinity of books, cats, music, and tea. Allison is currently finishing an MFA in Creative Writing at Hamline University

The Chorley

Rachel Ayers

Little Annamarie wore a mournful expression. "Mama," she said, "I can't find my Chorley." Chorley was a ragged stuffed elephant that the girl had had since she was two.

"Where did you leave it?" the Mama asked, the air of distraction hardened on her features. She had taken off the VR glasses that she customarily wore throughout the long hours of the day, and even the child could see that she was irritated by the interruption.

"If I knowed, I wouldn't be sad," the girl pointed out.

"Knew," Mama corrected.

Annamarie stamped her foot. "Mama, I need my Chorley."

Mama sighed and turned away from her desk. "Child, I'm very busy with a big project. If you need your toy right now, you'll have to look for it."

She went back to tinkering with the things on her worktable: an odd assortment of wires and pentacles and computer chips and silver. This was merely a ruse, but Mama did not want the child to consider that Annamarie herself was the true project of the day. The weird energy of the awful, ancient house had combined with the child's own latent gifts, attracting or creating a... thing. The thing came every night, and seemed to grow and fluctuate with the child's moods. It was intriguing, and unexpected, and Mama thought Annamarie might even have an early breakthrough, gaining a measure of control over her aura—most of the children in the Endeavor did not have any kind of control until they reached puberty. After weeks of monitoring it, she'd realized that the toy was somehow amplifying Annamarie's aural energies, and Mama decided that taking it would present the child with a fascinating new challenge.

It was not strictly prohibited in the Endeavor; side projects were allowed as long as they could be justified.

Annamarie spent a spare minute sulking before retreating in defeat; the Mama did not respond to this tactic.

Annamarie looked under her bed again, and in her closet. She was not, as a rule, a messy child, being rather precocious and having a strict Mama in the bargain. It was all the more mysterious that she couldn't find the toy, to which she had a deep attachment. She'd awakened from her nap to find it missing, and had looked all around their large and drafty house without a successful reunion with her lost Chorley.

At dinner Mama asked, "Did you look for your toy?"

"Yes, Mama." Annamarie was subdued.

Mama looked up from her soup and her newsscreen. "Did you find it?"

"No, Mama."

"Hmm. Well, I suppose you're too old for it, anyway."

This was grievously unfair, but Annamarie knew better than to remark upon it. Although she had an excellent vocabulary for a six-year-old, she could not explain to Mama that the stuffed toy had been painstakingly imbued with protective magic for the last four years, and that there were likely to be dire consequences if she were to retire to bed without it tonight. The spaces beneath the bed and within the wardrobe appeared to be perfectly mundane during daylight hours, but were in fact deep and dangerous repositories for the most nightmarish of creatures once darkness fell.

While she wanted to wail and kick her heels against the floor, Annamarie knew it would do no good; instead, she retreated to her bedroom. She looked around the familiar space, fighting the tears that threatened to fall down her plump cheeks.

She had a small desk, suitable to her short form, upon which she'd accumulated an assortment of electronic gadgets and loose ends from Mama's workshop, the yard, and the shadowy corners of the house. Annamarie had collected circuit boards since she liked the dark green shine of them, and countless wires, and other odds and ends, mostly gathered because of their interesting shapes.

There was a small, high window opposite the door, with a tattered pink curtain that hung limply over it. The curtain matched the quilt on the bed, and those two items were the beginning and end of any bright color in the room, except for, on a shelf over her bed, three other stuffed animals: a parrot, an anteater, and a jaguar. They had never held the special place in her heart which was reserved for the Chorley (named after the young elephant in the bedtime stories her Papa used to tell her).

She had two hours before bedtime, during which she was expected to study or, at the very most, quietly play. Mama was not supposed to be disturbed except during Meeting Times. Mama did not like other interruptions.

Annamarie pulled out her box of circuit boards, and a fistful of wires, and a small screwdriver she'd taken from the kitchen toolbox, and imitated the air of quiet contemplation Mama wore while she did her tinkering.

The girl frowned; she was missing something.

After a moment, she stood on her bed and pulled the other stuffed animals down to the floor with her. "I haven't knew you as long as my Chorley," she said quite solemnly, "but I still love you." She tapped her fingers against her lips, an uncommonly grown-up gesture. "I think you need to be boosted."

She selected a box-cutter—spirited away from Mama's worktable weeks ago—and ripped open the back of the jaguar without hesitation. Annamarie began to play intensely and with great purpose.

Mama, watching from the monitor, did not interrupt her child at bedtime. She was pleased and fascinated by this turn of events, which she had not anticipated, and she took notes for an hour, watching the child's selections and choices, enjoying the way the child mimicked her own work habits. The thaumo-meter hummed happily, measuring the surging energy around the child. Mama watched until the girl went to bed on her own initiative, the three newly modified stuffed animals arranged around her.

The thing that came in the night was perhaps more hungry than inherently evil, but still terrifying to little Annamarie. It oozed into the cracks created by darkness, nesting beneath the bed or curling in the closet. An unwary heel could be grabbed, tugged, and nibbled, if a dash to the bathroom was not properly executed.

The Chorley had protected her. The toy was alive with four years of devoted love; it was a powerful talisman against the thing, which was, after all, only acting according to its own nature. The Chorley repelled it, sent it scuttling for easier prey in other drafty houses. But now the Chorley was gone, and Annamarie had had to make do on short notice.

Mama straightened her glasses, ran her hands through her short-clipped hair, and turned on the dozen monitors which measured everything from the temperature of the room to the ectoplasmic content of the local atmosphere.

The other Mamas had much less to deal with. None of them had gotten stuck in a dark old house full of eaves and topped with crenellations—one variable too many, she'd argued, but been overruled—and most of the other Mamas still had their Papas around to help with their experiments. This Papa had gotten sentimental, protective of the innocent little girl, and that would not do. He'd been retired, peacefully enough. But then he'd tried to come back for Annamarie, and now Mama didn't know where he was, or if they'd even let him live.

She snorted to herself, turning off her computer screen and powering down her laptop for the night. She had a few hours of peace before the child woke. Annamarie was largely self-sufficient, but still required some persuasion in order to get her up and prepared to log in to her morning classes. Mama needed to sleep, but first she went through her own nightly ritual—which involved tea and a night light and a particular quilt, and which she never, ever would have admitted to performing to any of the other Mamas. She did not share anything with them beyond her notes on the child.

When Mama was fast asleep, and Annamarie tossed and turned beneath the surface of consciousness, the thing that came in the night began to ooze and creep into the girl's room. It had, as it always did, bypassed the lonely rooms of the house, and it moved by instinct away from the Mama's nightlight.

It slithered into the dark, cramped corner of the little girl's closet, watching her sleep. She was sweaty, muttering to herself and twitching—the best time, when it could invade the dreams and feed on the terror. An unwary foot was all well and good, but the thing that came in the night preferred fear to flesh. It liked to play with its food.

The child's talisman was gone: its bright blue glow, its glowering eyes, were not there to ward and guard the child. The thing that came in the night moved forward, undulating out of the closet, claws scraping into the cracks of the floorboards.

But it paused mid-rear before pouncing, studying the child on her bed more carefully. There was something wrong... something different.

The thing hissed, a slow angry boil of frustration and irritation.

Here were three new champions; and while they did not shine brightly, they cast their own faint glow through the room, and the edges of their light were painful to the thing that came in the night. They were nowhere near as strong as the Chorley, but they were vigilant, and there were three of them, and they were full of the love and playful energy of the child. Of course, Annamarie was extraordinary—or she would not have been chosen and taken for the Endeavor—and the toys were only one of the ways that her gift had manifested. That bright curiosity burned into something real, something that could affect the world in unexpected ways: it was exactly what the Mamas were trying to measure and control, with limited success. And now that power had been transferred into the toys, giving them a smaller measure of the child's aura, and granting her a sunny protection even as she slumbered.

The thing was forced to retreat, and it went, simmering with fury.

●

The Mama was unbearably smug during the conference call that took place during the early morning hours. She had every confidence that she understood the energies she'd measured.

"And she received no guidance from you on the matter?" the GrandMama asked.

"None at all," Mama assured her with a sniff. "She created three new guardians. All weaker than the one that's been soaking up her energy this whole time, but it was enough to get that... thing to leave her alone."

Another one of the Mamas spoke, hesitant. She was a new Mama, on her first child. "And you're certain that Annamarie doesn't suspect your part in any of this?"

"Of course not!" Mama said, though she did not really consider her answer before she said it. It had never even occurred to her as a possibility. Of course, the girl was precocious; all of the children were extraordinary. That was the whole point of the Endeavor. But they were still children, and Annamarie was only beginning to develop her talents.

"Keep a sharp eye on her," the GrandMama said. "The... thing is still a new development. We don't want your situation to go awry again."

The Mama schooled her face carefully, though she wanted to scowl. There had been no need to use that last word. This experiment was completely different, and Annamarie was far more talented than the last child the Mama had raised. It was hardly her fault that the last experiment had been abbreviated; of course, the child had died, so there was nothing that could be done about it except to move on. "I will certainly monitor the situation and present all my findings," she said. "On the child and the... thing."

She set aside her feelings of unease after the call. Certainly, there were more variables here than she had wanted, but she would work with what she was given, and she would be promoted within the Endeavor. If Annamarie lived, perhaps Mama could even move up with her. After all, she was the one who had thought of this experiment, and it looked like it might be just the emotional push the girl needed to advance her thaumatronics skills. If not with Annamarie, perhaps next time she could still begin with an older child, already aware of their aura; Mama had earned that much by now, surely. No more shepherding babies through their formative years. That would be a nice change.

●

For her part, when Annamarie woke, the girl was rested and relieved. The thing in the night had not gotten her, and her nightmares had been mild, even without her Chorley. She hugged her toys tightly in gratitude, and then got herself dressed and found breakfast and waited for Mama to log her into her class.

The toys were left to rest on the neatly-made bed, rather than the shelf above, and they were pleased with their change in status. It was not every day that a toy was elevated to best and beloved, and now that all three of them were now on the bed, well, they could not help but be pleased with themselves.

After her classes, and after Annamarie finished her walk—ten times around the yard, no more, no less—she took her nap with all three toys cuddled in her arms. None of them were particularly large, and with the modifications she'd made, they all had a few sharp edges and pokey bits. The girl didn't mind; she loved them all the more now that she'd made it through a night with them.

When she woke she had a little while before Meeting Time. Mama was busy in her office. She was very pleasant today, and had given Annamarie a cookie when she finished lessons. After her nap, Annamarie had an odd idea.

"Are you sure?" she asked the anteater, who seemed the wisest of the three.

The stuffed toy did not answer out loud, but Annamarie nodded reluctant understanding nonetheless.

Taking the jaguar under her elbow for courage, she crept out of her room, avoiding the creaking floorboards and slipping through Mama's bedroom door, opening it just shy of where it let out a long creaking groan. She rarely came in here; it was a cold room, always clean and tidy but never comfortable. Mama's bed was small, like her own, and although the room was much larger than Annamarie's, there was scarcely any more furniture in it.

Annamarie stopped, listening. She thought she heard a soft rustling from the darkness beneath the bed. She gripped the jaguar extra tight around the middle; the jaguar did not mind. Annamarie took comfort from his steady, stealthy presence, and edged around the room toward the closet.

This door let out a soft whine and Annamarie stopped with her head cocked, listening for Mama. She shivered and took one of the deep good breaths, and then she looked up on the top shelf of the closet.

There was her Chorley, carelessly flung so that it had toppled over on its side and lay on both of its own big, floppy ears. Annamarie let out a little sniffle at this pathetic sight. She reached her arms up, the jaguar still grasped by one ankle, and stood on tippy toes, but came nowhere close to reaching the stuffed elephant.

Annamarie left Mama's bedroom door propped open and crept back to her own room, sliding her bare feet along the rough floorboards where she knew they wouldn't creak. She gulped for air, back in her own room, and crushed the jaguar against her cheek for a final boost to her courage. Then she took the parrot and left her room again.

She paused outside Mama's office door; Mama was on the phone with someone, talking in one of the other languages. She was leaned back in her chair, with one arm over her eyes. While Annamarie watched, Mama straightened and lowered her arm, and her eyes brushed past the doorway where Annamarie stood.

But she didn't see Annamarie. She swiveled to face her desk, and Annamarie wrenched herself along.

She hovered uncertainly at Mama's closet door, looking at her Chorley. The one eye she could see—a scratched black button peeking over the edge of the shelf— implored Annamarie for rescue.

The little girl braced her feet evenly beneath her and tossed the parrot up toward the top of the closet. It was an impossible throw in the too-narrow space between the door and the shelf, and the elephant rested heavily and certainly on that shelf. Yet an instant later, both toys came tumbling back down and the girl caught them with no more than a muffled, feathery thump.

She heard a clunk and a clatter from Mama's office, and whirled around, clutching her toys. Another moment passed without a sound, and she tiptoed to the door, edging around Mama's dresser. When she passed the ugly little porcelain nightlight, the elephant's trunk snagged on the cord, and the thing tipped over with a *crunchthud.* The girl winced and froze. She set the light back upright, and fled to her own room. She did not tell Mama about the nightlight— Mama had taken her Chorley, after all, and could not be trusted—and there were no monitors in Mama's room, so, in later review, the other Mamas would never fully understand what happened that night.

When Mama came and got her for Meeting Time, the girl was on the floor, contentedly playing the coding game on her tablet. The parrot, anteater, and jaguar were ranged around her, as though they were participating in the programming.

"Make your bed more tidily tomorrow, Annamarie," Mama said. "It's very lumpy today."

"Yes, Mama," the girl said.

"Go and wash your hands and join me for supper," Mama said.

"Yes, Mama." She leapt up from the floor, grinning, but Mama had already started down the hall.

They ate a quiet dinner, and when they were done, Mama went back to her office and the girl went back to her room to do her homework.

When she went to bed that night, Mama was disgruntled to find that the bulb of her nightlight was not working. She gave a soft, muttered curse; she didn't have any spares. She'd have to get one tomorrow. Still, she was a grown woman, she reasoned. How much could a child's boogeyman really bother her?

At least she thought so, for a few more hours.

Annamarie slept blissfully well that night, with her modified toys ranged around her and the Chorley hugged tight in her arms. In the morning she woke late.

GrandMama was there. Annamarie did not like her. "Where's Mama?"

The old woman sniffed. "She's not… well. She won't be looking after you anymore."

"Will I get to see Papa?" A surge of excitement rippled through her.

"No," GrandMama said quickly. "No, you'll have a new Mama. I've come to take you to her." She glared around Annamarie's room; she found no fault with it, but still did not like the room… or the house, for that matter.

It took next to no time for Annamarie to dress and gather her things, hastily arranging her toys beneath her clothing. GrandMama recalled, uneasily, the Mama's report on how Annamarie had used her toys to channel her growing power… but with so many changes today, she would not take the toys from the child now. No, a smooth transition would be best; once everything else was under control, a new Mama could get the girl in line. GrandMama offered a hand, which the child reached to take, but a yucky jolt went through Annamarie's arm. She pulled back to grip her suitcase instead.

"Are you ready, then, child?" GrandMama asked.

Annamarie nodded. Mama had always told her that she had to obey GrandMama, but Mama had taken her Chorley. Annamarie made a secret promise to her Chorley that she would not trust GrandMama, not ever. Or the new Mama either. Annamarie walked down the steps after GrandMama: suitcase dragging behind her, and, tucked carefully into the bag over her shoulder, her Chorley.

Rachel Ayers' story "The Chorley" was originally published in Metaphorosis on Friday, 31 July 2020. See magazine.metaphorosis.com

About the author

Rachel Ayers lives in Alaska, where she writes cabaret shows, daydreams, and looks at mountains a lot. She has a degree in Library and Information Science, which comes in handy at odd hours, and she shares speculative poetry and flash fiction (and cat pictures) at patreon.com/richlayers

@richlayers

A Yellow Landscape

Sarah McGill

I dream of vast landscapes. The distance bends like cotton on a washing line or a rabbit vanishing down a hole. In my dream, women come, carrying brutally tined forks. Their hands crook around their bodies and somehow they are monstrous and too big. I walk, and I think I'm looking for a better landscape. Or only another landscape. This place is too wide and I pool borderless across it.

A woman draws her fork around her and says, "When I was a girl and I walked on the beach, I found a little house crusted in salt. I sat inside and ate lamprey and mint leaves. At dusk it flooded and I laughed, splashing my feet in the water. I grew into the shape of that house, ancient and mindful."

"My nana's house was a tent," I say and I am very proud. "I want to have walls like she did, but I don't know how to grow into the shape of a tent. She walked barefoot on the mountain with her mule. She made acorn flour and shouted *haloo haloo* to the thrushes in the valley." I am barefoot too.

"Well, it is good to love your great-grandmother. But there are loose rocks on mountain paths and tents aren't houses. They're unstable."

A woman says, "She must have been sad with no doorway to frame her and no walls to hold her. I suppose she was unhappy because she had no house to grow up in and learn to be herself."

I scratch the dirt with my toes and think they're wrong, but I don't know how. I don't know if Nana was happy. And I hadn't known that a tent wasn't a house. I wonder then what walls I can grow up into if not those. I turn around and walk away from their monstrous forks.

●

I lived in a house that wasn't my house, and I lived in a room that wasn't my room. Out the window was a hill the color of clay, covered in scrub. The bed was my cousin Mosi's, even though I slept in it with her. It was obvious it was hers because my blankets were yellow like soil. These were blue, like a bottomless lake. Mosi decided she liked blue when she went to school and the teachers told her the ocean was best. I kept my bird bones in a drawer with her shells and together we built white houses with bone frames and shell rooves.

Downstairs, someone knocked. Out the window, I saw it was a teacher and I hid in the cupboard in Mosi's room. The teacher came sometimes and said I had to go to school, but she couldn't come for me if I stayed in the cupboard. That's what my aunt said. She said the woman would always go away. That sounded true. The cupboard was the smallest place in the house that I could fit. I knelt, folded up over my knees. Sometimes it was suffocating.

My aunt told the teacher I didn't live in the scrubland. She said I lived with my parents in the mountains, even though that wasn't true and they were dead. When the teacher left, my aunt came and knocked on the cupboard. She opened the door and I spilled out. I sprawled, my legs and arms going as far as they could, all the way until they knocked against the walls.

When I went down to dinner, my cousin jostled me out of my seat next to my aunt and I went to sit out of her reach.

"Did you take the mule up to the hill today?" my aunt asked.

I nodded. "I want the hill to be as tall as the mountain Nana lived on."

My aunt served out the partridge's breast meat with pine nuts and pennyroyal. "If it were a mountain, at the top you would find the circle tent in the cloud, just like the hero Oupa did when he went looking for Buzzard. He lives there now and teaches everyone who comes to him."

"Nana met Oupa," I said, clasping my hands very seriously. "She laid down under a blanket and in her dream she was a kestrel and flew to the top of the mountain. Oupa smiled when he saw her."

My aunt pressed her lips together. "She told that story a lot."

"I want to do that. In my dream, I'll be a buzzard." I added pepper and rosemary to my meat.

Mosi laughed, leaning back in her chair to slap the rug hanging on the wall. Every time she slapped it, she grabbed a little thread and pulled, so that someday it would unravel and she wouldn't be embarrassed when her teacher came for dinner and frowned at the black goats leaping over the mountaintops.

"My teacher said that if you jump from the roof, you'll die," Mosi said. "She says it's a lie that Warbler jumped from a gable and learned to fly."

"Birds learn to fly by jumping from their nests," my aunt said, her eyes down. She ate with her fingers, the grease running down her palms. "You used to like the legends about Oupa."

"My teacher said bird meat is dirty." Mosi wrinkled her nose at the plate and wouldn't eat.

My aunt picked over her plate and I wished she'd say Mosi was wrong, but she said nothing.

●

In my dream, the sand is unfamiliar. Each time I kneel, I stand up far away from where I was a moment ago. I hate it.

I'm looking for Oupa. I think, far away, I see a mountain the color of sky. If I find it, I will find him and he'll teach me all the mountain's stories and how to be a buzzard. I don't look at the women when they come up behind me, although the terrible scraping of their forks makes my shoulders rise and my spine tingle.

"The wind is hard on my face," a woman says. "It burns my cheeks."

"You should wear a scarf like my aunt," I say. "It binds up her hair and keeps off the wind."

"Why don't you wear a scarf?" she says.

I put my hands up and I'm startled to find my hair uncovered, whipping around in the wind. "I lost it. I'll get another scarf, when I go home."

"What if you lose that too?"

For some reason I can't answer the question. It's too startling. Instead I ask, "If a tent isn't a house, then why does Oupa live in a tent?"

A woman laughs, so loud that the soil shakes from the mountain in the distance, cascading orange into the sand. The mountain is left bare and I see it's not a mountain, but only a rock, no taller than my hip. "Because he doesn't know anything at all," she says.

A woman spits. "It's too barren. Bring the ocean here."

I hunch my shoulder at the sprawling landscape. "I like the sand." But I reach into the soil where it's damp. A spring pops up as I pull back my hands.

A woman coos, "It makes me homesick. Oh, I miss squid."

●

Mosi came back to the house jumping, kicking up her legs to show off her new hard shoes. They glistened and I asked her if they were made of beetle carapaces.

"No," she said, and then wouldn't tell me what they were made of. She put her hands on her hips. "I'm going to the ocean."

"The mountain is better. In my dreams I'm going to the mountain."

"You don't really go places in your dreams."

I hurled sand over her shoes so they got dirty. "I do." I was so angry I almost hit her. "Just like Nana. I go somewhere else and you're not there."

"I'm going for real. My teacher says I'll like the ocean so much, I won't want to come back."

I crouched down in the sand. "Why did they come here, if they don't like it?" Many people came inland to escape the encroaching shoreline, the floods making the borders on the old maps all wrong, but there were still people near the ocean.

She licked her palms and leaned over to clean off her shoes. "Because they want to teach us to be good. The mountain people don't know how to be good. But if I go to school on the beach, I can be better."

"It'd be a long walk back in the evening."

She laughed and it was like the women with their forks laughing. "I wouldn't come home in the evening."

I held my hands in a cage at my belly, horrified. I didn't want to sleep in a house that was nearly empty, the wind rattling the loose windowpanes, or eat with just my aunt and the dripping dishes. "You aren't going."

She wrinkled her nose. "Yes I am."

"I said you can't go."

"I don't care." She clapped her hands in my face, like my aunt did when she was angry.

I pushed her hands away. "Your mama won't let you."

"It doesn't matter what she wants."

I lunged, grabbing her through her sweater. She hit me in the nose as we fell and she screamed about dirtying her uniform. I squeezed her around the waist. I imagined the empty house again and shook all over. I didn't want Mosi to leave me. I tried to map her body to mine, to match her concave belly over my hip, her spine around my arm. But she squirmed too much and when she hit my ear and set it ringing, I let go.

She scrambled to her feet, dust scrubbed into her uniform. Tears tracked down the dirt on her face. "I'm going to the ocean and I'm not coming back. No one can make me come back. I'll go to school there and be better than you." She turned and ran inside.

I curled up my knees and pretended I was in the cupboard, with the dark and the smell of pigeon. But it was too small, like I would never get out and would always be its cramped shape. I didn't want to grow into the shape of the cupboard. I sat up and wished a tent were a house.

My mule came around the house. She gnawed on the white shrubs beside me until I reached up and rubbed her flank. Her mane was full of dust. "Mosi doesn't mean it," I told the mule. "She won't leave. She'd miss the drawer with her little towels and the pegs to hang her shoes. The ocean is too wide and terrible for her." My mule gummed my hand.

When I came into the house, dirt up and down my knees, my aunt sighed. "I've told you not to jump on Mosi like that."

"She said bad things to me."

"What did she say?"

I didn't tell her. It would be more true if I said it. I would keep the words in my belly and make Mosi a liar. I sat in the corner and pretended it was a little house just for me.

"Can I sleep in the attic?" I asked while she stoppered the sink and poured in water. The attic had once been a dovecote. Doves were very sacred on the mountain, but I'd never seen one. "I'll sleep on a rug and hang walnuts and garlic like Nana did in the mountain."

My aunt shook her head. "I want Mosi to be in the room with you."

"Why? She doesn't get scared at night anymore. Not since her teacher told her Owl doesn't come at night to steal children's tongues. She says owls are stupid and crabs are better, because their shells are their houses and they fit inside them perfectly."

My aunt muttered something I didn't understand, which sounded ugly and mean. "She's still very young."

"She doesn't like me sleeping with her. I want to sleep in the dovecote." The dovecote roof came to a point like a tent. But it wasn't a tent so it could be a good house where I could learn how to be myself.

She handed me a dish and I just held it. "I need it for storage," she said.

She started soaping the dishes and I held the plate tighter. "But there's nothing up there. Just old rugs and baskets."

She made a *tch* sound with her teeth that meant she was done arguing.

I set the plate into the water, holding it with the tips of my fingers, hoping it would float. It didn't. I scrubbed with the heel of my hand. I felt bad for being upset and hoped I could make my aunt smile. "Were there really doves?"

She put her hand on my shoulder. "A long time ago, when I was a girl. We ate dove when there were guests and to celebrate the day my father came down from the mountain. He said coming down was a good decision. The traders liked him, even though he didn't eat their fish."

I set the plates up to dry on the rack. "What happened to the doves?"

"When I was eleven, I told my teacher I didn't want to go to school anymore. She said I had to. Until I was sixteen, I would go to school. But I wanted to stay home and tend to the doves. My teacher came for dinner and she said we shouldn't eat bird. It made our bones brittle. It scared papa and he got rid of all the doves. Lots of other families were told to get rid of their doves too and soon all the doves were gone."

I rubbed my thumb on the tines of a fork and made faces at it. "Why would everyone give their doves away?"

She crooked her chin into her shoulder and whispered, "I found a dove with a bullet hole in its belly."

"What happened?"

"Not everyone agreed to get rid of their doves." Her shoulders lifted gently, with a kind of long-drawn weariness.

"Was Nana upset that you didn't have dove for her when she visited?"

She clattered a cup into the sink. "Very angry. She called papa a weak son. She said he didn't respect his family's traditions. That's why she took me out of school and brought me up to the mountain, even when the teachers sent men after her to bring me back. We stayed away from them for three years."

I smiled. I'd never lived in the mountains. My mother was a little girl when she came down with her family. I thought sometimes that nothing would be the same if I'd been born in a bed, with walls to hold me like a second womb. Or if I'd been born in a cave, held by stone and a sheet of rain across its mouth. But I was born in a gully and I tumbled out like water from a pipe. The shock of me spilled over and soaked the landscape. I was a flooded road, shallow and clear and so still it was like a hole into the sky.

My aunt's stories about the mountains made me proud and jealous. I wanted to climb a mountain because it went on forever like the scrubland, but it had caves and cliffs and crags and definition.

She put her hand on my head. "Where's your scarf?"

"I lost it in my dream. The wind blew it away. Can I have one of yours?"

"You put it on the windowsill and left the window open, you mean. That was very clumsy."

I scowled. That wasn't what I meant.

She sighed. "Now I have to buy another."

"I'm sorry."

"If we were in the mountains, I would invite a woman to dinner and she would make you a good scarf."

"I'll go to the mountain in my dream and get a scarf."

She shook her head and I snuck guiltily out of the house with her green scarf that showed the coils of my hair underneath. I took my mule to the hill. Maybe I'd run away to the mountain to get another scarf. That was a bad thought, because I lay down in the heather on the hill and stood up hours away, the squat village like rocks among the yellow bushes. But the mountain was still far away, just a tear in the horizon.

My mule snorted as I mounted up. It took us a long time to get back. At the edge of town, a woman looked at us out her window and came out around the front of her house. I tried to turn away, but she came out too fast.

"Good evening," she said. It was the teacher who wanted to take me to school. "Not many people around here have mules." She leaned down and scratched my mule's jaw. "I hear they're not very cleanly."

I held tight to my mule's mane. "They're tenacious. She loves me and takes me where I want."

The woman flicked her fingers like she was dislodging dust and gnats from under her nails. She smelled like fish. "Are you from around here?"

I wanted to say yes. It was my town and I knew it very well. "No."

"Where are you going?"

"I'm riding through."

She smiled, her eyes pinching. "Haven't we met before? I remember. You said you were riding through then too."

"I ride through a lot."

"Mosi's mother wears a scarf like that."

"She got it from my mother. My mother makes these scarves. No one else makes them like this." I remembered then that my aunt had bought the scarf in town and flushed with fear.

The teacher locked her fingers together. "Perhaps you'd like to come in for supper."

I shook my head.

"I insist. You must be hungry. I have red tea, fresh from the fields, and sole fillet with mint."

"I don't like fish."

"You don't know how good it is. This is what happens, when you grow up on birds. Everything else scares you. You're flighty."

"I have to get where I'm going." I dug my heels into my mule's side, jerking her away from the woman. The woman watched me go, her stance trim and disappointed.

I rushed inside when I got to the house. It was dark and the walls stretched away into a terrifying vastness. It was like they weren't there at all. I climbed into bed with Mosi. She didn't like me holding her at night, but I squeezed up against her, staring until I found all the corners in the room.

●

It isn't my dream. Or I think it's not. The sands unravels behind me and I stand on the ocean shore. The water goes on forever, dizzying. It's unfair that I should find the ocean, when I can't find the mountain.

A woman stops beside me and jams her fork into the sand. She takes a deep and satisfied breath. *Ahhh,* she breathes.

"I'll send the ocean away," I say.

She gazes up, the skin crinkling around her eyes. "This is home, sweetheart."

I shake my head hard.

Her coat is like stone. "If your cousin goes to the ocean, you could go to school with her," she says. "Then you wouldn't miss her."

"But I would miss my aunt."

"If you were in a schoolhouse all day, you would be better. You would always sit in the same seat and know where you should be. And there's a drawer in the desk for you to keep your things."

"Can I lock it?" I've never had a thing before that I could lock.

"Good students can keep locked boxes inside their desk. If you went to school, you could bring your friends to the house and say, 'This is my home. This is where I live.' "

I like the idea. Then I could tell the teacher I live here and I'm growing into the shape of my house. "What about the mountain?"

Tsk, a woman says, *tsk*. "The mountain is a bad place to live. It's dangerous. There are no houses, so everything is unstable."

"Oupa lives in a big tent. My aunt says that's his house." But I don't feel very certain about it.

I try to imagine Oupa on the waves, kneeling in a boat, crouched on a reed mat with the sea birds and the white seashells. But it's impossible. My dream cracks around my waist, nearly breaking in half with the impossibility of it. Oupa can't come here, not ever. If he saw me now, he'd say I was the wrong shape and he couldn't teach me. I hold onto a woman's coat, wanting to step into the black recesses that are like tall walls, so that I don't crack all the way through.

●

My aunt stood with her hands hovering over the open cupboards. She stared at the lemons and the pepper and the barley flour. Her hands rested on a tin of red tea leaves, which she bought in the summer and said were very expensive. Her hands slipped to the dried mutton and salted pheasant.

I watched her from the doorway, my toes up against the lintel.

"If only I had a scrap of fish," she muttered.

Goosebumps ran up and down my arms and I put my hand on the doorframe so I wouldn't find myself a great distance away. "Should I kill a chicken?"

Her hands scrunched, fingers folding up tight against her palm. "Yes."

I killed a chicken outside and plucked the feathers, putting them in my pocket for pillows. Mosi came and crouched nearby, squinting. Her hair tumbled down her back, whipping over her mouth.

"My teacher's coming for dinner," she said. "Are you going to hide in the cupboard?"

I shrugged, even though I didn't want to go into the cupboard. There was a stiffness in my throat and I was afraid if I went in there, I would cry. It wasn't a good shape.

"How do you do that?" she asked

"Nana taught me." She died when I was young, but I remembered plucking birds was important. I held out the chicken and Mosi crept forward. I showed her how to grasp the feather so she wouldn't tear the skin.

When Mosi's teacher came, I didn't go to the cupboard. I sat in the closet under the stairs where I could look through a crack in the panels, and sucked on my fingers. If I decided I liked the teacher, maybe I could come out. The teacher came in a flower printed skirt, which flapped against her knees. She smiled and took my aunt's hand with only her fingers.

"I hope you don't mind," she said. "I brought a little something for dinner. I came home early today and I had extra time. I thought, wouldn't it be nice if I brought something to share?"

My aunt nodded, small. She picked up the chicken, which we'd cooked into a thick stew with bay leaves.

"Oh, no. I didn't mean to supplant your own meal." But she let my aunt take the stew away, and replaced it with her own plate. It was a fish of some sort, large and white and stuffed with sweet-smelling pears and apples. It smelled good.

The teacher insisted everyone wash their hands in the sink, scrubbing between their fingers before they ate. Everyone sat very quietly. My aunt didn't eat with a fork usually and she grasped the handle with her whole hand. The teacher held the fork with the ends of her fingers so that it dipped gracefully. She smiled at Mosi, who blushed and looked very proud. It made me jealous.

"Your daughter is a wonderful student," the teacher said.

My aunt nodded.

"You mustn't be concerned that I'm coming with bad news." She spoke with her hands, holding them out like she hoped my aunt would grasp them warmly. "Don't look so worried. I don't have one bad thing to say about her."

Mosi grinned at her mother, who didn't look at her. "Yesterday," Mosi said, "We learned about the new houses they're building on the coast to withstand the flooding."

Her teacher smiled encouragingly. I imagined building a small house out of seashells and the teacher looking at me like that. Maybe I could learn good things at the school and then grow into the shape of the house instead of its cupboards and closets.

"I'm very excited," the teacher said. "You see, there's a lovely boarding school by the seashore. Very safe, of course, and not too near the water. I went to visit last month. It's cleaned every day and the students can play on the beach. There's fresh fish in the morning and once a week they go fishing."

My aunt chewed fast, like she was trying to swallow before the teacher could finish speaking. But the fish went back and forth in her mouth and she couldn't seem to swallow.

The teacher beamed. "We'd like to send your daughter there."

My aunt coughed, spitting up a half-chewed piece of bone and fish.

The teacher jumped. I did too.

"I'm sorry," my aunt said. As if to remedy her fault, she cut off another piece of fish and put it in her mouth.

"That is to say," the teacher said, her hand on her chest, "all the students will be going there, eventually. But we'd like to send your daughter sooner."

"Mama, I have to go," Mosi said, hopping up onto her knees. A shock of horror went through me.

My aunt waved her back and Mosi slid down on her seat. When my aunt swallowed, it was like something huge was going down her throat, bulging the skin tight.

The teacher put out her hand. "I know it'll be hard for your daughter to move so far away. But you can visit. Or you can move to the shore, even. We'll help you buy a house and find a job, maybe skinning fish or somesuch."

"Yes, mama," Mosi said. "Come live with me."

My aunt stared at her daughter, her eyes wide and confused. "I've lived in this house my whole life."

"Your daughter told me that your father came down the mountain as a young man. Wouldn't it be following in his footsteps to move to the ocean?"

My aunt blinked at her. It was as if the woman had slipped her father under her nails like slivers of wood. "I could see Mosi then?"

I put my face against the panel, the wood smell strong in my nose. I thought of yelling to her that she couldn't go because then I would be alone. My body would spill over the scrubland and I'd vanish.

"Of course. It is a boarding school, so she'll sleep over. But she can visit you on the weekend, if she chooses."

My aunt set aside her fork. "I don't see any reason why she should go earlier than the other students."

Mosi gripped her fork, bits of fish still caught on the tines. "Don't you think I'm a good student?"

"Of course you're a good student," my aunt mumbled.

"Your daughter will benefit by going early. It's a better school."

"I don't want her to go."

The teacher folded her fingers together, poised over her fork. "There's another thing." She glanced around the house, frowning at the rugs on the walls, the sunflower seed oil on the counter, the unwashed dishes. I shrunk back into the closet. "Your niece."

"She doesn't live here," my aunt said automatically.

The teacher sighed, her shoulders heaving up in exasperation. "We've played this ruse for a long time. We've let you get away with it and we shouldn't have. We know your niece lives here, and it's illegal to keep her from school."

Mosi glanced at the stairs and squeezed down in her chair, shoving fish into her mouth. I was terrified that the teacher would stand up and thrust her hand into the closet and drag me to school right now. I wouldn't go to school if they meant to send me to the ocean.

"The next semester starts with the rainy season. Mosi will go to the school on the shore and your niece will start school here. It'll be better for everyone."

My aunt shook her head, but said nothing. The teacher wiped her mouth and popped up cheerily. "Thank you so much for supper. Please, keep what's left of the fish. It's my gift to you."

When she was gone, my aunt slid down until her head sunk into her arms. Mosi sat still, staring at her mother collapsed across the table. I leaned against the closet door, the doorknob pushing painfully into my hip, needing someone to say it wasn't true. Mosi stood, clenching her hands opened and closed, and left the room.

●

In my dream, the wind ripples the ocean waves, hushes, holds still. But then the tide gushes up the beach, washing over my knees, and I slosh out with the water, tumbling over the waves. I'm drowning. I catch my throat in my hands and bubbles pour of my mouth. There's nothing here to hold me. I spill until I am so big and thin that it's like I'm nothing at all.

●

I got up early so Mosi couldn't leave for the ocean without talking to me. My tongue was thick with salt. My aunt stayed inside, putting chicken stew into small pots sealed with leather caps. She moved slowly, stopping often to stare out the window. Mosi sat outside on her suitcase, rubbing her nose red.

"Do you think it'll be cold?" she said. "What if my sweater is too thin?"

"Wear a scarf over your hair." I scuffed my heels in the dirt.

"It's not allowed at the new school."

But she wore a scarf now, which she hadn't done in months. It tucked neatly under her sweater collar, crafted into a perfect curve against her back.

"You could wear it if you weren't being stupid and going," I said.

She stiffened. "I have to go."

I wrinkled my nose at the road winding toward the school and the car that would come for her. "I've never slept alone before."

"They'll make you go too."

I scratched my wrists and rammed my toes against the step. "Nana would be angry."

"Nana's dead."

I shoved her and she grabbed my hand, holding tight to my wrist. She looked at me and squeezed and squeezed. "Ow," I said. But she didn't let go, just kept squeezing until my wrist cramped. "Ow!" I shouted, jerking away.

She clasped her hands and stared down at her lap. "I wish you'd come."

"No. I hate the ocean. I hate it."

She buffed the side of her shoe with her wrist. "You've never seen it."

"I want to go to the mountains."

"What if there's no one left there anymore?"

I pushed my heels hard against the step. "They're still there. They'll teach me how to set up a tent and whenever I'm afraid of how big everything is, I'll set up my tent and sit inside."

Under her breath, like she was saying something forbidden, she asked, "Can you dream about the ocean and visit me?"

The sky spun and I had to sit down. I put my arm around her. "Yes."

She flushed and straightened her cuffs. "I'll write letters."

The door rattled and banged, catching on the frame as my aunt came out with a pot for lunch. Mosi put it in her bag. My aunt crouched behind us and fiddled with Mosi's scarf.

"What if we ran into the mountains like me and my grandmother did, when I was a girl?" my aunt said, very quiet.

I squeezed my hands shut. I wanted that very much. But my aunt would never go.

Mosi patted her bag, checking that everything was there. Then she stood, brushed off her uniform, and grabbed her mother around the waist. She held so tight her mother gasped and her hand fluttered indecisively over Mosi's back.

Then the car came and she left us standing alone on the stoop.

⬤

I sit in the surf, water dripping down my back and my clothes soaked through. When I twist out my hair, a river spills away. The ocean waves beat against my chest. I'm so angry I want to cry. All the ocean does is take people away. Nana wouldn't have gone. She knew the mountain was where she should be and was happy in her tent. Why couldn't a tent be a house? It was as much a house as anything.

The mud sticks and scrapes when I stand. But when I'm on my feet, I see something caught on the waves. I run to it and when I snatch it up, it's my scarf, the one I lost in my other dream. I wring it out and bind it over my hair.

⬤

In the morning, it started to rain. As I tucked my hair behind my scarf, I realized it was the scarf I found in my dream. I went into the kitchen and found my aunt opening drawers loudly. She hadn't slept. I'd heard her moving around all night, stacking plates and pouring water and then sitting at the table, the chair creaking when she shifted.

"You'll go to school today," she said.

I shook my head.

She rubbed her face, holding herself up on the counter with her left hand. "You have to go. I'll be arrested if you stay here."

"I'm going to be a buzzard!"

She stared down at her hand. "I'll still tell you stories about Oupa in the evening. We'll sit outside and look for his home in the clouds."

"They'll send me to the ocean." My arms flopped over the table like awful cooked fish. "I went to the ocean in my dream and I drowned."

Her hands went over the sink, rubbing and rubbing so it said *shush, shush.* "You didn't go anywhere. You just dreamed about it because you were thinking about the ocean."

"I found my scarf in my dream last night." I held up the scarf to show it was true.

She snapped her hands together. "You lost it under the bed or stuffed it into the bottom of your chest."

"No. Nana went places in her dreams."

"No she didn't. It was a good story. She couldn't do that." She grabbed a plate and set it down in front of me. Honey pooled over yesterday's bread.

I stared at her as she sat down and started eating. She didn't look at me. The corners of her mouth were firm and angry. I didn't understand how she could say that about Nana. It was the most impossible thing she'd ever said.

"You can't travel places in your dreams," she said.

I knocked against the walls. I spilled out the open door and the window. I drowned in the arid air.

I didn't finish breakfast. I packed lunch and extra food because I'd always eaten when I wanted and I was terrified of being told I could only eat at a certain time. Outside, through the drizzle, I searched for Oupa's circle tent in the clouds. It began to rain so hard the world turned grey and brown. My scarf plastered to my hair. I splashed through water, looking for my mule. Everything vanished into the downpour.

The house was dim and hazy. All the lamps were out and it was floating at sea, vast and empty. My heels sank into the mud and I was floating too. My skin crawled. The house was a bad shape. If I went in it again, it would crush me with its twisted rooms and slippery stairs and bent doorways. It was the wrong shape.

In the mountains, I would find a cave and the cave would hold me until the rains passed.

When I found my mule, I packed the saddlebags and mounted quickly, urging her on to the slippery road. The town was blue, vanishing in the coming tide. I could be anywhere, or nowhere. Water ran down my back and chest and my pants stuck to my thighs. My aunt would stay here forever, drifting aimlessly. I watched a buzzard fly under the clouds, its feathers black with rain. It was going toward the mountain. When it got there, people might see it and then tell how Oupa and Buzzard became friends. They would tell it inside their tents and they wouldn't mind that the walls flapped in the storm, because that was the shape they'd grown into. If I were there, I'd grow into that shape too, instead of a rigid, crooked house.

I pulled my mule around, digging my heels so hard into her sides that she leapt. She landed at a gallop and we pounded out of town.

"We'll go to the mountains," I said into her ear, mud from her hooves splashing against my shins. "Our family lived at the rim of the mountain and they weren't hard to find. Oupa will teach me to be persistent like Buzzard and strong like Nana. I'll sit in a tent and grow into it and it'll be my home. I think maybe tents aren't houses, but they can still be homes."

In the evening, the rain cleared. The mountains were white and red slips on the horizon, cutting out a small space for themselves in the sky. By morning they were bigger than even the women with their forks, and I could see smoke from cook fires. I imagined Oupa when he first came to the mountain, watching in wonder as Buzzard flew up and up and up and yet never seemed to reach the top. When Oupa finally reached the foothills, he put his hips and knees against the mountain crags and found that he fit. I reached the mountain that evening and as we went up the rocky paths, the peaks rose up like tents.

Sarah McGill's story "A Yellow Landscape" was originally published in Metaphorosis on Friday, 5 April 2019. See magazine.metaphorosis.com

About the author

Sarah McGill has published fantasy short stories in *Strange Horizons, Metaphorosis, GigaNotoSaurus, Not One of Us,* and elsewhere. She studies Medieval literature, but her favorite time and place is post-revolution France at the height of the Death Cabarets, mostly because the bohemians really did walk their lobsters in the rose gardens and pretend hydropathes were Canadian animals whose feet were made into drinking glasses. You can find her occasional ramblings at sarahmcgill.com.

Tell the Crows I'm Home

Laurel Beckley

There is a place where the lost go to be found.

It is a small farm tucked into a bend in Highway 38, between Scottsburg and Elkton—two towns barely on a map, and even less so after the earthquake shattered much of the West Coast. Once, this road was a bustling thoroughfare from the interior of the state to the coastal towns of Reedsport and Winchester Bay. Now it sits empty, giving more and more of itself to the hungry river it parallels.

The farm is nestled in a broad gap between the road and the river, hidden by swathes of shallow-rooted white oak, whose thick strands of sea-foam lichen and brown moss create their own ecosystems, creating space for the ferns and the birds and the insects, although there are fewer of all of those, now.

Nicole tends this farm, same as she has for the past forty years. She inherited it through a twist of fate and negligence after her parents passed, and then kept it with the stubbornness of a disowned queer child still tending old hurts. She replaced the hard memories with new ones, slowly rehabilitating the structures of her home and her soul.

The first few years were hard: relearning the lost skills of childhood, accepting the weird things found in her pockets and glove box and shoes, navigating the conservative mindsets of her neighbors—who knew the reasons for her leaving and still disagreed with her lifestyle upon her return. Life got a little easier as muscle memory took over and the collective current turned grudgingly towards acceptance.

What never changed was being viewed as an outsider. Ten years away transformed her into a stranger, despite being practically immortalized for a high school track record that remains unbroken nearly fifty years later.

The gym with her record etched onto the walls flooded in the quake of '22, erasing history but not memory. The football field and high school have been reclaimed since the flood, but the town dwindles with each passing year.

Those old enough to remember Nicole's parents have died off or moved on to nursing homes in Roseburg or Cottage Grove or Eugene. Most of Nicole's former classmates left when the nearest hills were stripped in the first gasping resuscitation of the after, when everyone scrambled to take what they could while they could, before the fires devoured everything or another quake hit or the Yellowstone caldera finally blew or another recession or, or, or. The reasoning was endless and short-sighted. Consideration of replanting and maintenance vanished, along with the northern spotted owls and the wineries and the frogs and the Roosevelt elk.

Nicole stayed, even as the years passed and friendships eroded and the pile of lost things grew. She stayed, though each winter the river takes a swallow of asphalt, another gulp of concrete and mud sluicing off the hillside into the brown water below, until the highway is barely passable by car, no matter what season. There are no funds to repair infrastructure, much less to fix a road leading only to graves and ruin.

It has been ten years since the last clear-cut, and life is slowly returning to the hills north of Highway 38, beyond Nicole's farm. Spindly Douglas fir compete with red-bark madrone and scrub. Hidden trilliums emerge in the springtime deep in the groves of mixed forest old-growth, and sometimes she finds shooting stars in the middle of July. Their vibrant purple headdresses and black-tipped noses give her small bursts of joy, tiny pockets reminding her that while the air pollution is high and the temperature scorching, life continues. Life will continue, even after the end, because nothing truly ends. And that is a small comfort.

Despite her isolation—with the road conditions and few connections to the rest of the world, the five miles into town is a day-long excursion, never mind the hurdles she must jump to arrange transportation to the nearest grocery store in faraway Sutherlin—Nicole is not lonely. Nor alone.

Finders are never alone.

This is what she tells herself.

This is what she has told herself for so long she believes it.

There is a routine to the seasons, and to the things she finds, and she's fallen into the rhythm of her life without quite realizing the rut she's dug.

Each October, a new band of Canadian geese arrive dazed and confused and diverted, and depart happily fat in April. April is also kitten and cat season, when mamas have babies and humans abandon the fanged teenaged terrors they had assumed were cuddly fluffballs. Dog season is year-around; runaways fleeing the terrors of a thunderstorm or wanderers ditched by their masters, for whatever reasons people leave their furred family members.

Nicole finds them all, save for the crows, who do not appear to be bound to the rules of the farm, and come and go as they please. Like Nicole, a crow is never lost.

She used to have quite a few human visitors, back when the world was only half broken. And a variety. More than one flying craft has made an emergency landing in the narrow, flat field that used to provide hay but now lies untouched. After the sixth time a lost pilot insisted they were in a different region of the county, Nicole learned to keep a map handy in her tractor or a back pocket, just in case. Summer was for lost kayakers and inner tubers, back when folks floated for fun. They'd put in around the high school to catch the rapids and came ashore on the lower pasture's pebbled beach convinced they'd arrived at Umpqua Myrtle State Park.

Her wife, rest her soul, stumbled upon the farm by chance after taking a wrong turn in 2006 while searching for a bed and breakfast in Scottsburg. It was raining, and late winter, and the banks of the river were rising. Nicole invited this stranger inside, and Christine never left until the day she took her last breath, two years before the quake.

Even now, a traveler might get caught out late at night, far from where they are meant to be, and see Nicole's porch light through the trees—a trick of the eye or the vegetation, as her house is guarded by a stand of fir and oak and hedges. She always keeps the guest bedroom ready, and has grown to read the signs of a new arrival's approach. She knows, with bone-deep intuition, if the visitor will go, or if they might linger a while.

Some visitors, like Christine, stay longer than a night. Some find what they are looking for, but most don't. Eventually, they depart, and never return.

Nicole stays, and she waits for her next visitor, even as the years stretch on and on, and the ache of loneliness morphs into something else. She knows there is a world out there, but she has convinced herself the larger world is not her purpose. She stays so she may find the lost and missing, like a lighthouse along a dark stretch of shore, a stationary point for the lost to be found, to reorient themselves and move on, in whatever way moving on means. Christine used to tease her about being a witch, but that's not accurate. Lighthouses are not magic, and neither is she. They just are. Nicole is a finder and crow-friend and sometime farmer and old woman in the woods, and that is enough.

This is what she tells herself.

●

It is early fall in Douglas County. The first snap has hit, a wet cold that seeps through clothes and penetrates deep. Nicole's root cellar and pantry are well stocked for the winter, although her arthritis has turned screwing lids into an ordeal, and her hip aches when she sits or stands or sleeps or moves.

This morning she found a set of car keys from a Mercury Cougar in her left house-slipper, and there's a white-tailed deer in the barn, sleeping between two milking goats. It raises its weary head when she arrives, blinking in exhaustion and covered in soot and ash. The nearest fire is fifty miles away, and its smoke has traveled to the valley, layering everything with a hazy smog that brings brilliant sunsets and displaced wildlife.

Nicole admires the deer's antlers as she feeds her small flock. First the cats, because they demand to be first in everything. Then the crows, who really should be first but who understand the cats in ways no other animal should. Then the goats, who eat and are milked, as much as it pains Nicole's hands—a part of her wishes another runaway teen would arrive, not because she wants to put in the emotional energy of caring for a sullen and scared and bewildered child, but because she wouldn't mind someone else doing the milking or morning feeding—and lastly the dogs and whoever else has wandered in during the night and refuses to feed themselves.

She is about to head into the house when a crow swoops, wings brushing her cheek as it lands on her shoulder, clawed feet digging through her jacket. It nuzzles her gray hair and chirps the word for *stranger*.

With a sigh, Nicole trudges out to the front, rubbing the side of her hip, pushing aside a feeling of trepidation. The crow remains on its perch, although its fellows have gathered on the eaves to watch the newcomer.

A car is parked outside the house, which means someone has fixed the roads. The car's engine ticks in the cold, steam rises from the hood. A person huddles against the passenger door, arms wrapped about their stomach, tucking their tan jacket to their body. Their pale face is drawn and tense, as if they are preparing themself for a task. Their brown hair is cropped short, highlighting round cheekbones and thick eyebrows. Their head jerks, eyes widening as Nicole emerges from behind the house.

"Aunt Nicole?"

Nicole's chest tightens. She does not know this person. She's taken in a lot of strays, and only the human children refer to her as *aunt*—the easiest term to explain if anyone questions her foundlings. But none of the children ever return when they finally leave. No one returns. That's the rule, unspoken and unwanted, but there all the same.

The person shoves off the car, shuffling toward her. Their bare hands are still tucked into their armpits. They are in their early twenties, maybe, or they might be forty-five, or thirteen with a stolen car. Nicole is bad at determining ages. At this point, everyone seems impossibly young.

"Um, you don't know me," they say. Nicole's left eyebrow crooks, and their shoulders hunch, as if they are trying to make themself small, either to be non-threatening or to diminish themself before her. "But my mom talked about you. A lot. Jessica? Jessica, uh, her maiden name was Canby?"

Nicole waits. She doesn't remember a Jessica Canby, but she has known a lot of Jessicas. Most of her strays don't have last names, or they give false ones, and often, she recommends they tell her their destination dream, and that becomes their last name. She has known quite a few Austins and Portlands and Harvards.

The person fidgets. "She um, she said a lot of things about you, and I think she was here when she was a teenager? She'd run away from home and you, uh, you gave her a place to stay. I think it was in 2010 or something? I don't expect you to remember—it was a really long time ago." There had been two Jessicas in 2010: Cornell and Seattle. "Anyway, I um, I'm Aubrey, Jessica's daughter. My pronouns are she or they."

Nicole nods, smiles despite her uneasiness. Most times she knows what her visitors will need. A place to sleep, a hug, a cup of coffee to keep going, a map, a spare tire, a band-aid, a locked door, even a quiet morning alone on the porch, listening to the crows and robins talk to each other in the garden. Some just need to be seen and heard. But for the first time in a long while, Nicole doesn't know what this lost person needs, and it scares her. Still. The child is lost, and Nicole knows her purpose. "Come inside, Aubrey. Let's warm you up."

Aubrey fiddles with a peeling strip of paint on the kitchen table, not meeting Nicole's gaze. Aubrey seems fascinated by the table—one of Christine's first furniture renovations, where she transformed the source of so many of Nicole's shitty memories into pure pride—and her finger moves down the red stripe, then the orange, tapping each color of the rainbow. The table was painted before the intersectional flag, and lacks the now-ubiquitous brown, black, white, blue, and pink triangles.

"I'm not lost, you know." *Tap, tap, tap.* "That's what Mom said? That you find the lost."

Nicole's hands tighten around her mug of tea. "Did she, now." The crow, who's followed her inside and hopped from her shoulder to a perch on the sink's edge, clacks its beak. "How is your mom?"

Aubrey winces, and Nicole bows her head. Well.

"I'm sorry," Nicole says. The words are inadequate. They are always inadequate. Most times she finds the right words, but this time the well inside her chest grows, choking off platitudes, and she stays silent.

"She passed away in April. Cancer. It was—it was quick." Aubrey still doesn't meet her eyes. One fingernail continues to worry the red strip, the paint separating further from the laminate. "I tried to keep going. College, chin up, all that shit." Aubrey looks up, gaze fierce. "I'm *fine.*"

Nicole nods. Aubrey is very clearly not fine, but Nicole doesn't think she needs comfort.

"She said you were her only family."

"Many do, I imagine. Where did she end up?"

"Pittsburgh." Aubrey breaks a chip away, and bites her lip as the scrap flutters to the ground. "She wanted me to find you. Tell you she, um, she appreciated it."

"That's a long journey." Pittsburgh is a lifetime from here. Dark shadows line Aubrey's bloodshot brown eyes, and she reeks of greasy fast food and unwashed flesh and hard journey. Nicole's instincts tell her to get this child into a bath and then bed, but there is something off. No one has ever traveled here *intentionally.* Not even neighbors, back when she had those. "Did you get lost along the way?"

Aubrey's chin jerks up. Her lip curls. "No. I knew exactly where to go. I always do."

Nicole exhales, long and slow. "I see."

She does not see. She's accepted her place for so long that she's stopped questioning. Reopening that part of her mind is hard, as it involves grappling with concepts and ideas and implications she has buried for decades. She knows her purpose, has accepted her strange gift, and that is enough. She stands up. "You must be exhausted. Let's get you a bath and a nap. We can talk later."

●

Aubrey sleeps for two days, and when she awakes, she's like the river—pushing beyond her boundaries, slowly carving new places and insights, whittling away at Nicole's reserve and resolve, always hungry for more and more and more. Seemingly determined to shove her history into the past, she follows Nicole, learns how to run the farm, how to prepare for a wet winter or a drought, how to gather the last of the berries and the vegetables. She refuses to talk about returning to college or next steps, but seems content to stay.

She roots through the house, relentless, curious. Over the years, lost items have found their way into Nicole's home: inanimate objects she doesn't recall bringing back but which somehow squirrel into drawers or a back closet or her root cellar, and are then dumped into the guest bedroom and spare closets. Aubrey seeks it all, fascinated by everything from spare change to baby clothes to shipping manifests to credit cards to half-filled day planners to stuffed animals to thirty-day return receipts to cell phones, but it is the stuffed and mounted six-point buck's head that really catch her attention. Nicole has to explain how it showed up on the hood of her car in 2003—or what it 2004? Time is strange—and the explanation drifts into the whole debacle of her attempt to find the trophy's owner.

Aubrey brings order to the clutter, the bits and pieces that were once content to stay crammed into overflowing piles but now seemed to scream for attention, for organization. She even finds the plastic tub filled with old coins, invaluable gemstones, and an ancient dented goblet. "Is this what I think it is?" Aubrey asks, tilting it back and forth, staring at the etchings from an ancient language.

"Most likely," Nicole replies, and Aubrey replaces the goblet into the bin reverently, returns the tub back to its place. She seems to understand that some things are best hidden from prying eyes. Nicole likes that.

But Aubrey's incessant desire to seek grates, and Nicole's unease grows as Aubrey comes to life over the winter, blossoming as the world dies down and the rain-bearing clouds leech color, turning the countryside brown and grey and damp. Having organized the house and the barn and the toolshed—even cleaned out Nicole's rusting solar-converted car—Aubrey crosses the abandoned highway, moves through the woods with the enthusiasm of an explorer, and returns with truffles and mushrooms and late-season elderberries.

Then Aubrey begins venturing into town, navigating her car over impossible gaps and washouts, returning with pizza and canned peaches and secondhand stories of community as December sprawls into January.

"Come with me tonight." Aubrey's breath wisps before her, twining through her hair and cold-chapped cheeks. She has taken over milking duties and many of the more physical chores, completing them before vanishing on her next adventure. She's explored the remnants of Scottsburg, and is now fascinated by the folksy vibes of the townsfolk of Elkton. The apparent ease with which Aubrey moves through the world is irksome and brings up feels of inadequacy and loss, and yet each time she leaves, Nicole worries. Despite her mixed feelings, Nicole...enjoys this strange person. She likes the company.

"Come where?" Nicole asks, although she already has an idea. She finishes feeding the goats, and massages her stiff hands. Aubrey's back is toward her. Hunched over as the girl is and dressed in Christine's jacket, Nicole can pretend—for a moment—that she is talking to her wife. Then the moment is gone and she is in a barn with a young twenty-something, instead.

"There's a basketball game at the high school." Aubrey turns. Her nose is pink from the January cold, and her cheeks are two round red apples. "It should be fun. You haven't left the farm since I got here. It'll be good to get out."

"I haven't left because you get everything we need." And the thought of leaving scares her. She hasn't stepped foot off the farm or seen a human face that is not Aubrey's since July, and Aubrey's relentless pursuits underscore Nicole's commitment to not leaving her home, solidifying and entrenching her position and reluctance and sense of place. Nicole has told herself the same things for forty years, and will not fathom a paradigm shift, even as the fear of *something* ending burrows deep into her core. She doesn't want to know why Aubrey's presence bothers her so much, because looking means digging deep enough into herself, uprooting her stories and unearthing the passivity of her existence. What will her roots look like? She doesn't want to know.

And yet.

The fact no one from town has come to check on her gnaws on that small place she keeps buried. She's an old woman who's had a strange youngster come along. It should send up red flags among the townsfolk, but then, Nicole is known both for being reclusive and for her mysterious, extended family. Aubrey's words sink in, though. "A basketball game?"

"Yeah. The girls are playing some team from Oakland? They're undefeated. It should be fun?" When she's nervous, Aubrey's up-talk returns, twisting her sentences into uncertainty.

Nicole has no desire to see the people of Elkton or anyone else. "It'll be dark when we return." It's a paltry excuse, and they both know it. Still. She has no idea how Aubrey navigates the roads. Last month she crept to the end of the driveway, and discovered the large washout was still there. It was impossible to drive around, much less over.

Aubrey smiles. "Already covered. Andrea Gardner says we can stay with her."

Andrea Gardner is the granddaughter of Molly Springs, who spat on Nicole in sixth grade and then outed her their senior year. When Nicole returned, Molly welcomed her back into the community, all smiles and acceptance and bygones being bygones and no apologies ever given or faults acknowledged. Nicole did not attend Molly's funeral, claiming the roads were washed out, but really, she has not forgiven her bully. This offer is uncomfortable, but perhaps there is change between generations. And if she bends on this request, perhaps Aubrey will find what she has been seeking.

Nicole tilts her head, and Aubrey's face lights with joy.

Trepidation builds as the day draws on. Nicole tries to push down the feeling this is the last time she'll feed her goats or walk this path or pet a crow or find a wheat penny, that this is the end of something. The emotion she's been suppressing all fall and winter, tamping down alongside all her other fears, bubbles over, churning acid up into her throat. She wants to hold on to everything all at once, and the pain in her chest builds until there is a bowling ball on her sternum, slowly crushing her. It doesn't help that everything she finds is trash—a mummified, half-eaten Snickers bar in her left shoe, someone's Walmart receipt for oranges bought in 2004 crumpled under her hairbrush, a used condom. She gingerly places everything into the trash and spends the rest of the day locked in her bedroom, staring out the window at the crows huddled on the fencepost.

But Aubrey steers her into the car an hour before the game, and glares until Nicole buckles herself in with shaking hands. As her house slips away behind the oaks and the ferns, the fear she'll be unable to return increases. Aubrey taps her on the arm, and points ahead as they bump and jolt down the driveway. The crows are gathered along the branches of the trees, watching them turn onto the pothole-filled highway, wings flapping in farewell.

Nicole closes her eyes as they near the washout, unable to comprehend the how or why or what of Aubrey crossing an impassable gap in the road. She leans forward, pressing her fists against her closed eyes. Purple stars dance against the thin flesh of her eyelids, little shooting stars shouting in fear instead of joy. Each breath is a rasping sob, a half-groaned *I can't*. This cannot be her end. Not now. She is not lost—she is *never* lost—and her home is *for* the lost and those who are found can never return. What if she *can't* go home? She's not lost. She's not *lost*. She's *not* —

"Aunt Nicole, are you—" The car stops. "I'll turn around."

Nicole stays hunched over, trying to breathe through the fear and the pain, until she feels the switch from asphalt to dirt. She holds her breath, peeping between her fingers until she sees her farm, her house, her fields, and all that is familiar yet again. Aubrey taps the brake as the house comes into view, and Nicole launches for the door release. The seatbelt pulls at her midsection, refusing to free her, until Aubrey presses the button and Nicole shoots out of the car, gasping, free, and home.

She presses her hands to her chest, breathing in the familiar air. The crows squawk overhead, wings rustling, and Nicole stumbles forward to lean against an oak. The brown moss squishes and crinkles under her hand, the opposing sensations grounding her. She is *not* lost.

The driver side door opens and closes, and Aubrey edges forward. "I'm sorry."

"Don't be." Nicole can't face her. Can't let her see the fear that's been brewing since September. Fears long dormant, fears she's pushed aside, that have risen and flourished. "It's not your fault."

It *is* her fault. Endings always have beginnings, and this the beginning of an end.

Nicole is so comfortable here, in her home, where she knows everything and everyone, where she maintains the memories and keeps the lost, and she does not want to leave. She does not want to see people who don't need her or understand her or who keep her at a distance. She does not want to take the chance of leaving, because she might never return. She cannot squash the fear of being replaced by someone who can bridge the gaps she cannot.

Footsteps crunch behind her, and Aubrey's hand presses against her back, tentative and comforting. "You know, when I was little, I never understood how people could get lost. I kept running into people who couldn't find their way, or their keys or their purpose or whatever, and it was so weird. I always, always knew exactly where I was and where to go."

Nicole stays silent, unsure what Aubrey is saying. Unsure how this relates to anything. How this is supposed to soothe her fears.

Aubrey continues, "I didn't know what being lost meant. Then Mom died. I knew exactly where to go, except for the first time there were two paths instead of one. I tried the first and it didn't work because it was the path I'd been going on, and it wasn't mine anymore." She takes a deep breath, releases it. "So I took the second path and came here. And I met you."

Nicole laughs. "And you think I'm lost?" The thought is absurd. The lost come to her to be found. She knows where she is. She always has. She has told this story often enough that she believes it.

"I think there are different ways of being lost." Aubrey's toe scrapes a circle in the dirt. "And, maybe, different kinds of being found?" Another scrape. "I know you're nervous and you've kept yourself isolated here for so long, but I thought—"

"You thought a basketball game would help?" Nicole turns, faces Aubrey. This kid can't be serious.

Aubrey twists her hands together. "No, the basketball game was an excuse. I found your name on the gym wall. For athletic records?"

"The quake flood destroyed everything."

Aubrey crosses her arms over her chest, hugs herself. "Well, turns out there was this sophomore who went digging through the old internet archives. She found the records and convinced the principal to put them back up. And she saw your record and how long it's stood, and she's thinking about trying to beat it." Her eyes dart to the right. "She's a junior now, and going to play in the game tonight, and I thought it might be interesting for her to meet you. Put a face to ancient history."

"Before she erases it."

Aubrey rolls her eyes. "Before she beats a fifty-year-old record! That's huge—for both of you."

Nicole steps back, towards the trees. The fear is back, although now it's competing with irritation and another worry. First the world ended, but everything was fine because Nicole found lost things and made a place for them, or gave them the space to find themselves and move forward. Now Aubrey is here to replace her, and this new child is going to remove her from history completely, never mind that she is erased already. She is a myth, a rumor, the old woman who lives with the strays on an abandoned stretch of highway. She finds the lost and has become lost in return.

Nicole finally sees the trench she has dug for herself. Years upon years of self-soothing stories, of unthinking rhythm and routine, of refusing to look outward, have built a fortress of isolation wrapped in false purpose and a fear of her fiercely protected comfort vanishing in a return to past prejudices. But she also sees that the walls are not so high she could climb out, if she had help.

"Please?" Aubrey asks.

Nicole stares at the branches, at the crows. She rocks side to side, hyper-focused on the black wings, the clacking beaks. They are not agitated, as she had thought. They are reminding her that all things end, and the ending makes space for beginnings. They are telling her there are finders, and there are seekers. There is alone and there is loneliness. There is family and there is community. There is fear and there is courage. There is the past and this is the present. They are saying *happy hunting* instead of *goodbye forever.*

This is a new beginning. A new story she can tell herself, over and over, until she believes it. This time, she will have help in the telling.

Nicole takes a deep breath and gets back into the car.

Laurel Beckley's story "Tell the Crows I'm Home" was originally published in Metaphorosis on Friday, 22 October 2021. See magazine.metaphorosis.com

About the author

Laurel Beckley is a writer, Marine Corps veteran, and librarian. She is from Eugene, Oregon, and currently lives in northern Virginia with her wife, fur creatures, and a collection of gently neglected houseplants.

thesuspectedbibliophile.home.blog, @laurelthereader

Leiprenese 101

Jason A. Bartles

I scrambled to find the arm hole in my gown as I ran toward Zorah's office apartment. Synthetic fabric should not get this twisted, but the wind tested my best efforts to arrive precisely on time. Zorah lived in the central Administration Building that towered over Mount Leipren University. They occupied the second-highest floor, but unlike the Chancellor right above them, Zorah invited their students and coworkers inside. I untangled the gown and situated the cap, trying to catch my breath. Then I checked my watch. A minute to spare. As I waited for the elevator, I reviewed my mental checklist for the final interview that stood between me and tenure.

My blood pressure rose with each passing floor. An MLU professorship was not a job for the lazy, the purposeless, or even the decently competent. Imposters and flakes were weeded out. It was tenure or bust, admission into the inner circles of academia or irrevocable banishment from this campus and this career. I could not fail now.

The elevator chimed, and at exactly six o'clock the doors opened to reveal—*you've got to be kidding me*—not Zorah, but Rafa.

"Good morning, Charlie!" Rafa practically burst with self-satisfaction. They had been waiting in front of the elevator to gloat. I could have sworn I had reserved the earliest office hour. I wanted to set the bar high, to become the standard against which others were compared, but Rafa had outmaneuvered me. "Good luck," they said insincerely and squeezed past me to take the elevator down.

I shot them a fake smile and stepped into Zorah's foyer.

"Come in," Zorah called, and a door opened at their command. I shook my wrists and took a deep breath before proceeding to their study.

"Good morning, Zorah. Thank you for meeting with me so early," I said. I had planned that greeting, but after Rafa's surprise attack, my words took on a double meaning.

"Never mind about Rafa," Zorah began. They had anticipated my reaction. "Everyone assumes going first gives you a leg up, but the truth is," they leaned forward and gestured for me to sit, "the patterns of the recent past are no guarantee of the present."

Zorah was dressed in the finest regalia. They sat behind a grey marble desk. On either side, bookshelves lined the walls. They were crammed with old lesson plans, monographs overflowing with sticky tabs, and personnel files. Somewhere in there, I thought, must be Zorah's field notes for the first English-Leiprenese dictionary and countless other treasures. Behind them, floor-to-ceiling windows opened onto the Appalachian ridges that wrapped around the campus.

The view from this elevation, and Zorah's reassurances, washed away the disappointment and most of my nerves. They had a way of making the world feel right again.

"Let's get down to business," said Zorah. I took a seat, while they opened my file. Zorah skimmed the summary of my publications, peer evaluation scores, and the data collected about my work-life balance. They mmhmmed and appeared to be quite pleased with my performance over the past decade. Then they tapped the page with their finger and looked at me over the rim of their glasses. "This says you have a new essay forthcoming. A report on the influences of Leiprenese on Earthling languages?"

"Yes. It will be published next month."

Zorah gestured for me to explain the work. This was an interview, after all.

"Right. Leiprenese is a pidgin language developed by the Renner to facilitate the colonization of Earth. At first, the Renner envoys used it to communicate with Earthling leadership about commercial matters. For the Renner, Leiprenese was an undignified but necessary mode of speech."

"Some of your peers would disagree with that statement," Zorah interjected.

"Well, they would be mistaken. There is a somewhat popular, but unfounded, notion that the Renner cherish Leiprenese for its simplicity. However, such scholars fail to distinguish the moral value the Renner assign to efficiency from their own yearning to be respected by the Renner. It's pure solipsism."

"Let's assume that's true. How, then, do you explain the Earthling desire to borrow from a language of such low esteem?"

"Earthlings are banned from learning any of the Renner's native languages while on Earth. The Renner have always insisted on maintaining a certain distance from their colonial subjects," I explained, and Zorah finally nodded in agreement with something I had said. "On Earth, Leiprenese was, and still is, the only possible means of communicating directly with the Renner. Speaking the language provides a way to improve one's station in life. For those born around the time of Earth's discovery and who came of age just as the Renner reconstructed the economy to ease its entry into the galactic marketplace, Leiprenese became associated with the progress and prestige of the Renner and their Homeworld."

"You're speaking of my generation."

"Precisely. In fact, I analyzed many of your early speeches."

"Is that so?"

"Yes, as if overnight, you stopped using gendered language."

"That was intentional. The Renner practically demanded it. Are you arguing that all of the changes were conscious?"

"Of course not. Most occurred over time as the result of code-switching, of constantly living between the two languages. Over a span of ten years, you adopted new vocabulary and even smoothed out some of the harsher consonants not used by the Renner. The *th*, for example, became an aspirated *h*."

"And?" Zorah prodded.

"And the hard *k* softened into sibilants."

"When I think back to how I used to speak, these changes seem drastic," said Zorah. They traded the steely gaze of peer review for a more wistful expression. "But I suppose those born into this world never knew anything else."

"Now you're speaking of my generation," I replied with a wink.

"And speaking of your generation, I have to say I'm quite impressed. With two of you anyway. You and Rafa can count on my endorsement."

"Thank you, Zorah, that means a lot." I could have melted in relief.

"You've earned it," they added.

"What about you? Is there any news about your ascension to the Homeworld?"

"You never know about these things," Zorah said cryptically. Without a doubt, they were the most qualified candidate. Every year, the Renner chose one professor from each planet in the empire to retire among them. Zorah had been favored for last year's opening, but at the eleventh hour, the Chancellor received word that the Renner had suspended all ascensions due to unforeseen circumstances. Something about the collapse of the housing market on a distant planet. Zorah stood and turned toward the windows. "But I try to remain optimistic," they said and invited me to join them.

"I'm sure this will be your year," I said as I approached the wall of glass. "I can't wait to be where you are. I lie awake most nights and dream of escaping this backwater planet."

"I take it you've watched the latest video of the Homeworld?" Zorah's gaze rose toward Renner Hall as they spoke, and mine followed. Perched on the highest peak, the site where the Renner had made first contact almost fifty years ago, its gold-plated facade reflected the sunrise over the entire valley. Originally, the building had been reserved for Renner envoys, until they stopped visiting the planet in person. Ever since, the hall had taken on a ceremonial role, housing the person chosen to ascend for their last night on Earth. The rest of the year, it looked down on the campus as a comforting reminder of the Renner's promise: Paradise awaited those who worked with passion and perseverance.

"Who hasn't? Rethinking your plans now?"

"Absolutely. I had always wanted to stay in the capital. I love living in the mountains, but I thought for my retirement I'd try something new. The sprawling city with its glass towers and plastic-lined boulevards. The personalized pods to carry you to the Anthropological Museum of the Galactic South and then to the beauty spa for a quick chemical peel. I'd watch the sunset in one of those open-air wine bars in a heated pool near the coast. But that train, is that what you would call it?"

"I suppose. There weren't any tracks, or at least none I could see."

"It made me rethink everything. Having your own private car while touring the planet," Zorah's voice soared with their imagination. "The quartz canyons, the cloud forests, the petrol rivers."

"I had no idea those even existed."

"No one did. And being granted permission to study the local languages as you pass through each region."

"It's a dream come true for language nerds! Any favorites?" I asked.

"I'm partial to Milonian. I find the short, shocking phonemes to be an irresistible challenge for my palate."

"Hacher would be my choice."

"The language of austerity," they added. "It all sounds marvelous."

"I wish they'd allow for more opportunities to visit the Homeworld. You'd think if people got a taste of that lifestyle, they'd be more motivated to develop their own planets."

"I'm sure they have their reasons," cautioned Zorah.

"Of course," I agreed and shifted the topic. "It's exciting to think I could get tenure the same year the Renner choose you to join them."

"That would be nice." They spoke in hushed tones, as if another line of thought were running under the surface. "You're following closely in my footsteps."

"I've had a fantastic mentor in you," I said, at risk of crossing that line between gratitude and groveling.

"But best not to get ahead of oneself. There's still plenty of work to do here."

I watched as Zorah traced a finger over a hairline fracture in the window. The gesture was unassuming, as if out of habit, but it left me uneasy. I couldn't help but imagine the entire pane shattering into a million shards and pelting the ground below. I took a step back from the edge and returned to the other side of the desk.

"Look at the time," Zorah said as they turned toward me. Their voice helped shake the irrational vision from my mind. "I have eight more interviews to complete, and you have a class to teach."

"Thank you again." I bowed in deference and left Zorah's study. For a moment, it felt as if everything were lining up just as I had planned.

●

The students in my Leiprenese 101 class were arranged in their mobile desks like ten little bowling pins. It was my job to knock them down in order to build them back up. Now that I had secured Zorah's endorsement, I could focus on defending the record I had set years ago as a student in this very classroom. Today's unannounced oral exam was designed to do just that.

"My value is my work," declared Student 1, leading the repetition of the weekly motto. Rankings were all that mattered at the introductory level. Scores were tied to biometrics, and only the top twenty percent would survive the first year. Only then would I bother with their names.

"My value is my work," said the other students in unison.

Student 1 had been Student 1 for almost a month, which gave me until the end of the week to depose them. They knew I would be relentless to them in defending my title, while lobbing easy questions at their competitors.

There were no friends in that classroom. Only ten adversaries. And I had all the power.

"Today, I will assess your understanding of pronouns," I said. "Student 1, are you ready?" I had switched to Leiprenese, and they knew resorting to English would move them immediately to the back of the class.

"Ready," they responded.

"Student 1, fill in the blank: The employee is late. *Blank* lose ten percent of their wages."

"*They* lose ten percent of their wages," they affirmed with annoyingly accurate pronunciation.

"Correct. You earn one point." I pursed my lips.

"Student 2," I said, slowly and in English, freeing them to respond more easily. "True or False: *I* is the first-person singular pronoun."

"Umm."

"Student 2, you have three seconds."

"False?" Their voice cracked with uncertainty.

"Such a maynard," mumbled Student 1. "Pathetic."

"Wrong," I said in disbelief. "Did nothing trickle down from my recorded lectures? Minus four points."

At my command, the scoreboard in the front of the room docked four points from Student 2, who became Student 4, though they deserved to be in the back of the class. As always, I had been too generous. The desks rearranged themselves, moving Student 2 back a row and sliding Students 3 and 4, who became 2 and 3, into higher-ranked positions.

Just then I noticed Rafa lingering in the hallway, checking to see if Student 1 had outperformed me yet. Time to strike.

"Student 1," I said, returning to Leiprenese, "Fill in the blank with the proper first-person plural pronoun: *I* am the foreman. *They* are the Manager. *Blank* always reward efficiency."

"*They*, wait—" the student's eyes popped as they began to self-correct. I had my opening.

"Sorry, Student 1. The correct answer is: *I and they.* Minus—" I turned to look at the scoreboard. Student 1 was now in the lead by twenty-four points. "Minus twenty-five points."

The star student became outraged at their failure to best me. While the chairs for Students 1 and 2 swapped places, I walked toward Rafa, winked, and shut the door in their face. I would count this as payback for the little trick at Zorah's office.

"You'll just have to try harder, Student 2," I said as I turned. It was better they learned how the world worked under my guidance than on the job. This was for their own good.

●

The day of the Promotion Ceremony had finally arrived. I and Rafa and the other eight candidates for tenure waited behind the auditorium with luggage in hand. Anyone not tenured would be escorted from campus immediately. A lucky student had been assigned to usher me and the others through the loading door and into the wings. In the audience, the tenured faculty were arranged by rank in the shape of an inverted pyramid that pointed toward the stage. At stage left, the Chancellor teetered behind a podium, while Zorah oversaw a folding table draped with purple fabric. It bore the MLU sigil of a black bear under a maple tree. I counted two golden sashes and two flower crowns.

I and the other candidates drew lots to decide the seating arrangement on stage. I drew a front-row seat, and Rafa, poor thing, would have to sit behind me. As they settled in, their shoe kicked my chair. It was not an accident. I was used to the spats, the little digs at every turn, the subtle, but not unnoticed, affronts. It would be a long road beside them, but then again, every Arguedas needed their Cortázar. Rafa's disparagement drove me to new heights, to push harder than I ever imagined as I worked to outshine them.

The Chancellor tapped the mic. They praised the faculty for their increased output and commitment to student success, but then they deviated from the perennial format of their speech. "This year, I'm proud to report a special honor bestowed upon the campus." The auditorium brimmed with anticipation. This must be Zorah's moment, I thought. Zorah took a step toward the podium, and a hush fell over the crowd. "Mount Leipren University," the Chancellor continued, leaning toward the mic, "finally pushed into the number one spot for most accumulated unused vacation days on the entire planet."

The faculty cheered as a wave of ceyah washed over the room. Such a frugal loan word from the Leiprenese. It named a feeling that had become prominent under Renner tutelage. Ceyah is similar to pride, but without the enduring sense of satisfaction, because no record is ever unbreakable, no limit impossible to surpass. Ceyah is that brief moment you celebrate before going back to work.

"Now, on to the final event," they said.

The faculty were caught up in their own success, but I kept my eyes on Zorah. They would not ascend yet again this year. They appeared sullen, as if something had broken, as if they had known it would slip from their hands but picked it up regardless, only to watch helplessly when it crashed to the floor. As the lights dimmed, they stepped back to the table and tried to put on a brave face.

Suddenly, my chair began to move. I and Rafa and the others swirled and rotated around one another at center stage. The big reveal had begun. My chair pulled me upstage, and my pulse pounded in the side of my neck. This was the wrong direction. I felt the blood drain from my cheeks, and Rafa rolled beside me. The others enjoyed the view from downstage. I stared at Rafa, and they at me. An uncharacteristic nervous sweat had beaded around their brow. At least if I were being banished as a failed professor, I thought, so were they. But to my relief, the bigger group was then split in half and dragged toward the wings. I and Rafa were pushed through the open space between them, and in a reversal of fortune, the undeserving eight were swept from the stage entirely. I dared not turn around for a final look at my former colleagues.

The spotlights landed on me and Rafa. I stood to receive a handshake from the Chancellor and my sash and crown from Zorah. Rafa received the same in reverse order. This was the moment I had been working toward my entire life. On paper, it was my greatest achievement. I was happy, or I would be, I told myself, once the reality sank in.

Still, there was no denying this competition had taken its toll, and it was far from over. Earning tenure had been a simple sprint. Now, I would need to adopt a new regimen if I wanted to beat Rafa—and if I hoped to avoid Zorah's fate—in this marathon toward the Homeworld.

●

I unclenched my toes and let my head drop onto the pillow. Rafa rolled off my bed and rebuttoned their shirt.

"That was productive," they said, hopping as they pulled their too-tight and too-short pants up to their waist. "What are you going to work on tonight?"

I usually experienced a renewed clarity as soon as I and Rafa finished, sometimes even a hurried need to start drafting a new lesson plan before they were out the door. But my mind felt mushy.

This rivalry paused twice a week. Wednesdays I visited them, and Saturdays they visited me. The calendar was marked for a strict twenty minutes. I and they toasted to recent accomplishments, in this case tenure, and allowed for a quick release.

"Afraid I'll steal your next great plan?" Rafa prodded.

"Please, you couldn't scoop any idea of mine."

"Then tell me." Rafa almost knocked over a stack of journal articles piled on the nightstand as they bent over to pull on their socks.

I didn't know what to say. For the first time in my career, a blight had spread over the vines where my upcoming ideas usually ripened and waited to be plucked. "Didn't you—" my voice trailed off as an impossible idea skulked around the corners of my consciousness.

"What?"

"Expect the Chancellor to announce Zorah's ascendance last week?"

"The thought did cross my mind."

"They should have ascended last year. To be passed over twice is incomprehensible. If Zorah can't make it, who can?"

"I can," declared Rafa. They never missed the chance for self-promotion.

"Seriously, the Renner have to realize Zorah is unsurpassed in their generation. No one at those old-world Ivies even comes close."

"That entire generation began to slack the minute they got promoted. I and you both produced more plans and better research than Zorah last year. The way I see it, none of them have earned the right to get to know the Renner in person. They were just lucky enough to not have serious competition."

"Still, I wonder—" I sat up and pulled on my undershirt. There was a tear in the seam under the arm. I would have to get this mended.

"Out with it, Charlie. The clock is ticking."

"Maybe ascendance isn't worth it."

I watched their mouth droop a bit. The thought had never crossed Rafa's mind, and it ought not to have crossed mine either. The mere doubt in my voice approached the treasonous.

"That's absurd," Rafa scowled.

"I just mean—" I tried to backtrack. "I thought this would be Zorah's year."

"Yeah, well, it wasn't."

My proposition had been outlandish, mindless, even violent. If I were Rafa, I would have been over the moon, plotting the best strategy to reveal my great mistake.

"It was a dumb thought. Don't pay me any attention."

"Sure thing," said Rafa as they opened the door. They chose not to confront me in private. Their energy would be better spent on a whisper campaign that would slowly erode the high hill on which I currently stood. For now, they shook their head and slipped out the door.

I should have been panicked, or angry, or rushing to preempt Rafa's next move. Right then, for a reason I could not explain, it just didn't seem to matter. The calendar alarm sounded, but instead of getting back to work, I sat on the edge of the bed and stared blankly at the reflective poster of the Homeworld hanging over my desk.

●

A sea of purple caps and gowns with golden doctoral stripes packed the roof-top deck of the Administration Building. I stood with my back to the party, sipping champagne, and stared out at the campus. The valley shone under flood lights on this chilly evening. Going into the New Fiscal Year, I had to reclaim my sense of purpose.

Looking for inspiration, I turned toward Renner Hall, but the campus lights had imprinted on my vision. I lowered my eyes, blinking away the glare, and noticed a crack in one of the deck boards. It appeared to be quite deep, like a fault line on the verge of fracturing. I traced it as it zig-zagged beneath my colleagues' shuffling feet, but I couldn't see where it led.

I was taking another sip when a hand landed on my shoulder. I recoiled, and champagne dribbled down my gown.

"Charlie, hi, sorry, didn't mean to startle you," said Zorah. They reached for a cocktail napkin and dabbed at the wet spots.

"No worries," I said. "It won't stain."

Still, they folded the napkin and patted at the spot once more. "Why are you standing over here all alone?"

"I'm just in my head tonight."

"I know that feeling."

They noticed the doubt in my silence.

"Seriously," they said, getting quieter as they rested their lower back on the bannister and crossed their arms.

"Did something happen?" I asked cautiously.

"The Chancellor informed me the moratorium on ascensions has been extended indefinitely."

"Let me guess, another unprecedented crisis on the other side of the galaxy means Earthlings have to tighten their belts?"

"Pretty much."

"And by indefinitely, they don't just mean a year or two, do they?" I turned to look back at Renner Hall as I asked. Zorah should have been spending their last night on Earth over there, waiting for the shuttle to pick them up first thing in the morning.

"It could be five, ten years. Maybe never. Who even knows?"

Zorah turned around with me. As their words echoed in my thoughts, the future I had imagined, the one the Renner had promised, slipped from my fingers like a balloon from a child's hand.

I felt dizzy and braced myself on the bannister. "This champagne is strong."

"I don't think it's the champagne," replied Zorah. "A little birdie told me you're also having some doubts."

My face burned, and my shoulders went stiff with the thought of Rafa's version of the events. I tried to strategize a counterattack, still unsure of Zorah's motives. Before I could muster the energy, they reached out and rested their hand on my upper back. Their touch, friendly, released some of the tension and quieted the growing sense of abandonment.

"Rafa, blissfully unaware, approached me the day after your accidental revelation," Zorah said, laughing a bit.

They stood beside me and waited, patiently, as I debated what to say next. Even if this was a trap, I thought, even if confirming Rafa's accusations meant some sort of punishment, I decided to risk it. I couldn't hold back any longer.

"I can't explain it, but this—" I looked around.

"Doesn't seem worth it?"

I almost dropped the glass, so I set it on the bannister. "How did you know?"

"Because, Charlie," they sighed and paused. Exhaustion settled in the crow's feet around their eyes. Meanwhile, Rafa kept to the opposite side of the deck. The busybodies kept buzzing around them, perpetually reconfiguring the dynamics of the swarm. "It's not worth it. Only a handful ever made it to the Homeworld. And the rest, what did they get? What did I get? What will you get? I'll tell you what. Nothing."

Zorah's words confirmed a fear I had so far kept from surfacing.

"The Homeworld is a lie," I mumbled, still concerned I might be overheard. Worse, I realized, is that I would never get the chance to prove to the refined and upstanding citizens of the Homeworld that I was an elevated example, if not an exception, to the human race.

"The Renner withdrew long ago," said Zorah. "Yet, they control every dimension of this little planet from a distance."

"So they don't have to get their hands dirty?"

"Yes, and also to avoid being blamed for the world they built. Today, Earthlings discipline and drive other Earthlings. As professors, I and you play a key role in churning out the managerial class that keeps this system humming along. One of the strategies the Renner developed was to prohibit the use of Earthling languages in the workplace. They believed they could prevent, or at least slow, any nascent sense of solidarity by alienating the workers from one another. Of course, the crushing debt they acquire just to make ends meet and the lack of alternatives keep most people from stepping out of their assigned role. Not to mention the threat of being sent to the mines. Meanwhile, the Homeworld keeps those who are better off shut into the system, running in circles to achieve a vague promise of another world, another life."

"Not just running, but constantly trying to outpace everyone else," I added.

"Right. The Renner never force you to run faster, technically speaking. They don't crank some knob. The faculty here do it to themselves. All in pursuit of a dream that was imagined by another. Meanwhile, the Renner sit back and feast on the fruits of Earthling labor. And every time the Renner move the goalposts, everyone accepts this as a greater challenge. Look at Rafa."

"Between my blunder and your failure, Rafa couldn't be more motivated."

"You can't blame them. I've been in their shoes and acted no differently. Everyone is playing the same game here. But I think, Charlie, like me, you're growing tired," Zorah offered.

"I am."

"You know, you and I really are quite similar."

"Do you think—" I started to say. "Wait." The word order was wrong. "What did you say?"

"You heard correctly, Charlie." Zorah smiled and took my hands in theirs as the unnoticed anagram unscrambled itself. "You and I," they repeated.

Zorah's words sprouted before my feet. Their syntax went against everything I had believed, everything I had been taught. Yet somehow it perfectly described one of the many sensations that had been surfacing since the Promotion Ceremony. I let my toes inch their way toward that new growth. It was soft and squishy, like a bed of moss. Zorah, quite literally, had put me first. Not their work, not their own interests or ambitions, but someone else. I felt light as air and stood tall.

"Yeah, you and I," I repeated slowly. "You and I." I had to untrain my mouth to break the deeply ingrained grammar, but with practice, the words would take shape, and one day I might be able to return that generosity or pay it forward.

Zorah squeezed my hands once more and then, as the final seconds of that year wound down, left me to make a decision for myself.

●

"In the year 2035," I recited in slowly enunciated Leiprenese, "the Great Navigator discovered a primitive culture with the potential to be molded." I paused. The students, arranged before me in two opposing lines, furiously transcribed my every word. They were competing to reproduce the most accurate text in the least amount of time.

In the interim, Zorah's "you and I" kept rattling around my brain.

I read the next sentence. "Upon contact, the Renner demonstrated the benefits of cultivating a highly intensive culture of achievement."

Such a clunky phrase, "you and I". A more succinct way to express that idea, that connection, had to exist. It was on the tip of my tongue.

"The Great Spaceship dropped through the atmosphere to the wonder of all Earthlings, who freely offered—" I stopped the dictation mid-sentence and looked out at the obedient students. I had to stop repeating the Renner's lessons. This could not go on.

One by one, each raised their head wondering why I had paused for so long.

"Professor, you may continue," the student currently in first place informed me.

I would not go on. There were no words, in Leiprenese or any other language, that could reach across the void and explain to the students I had trained so well what I was about to do. Out of habit, I gathered my notes from the podium, tucked them into my briefcase, and walked silently out the door.

I could hear the disbelief in my wake. A few sat frozen. Others buzzed with gossip, and one suggested they follow me outside.

Renner Ridge surrounded me. Even from my relative elevation at Leiprenese Hall, it was impossible to look off into the distance. There was no horizon here, only a barricade sealed by Renner Hall. If someone happened to let their gaze wander beyond themselves, their work, and their rank, the building's shiny walls would grab their attention and redirect it toward thoughts of the Homeworld.

That was where I needed to go.

The Hall could only be accessed by a narrow staircase. I hopped the gate. Before my little stunt, no one had imagined a need for greater security. The minds of each member of this campus blocked access better than any physical barrier.

My gown whipped in the wind as I plodded along. I clutched my cap reflexively, but then I ripped it from my head and tossed it over the railing. It soared above the campus for quite some distance before landing in a thicket. A student, still playing by the rules, rushed over to retrieve it.

Higher and higher, I climbed until I finally reached the launch pad next to Renner Hall. For a second, I saw myself from the outside. I laughed at the absurdity of it all. Here I was trespassing on consecrated grounds during a workday for no apparent reason.

Up close, Renner Hall did not look the same. The façade was scratched, and the shiny surface only coated the walls that were visible from below. The others, made of concrete, were covered with mold and old growth. I had an urge to smash the windows, but I changed my mind when I noticed they were made of plexiglass.

For the first time, I saw Renner Hall for what it was. A vacant tower. A few crumbling walls coated in fool's gold. A monument to deception and exploitation. A cardboard box left out in the rain.

I walked back to the stairs, peered over the railing, and saw bodies pouring out of every building. They gathered around a central figure—Rafa—who steered the swarm's bewilderment. They directed outraged hands and fingers to point in my direction.

A corrupting influence on such impressionable minds!

A defender of society hiding in plain sight!

Meanwhile, the briefcase tugged with the weight of the world below. *Why was I still holding on to this?* The lesson plans and ungraded essays begged for their release, so I popped the clasps and dumped out the contents. Pages and pages burst from their folders and fell out of rank. As the papers hung over each stunned student and staff member, time itself lurched to a halt.

An irreversible first strike, for those below. From here, a moment to contemplate the slow beauty of my disruption.

The sheets fluttered in the wind. Some drooped toward the crowd and caught in treetops, while others glided into the distance. I dropped the empty briefcase and stripped off the gown as I walked to the other side of the launch pad. There, I climbed on the railing and sat with my feet dangling over the far edge. My idleness occupied a forbidden space and time. But it also revealed a horizon that had been missing from my life.

A hand touched my shoulder, and I steeled myself to be cuffed and dragged back down the mountainside.

"Charlie," said Zorah.

"Don't try to talk me out of this," I shouted, but they shook their head.

"I had no such intention." They climbed on the bannister, took a seat beside me, and removed their cap. They had not come to stop me. They had been waiting for me to join them. "You and I sure are going to give them something to talk about today."

"*You and I.* My mind resists that phrase at every syllable, and yet it feels somehow right to foreground you instead of me."

"*I and you* wasn't always the grammatical order," Zorah explained. "It was imposed by the Renner in the early days, and I thought, just maybe, you'd have noticed in that last article you wrote."

"Oh really? No, there are no oddities in the use of pronouns in your recorded speeches."

"In the ones that still exist. Many documents from the first years were purged, and by the time you were born, those changes had already taken hold. They were taught to you in school and in every interaction. They even reflected the hierarchies and values built into the environment all around you. But language cannot be controlled completely from above."

"It was so disorienting, and yet freeing, when you said 'you and I'. You named this thing I couldn't quite put into words, this thought I didn't know how to express. I sensed there had to be more than this competition, this life of working without rest. There had to be more than my little academic achievements."

"See, you get it."

"You're the one who invited me to hop off the treadmill. There was no going back after that."

"Indeed."

Zorah took a deep, renewing breath.

I did the same.

It was quiet here, calming. There was an ease to it all.

Mountains stretched before Zorah and me. I could have stared at those blue ridges for days. No roads or trails pointed the way. No rope guided my descent. Only a steep drop, and beyond that, the open woods. Not long ago, the thought would have terrified me.

"What now?" I asked. The timeless questions had resurfaced. "How do we undo all of this? How do we build something better?"

"*We*, Charlie. You do know that word after all."

"We!" I shouted in surprise at myself. The ancient pronoun had crept up from the back of my mind. Not *I and you.* More than *you and I,* even—Zorah and I became *we.*

The word echoed in the distance. So elegant and unassuming. It joined, not through isolating chains of conjunctions that mark order, but by allowing individuals to come together in a collective syllable.

We sat here together. We were exhausted and burned out. We let ourselves, *ourselves!* We let ourselves rest, shoulder to shoulder, and for a moment, we chose not to do anything at all.

Our collective inaction sent a shudder through the campus behind us. We had opened a hairline fracture in the foundations of this place. We had cracked open a door. There would be no guarantees, of course. It would take more than two to change the world, for we could easily be discredited, cast out, and replaced.

Yet, for us, being tired together formed the strongest bond we had ever known. This was our first real lesson, one we were writing together. Ours was a small offering, intended as only one of many more to come. For now, though, we would wait here on the cusp of something unforeseen as long as we could. We would invite others to take a seat beside us. To rest and linger here for a while. To contemplate a new sense of time, one that did not consume, but endured.

And after that, we just might have the strength and the stillness of breath to speak with one another and imagine where we go from here.

Jason A. Bartles' story "Leiprenese 101" was originally published in Metaphorosis on Friday, 21 May 2021. See magazine.metaphorosis.com

About the author

Jason A. Bartles (he/him) is a queer SFF writer and academic. Originally from West Virginia, he now calls Philadelphia home. He is a Clarion West '23 alum. As a researcher of Latin American literary and cultural studies, he published *Arteletra: The Sixties in Latin America and the Politics of Going Unnoticed* (Purdue University Press 2021). This book received an Honorable Mention for the Best Book in the Humanities Prize by the Southern Cone Studies Section of the Latin American Studies Association. He has authored numerous essays on literature, film, philosophy, and video games. As a creative writer, his short stories have appeared in *Daily Science Fiction, Utopia Science Fiction Magazine*, and *Little Blue Marble*, in addition to his debut paid publication in *Metaphorosis*. In 2024, his debut novel, *A Valley to Harness*, will be published with Two Doctors Media Collaborative.

194

Freely Given

Connor Mellegers

Forty ravs on the Bone and it was all the Tech could talk about. Taye had done it, so said everyone. His name was on the lips of every student at the Tech the same as if he'd given the money straight to them. Forty ravs. Enough to live on for years if you were careful, and he'd given the lot to the Bone as if it were nothing. Sheena said Taye had shown her the scars he'd gotten on his hands and knees working to earn it through all sorts of hard labor. And now the secret was out, and students and instructors alike were lining up to shower him with praise and affection and gifts of their own. Already, stories of the gifts he'd received were spreading like wildfire, fueled by the fact that he made a grand display of denying that he had donated anything at all. Genuine humility, of course. Someone like Taye would never aggrandize. After all, he'd given forty ravs to the Bone.

I met Joan in the gymnasium of the Three Oaks community center. The huge wooden room was empty save a few stray balls and frayed mats scattered across the floor. Normally, the floor would be covered in the refuse of after-school activity: pylons, hoops, balls of all shapes and sizes, but all of those were neatly away in the storage room, which meant Joan had gotten a serious head start on me. I rushed to the supply closet and grabbed a push-broom. By the time I got back, Joan had put everything away and had already begun disinfecting the equipment. I put my head down and began sweeping.

Joan and I had been assisting the center managers for years. The managers were responsible for the center's operation, of course, but between managing their programs and supporting the needs of their visitors, they barely had any time to keep the facility clean. We provided our labor as a gift to the managers, and they kept the center running as a gift to the entire community. After our labor, we would record our gifts in the official registry. Both of us checked off what we had each done of the sweeping, mopping, sanitizing, etc. The work each of us did affected how much official credit we would receive and thereby the gifts, respect, and esteem that would follow in equal measure. Unofficially, what we did affected how the center's managers saw us. You could see them following your pencil as you marked off what you'd done, raising their eyebrows in appreciation, or letting them furrow in disappointment. You could hear it in their voice, too. "Thank you for your generous gift to Three Oaks *and* thank you for *yours*." It was all in that *and*. I couldn't be that *and*. Not today. Not after Taye had given forty ravs to the Bone.

Joan started mopping the second I'd swept up the dust and dirt. I nearly ran to fill another bucket and begin mopping from the opposite side. I kept my head down, my motions fluid and perfect. Mopping half a gym might only have been worth half the credit, but if I was quick enough, I could get to the next task before Joan and have a chance to catch up to her. After five minutes mopping in silence, I finally turned to look at her from across the room. She was grinning.

"What?" I said, turning my eyes back to the floor, desperate for this chance to clean while she was distracted.

"You heard about Taye," she said. I groaned and she laughed. Of course. She knew exactly why I hadn't taken a breath since I arrived. She'd been laughing at me the whole time.

"Everyone heard," I said. "Very generous of him to give all that money. Thirty ravs, was it?"

Her smirk made my stomach jump. "Forty. And you don't have to rush, you know. I'll split credit with you, whatever we've done."

I mulled it over. It was clever of her, but that was no surprise coming from Joan. Splitting credit meant that officially we'd done the same work and would share whatever esteem we'd earned in the eyes of the community. Considering how much she'd already done, that was a generous gift, though a gift to one person was nothing compared to a gift to the entire community. I could refuse, but that would be disrespectful. Perhaps doubly so for the base intentions with which the gift would have been received.

"Oh please, Ev. I won't tell anyone," she said.

Another gift, this time hidden. At this point, refusing would be irresponsible.

"Thank you," I said.

"Taye won't get official credit without disclosing openly," Joan said.

"And that just makes it more impressive."

She nodded and scrubbed at a stubborn spot on the floor. Anonymous gifts were often the most worthy. Little chance of credit meant that a gift could truly be freely given. But they were rare. A gift-giver deserved their credit and had a right to it. Earning official credit meant that everyone could see what you'd done. The higher your credit, the greater the gifts you would receive from those around you. Everyone wanted to give to the most generous and share in the righteousness of their generosity. But Taye had given a massive gift in near-perfect silence. And he'd given to the Bone. Few ever gave to the Bone and what little they did was rarely worth having. Anyone could take from the Bone — whatever they wanted and however much they wanted. A crowd of takers, ingrates, and even hoarders could enter that sad little building on the edge of town and walk off with all forty ravs without so much as a reason. Few had it in their hearts to give to those who took from the Bone. To give cash was even more unheard of.

But Taye hadn't cared. He must have labored for wages for months — hard, thankless work without any credit or respect — just to anonymously dump it all directly to the Bone. And his gift would never appear on the official ledgers or records. Those takers and hoarders would never know who had given them all that money. A gift like that was unheard of. But we had heard of it. And now, official credit or not, everyone knew what he had done. It was genius. Genius and risky. Hell, who wouldn't be impressed? Even I'd go out with Taye if he asked me, not that I was looker enough to be asked. If he did, it would just be another gift to his credit.

"It is *very* impressive," Joan agreed. The edges of her curly black hair bobbed into the soapy water as she bent over the bucket. "But it's hard to believe Taye could earn that much money through labor alone."

"Sheena saw the scars," I reminded her.

She scoffed. "Everyone has scars, they don't mean anything just because a credit-hungry looker like Sheena thinks they do. Any labor worth doing is given as a gift. Earning wages like that means taking on labor no one else wants to do, work in a factory or mine, or some other horrible place. Taye's a shrimp from a good family. Wage labor enough to earn forty ravs would break him." She snapped up and her eyes landed on mine. "Unless he had help. Or maybe it was a gift. Maybe he wasn't the one who made the donation at all."

My mouth dropped and my feet squeaked on the gym floor. A gift gifted. Credit for an incredibly generous donation freely given away. That wouldn't just be impressive, that would be astronomical. Untouchable. Worth all the respect you could imagine. Even without official credit, if that leaked, you'd have more than just half the Tech longing for you. Hell, even the instructors might go for you.

"You heard something?" I asked.

"No, I didn't hear anything," she said.

I huffed and slammed my mop into the bucket, splashing water all around me.

"Then why even bring it up?" It was hurtful to get my hopes up like that. That kind of gift would be fantastic to witness. To even be in the presence of that kind of generosity is something everyone dreams of.

Joan sighed one of her big sighs. Older-sister sighs, I call them, even though we're not related and my mom sometimes makes gifts of meals to her family. All the more significant for the fact her family isn't offered many gifts.

"What I mean, Ev, is no one has heard anything, *yet*. But maybe they could. And who knows what name could be attached. I mean, there's no official record; anyone could have done it."

I stared at her for a long time. Joan wasn't a looker, same as me. She wasn't particularly athletic either. Her math and writing, though better than mine, were hardly enviable and no student at the Tech would want to trade places with her in a million years. But she had these ideas sometimes. Wild ideas. Ideas so twisted it hurt my brain to try and wrap itself around them.

"Anyone could have done it," I said, my mouth still failing to close.

"Anyone," she agreed.

"Like you?" I asked.

"Oh no," she shook her head in big arcs. "Who would believe that? My family are known takers," she said.

I nodded and turned away. We never talked about it. It felt shameful to even mention. Her parents accepted any gifts they were offered and even took from the Bone: money, food, furniture, whatever they needed. But they never gave to anyone. They never seemed to labor at all. True takers. What little they did receive was the result of Joan's labors at Three Oaks and her gifts to fellow students. But even so, she carried the stain of her parents' greed. No one would believe she was capable of such generosity.

"But you could have done it," she said.

I scoffed. I wish I'd done it. I wish I could have done it. I'd never had anywhere near forty ravs in my life. I only ever labored as a gift. I never needed to work for anything so shameful as pay.

"Your grandmother visited last year, didn't she? I heard she was a hoarder."

I tried to scoff again but my tongue was heavy and dry. Joan was really saying this. Grandma Ross was a hoarder and a wage taker. It had always brought my dad shame, but he still invited her to stay with us every year. Hoarders sometimes gave chunks of their fortune to family members. It was known to happen. It might be believed. But to really suggest taking credit for someone else's gift? I'd never even heard it done before. A credit thief would be below even the least remorseful takers.

"Taye earned his credit, Joan."

"Did he? Because he donated it all at once? Because it was some grand gesture of a gift? We give away our labor every day and who notices? I'm still a taker and you're still a laggard. But Taye gives some money to the Bone and suddenly he gets gifts and respect you and I could only dream of. Why does he deserve the credit more than you, Ev?"

This was too much. What she was saying was ludicrous. Taye had been generous. He deserved whatever anyone wanted to give him. "It was an impressive gift," I said.

"All gifts are impressive. Sheena's kind only care about what's novel. What draws enough attention to earn them praise. Perhaps they'd like to hear something even more novel."

My heart felt like it might leap out of its chest. I kept my eyes focused on the floor. "Joan, we couldn't..."

"Couldn't what? Tell people what we might have heard?" She laughed, picked up her mop and bucket, and left the gym, leaving me behind to stare. She didn't look back.

●

Billy was the first. Then Eliza-Beth. The king and queen of lookers at the Tech. Then the rest followed: Cara, Saraisa, Johanssen, Themi, all the lookers worth seeing lined up outside my locker between classes. And the instructors. The grins they gave me when I passed by could light up a room. Huge, massive things that made you feel like the smartest kid in the Tech. And suddenly I was, however you sliced it. My grades went through the roof. Study notes from lectures I'd never heard and essays I didn't remember writing popped up in my bag and my locker, gifts from instructors and students alike, freely given and taken. And yet, even accepting them, my collateral didn't drop. It couldn't. My gift had been that big, that selfless, that colossally unheard of. A donation that large and the credit for it freely given away. I could take jobs for wages. I could take gifts from anyone who offered. I could be the biggest hoarder there ever was and I'd still be the greatest gift giver the Tech had ever seen. I was infallible.

One day my dad called me in after school. He's a big man, tall and grim. He has a massive smile, the kind like Eliza-Beth's that could light up a room with only the flash of a few teeth. But we never saw it at home. He always said his smiles were gifts and too precious to waste on family. But that day he smiled. Mom too. Even Geoffrey, who'd never given or accepted anything from me a day in his life, was smiling. They all had gifts in their hands. Delicately wrapped in the paper and ribbons you saved for really special occasions. I smiled back at them.

"Here are some small tokens of our appreciation," my father said. Small tokens. He *actually* said that! My father had met mayors he was less respectful to, lifelong dedicants and gift-givers of the highest order who didn't hear such words, but he said them to *me*.

Of course, not all those who looked were lookers. I once saw Taye from across the Tech cafeteria. His stock had fallen dramatically after everyone found out it was me who had given 40 ravs to the Bone and not him.

I was surrounded by people. They jostled to see who would be able to give me lunch. They pressed around me, beautiful meals made with love offered up with admiration and desperation. Whatever lunch I accepted bathed the giver in the light of my generosity, earning them the highest credit possible from one small gift. I took one, a dal made by a looker named Kiel. It smelled amazing. The others pulled back, staring crestfallen at their unaccepted meals.

Across the cafeteria, Taye pulled out a brown paper bag. Eating one's own lunch was something only takers and those most pathetic were ever forced to do. No one cooked for themselves by choice. Back before my star had risen, Joan and I would swap meals we had each made. It wasn't prestigious, but at least it meant we ate through the generosity of those around us and not our own petty labor. Joan would scoff every time. She thought it was pointless and silly, but I always insisted. Even so, whatever she had cooked was always made just the way I liked it.

My stomach flipped as I watched Taye open his crumpled paper bag. I thought of asking one of those I'd rejected to give their lunch to Taye as a gift to me. But then I saw him slide his bag across the table as someone else did the same. I couldn't make out who it was before Kiel pulled me to their table and into that afternoon's gifts.

●

I was laying on the hill outside of the Tech with Billy and Eliza-Beth. We were drunk and sweet off compliments and the summer air and all sorts of gifts freely given and taken and given back in return. Joan walked up the hill to greet us. We were covered only by a thin, white blanket. She smiled and the three of us giggled. Joan was from a family of known takers. Even a giggle was a gift.

"Enjoying your afternoon?" Joan asked. I hadn't seen her in ages. Our work at Three Oaks was a thing of the past, just as needing to labor for credit was a thing of the past. The three of us stared at her, smiling and unblinking.

"It's funny," Joan said in her older-sister tone. "How much a gift can change your life. Receive the right gift and you might find yourself surrounded by friends you never even knew you had."

Billy barked a laugh. "And what would you know about giving gifts?" he asked.

"I know that accepting them can cost just as much as giving them," Joan said.

Billy and Eliza-Beth both laughed maniacally and rolled into each other, pulling me back into a pile of kisses. They both joked, as we rolled around, about the taker who thought she could educate us on gifts.

I tried to let the sun and grass and attention wash over me, but Joan's words flew around my mind long after she'd left our private hill. I had forgotten. In the face of the gifts, and attention, and love that felt so right, so perfectly right, I had forgotten where they came from. I had let myself believe that this was my life, finally earned after years of under-acknowledged labor, creativity, and kindness freely given to those around me. But in reality, it had been a gift, one bestowed on me by Joan through the rumors she'd spread.

It is not a bad thing to accept a gift. But to take more than you give, to think only of what you can take, that is what makes a taker. When I had ascended to the ranks of the most generous, I gave a few rare gifts where I could. But I now realized I hadn't given enough. I had forgotten that I had taken a gift at all. It had been freely given and freely taken in return, but it was wholly unreciprocated. Joan had given me the greatest gift of my life and I had ignored her completely and allowed myself to become surrounded by those who had never even seen me before I was someone to be seen. She was right to chastise me. This gift had cost me my generosity. I had become a taker and it was time to give again.

●

Even with the free time granted by the gifts of grades and papers, the desk had taken three straight weeks of labor. It was the most beautiful gift I had ever made: compact, lightweight, strong, with discrete cabinets and a beautiful blend of colors. Its manufacture had attracted more than a little attention and there was a small crowd gathered around me to see who was lucky enough to receive it.

I waved Joan over as she exited the tech. Her mess of tight curls shrouded her face, and I could hear the onlookers whisper "taker" as she came up to me.

"Joan, I would like to give you this desk. I can think of no one more worthy of it. You have given me many gifts over the years that I could never repay. Your gifts to this community, including your tireless work at Three Oaks, are far too often overlooked. I hope this desk can help you in your studies and that it properly conveys my gratitude."

I had practiced the speech the night before. It was the same as what I had written in the official gift registry. The words were important. The gift wasn't just the desk itself, though it was no small thing, the real gift was my acknowledgment of her. My status gave those words serious weight. With one gift, I would hitch her to my rising star.

The tiny crowd froze behind me. They were as eager for Joan's response as I was. They were eager for her gratitude, eager to acknowledge her as someone worthy of such a spectacular gift.

But Joan didn't embrace me. She didn't cry tears of joy and clap her hands. She simply looked at the desk and said, "I don't need a desk," then walked past me and my tiny crowd. Over her shoulder, she shouted, "Give it to one of your pretty new friends."

The onlookers and I froze, then their snickering filled my ears as the crowd petered out behind me. Cold tentacles of fear crawled up my back. No one refused a gift like this, whether they needed a desk or not. The real gift was far more than mahogany and brass hinges, it was my presence, acknowledgment, and friendship. She had turned all of these down without a second thought.

I had been wrong. Joan didn't want me to give again, to reciprocate to her and others as was right. That visit on the hill hadn't been a reprimand of my greed, but a reminder of what I owed. She alone had given me my new life and she alone knew it didn't belong to me. I owed Joan a massive debt, and she would decide when it was paid.

●

Money is not something I'm used to dealing with. My food, my home, and the things that fill it are all gifts. Gifts given by people that knew I would give everything I could back in return. A family like mine has little use for ravs; we are generous enough to need only the generosity of others. So, it was beyond strange to be holding twenty ravs in my hand and even stranger to slip them through the slats of Joan's Tech locker. I'd sold the desk and half the gifts I'd received in the last few months to get the money, including an ornate candleholder Billy had carved himself and a crystal beaded necklace made by Eliza-Beth. I received strange looks when I sold these precious gifts for cash, but I'd had no choice. Joan had refused my gift and all that came with it. Joan was not simply content to let me live the life she had given me. She had shown me that much. She had no interest in sharing in the light of my generosity, but money was another story. Money could buy all the food, clothing, and comforts her family only received when the Bone was full or when Joan's labors at Three Oaks elicited some token of generosity. They would still be takers, but fed takers, comfortable takers.

The coins rattled as they fell into Joan's locker, and they rattled even louder when they spilled out of mine later that day. Heavy, loud, obnoxious things. Twenty ravs, enough money to buy her family food for a year and she had given them back like they were nothing. There was no note with my ravs returned to me. The only response was the money itself — a clear message that Joan would rather she and her family suffer than take anything from me. Even this small fortune couldn't buy me out of her debt.

●

Joan was attacking the floor with her mop when I arrived. She had already cleared the equipment, swept the entire facility, and begun mopping while sunlight still poured through the windows. I joined her from across the room, trying to match her pace. She didn't acknowledge me. After only five minutes with the thwack and splash of our mops to occupy my attention, my mind began to ache. I threw my mop down with a huff.

"What do you want?" I whimpered. "What do you want from me, Joan?"

She leaned her mop gently in the bucket and smiled. An ugly grin, all teeth. "Want from you? Surely the generous Ev would not be so base as to offer an exchange. If you offer a gift freely, I'm sure I will accept it freely."

"You didn't take the desk."

"I have no need for a desk."

"It was a gift.

"One I had no need for."

"You didn't take the ravs," I said.

She sneered. "The twenty ravs tossed in my locker without even a note? The twenty ravs you no doubt earned off of Taye's labor? I don't want your money, Ev."

"Then what do you want, Joan? If you don't want gifts or credit or money, what do you want from me?"

"I want to finish cleaning, Ev. It takes twice as long without you here."

I looked down at my hands. Without my regular labor, they had lost all their long-held calluses and were aching already.

"Joan, you spread the rumors. You gave me the gift," I said.

Joan nodded. "And you took it. You took from Taye, desperate and greedy, just like all your pathetic lookers would have done. And now you call me taker behind my back."

I opened my mouth to protest, but I couldn't force out the lie. "What was I supposed to do?"

"Did you know Taye doesn't care that you took the credit from him? I told him what we did. I apologized for stealing his credit and having you waste it on your lookers and trinkets, but he says he doesn't need it. He says that as long as he has enough to survive, he's happy. We trade lunches now most days. He even labors with me here sometimes, not that anyone notices."

My heart fluttered. If she had told Taye, she might tell anyone. She could crush me with a few well-placed words. "I didn't take the credit," I muttered.

Joan smiled. "But you did, Ev. And you didn't do anything with it. You weren't generous, you weren't kind, you didn't fight for anyone, you just left. You became one of *them*, whose every breath and whimper is a gift, and you laugh at us who labor every day for your scraps. And you never came back."

My eyes filled and my throat became tight and scratchy. It wasn't true. I had tried to give. I had tried to be generous. "I gave you a gift in return," I said.

"The gift of joining your sycophantic circle of lookers. The gift of laughing at my parents and Taye and anyone else you choose to look down on. Keep your gifts, Ev. Keep your life. You earned it."

I begged her to leave me be. I begged her not to destroy me, not to take what she had given me, but she just laughed and shook her head. Eventually, she turned and mopped her way out into the hallway. I followed her, but she wouldn't even look at me. After a few minutes, I dumped out my bucket and left.

●

This time it was harder. My stock was still high, but my renown wasn't what it had once been. I sold all the gifts I'd acquired and begun laboring in a heavy-manufacturing plant. The looks to and from work stung, but I knew they were worth it. I needed the money and the labor it took to earn it. The gift from Joan had turned out to be no gift at all. It was a yoke, one that tied me to her crime for as long as I wore it. She was a credit thief. She had taken the credit that was rightfully Taye's and given it to me. I had accepted it without question and become the greatest taker the Tech had ever seen. And Joan knew it. She wouldn't take my gifts; she wouldn't accept my friendship. But she wasn't gone, either. She stayed on the edge of my life, threatening it with every breath she took. If I couldn't convince her to join in the spoils of what we had taken from Taye, to mire herself as I had done, I would have to give what I had taken. I would force her to become a taker as she had forced me.

The news made the Tech even wilder this time. Sixty. Sixty ravs to the Bone and they were alive with the buzz of it. The work that must have taken. The respect hidden within. And before the end of the day, everyone knew who had done it: two quiet takers named Taye and Joan.

I was relieved. Tired and relieved. My own stock had fallen far after news of me working for wages had gotten out. Further than I ever expected it could, and I now stood little better than I had before all this began, but I had repaid the gift in kind. I had done the work and given back what I owed. And now Taye would receive the credit he truly deserved, and Joan would receive credit for a gift she hadn't given. She would become a taker, same as I had been, and I would be free. This was a gift she could never refuse, not without harming Taye, who had done nothing but give.

I had been freed from her debt, and the relief settled over me and flushed the shame from my core. I had given much of myself, not only my labor, but the credit, gifts, and status I had always wanted. And now I was a taker no longer. I was excited to see no one waiting for me as I exited my classes. I was relieved at the prospect of cleaning Three Oaks tonight. Everything was as it should be.

I found Billy and Eliza-Beth standing in front of my locker at fifth bell. They, like all the other lookers, hadn't spoken to me for months. Today they came up to me fawning, delicate, and smelling of roses.

"We heard what you did," one of them said. Then all of them said it, one by one. All the lookers. Then all the instructors. Then everyone else. Joan had set the record straight. She had told them about all the money I'd given and how I had tried to give her and Taye credit. They surrounded me at the steps of the Tech. Thousands of them. I could even see my parents in the crowd. A hundred ravs to the Bone in under a year. An enormous sum given to those few dared give to, and I hadn't even kept the credit. I had thrown it away like it was nothing, to two people who could hardly have deserved it. I was more than a giver. I was a legend reborn. I was fantastic. I was nothing they'd ever seen before.

Joan stood at the edge of the crowd. She wore a huge smile. Twice now, she had openly refused my generous gift freely given. She was an ingrate of the highest order and an ungrateful taker at that. She had taken on a status so low she could never crawl out from under it. She had accepted a life of pity and the Bone rather than take a gift she didn't want, and she smiled as if it were the greatest day of her life. I stared at her while the crowd pawed at me. I saw now that my gifts had never been meant for her. I had only ever tried to free my conscience and secure the life I always wanted. And by refusing them, she had let me. She had shown me who I wanted to be and let me become it. I was fantastic now and forever. I was a taker, now and forever.

I saw Taye join Joan at the edge of the crowd. They smiled at each other, then they smiled at me. The crowd surged forward to surround me and I lost sight of them.

Connor Mellegers' story "Freely Given" was originally published in Metaphorosis on Friday, 18 February 2022. See magazine.metaphorosis.com

About the author

Connor Mellegers is a freelance writer living in Toronto. When not writing speculative fiction, you can find them reading, cooking, and struggling to grow a garden.

@cmellegers

Useful and Beautiful Things

E. Saxey

This suburb has rows and rows of identical 19th century houses, but when any single home is opened, it can contain wonders.

It's late in the hot afternoon when I report to the address the Guvnor sent me. A mahogany behemoth is escaping through the ground floor sash window: a George III wardrobe with claw feet. A remarkable piece of furniture, requiring a gang of four sweaty men to wrestle it through the window.

"Frankie!" I recognise one of the men as the Guvnor, the gang's coordinator. He's hauling at a claw foot, struggling with the weight. "Give us a hand, girl?" I step in and take some of his burden, protecting the wardrobe from damage as we bring it down to the ground. The men are thankful, if confused. I'm stronger than I look. The Guvnor slaps me on the back. "Ta, Frankie. This is a hell of a house. There's so much bloody junk, we've only got half of it out."

I follow him up the garden path. The back of his T-shirt reads 'St Lucian 'till I die', providing his own provenance. Alongside the path, I see marvels: a Chinese *famille-verte* floor vase, which shouldn't be standing up on the uneven lawn like that. I lay it gently on the grass. Sheltering under the hedge is a herd of six dining chairs, Queen Anne style, two of them stacked awkwardly, like animals mating.

"Sorry about your Ma, Frankie," calls the Guvnor. "You doing alright?"

I catch his anxiety and reassure us both: "I can work solo."

The Guvnor beckons me indoors, and upstairs to a sunlit study. "This place is a total hodgepodge, Frankie." He flaps his hand at walls, which are lined with shelves. Most are packed with books, but one shelf holds statuettes of gods, a dozen of them, an international pantheon. "It's a bad scene."

I wonder why he sounds dejected. There's death, here, certainly, I know the signs. This house was a man's home, he was the gravity which kept these objects together. Without him, they spin off and spill into the garden, and get damp and chipped. But estate sales are bread and butter to the Guvnor; he's a genius at house clearance, he can strip a place in a day. He helps to mitigate the tragedy of death by finding every item a new home.

"What have you found?" I ask him.

"We put it over the back, there. For safety."

Pushed to one corner of the study is a small low table. My discernment stirs: the table is circular and wooden, satinwood, 19th century—yes, 1860s—with a *pietra dura* marble chess board in the centre. My skills still function, thank goodness. Despite the worries of the last few months, I can do my job.

A chess set made of stone is laid out, ready to play.

I stop dead in the middle of the room. I can't intuit anything about the chess set.

I recognise the shape of the pieces—the nobs and planes of the ultra-traditional Staunton design—but little else. I suppose the translucent pieces could be rock crystal from South Asia. Too vague, much too vague! I try to keep my heart from tick-tick-ticking in panic. The set is slightly uneven, the pieces not symmetrical. Handmade, perhaps by an amateur; such objects are always hard to identify. The dark pieces are carved from malachite, dark green with vivid spots like moss or mould.

"What's wrong with it?" I ask.

"Three of my boys couldn't put this bloody thing away," the Guvnor informs me. "I'll show you what it does." He plucks the dark green queen from the table, blinks, puts her back, nods. "Here, I'll show you." Picks up the queen again and replaces her. He remembers nothing, resetting before my eyes. "Wait a mo, I'll show—"

"You showed me."

"Damn! Did it mess me around, again? Well, you get the idea."

"What do the other pieces do?"

"Not a clue. But one lad who touched them was acting so funny, I had to send him home. It's all yours, if you want it. Usual terms? You take it away, fifty-fifty if you sell it on?"

That's fair, so we shake on it. The Guvnor leaves me to my work. I slough off my backpack, tie back my hair. I don't go back to the chess set, at first, but poke through the bookshelves in case there's a box for the set, or any provenance or context.

"Hey! You can't take any of those."

I jump back. I overlooked the person frowning at me from the far corner of the study, because she wasn't part of my jurisdiction. I take her in: rounded, wearing dusty dungarees, about three decades old, but people are hard to date. Her dark brown hair, in a shaggy bob, is a couple of inches longer than when we last met, and her expression is more combative.

"My employer has an agreement for the books," she says. "I work for Sotherans. I'm Tamsin Zhang."

"I know. I mean, we both worked on the Griffiths estate, in Portslade. I'm Frankie Cornish."

"That was woman with you, an older woman. She got the *Mabinogion*."

"My colleague." My mother. Yes, she took the *Mabinogion*, an 1880 edition, lavishly illustrated, cloth-covered in green. What a memory for an object Ms Zhang has. I recognise a kindred spirit. I need to reassure her. "I'm only taking the chess set."

She walks closer. Her spectacles are round, with faux tortoiseshell and strong lenses, and I think I come into focus for her because her frown relaxes.

"Oh, yes! I remember you. Why are you in my books, then?"

"Looking for anything related."

"The dead guy had a secretary, who took all his papers."

I sigh at the news. She could go back to her work, but she lingers, perhaps regretting her initial hostility. "What's so important about the chess set?" she asks, peering down at the pieces. She is 5'3", not as high as my chin. "They carried it in here like it might explode."

"I'm disposing of it."

"You're throwing it out? Can I have it?"

"No! Sorry. I mean, I'm taking it away with me. To evaluate."

"Are you taking any of this other stuff? This house is ridiculous. What was he doing with all these?" She points at the shelf of gods, where a fist-sized blue baboon (sixth century BC) hides in his newspaper wrapping from a bronze leopard (17th century, probably stolen in the sack of Benin City). Some of the gods are genuine and some are replicas, and nobody will want the whole mismatched collection, but the Guvnor will find each god a new owner.

In the second during which the gods distract me, Tamsin reaches for a chess piece.

"Don't!"

"I can be careful. I handle fragile books, that's my job." Tamsin is so sure of herself, so indignant, that I pause. She plucks up the green queen, places her down again, blinks and resets. "I'll be careful." She picks the queen up again, puts it down. The possibility of danger overrides my manners, and my hand shoots out to grab her wrist, to stop her third attempt. But Tamsin is already drawing back, and my hand closes on empty air. "Ooh, that's weird. That's *clever...*" She touches the head of the green queen, blinks a few times and laughs in astonishment. "Bloody hell."

"You have to stop. It might not be safe." I sound priggish. She doesn't seem to take offence, but does give me a hard stare, eyes huge through her distorting spectacles.

"Did you know it would do that?"

There's no chance of bluffing, she's felt the weird effect herself. "I knew it would do *something*. That's why the Guvnor called me in."

"Does this kind of thing happen often?"

"To me, yes." She looks at me with avid interest.

"So how does it work?"

"I don't know." I have a handful of hypotheses. "I have to take it away and test it."

Her frown returns, similar to when she mentioned the *Mabinogion*: unwilling to let go. "Wait! I have something that might be connected. We can investigate!"

I am so used to working with my mother that the offer of collaboration is a comfort.

●

The owner's name is Magnus Owens. Earlier that day, Tamsin found his diaries, which were shelved with his books and thus escaped the notice of his secretary.

"Check these out," Tamsin says. They're half-bound in Moroccan with blind tooling. "Bit creepy, other people's diaries. Not my area."

She passes me a volume. Diaries are the most personal, the least transferrable objects. I know these ones may not find a buyer, despite their fine bindings. "Are there family members who might be interested?"

Tamsin shrugs, indifferent. "Dunno. Owens doesn't mention having a wife or kids, in the parts I read. He was mining graphite in Sri Lanka, obsessed with his collections. He lists all the things he buys, there are cross-references to a stack of auction catalogues, I showed them to the Guvnor." I'm glad. That will help him re-home the objects. "But look at this." Tamsin stands close to me, turns the pages of the volume I hold, and points to the notes and number at the foot of each page: *Won in 22, Sicilian Defence, Smith-Morra Gambit. Lost in 10, Dutch Defence.* "This is the main thing, apart from collecting, that he bothers to write down. It's a record of chess games." She flips forwards, backwards. Numbers on every page.

"He played every night?"

"Yeah, almost. So, do you think he made this freaky chess set to confuse his friends? To win more games. Maybe to win money?" I admire the leaps of her logic. But there's no money mentioned here, only a tally. I flick the pages, find a month when things improve for Owen: *Won in 12. Won in 10.* Only a week before, I find a description of his chess set arriving from Rajasthan.

As soon as I read the place-name, I am flooded by images of Rajasthani stone-carving: Jali screens framing the sky in a lattice of stars. A provenance! I feel it like a delicious cool wave. My heart calms. And the diaries have proved useful, after all.

Tamsin quizzes me, as I take photos of the relevant diary pages

"So do you ever get called in to deal with books? Books which do weird things?"

"Sometimes."

"Magic books?"

"Not magic."

"Alright, *freaky* books. Do you have any? Could I see them?"

"Thank you, but I'm not planning to sell any. You're with Sotherans? I'll think of them, the next time I have one." She looks a little annoyed. I suppose it would have been a professional coup, for her to bring in an unusual tome. I pick up the green queen and stow her in my backpack.

"Hey. Frankie!" She touches my arm, suddenly agitated. "How can you touch the pieces, like that?"

I've made a foolish mistake. Normally I'd wear gloves, to keep up appearances. "I have a high tolerance."

"For freaky stuff." Tamsin's eyes shine. "It doesn't do anything to you?"

"I'm not very sensitive." The room is too hot. If I were staying, I'd throw up the sash windows, invite a breeze in to ruffle the packing paper. But I'm leaving.

Tamsin asks: "If you're not *sensitive*, how will you find out if the other pieces do the same thing?"

She notices too much, and she thinks too fast. I look at the ranks of chess nobility, slightly askew as if drunk, gazing over their pawn army. Each piece could be hazardous. Normally, my mother would test the pieces, at her workbench back home, with great interest and care.

"I'll help you," Tamsin offers.

"You can't."

"I can. They won't do me any real harm, will they?"

"One of the Guvnor's boys went home, sick."

"He might have skived off to enjoy the weather. I'll help you find out."

I have a book of contacts, from my mother, listing trustworthy people who buy strange things. I have storage facilities, and a network of folk (including the Guvnor) who put interesting artefacts my way. What I don't have is someone to do what my mother did: interact with objects, and let them work on her, demonstrating their properties. The nervous ticking fills my chest again.

"I won't *steal* them," she protests. "I'm a *book* person!" I think she's teasing me. I find her hard to read.

"Maybe, thank you. Yes." I make one stipulation for safety: "But not until the house is empty."

●

For the next few hours, Tamsin works at the far end of the study, chatting with me between periods of intense concentration. She asks me again about unusual books, and I describe a handful that I've seen, and their hazards. I tell her in the hopes she will respect my expertise, as I respect hers, but she seems unsatisfied.

At six in the evening, the shouts and crashes downstairs die away. The Guvnor hands me the keys, and the house is silent.

"So I pick the pieces up," asks Tamsin, "One at a time?"

I hold my notebook and pencil ready. "And tell me the effect."

"Just the greens, or do you think the whites do anything?"

I try to think like Magnus Owens. "He wouldn't want to disadvantage himself."

"Yeah, but could the white pieces do *positive* things?" She puts herself in the shoes of the dead man, so easily.

"Perhaps. Let's try them first." I sit on the floorboards, cross-legged by the chess table. In my experience, it's better not to have too far to fall. Tamsin sits down, not across the board where an opponent would be, but on the adjoining edge to me, our knees almost touching.

I can see how deftly Tamsin must handle delicate books. She walks her index fingers with care along the heads of the pawns. King's pawn: "Nothing." Knight's pawn: "Nothing." I write, for both: *No effect.*

Bishop's pawn: Tamsin sneezes violently. Her bobbed hair falls forwards. "It wasn't the pawn! It's dust." *No effect/allergenic?*

Rook's pawn: "I feel calm. Really chill." *Relaxing?* Then she looks about the room and sighs. From up on the shelf of gods, the small blue baboon watches us. "This damn house. Why don't I have a house like this, a collection like this? Oh, hang on." She throws the pawn from hand to hand. "It's this piece. It makes me feel like I deserve everything."

"Confidence?"

"Entitlement. Resentment."

Queen's pawn: "Oooh. This one feels *nice.*" Tamsin clutches it to her chest. "Satisfying. Like dumplings. Maybe I'm just hungry." She lifts her arms over her head, savouring the stretch, and regards me with a catlike smile. *Sense of wellbeing?* "What do you want?"

"Sorry?"

She's taken out her phone. "Wonton soup?"

"Dim sum," I say, for the sake of appearances.

"It'll be here in half an hour, you owe me a tenner." Her fingers take three last steps along the front rank of pieces: rook's pawn, bishop's pawn, knight's pawn. "And these are all duds. You could let me have one as a souvenir."

"I have to keep the set together." But perhaps I should pay her half of what I make from the set, because her evaluation will inform me about how to sell it. Not on the open market, of course, but using my mother's list of trustworthy collectors. I would have to stay in contact with Tamsin, to arrange payment. The prospect cheers me.

Tamsin plucks up the white bishop and squints at a bookcase, more than three metres away. "I can read all the titles." She takes off her glasses. "Hey, my eyesight's fine. Holy crap! Has this thing fixed my eyes?"

"It may have optimised how your brain works with your eyes." *Positive minor visual effects*, I write.

"Wow. Can I buy it, seriously?" Her glasses have left a pink dent on each side of her nose. "My eyes are so rubbish, this would be a life-changer."

"We don't know how it works. It could be doing terrible damage to your brain."

White bishop is grudgingly replaced, as are Tamsin's glasses, and she scoops up the white knight. "I feel confident." She chuckles. "No, I feel *lucky*."

"Shall we test it?" In my pocket, I find two dice and hand them over.

Her expression is sceptical, but she sends the dice rattling across the floorboards. Two sixes. I retrieve them, and Tamsin rolls them again. Double sixes. I write *positive effect, good fortune* while she glares at the white bishop, its eyeless face and aghast mouth.

"So this little blobby boy is actually affecting the world," says Tamsin. "But double sixes are a completely arbitrary symbol. How does it know that they're lucky? Wait, are those dice loaded?"

"I can give you a coin to toss, if you'd rather."

She stands and paces back over to the bookshelves. Impossible questions are grinding together in her mind. She's probably going to leave, now. I may not see her again, except at contentious estate sales, at intervals of years. That's alright. People are allowed to relocate themselves.

Tamsin uses both hands to unshelve a large dictionary, Bosworth and Toller's Old English, cloth-bound in burgundy, and carries it back to me. She opens the cover carefully. Inside, the pages have been hollowed out to hide a flat bottle of Talisker 25 year single malt whisky. "I found it this morning. Isn't it tacky?" She upends the bottle into her mouth and there's an audible glug. She hands it over to me.

"I don't know if we should combine alcohol with..."

"We totally should, because people are going to play with these pieces when they're drinking sherry, or what-have-you, and you need to know how bad that would be." She folds her legs up and re-joins me on the floor. She's misjudged our proximity, and now her knee presses mine. "I bet Owens got his friends drunk, the filthy cheat. Why do you have dice in your pocket? Does this kind of thing happen to you a lot, eh?"

"I have some cufflinks which work the other way. Gold with blue enamel." Translucent lapis blue over hatched engine-turning. They're in my mother's permanent collection, never to be sold. "Fabergé."

"Unlucky cufflinks?"

"Three owners found them… difficult." I realise I'm showing off. I shouldn't. It's dangerous to invite her to look closely at my life.

"Wow. *Terminally* difficult? And you kept them? William Morris wouldn't like that." She prods my shoulder and takes back the whisky bottle from my hands. I want to share her joke but I can only think of William Morris' floral patterns, looping across mid-C19th sofas.

"Why would he care about my cufflinks?"

"He said you shouldn't have anything in your house that you don't know to be useful, or believe to be beautiful. But your house is full of *awful* stuff, by the sound of it. Am I right?"

I think of my mother's workbench, and all the artefacts my mother restored and rehomed. Then the wall of strongboxes, one of which will hold the chess set. I picture the peace that will fill me when I close the lid. "It's a very useful place, overall."

"Oh, Frankie, you should have a beautiful house!" This time it sounds less like a scolding than a wish: Tamsin thinks I deserve a beautiful house. Before I can ask her, she adds: "What's your favourite thing that you own? Is it a book?"

I've never thought of that. I don't truly consider the objects in my collection to be mine. They're only resting with me because nobody else can own them, at present. "I don't have a favourite."

"Not even that *Mabinogion* you snatched?" Another nudge on my shoulder. "Was it freaky? What did it do?" It could be a joke, but perhaps her excellent memory for books is supported by a great capacity for grudges. I shake my head.

White rook: "Nothing. No, wait." She holds out her wrist. Should I admire her bracelet of 1970s cloisonné beads, patterned with bats? "My pulse. Feel it."

I touch her warm soft wrist, and the flicker I find there slows and slows. "You should put the rook down."

"But I feel really calm. Really on top of things..." I pluck the rook from her hand. *Induces catatonia?* "Spoilsport," she accuses, rubbing her wrist where I touched it. "The queen's got to be the most powerful one, right?" She lowers her fingertip onto the milky crown of the white queen. "Oh. I'm the most important person in the world. Anything I do for my own benefit is just fine. Cool." *Solipsism?*

White king: "Wow. The board just lit up." Tamsin sits bolt upright. "I can see all the moves. I haven't played chess since I was ten, but I can see every way it could possibly go..."

She turns her gaze on me, and lapses into silence.

I write down *strategic foresight.*

"How do you get into a job like yours?" she asks, still staring.

I write *overly curious,* because I know she's reading it.

"No, but seriously. It can't just be because you're *insensitive.*"

Persistent intrusive questioning. I shouldn't have shown off about my cufflinks. I need to turn her attention aside. "Is there more whisky?"

Tamsin reluctantly relinquishes the white king. "I can't keep it?"

"It might give you something like concussion."

"But you're still going to sell the set?"

The list of people I would trust with them has dwindled with each piece, each power. "I'll see."

"Or get rid of them. Throw them away."

"No! Don't say that!"

"Why not? God, you sound like those people who get sentimental over books being chucked out. Do you know how many terrible, waste-of-space books there are? You can't hang on to *everything,* you can just bung stuff in the bin..."

I shake my head, over and over. I worry I might scream.

A chime rings round the room. Tamsin springs to her feet. "Food's here!"

Tamsin thunders down the stairs, and the vibrations set one of the shelf-gods wobbling. I nudge it further back, to safety. I would love to have a day to hold each of the small statues in my hands and know who they are, where they come from. But they're not dangerous, so they're not my business.

I should be wary of Tamsin. She lulled me into thinking of her as my work partner, but I didn't choose her. She keeps teasing me and touching me, but I should keep a level head. I hear her chatting with the delivery man, which gives me time to pluck up all the pieces we've tested and stash them in my bag, away from temptation.

When Tamsin returns, her face is somewhat pallid. "The delivery guy told me that Owens *died* here. In the house."

I remember the Guvnor saying this was a *bad scene*, and wonder if he meant the manner of Owen's death. "It's understandable." People die. Things endure.

"It's grim." Tamsin lays the pots of food out on the floor. "Hey, where did the white pieces go?"

"They're safe. What do you think Owens was like?" I ask, to distract her from my tidying, and from the fact that I won't eat the dim sum. And because I want to know her opinion.

"An English man collecting colonial curiosities to make his Englishness more interesting." She puts herself in Owen's place, then puts him in his place, too.

"Did you get that from his diaries?"

"I got that from his book collection—lots of international publications, lots of uncracked spines. Don't be sad! All the better for my bosses, to have pristine Bengali poetry. *Gitanjali* will end up with someone who appreciates it."

I wait until Tamsin wrangles a steamed dumpling into her mouth. "The green pieces," I say. "I shouldn't let you test them."

"*Let* me, hah." She can still argue with her mouth full.

"The green ones may be terrible."

"No, because look..." She swigs her coke. I've hidden the whisky under my backpack. "They can't be that godawful, or nobody would ever play chess with him twice.

They're not going to make you cough up your lungs, are they?" She's three moves ahead of me. "And *you* need to know how they work. Don't you? To be a good caretaker."

I need to know the full extent, to judge what to do with the set: who might safely buy it, or more likely, how I can store it. Whether to seal it in clay or submerge it in running water. But must I rely on Tamsin?

"Let's just do the pawns," she offers, as a compromise. "They're only small."

The pawns will perplex us both.

●

King's pawn: "Nothing." No effect. "It's not doing anything at all." She chuckles slyly.

"Tamsin, are you lying?"

"Nooo, heh-heh." I write *Induces duplicity/hysteria?* Tamsin shivers. "Holy hell, that was stranger than the eyesight thing."

"And it made you lie?"

"It didn't do anything! I was fine. Heh-heh."

I reach to take back the pawn, and she makes a fist, twists and turns, play-wrestles my fingers with her own. I don't like to look strong, and she's wily and enjoying herself, so the fight goes on for longer than it needs to. When the pawn is out of her hand, she asks: "Why would that help Owens win? I suppose it would encourage his opponent to cheat."

Bishop's pawn: Tamsin sighs. "I'm rubbish at this, anyway."

"At chess?"

"At everything." *Hopelessness.*

Knight's pawn: "I want to bet you a lot of money that I'm going to win." *Risk seeking? Over-confidence?* "What happens if—" Before I can stop her, she's palmed two pawns simultaneously. "Ha! I think I'm going to lose and I don't care, I still want to bet on it! I wish you could feel this!" Her grin is contagious, her eyes are alight. This is all irresponsible, reprehensible. I should be working alone.

"Stop. Please." Thankfully, she does.

Queen's pawn: "It's telling me just do anything, move wherever, don't overthink it."

Hazardous rashness. "Does it have a voice?"

"No, it's just a feeling. Do some things have voices?"

I think of the rooms in my mother's house—my house —filled with items that charmed and berated her, to which I am blessedly oblivious. We were perfect colleagues. "Sometimes."

She leans in closer to me. Does she want to be hugged? I could do that. She swipes the whisky from under my bag. "Queen's pawn makes you thirsty."

Rook's pawn makes Tamsin jump to her feet, knocking over the remnants of her takeaway. "Sorry! I can't sit still." *Restless.* "Why does he get all this stuff? How can anyone deserve..." *Psychologically restless?* "I feel small. Do I seem small?"

"Not more than you—no."

"You're not taking me seriously!"

I should have said something kinder, more respectful. "I'm sorry. Put the pawn down?"

Instead, she sweeps up more pieces, handfuls of them, stuffing them into the pockets of her dungarees, and runs.

I lunge at her but she's quicker. She's off down the stairs, almost flying, bursting out of the back door and vanishing into the overgrown garden.

I have to follow. It's dusk, and the trees cast deep shadows. There's a pale path, but as I run down it, chasing her, I feel thorns catch at my clothes. I hear Tamsin, rather than see her, ahead of me. Please let her not be hurt. Let her not drop anything, either. Let me not have to hunt for the dark green chess pieces amid brambles in the dark.

My eyes adjust and a movement draws my gaze to Tamsin standing in an old wooden gazebo. I should jump at her, pin her arms, make her release the rook's pawn. But I can't imagine hurting her.

"Come on! Take them off me." She raises her fist and waves it from side to side. "This is most the important thing, right?"

It is an accusation, but it is true. People pass, things endure; my responsibility is to things. While I hesitate, I see a quick arc in the dark, her arm as she flings the pawn of low self-esteem far into the garden.

Her penitence is instant. "Oh, God, sorry! Shit! I'll find it!" Her face glows in the light of her phone. "It went in that direction..."

I have a keyring torch, and I spot the pawn before she does, resting in a patch of dandelions. I turn my back to Tamsin before I stoop to pick it up. I need to keep it secure. I dust off the dirt and place it on my tongue, force myself to swallow, feel the nobbles as it slides down my throat.

"Found it," I call.

"I've found something else." Tamsin has her phone light trained on a flickering tail of plastic tape in the bushes, with lettering: POLICE LINE DO NOT CROSS. "I think he died in the garden. Owens." Tamsin stares up at the house, the sash window glowing with light. "Maybe he jumped out of the window of his study. Do you think the chess set killed him?"

I thought not: he should have known its properties. But what pieces might he have touched by accident, in what combination? Did he grab recklessness, self-doubt, and foresight all in one hand, and throw himself away? And now all his possessions have followed him, flung outwards, dispersing.

Tamsin, standing beside me, says: "You'll get rid of it, won't you?"

"Don't worry. I won't pass it on to another owner."

"No, I mean you should trash it. Smash it up and bury it."

I dislike this line of thought. I dislike it very much. Inside me, things tick painfully fast.

The horrible plastic police tape dances about in the wind. I am seized by a pang of fear. I'm not mourning Owen, or thinking of the ways he might have died; I'm empathising with the objects he's left behind. I never want to be wrapped in a rug, left on a lawn. I don't want to be forced to seek someone new, someone who appreciates me enough to keep me.

My internal mechanisms are spinning wildly. I need to be calm. I remind myself: I may not have an owner, but I have a place in the world. I have earned it.

I duck into the gazebo and sit on the bench I find inside. "You can't throw an artefact away," I say. "Just because you don't have a use for it at the moment." I'm speaking to myself more than to Tamsin.

She hears me, though, and shouts back: "But you can't hang onto it indefinitely, either. Not if it's toxic!"

"I'll keep it safe."

"But you won't live forever, will you?"

I don't know the answer to that.

Tamsin stumbles into the gazebo and joins me on my bench, pulling out her bottle of coke (into which, it occurs to me, she has poured a lot of the whisky) and drinking deeply.

"Let's do the rest of them quickly," she offers.

I shake my head.

"But we're almost done." She points to her dungaree pocket. I see the bumps of the stolen pieces through the denim. "You get them out."

I work my hand into her pocket, ignoring the warmth of her body, and retrieve them. I line them up on the bench, within arm's reach, and lay my torch alongside, to light them. I take out my small notebook and pen. I can complete this quickly and depart.

Green rook: "I shouldn't be here," says Tamsin.

"The same as the rook's pawn?"

"No, that was just twitchy legs. This is: I need to get away, right now! Shit, do you think this is the one that killed Owens? Sit on my feet. Come on, it'll slow me down if I try to run off." She's tucking a foot under the bend of my knee, wriggling it until it's wedged. "There, like that."

Need to be elsewhere? Self-destruction? My handwriting is not neat.

Green bishop: "Do you ever wonder what you're for?"

I did. I do. Has the bishop given her telepathy? If so, does she know how conscious I am of her wriggling foot?

"Go on, write down *existential doubt*. Or *moody cow*."

Green knight: "I want to fight you. I hate you!" She wrenches her foot free from under my leg, but falls backwards to the floor. I spring up, hit a gazebo pillar and shake down cobwebs and dust onto both of us. I want to help Tamsin stand, but her arms are flailing, she is still furious at me. She takes a wild swing. The chess piece flies from her hand. "Gah! Vicious little horse bastard!" she cries.

I crouch down to pick up the knight, and quickly swallow it, to join the pawn. I am the safest temporary store for small, wicked objects.

Before I can stand, a hot hand lands on my back. I hear Tamsin's breath. Her hand slides up, she slips her fingers into my hair, to stir deliciously against my scalp.

"You're a very attractive—whatever you are. A very cute curator."

Her voice is low and tender, all her rage boiled away, and her heat warms me. But only one of her hands is in my hair.

She's holding the green king in the other.

It's not fair to let this go on. I twist around and prise her fingers open as gently as I can.

I know it's worked when I hear her swear, and she pulls away from me and stomps to the other side of the hut.

I eat the green king. I focus on finding my notebook. I write: *Emotional connection?* A euphemism. The lust-inducing king is even less explicable than the rage-knight. Would desire distract your opponent? It's distracted Tamsin, who is holding her head in her hands.

"Is that the last one?" she asks, flatly.

"There's only one piece left, and we know what she does. The green queen. Amnesia, or confusion."

We are confused enough. "Yes."

Tamsin raises her head, sucks in the night air. The aphrodisiac effects of the green king have disgusted her. And I'm to blame, I wanted to impress her by my association with wonderful things. My back feels chilly, now, where her hand had rested.

Tamsin raises her head, sucks in the night air. "Is that the last one?" she asks, faintly.

"There's only one piece left, and we know what she does. The green queen."

"Oh! Her." The monarch of forgetting and re-setting. Maybe Tamsin would appreciate some amnesia.

I look back to the house, and through the back door glimpse floorboards of rich golden oak. Carpets fade and moths consume them, but wood goes on for centuries. Until you burn it. Even then, it's useful.

"You have to get rid of them all," Tamsin instructs me. "Apart from the one which fixed my eyesight..."

"White bishop."

"You could give that one to a doctor. All the others, though, they need to go! You can't let people use them to start fights, or win elections. Or as a bloody truth drug."

I can't read my notebook, so I double-check my mental list of the pieces; none of them worked as a truth drug. Her anger's making her exaggerate. "I'll keep them away from anyone," I promise her, as I pick up my backpack. "I'll use my best strong-room."

"But you could fall under a bus tomorrow. They'll get out into the world again. Why not destroy them?"

Tick-tick-tick, my heart stutters, faster than I've ever felt it. I can't speak my objection.

"They're lethal!" she insists. "They might have killed their last owner!" I know the fuel for her hate isn't the self-destructive bishop, or the aggressive knight. It's the green king, the piece that made her want me. "*And* they're ugly! They're failing the William Morris test on both fronts."

"I do believe that almost everything can find a new owner."

"Really? How long have you been hoarding those murderous cufflinks? Objects have to earn the space they take up in the world! Things have to be useful..."

And to my surprise, tears well up in my eyes and drip onto the golden oak floorboards.

"Not you! I didn't mean you! Oh, damn..." She scrambles across the bench to wrap her arms around me. "You're remarkable."

"Am I?" My mother did a lot of work to make me appear ordinary. "Is it obvious?"

Tamsin continues her clumsy hug and clumsy reassurance. "No, no, not unless you look really closely." People don't usually look at me closely. "I'd never have noticed, except the white king made me understand how things worked. Oh, and then you ate those chess pieces."

I clear my throat. "I've lost my mother." My co-worker, the one who restored me. Almost all my memories are from after she mended me. "She died, two months ago, she died."

"I'm sorry."

"This is the first job I've been on, without her. I need to know I can still do the work, that I'm useful."

Tamsin loosens her grip and I think she'll let me go but she settles into a more sustainable embrace. "I understand. Everyone wants to be useful."

"But every thing *needs* to be useful."

Tamsin shakes her head very hard, brushing her face against mine. "No, no, no. You don't need to be useful."

"I do."

She is trying to think of arguments against all her earlier pronouncements. "Beautiful! You could be beautiful, instead."

I want to correct her: no, someone else must *believe* I'm beautiful.

I want to ask: does she believe I'm beautiful?

Instead, I ask: "Which chess piece makes you tell the truth?"

Tamsin buries her face in my shoulder without answering. It is the green king, then. I study her cloisonné bracelet in the dimness and listen to the tick-tick-ticking of my heart.

E. Saxey's story "Useful and Beautiful Things" was originally published in Metaphorosis on Friday, 22 December 2023. See magazine.metaphorosis.com

About the author

E. Saxey is a queer Londoner who works in Universities and volunteers in libraries. Their current writing desk used to belong to the Ancient Order of Druids. thelightningbook.co.uk, @esaxey

A Wizard Comes to Shorehaven

L.J. Wetherby

Many years had gone by since a wizard last dwelled in the small seaside town of Shorehaven. It had been so long, in fact, since the town had enjoyed the presence of a wizard, that the people of Shorehaven had begun to forget why a wizard was such a desirable thing for a town to possess.

Children would finish their bedtime prayers with the words, "and please send Shorehaven a wizard before too much longer", but the words meant almost nothing to them, and little more to many of their parents. Wizards, as far as the younger generation of Shorehaveners was concerned, were a fantasy; something nice to dream of, but never seriously expected to come to pass.

The townspeople were surprised, then, when a wizard arrived one day. She was of middling height, with long twisting hair that was brown, grey, and white in different places, and wearing long robes the same colours as her hair. She looked very, very tired.

The only question on the town's lips was whether the wizard had come to stay or she was merely passing through. She spent her first night in a boarding-house, where (to the tremendous disappointment of the proprietor and the other patrons alike) she requested a private room and took all of her meals within it, never venturing out into the common areas. There were many in the boarding house that night who hoped for a chance to converse with the wizard, or at the very least to catch a glimpse of her, and there were many in the boarding house that night who went to bed disappointed.

The following morning, the wizard walked past Marsh's Stores in town, examining the glass-fronted noticeboard outside the shop and taking down notes in a small leather-bound book that she kept in the pocket of her robe. Then she walked out of town along the north road, towards the coast.

A few Shorehaveners were sufficiently intrigued by the wizard's arrival that they attempted to follow her out of town, but ill luck befell all who tried. Gordon Harris the baker's son stepped into a bog and ruined his socks and shoes. Amelia Connor the seamstress got her skirts so badly caught up in a patch of brambles that it took her almost an hour to free herself, and she came home scratched and bleeding. And Ghislaine Willis, who fancied herself something of a hedge-witch, became so lost while trying to follow the wizard that she found herself walking back into town along the south road, miles away from the north road that she'd taken out towards the coast in the first place.

A single cottage sat at the very edge of the cliffs, past the point where the north road ceased to be a road and turned into a path. It had lain empty for many years, almost as many as the town had been without a wizard. The notice announcing that this cottage was for rent was one of the oldest advertisements on the board outside Marsh's Stores, with its print almost completely faded and its edges yellowed and curled.

The wizard decided almost immediately after viewing it that she would take the cottage. She made one last trip into town, to put down a year's rent and to purchase some provisions from the store.

By this time, many of the townspeople were curious about the wizard, but everyone who attempted to walk out as far as her cliffside cottage to get a better look at her ran into the same kind of trouble as those who'd followed her out of town the day after her arrival — minor injuries and misfortunes, the sudden loss of their ability to navigate familiar roads, and in some cases a profound urge to turn around and check that they hadn't left the front door unlocked or a pan boiling dry on the stove. Eventually people started to complain about the situation, lamenting that after so many years of waiting, they should suffer the misfortune of only a very unsociable wizard arriving in Shorehaven.

The Mayor was a popular person to complain to, because he was ostensibly the most powerful man in town. In his private moments the Mayor would laugh to himself about this assumption, knowing as he did that being the Mayor gave him no power whatsoever — it merely made him responsible for dealing with all the problems that other people couldn't or wouldn't deal with themselves.

For the first week, the Mayor listened to the town's concerns about the new wizard with a solemn expression. He told each of them that he understood why they were worried — that he, too, was interested to learn more about the wizard — but that since it had been such a long time since the town had had any sort of wizard at all, everyone must be very patient. The wizard would reveal herself in her own good time; he was certain of it.

After three weeks had passed and there had been neither sign nor word of the wizard, however, and no further orders placed at Marsh's Stores, even the Mayor began to lose his patience. He decided that the townsfolk had been respectful enough of the wizard's privacy: he would force the issue. A wizard could hardly refuse an official visit from the Mayor, after all. And it would have been deeply undignified for the Mayor to have returned from attempting to visit the wizard with his legs scratched to pieces by thorns, his memory strangely absent, his socks and shoes ruined, or his sense of direction temporarily suspended, so he took Leonie with him as insurance.

Leonie was his only child, a quiet and unassuming person of around twenty-four years of age, who possessed a certain subtlety when it came to magic — it was said that Leonie's mother, who by this time had been dead for almost as long as she'd been alive in the first place, had been a distant relative of the town's previous wizard. The prestige of this connection had been one of the many reasons the Mayor had married her, and the fact that their only child showed the faintest hint of this familial skill had always been a source of particular pride for him.

Over the years, his child's ability had manifested on only a few occasions. Once, when the town had been suffering a drought, Leonie had managed to sense a raincloud nearby, tugging it by some unseen means towards the wheat fields that lay beyond the town. And there had been the time when a very young Leonie had managed to calm a rabid dog that was blocking the road to the schoolhouse simply by speaking soothingly to it, in a voice that sounded strangely ethereal, and nothing at all like Leonie's ordinary speaking voice.

Leonie did not enjoy being the Mayor's daughter, in spite of the Mayor's pride. For as long as Leonie could remember, people had watched constantly to see what the Mayor's daughter might do, and to ensure she comported herself with the same dignity and respect that the Mayor himself assumed. Something deep within Leonie writhed and squirmed away from this attention, seeking out a more dark and private place where it could merely exist, unobserved. The demands of the position sat very uneasily with the Mayor's daughter, who felt as an adult only very slightly mayoral, and not at all daughterly.

Leonie and the Mayor took their time walking along the north road, for Leonie had been born with one ordinary leg and another that tapered into nothingness halfway down the thigh. Leonie had hardly noticed this difference until the Mayor had made it clear that it was something to be managed carefully; as an adult, Leonie wore a prosthesis so artfully constructed that it was indistinguishable from a full-grown leg in every way, except for the fact that it caused Leonie to walk a little more slowly and carefully than other people. The small amount of magic that Leonie possessed had been very fortunate on the day when the rabid dog had wandered into town, given that running away at any speed had been out of the question.

Leonie could feel the wizard's presence all along the north road, even before they made it past the edge of the town. The charms and glamours that had prevented curious individuals from trespassing upon the wizard's hospitality until now were obvious to Leonie, glimmers faintly perceptible to the corner of the eye and easy enough to work around. They arrived at the wizard's cottage just after midday, picking their way through the nettles and weeds that had grown over the path to the cottage door, which was closed.

The Mayor knocked, with an amount of force and ceremony befitting his status in the town. There was no answer. He knocked again, but still no answer. After his third knock was similarly ignored, he motioned to Leonie. Leonie's knock was soft, gentle, and hesitating. After it had sounded, the wizard called out.

"It's open. You might as well come in."

The Mayor was old enough to remember a time when this cottage had not stood empty. It had been a pretty place then, full of light, with a lush garden surrounding the house on all sides. Now, even though the new wizard had been in residence for almost a month, it seemed a drear and dingy little hole. The floor had not been swept, half the shelves were bare and lined with a thick layer of dust, and the curtains, old and frayed and stained as they were, did a very thorough job of preventing any light from entering the house.

There were three rooms downstairs, the right-hand side of the cottage divided into a kitchen at the front and a sitting room at the rear, looking out over the sea. On the left side was one long room that the original owners had used for dining and entertaining. There were two bedrooms upstairs, but the Mayor assumed them to be out of use, given that the stairs had rotted and fallen in and no one had repaired them.

The wizard's voice had come from the room on the left, but when Leonie and the Mayor went in, there was no sign of anyone there. Just as they were about to check the kitchen and the sitting room, they heard a groaning sound from the corner of the room.

There they found the wizard half buried in a makeshift bed, beneath a bundle of blankets on top of a broken old sofa.

"I ought to get up and greet you properly, I suppose, except I don't want to," said the wizard, an unseen hand pulling at the pile of blankets to reveal her mouth.

There were a few chairs scattered here and there around the room, and Leonie and the Mayor selected two of the least dirty and broken ones and pulled them over toward the sofa where the wizard lay.

"I am the Mayor of Shorehaven," the Mayor began, in his most mayoral tone. "I would like to formally extend our warmest welcome to you on behalf of the town. It's been a very long time since we've had a wizard dwelling near Shorehaven."

"Oh dear," said the wizard. "I was afraid this might happen."

"Afraid what might happen?" asked the Mayor.

"That you'd all assume I've come here to be your new wizard," said the wizard.

"Well, what have you come here for, if not that?" asked the Mayor, trying to hide his disappointment.

The wizard took a deep breath beneath her pile of blankets.

"I have come here to die," she said mournfully.

The Mayor stared at Leonie, hoping the wizard could not see his expression.

"Oh," he said, after too long a moment had passed. "Well, I'm very sorry to hear that."

"Not as sorry as I am," said the wizard. "My only wish is to die here in peace, but the people of Shorehaven keep bothering me."

"We meant no disrespect," said the Mayor.

"Ah, but respect is poor currency for a dying wizard to hoard," said the wizard. "I neither relish nor require your respect; I merely ask to be left alone."

The Mayor did not know what else to say. He had rehearsed a number of talking points that he imagined might make suitable conversation in the company of a wizard, though he'd been but a small boy himself when the old wizard had died. Now, with the new wizard apparently nearly as dead as the old one, the thought of attempting to make polite conversation suddenly seemed ghastly.

"Anything you need, anything that the town can provide for you," he said instead. "You need only ask."

In truth, the Mayor was not feeling particularly generous — he'd expected a healthy wizard with many long years of wizarding ahead of them, and he'd already overexcited himself at the thought of the benefits that such a wizard might bring to the town. Now, with those hopes dashed, there was a part of him that wanted nothing more than to leave the cottage and pretend that the dying wizard had never come to Shorehaven. But he feared for the town's reputation; if word got out that a dying wizard had been treated with such disrespect, Shorehaven might never again attract a healthy one.

"Thank you," the wizard groaned, "but I require nothing except privacy."

The idea of staying when they were so clearly unwelcome made the Mayor feel awkward and uncomfortable, sensations that his position in the town normally insulated him from rather effectively. He cleared his throat, stood up, and motioned to Leonie to do the same. They left the wizard in a pile on the broken old sofa and went home.

Dinner that night at the Mayor's residence was a dour affair, and not even Leonie could brighten the Mayor's spirits. They both went to bed gloomy, and the next morning at breakfast it was clear that a good night's sleep had only compounded the Mayor's concerns about the wizard.

"It doesn't seem right," he said, applying a thin layer of marmalade to his crustless toast. "That she should come all the way here just to die alone in that cottage up on the cliffs."

Leonie nodded and murmured and made all of the noises the Mayor expected from his only child.

"If only there were something we could do," the Mayor continued. "Some way we could help."

The Mayor looked up from his toast just as a ray of morning light struck the window of his breakfast room. Framed by this sunbeam, Leonie seemed gently radiant, and an idea formed.

"What if you were to go and assist her?" the Mayor asked.

"Me?" asked Leonie.

"Precisely," said the Mayor. "You're a great help to me here, of course, but I'm still comfortably within my prime. I could do without you for a few months; certainly long enough that the wizard might pass peacefully."

"I thought she made it very clear that she didn't want to be troubled by anyone from town," said Leonie.

"Even so," said the Mayor. "Think how it might look if people found out that we had a dying wizard staying just outside Shorehaven and we did nothing to help her."

Leonie knew the Mayor well; well enough to know that when he said things like 'think about how it might look', he was thinking not only of the reputation of the town, but also the reputation of its Mayor. Although Leonie's father had been Mayor long enough that many of the townsfolk had never known any other Mayor, he was constantly anxious about his position. He did not want to end up out of a job and forced to cut the crusts off his own toast, rather than having them cut off by someone else and served to him on a silver toast-rack.

Leonie did not want to go and help the wizard. Not because wizards were uninteresting, but because this particular wizard had made it abundantly clear that she wished to be left alone. The last time the Mayor had asked Leonie to do something unpalatable and potentially embarrassing, his only child had made the private decision that it would be the last time, and that next time, "no, that won't be possible" would be the only answer given. But the Mayor was very persuasive, and his only child had little experience of disappointing him; the middle of the morning found Leonie walking up the north road again, this time with a letter in hand.

It was easy enough for Leonie to avoid the additional charms and hexes that the wizard had put up since the Mayor's visit the day before, though the work was impressive for a wizard running up against the end of her stamina — once again they glinted, slightly listlessly, in a way that only the corner of Leonie's eye could perceive. It was a sense that Leonie was well aware that most people in Shorehaven did not possess or even understand; one of the many strange feelings and sensations that Leonie had grown used to never talking about with other people, lest they distract from the importance of adequately performing the role of Mayor's daughter in public.

When Leonie arrived, the door to the cottage was still unlocked, and the wizard lay in the exact spot where they'd left her the day before.

"I thought I told you to leave me alone," said the wizard from beneath the pile of blankets.

"That would have been my preference too," said Leonie, placing the Mayor's letter on the end of the sofa nearest to the wizard's head.

A skinny hand crept out from beneath the nest of blankets and snatched at the envelope.

" 'Please allow me to lend you my girl to ensure your comfort at this sad time, yours sincerely, the Mayor of Shorehaven'," she read aloud.

Then the skinny hand crumpled up the piece of paper, which had been embossed with the Mayor's name, title, address, and official seal, and tossed it into the fireplace.

"Fool," she said, as Leonie continued to stand around, unsure whether to say or do anything. "To call you his girl. As though you were a girl. As though he owned you."

Leonie felt very odd at that moment, as though the wizard had stumbled upon an unexpectedly pertinent truth.

"What do you mean?"

"You're old enough to be a woman, for starters," said the wizard. "Except you're not a woman, are you? Or a man, either?"

"I'm not," said Leonie, a strange feeling bubbling within that might have been anxiety or relief. "Is that what's always felt wrong about being the Mayor's daughter? Everyone has always assumed..."

"To hell with their assumptions!" cried the wizard, with more vigour than Leonie had realised her capable of. "You are what you are. Doesn't matter what people think you are, or what they expect you to be. Now, tell me how you managed to get up here today. You weren't deterred by my trickery yesterday morning, but the hexes I put down in the afternoon to stop anyone else approaching were sound."

"I don't know," said Leonie, still reeling from the wizard's previous observation. "I suppose I've always been able to perceive magic better than most people in Shorehaven."

"Well, if someone has to come up here, I suppose I don't mind as much if it's you. It was everyone else that I was trying to keep away."

"It seems a lonely thing, to die up here on your own," said Leonie wistfully. "I'd be happy to keep you company."

"Company is the last thing I need," said the wizard. "If I needed company, I'd seek it out. But since you're already here..."

Leonie took the hint. The cottage was in such a state of disarray that it was easy to find a place to start, because everything needed doing. First, Leonie swept the dust from the empty shelves and the corners of the room. Then they checked the wizard's pantry, making a note of anything that might be needed from Marsh's Stores in town. They boiled up a great quantity of hot water, reserving some of it for mopping, some for wiping down the windows, some for laundry, and the last of it for making tea, which the wizard accepted gratefully.

While the wizard drank the tea, Leonie carried on dusting, wiping, sweeping, and washing. By the late afternoon, the cottage was already looking significantly more presentable, even though there was still plenty more work to be done. The wizard didn't have much food in the house, but Leonie did what they could, making a big pan of porridge and leaving a bowl of it near the wizard's nest, covered with honey and nuts.

"I'm going to go back to town now," they said in the late afternoon. "I'll order some more things from Marsh's Stores and bring them up, and I'll speak to the carpenter about repairing the stairs. I'll be back tomorrow morning."

"Suit yourself," said the wizard from beneath the pile of blankets where she still lay, unmoving.

Back at the Mayor's residence, the Mayor was delighted to hear of Leonie's progress and he encouraged his only child to go back to the wizard's cottage first thing in the morning. And so Leonie did, carrying the supplies from Marsh's Stores slowly up the north road. They found the wizard exactly where they'd left her the night before, but the bowl of porridge had been consumed entirely and licked clean.

Leonie spent the morning clearing out the kitchen and arranging the groceries in the pantry. With fresh provisions laid in, they were able to make a much more interesting lunch for the wizard than mere porridge: fresh mushroom stew with wild rice and a green salad. Again, they left a bowl and a plate near the wizard and went off to do other things, and again, when they returned, the bowl and plate were clean. Whatever fatal concern was troubling the wizard, Leonie mused, her appetite was certainly remarkable.

On the third day, Leonie walked up from town with the carpenter's apprentice to make sure he found his way past the wizard's enchantments. They spent much of the day weeding, raking, and digging in the garden that surrounded the wizard's house on all sides while the carpenter's apprentice sawed, hammered, and sanded.

The wizard did not make herself visible when Leonie brought in her lunch — soup made from the remains of the mushroom stew with fresh-baked bread — but when they brought her a cup of tea at the end of the day, after the carpenter's apprentice had finished the job and gone home, the wizard's head emerged from the nest of blankets, and she motioned to Leonie to sit down in the chair nearest the sofa.

"I'm glad all of that hammering and banging is finished," said the wizard.

These were the first words she'd offered that weren't in response to a direct question. Leonie nodded.

"Why don't you sleep here at night, to save you dragging that leg up and down the road to town twice a day?" the wizard continued.

Leonie was startled. They'd mentioned nothing of their leg to the wizard, and indeed they'd been using the prosthesis for so many years that it now formed a well-integrated part of their gait; they were surprised that the wizard had been able to tell.

"It doesn't trouble me," they said.

"Of course it does," said the wizard. "The ache in your hip. The tender part that sits in the socket all day, that you cover in socks and bandages so that it doesn't ever get rubbed completely raw."

Leonie looked at the wizard again, no less startled.

"How could you possibly know that?" they asked.

One of the wizard's particular skills, and a focus for her magic, was seeing people exactly as they really were — something she'd hinted at the first day Leonie came up to the cottage on their own, when she'd debunked the myth of the Mayor's daughter. She was adept at looking past the layers that everyone dressed themselves in, the faces and façades they wore for the rest of the world, in order perceive their deepest essences. That was how she'd known that Leonie wasn't really a girl, even if they kept pretending they were for the benefit of the Mayor and the town. And the outline she'd perceived of Leonie with her magic, rather than with her eyes, included a leg that ended where nature had ended it, far short of the ground.

The wizard was loathe to explain how her magic worked, however, so she merely shrugged.

"The offer's there if you'd rather not keep making the journey," she said instead. "And if you want to take that leg off for an hour or two to give yourself a break, go ahead. It doesn't trouble me."

The idea of removing their leg in front of the wizard was on a par with the idea of removing all of their clothes and underwear, as far as Leonie was concerned; something they had never considered doing in front of any living person before. Their father loved to see Leonie walking proud and upright without any hint of pain or fatigue, and they had mastered the art of this performance so thoroughly that the idea that they might choose to stop performing it seemed entirely out of the question.

Their father hated to be reminded of his only child's disability, and in the years since the first in a series of legs had initially been crafted for Leonie, they had never once taken any of them off in his presence. They knew, somehow, that to do so would be to violate a holy and entirely unspoken expectation that stood between them.

It was also one of the many reasons they had never seriously considered forming a romantic attachment with another person. No one, as far as Leonie was concerned, wanted to see their body as it truly was, and they had taken on the idea that it was their own profound responsibility to manage their body in such a way that it might not possibly offend anyone. This had grown to the status of another holy and unspoken duty, one to be performed privately and in silence, the pain and effort of it never to be hinted at in front of anyone else.

"It doesn't trouble me," they said again, more quietly this time.

The wizard did not believe them, but neither did she press the issue.

Leonie kept returning to the wizard's cottage every morning, where they continued to put the place in order, and dreamt up meals to tempt even a dying wizard's appetite. And every evening, when they returned to the Mayor's residence, the Mayor asked them how the wizard was getting along, and whether they thought there was any chance of the wizard doing a spot of wizarding on behalf of the town at some point in the near future.

"She's dying, Father," Leonie would say every time the Mayor asked, which stunned him enough to prevent him from asking again the same evening, but not so much that he would not ask again the following evening.

And every afternoon, when the bulk of the day's work was done, Leonie would sit with the wizard and drink tea. The wizard gradually became more communicative as the weeks went on, and she began to sit up properly in order to drink her tea, rather than sipping at it from the side of her mouth as she lay on the sofa. Indeed, as the wizard's surroundings began to brighten up, so did the wizard.

And just as the wizard responded to the improvements that Leonie had made to the cottage, Leonie began to respond to small signs of improvement from the wizard. She mentioned one day, in passing, how much she might enjoy a scone with her afternoon tea. From that day on, during the quiet hour after lunch when the wizard took her nap, Leonie would stand in the kitchen conjuring up sweet things. It turned out that the wizard enjoyed cakes, biscuits, and brownies as much as she enjoyed scones, and Leonie enjoyed making them for her, and sitting with her in the late afternoon looking out over the ocean as they ate something fresh and small and sweet and drank their tea.

"Do you mind me asking what's wrong with you?" they inquired one afternoon, no longer able to suppress their curiosity about what possible condition could be killing the perfectly healthy-looking wizard in front of them.

"It is a long, sad story," said the wizard.

"I'd like to hear it, if you're willing to tell it," said Leonie.

The wizard sighed, and took a deep breath.

"Many years ago now, when I was a much younger wizard," she began, "I wandered all around this world until I came to a forest. For as long as I could remember, my head had been full of spells and noises, wonders, and curiosities. But when I sat for a while beneath a great ancient tree in that forest, for the first time in my life I felt at peace."

The wizard sighed again, more tenderly this time, before she continued.

"Given how thoroughly that sense of peace had eluded me until then, I began to imagine crafting a life for myself in those woods. I slept out beneath the forest canopy that summer, building myself a small hut day by day. There was a brook nearby, and in the evenings I would sit with my feet in the water, resting my body and allowing my mind to wander.

"One evening, I felt the presence of another with me on the bank of the stream. Every time I thought I was about to catch a glimpse of her, she slipped away from me. But I kept returning to the brook every evening, and eventually she took form one night, and sat beside me.

"She was a spirit of the forest, as curious about people and their wizards as I was about forest spirits and their magic. We danced around one another for months — metaphorically speaking, of course — before she finally kissed me. My hut was complete by then, and she agreed to live with me there for a time, to learn on an intimate level how human wizards conduct their private lives.

"We were very happy there together, for many years; I should have known that it would not last forever. No one has ever managed to keep a forest spirit captive for very long, not that I wanted to imprison her. I suppose it is a miracle that she stayed as long as she did. For what felt like an age, we lazed in the grassy glades together, splashed one another as we swam in the brook, slept beside one another each night. And then, one day, she was gone.

"I could not stay. The hut seemed empty without her. The whole forest seemed empty without her, even though I knew she lived on somewhere within it. The days of her sharing my life with me were over, and I was utterly bereft.

"It is said among my people that when a wizard tires of life, death must surely follow, and swiftly. After she left, I was more than tired of life. I felt nothing but emptiness. I ate little, slept either too much or too little, and as my strength waned, so did my magic. That is why I came here to Shorehaven to die, for there are few trees along the clifftops. I wondered if it might be easier to forget her in a place like this. To live out the final days of my diminution here."

Leonie listened to the wizard's story with interest, and they sat silent for a long time after the wizard had finished speaking.

"I'm sorry you lost her," they said at last.

"So am I," said the wizard mournfully.

"Is it not possible, though," said Leonie, "that you might have been mistaken about the nature of your illness? I understand why you felt as though you were tired of living after she left you, but I've seen a great improvement in you since you came to Shorehaven."

The wizard took offense at this, and made a huffing noise.

"I have been a wizard all my life," she said. "Surely I ought to know whether or not I am dying."

Leonie said nothing, nor did they give the wizard the pointed look that they strongly wished to. From their perspective, the wizard had only grown in strength and vigour as the weeks passed. She seemed less gaunt now, and her hair was shinier and less tangled, and she had even begun standing up from the sofa from time to time and walking out as far as the end of the garden behind the house to look out over the sea.

After this conversation, the wizard kept firmly to the sofa for several days, reverting to her previous position beneath a tangle of blankets, as if to prove to Leonie that she was indeed dying. Leonie considered asking the wizard whether she'd ever experienced a spell of low spirits before, if it might be possible that she'd mistaken the despair of such an episode for the fatal certainty of her own impending demise, but again they held their tongue.

Instead, Leonie set about clearing out the rooms on the upper floor of the house, which were now accessible thanks to the work of the carpenter's apprentice. The bedsteads that had been left up there by the cottage's previous inhabitants were still perfectly serviceable, so Leonie ordered new mattresses, linen, and curtains when they were in town, and asked to have them sent up. The wizard grudgingly agreed to temporarily remove some of the protective charms and spells along the road to the cottage so that the delivery people could bring up the mattresses.

"There's no way I can manage those mattresses myself," said Leonie sheepishly.

"There's no need for you to walk up and down the road to town every day," the wizard replied sharply. "Especially now that there's a bedroom for you upstairs if you want it."

Leonie said nothing, although they'd considered taking up the wizard's previous offer. It *would* save them a lot of walking every day, and their father the Mayor had only become more insistent as time had gone by that the wizard ought to begin to do at least some wizarding for the town, regardless of the state of her health.

And they were tired of the Mayor referring to them as his 'darling daughter'; ever since the wizard had confessed her perception of their true self to Leonie, they'd found it increasingly difficult to carry on the pretence of being the person that Shorehaven expected them to be. Life was slow and gentle up here on the cliff edge, and for the first time in their life they felt entirely unobserved.

"I'll think about it," they said this time, instead of ignoring the question altogether.

When they arrived at the cottage the next day, Leonie was surprised to see the wizard standing up near the window, wearing more than just a nightgown and looking out over the sea.

"Do you have much work planned for today?" she asked.

Leonie shrugged.

"Dusting, decorating the bedrooms, making an apple cake," they replied.

"Anything you can't put off until tomorrow?" the wizard asked. "Apart from the apple cake, which I'd very much like to eat later. Can you put together a picnic lunch while you're at it?"

Leonie agreed to postpone the dusting and bedroom-decorating, and set about preparing the requested victuals, curious about the wizard's intentions. When the apple cake was cooling on the kitchen windowsill and the picnic lunch had been packed up in a basket, the wizard nodded her satisfaction and strode out into the rear garden towards the edge of the cliff, which she stopped to look down over.

"Is there a path to the beach?" she asked.

Leonie shook their head.

"We'll see about that," said the wizard.

She knelt down at the far edge of the cliff and planted her hands firmly in the thin layer of grass and soil, massaging it gently. At first there was a faint vibration that grew more rumbling and distinct as the wizard continued her work; Leonie felt it radiating up through the bones of their right leg, and buzzing furiously where the prosthesis met the terminus of their left leg.

Slowly the edge of the cliff began to change shape, the rock rearranging itself beneath the command of the wizard's fingers until a new form emerged amidst the cliff face: a narrow staircase that looked as though it had always been there.

"Can you manage?" the wizard asked.

Leonie looked at the staircase, anxiety creeping over them as they considered just how many steps there were, and just how uneven most of them looked. The Mayor had drilled into them over and over again how important it was that his daughter appear normal in public. 'Normal', in the Mayor's eyes, meant things like never walking with a visible limp, and taking any number of stairs with equal amounts of agility and cheer. Leonie had internalised these lessons so deeply that most domestic staircases posed no challenge, but the stairs the wizard had just summoned into existence were an entirely different proposition.

They realised, however, that they were not exactly 'in public' out here with the wizard. Nor did they seriously feel compelled to maintain the pretence that they were the

Mayor's daughter, especially not so far out of sight of the rest of the town.

"I'll be honest, I think it's going to be a struggle," they replied. "The leg is fine on shorter staircases, but this one might be beyond me."

"How would you approach it if the leg wasn't in the picture?" asked the wizard.

Leonie was instantly transported back to early childhood, a time they hadn't thought about for many years, when they'd accepted their body exactly as it had been, and they'd had no concept of legs or propriety or the role of a Mayor, or indeed the role of a dutiful daughter. They'd been more than happy back then to pull themselves up and down staircases in a seated fashion; it was the Mayor who'd insisted they learn to walk up and down the stairs like any other person.

They took a deep breath. Then they began to untie the leather straps that anchored the leg to the girdle they wore just below their left hip. Once the straps were loosened, they tugged at the socket of the leg until it popped off, and then slipped off the thin covering they wore over the tapered area where the end of their natural leg met the beginning of the prosthesis. Instead of placing the leg down carefully, as their father had always insisted they do, because of its great importance and the tremendous expense of its construction, they let it fall to the ground with a thud.

Standing before the wizard without their prosthesis, Leonie felt strangely exposed, but the wizard merely nodded and smiled.

"It's nice to see you as you are, for a change," she said.

Then the wizard began to clamber down the steep, narrow staircase towards the sea, hitching up the skirt of her robe and carrying the picnic basket while Leonie followed on their backside, their trousers rolled up as far as their right knee and the terminus of their left leg. By the time they reached the short pebble beach that lay between the base of the cliff and the sea, Leonie's arms burned from the exertion, but the effort left them feeling strangely exhilarated rather than worn out.

They followed the wizard down the beach, the sensation of the smooth pebbles beneath their right foot a delight as they hopped along. The Mayor had disapproved of hopping almost as much as he'd disapproved of taking staircases from a seated position; Leonie was surprised to find that they were easily strong and agile enough to hop the distance to the shoreline comfortably. The Mayor had been so insistent that they needed the leg in order to function that they'd never stopped to consider whether this was actually true.

The sea was fresh and salty and just a little too cold for comfort. After stripping off her clothes and leaving them just beyond the reach of the waves, the wizard began swimming, and Leonie joined her. They swam side by side for a while, pausing occasionally to tread water, and then they returned to the beach, where they lay in the sun until their bodies were mostly dry again.

The wizard rolled towards Leonie, stroking their arm, her lips parted and her eyes questioning. Leonie shrank away from her touch, not entirely understanding the expression on the wizard's face. They turned onto their left side, covering their thin, short left leg as much as they could with the sturdy bulk of their right. The wizard took Leonie's cue and did not pursue the matter; when they went back up to the cottage in the late afternoon, she strode on ahead as Leonie worked their way up backwards. At the top of the cliff, they sat on a rock and reattached the prosthesis, easing the end of their left leg into its socket and feeling the dull, familiar pain in their hip as they stood and began to bear weight on it again.

The wizard attempted no further advances that afternoon. Leonie finished up a few chores and left the wizard some supper. The wizard did not want to appear as though she was watching them, but she couldn't help noticing how they'd turned inward after she'd reached out to them: the pain and confusion visible on their face in moments when Leonie believed the wizard was not looking, the fact that their gait seemed clumsier somehow now that they'd reattached the leg. As they went to leave, the wizard caught their arm.

"Are you sure you wouldn't rather stay the night?" she asked.

Leonie pulled away again, their eyes flushing with hot tears even as they tried to blink them back. On the return journey to town, their mind swirled with memories and emotions, things they'd steadily and dutifully repressed in order to more deeply inhabit the role of the Mayor's daughter. A single, sweet kiss shared with a girl from school, never repeated for fear of what people might think if they found out. Their leg, and the extent to which they'd allowed themself to turn it into an excuse never to become intimate with anyone. But the wizard had seen them without it, and hadn't shied away; she had perceived their lower left leg's absence as a core component of Leonie, a radiant part of their truth rather than something to be obfuscated.

Dinner at the Mayor's residence that evening was subdued. The Mayor could tell that something was wrong with Leonie, but couldn't fathom what the problem might be. When he enquired as to whether the wizard was dying at long last, Leonie's response surprised him.

"No, father, it's not the wizard. She's doing well."

"Then what is it that troubles you, child?"

Leonie's next response surprised even Leonie.

"My hip aches terribly from all the walking I've been doing back and forth to the wizard's house, and I'm afraid that a sore patch is forming where my leg sits in the socket of the prosthesis."

The Mayor's eyes widened, and an expression as sad as the one Leonie had been wearing all evening crossed his face. But he said nothing more about the wizard or Leonie or their leg, just as Leonie had expected he wouldn't. And in that moment, they understood that a decision they hadn't even realised they'd been contemplating had just made itself.

The following morning, the wizard stood anxiously in the cottage doorway. Leonie was late, much later than usual, and the wizard was afraid she'd driven them away with a single wordless touch on the beach, and that they might never come back. As she watched, however, a figure emerged along the road from Shorehaven, moving slowly and springily. As the figure drew closer, the wizard saw that it was Leonie hopping along the road, the prosthetic leg and a pair of crutches that the Mayor would have preferred them not to own strapped to their back.

Leonie was annoyed at how long the journey had taken, even though they'd set out with plenty of time to spare. It was only a small annoyance, though; it paled in comparison to their delight in finding that they were easily fit and strong enough to make the journey from town without the assistance of the prosthesis.

Leaving town, they'd seen people they'd known their entire life staring at them and whispering. And although they couldn't hear any of those whispers, they could easily imagine what the people of Shorehaven were saying. *Goodness, there goes Leonie-the-Mayor's-daughter without her leg. Perhaps it's broken. Maybe that good-for-nothing wizard is going to fix it for her. Poor little dear. What a shame.*

But each hop they'd made past the town boundary had felt like a leap of triumph, the energy and propulsion of every successive step batting away the dreadful comments they imagined the townsfolk were whispering to one another. Every time their right leg landed on the road, it seemed to reinforce some deep, unadulterable part of themself: they were not the Mayor's daughter, there was nothing broken about the leg that nature had given them, nothing about them was a shame, and they were categorically not a poor little dear.

The wizard tried to appear nonchalant as Leonie approached the cottage, though her face was somewhat flushed. Leonie did not immediately comment on their journey or the leg, which they left propped in the hallway for the time being, but they did announce a change that made the wizard very happy.

"I've told the Mayor not to expect me back tonight," they said. "Assuming your offer of an overnight stay still stands?"

"It does," said the wizard, and when she slowly approached Leonie and placed her hand around their waist, they did not pull away this time.

As they kissed, Leonie realised that their anxiety at the thought of being intimate with another person had melted away entirely, only to be replaced with a different concern.

"I'm not sure I can measure up to a forest spirit," they said, blushing.

"If I wanted to be with a forest spirit, I'd go back to the forest," said the wizard. "I like you just the way you are."

The people of Shorehaven complained at length about the town's great misfortune during the many years that followed. To have been without a wizard for so long, only to have one arrive who showed no interest in using her magic to benefit the town or its people was a heavy burden for any town to bear. They felt tremendously ill-used, both by fate and by the wizard herself, and rather than teaching their children to pray for a wizard to come to Shorehaven, they now taught them to curse the wizard who *had* arrived, for her selfishness and lack of community spirit. Some even said that they wished the wizard would hurry up and die, as she'd said she was going to, for she had done absolutely nothing to help the town, nor any of its inhabitants.

That was not true, however; Leonie blossomed at the cottage on the cliffside. They managed to persuade the wizard to make an exception in her charms and hexes for their father, that he might come up and visit them occasionally, and the wizard agreed, so long as Leonie wasted no further energy pretending to be the Mayor's daughter.

The Mayor was made to understand that Leonie would no longer live with him, that they had tried a life of service in the town of Shorehaven and it had not suited them, and that they did not particularly enjoy being called "she" or "daughter" when those ideas were so foreign to the sense of self that the wizard's love and company had solidified within them.

The Mayor was also made to understand that the wizard would not live to serve the town of Shorehaven either, even though the wizard was indeed not dying, and no matter how much the town might desire her service. Much of the Mayor's professional life from that point on consisted of placating the townspeople on behalf of the wizard, and it was true that he did not enjoy his job quite so much once the town realised that the wizard was not inclined to help them in any meaningful way. He tried to point out to the townsfolk, as the wizard had pointed out to him, that they had managed perfectly well for many years without any wizard at all, but this was cold comfort as far as most Shorehaveners were concerned.

Finally, the Mayor was made to understand that any future wearing of the prosthetic leg would be done entirely on Leonie's terms. The first time he visited the cottage, they sat in a chair with the leg leaning against a bookcase in the living room, hopping into the kitchen as needed. It seemed to pain the Mayor to see this, but when he asked whether there was anything wrong with the leg, Leonie told him unceremoniously that they would no longer be wearing it purely for his comfort — only for their own, on the occasions when it was truly comfortable to do so.

And the Mayor had wrung his hands together, and said that he'd only ever wanted his only child to be happy and comfortable — and that surely the key to being happy and comfortable was to be as much like other people as possible, which was why he'd always insisted about the leg. But he was capable of understanding that he had been wrong, and of realising that the price of a relationship with his only child meant never mentioning his own preferences regarding their leg, or calling them "daughter".

And so Leonie remained in the cottage with the wizard, baking cakes to enjoy with her in the afternoon, swimming in the sea with her as often as they liked, working alongside her in the garden and talking about magic in a way that they both knew no other Shorehaveners would understand. Up on the cliffside, surrounded by the peace of the wind and the waves, they set aside all thoughts of how a Mayor's daughter ought to appear or behave, and allowed themself merely to be.

L.J. Wetherby's story "A Wizard Comes to Shorehaven" was originally published in Metaphorosis on Friday, 6 August 2021. See magazine.metaphorosis.com

About the author

LJ Wetherby (they/them) is a non-binary writer living in Cambridgeshire, UK, with a focus on speculative and historical fiction that centres queer characters. ljwetherby.com, @ljwetherby

254

L.J. Wetherby   Queer Metaphorosis

About the author

LJ Wetherby (they/them) is a non-binary writer living in Cambridgeshire, UK, with a focus on speculative and historical fiction that centres queer characters. ljwetherby.com, @ljwetherby

Superbloom

Lynne Peskoe-Yang

The call comes in the evening, though it's morning on the other side of the world. K. is demanding that I leave my study right this minute to look at the sea. I grab my sample bag and rush outside, too curious to argue. It takes less than a minute for me to jog from my house to the end of the jetty.

I peer down at the surface of the water. I can't see much; the sun set ten minutes ago.

"What am I looking for?"

"Look at the water. What color is it?"

I fumble in my bag for my good flashlight—one I made myself, with a patented triple lens—and turn its ultra-sharp beam on the ocean.

"Why is it doing that?" I whisper. "Why is it just sitting still?"

"What color is it, D.?"

"Green. The whole thing is just solid green."

A long, textured sigh issues from my earpiece. "God," K. hisses. She seems on the verge of tears, but with some effort she controls her breathing.

I can't wait. "Is this that algae bloom of yours? What the hell is it doing here?"

She inhales purposefully. I hoped she'd have to pull herself together to correct me, and it works; when she speaks again, her voice is steady.

"Not algae. It's a lichen—or it was when I started studying it. I've got no idea what it's doing there, other than growing. I'm still making sense of it myself. Do you remember my dissertation?"

Of course I remember. A year ago, K. printed out that dissertation and mailed it to me personally, neatly stapled and, I thought, perfumed. I read the abstract a dozen times before I gave in and called. She explained it all to me, in her laughing-brook voice, with a patience I hadn't been shown since I was a girl.

She had found me in a directory of remote researchers and wrote to ask me to photograph some of the lichens in my little biome, which was, she pointed out meaningfully, on the exact opposite side of the world from where K. herself lived, in New Zealand.

In the dissertation K. had referred to the floating, living islands that popped up along the northwestern coast as "ur-lichens", or, in more casual contexts, "super-lichens".

It was the second name that caught on in her small collective of Māori ecologists, the only ones paying attention at first. The super-lichen was a local disaster, overshadowed by the death rattle of the oceanic coral reefs. The collective relied on a growing network of citizen scientists to track the expansion—what they came to call the Bloom—as it spread unchecked along the coastline.

K. had volunteered to make contact with someone who could keep the last watch, as far away from the origin as possible. My island outpost, her own antipode, would mark the finish line for a fully global superbloom, if it ever got that far. I didn't ask her what good it would do anyone to know how much of the ocean was lost at that point. I don't think either of us expected that such a thing could actually happen in our lifetimes.

When the Bloom began to move down the northwestern coast of New Zealand, K. packed up her belongings and moved with it. She still called me occasionally to ask for updates from my side of the world. I would take the call on my headset while I worked the glass.

"A fungal spore sends its hyphae into the algae," she'd say, drawing out the Greek ending—*hy-fee*—in a grin that I could almost see. Through my headset I could hear her, even while I sanded finished prisms or made coke fuel for the forge. Sometimes she asked me about my work, but I had no talent for translation.

Instead, I sent photos, both of the growing lens and the lichens—no samples, she said, as the risk of contamination was overwhelming. I also sent her tools. Funding was scarce for lichen-watching, but I had all the raw materials at my disposal to replicate and improve every piece of glassware K. needed, and shockproof shipping was free under my contract. When K.'s digital microscope was stolen, I sent her a replacement—a bespoke mechanical version from my own workshop, with a hardwood carrying case, hand-engraved with her initials.

After that, the calls were daily. My ears adapted to the sound of K.'s voice and listened for it even after we hung up. I could not help but absorb her passion, her creeping panic, over the terrible might of the Bloom. Alone of ocean beings, it seemed to delight in the spiking acidity caused by human pollution. The Bloom was so good at growing, so blazingly energy-efficient, especially near the surface, that huge mats of it emerged in shallow waters around dozens of islands in the South Pacific. Where they met the coasts, the floating mats merged, surrounding whole archipelagos in swamps that turned alarmingly toxic.

I asked K. how it reproduced.

"This one doesn't," she said. "It only grows."

●

This is what I learned in those months of building: a lichen is not an organism, but a community of organisms acting collectively. The photosynthetic members, single algae cells or long strands of sun-loving cyanobacteria, feed the fungus via the hyphae, which penetrate the algae's cell walls to extract their sugars. In return, the fungus offers a safe habitat for its support organisms. Together, the hyphae and the photosynthetic cells make a single continuous unit of life, self-replicating and infinitely adaptable.

"On its own, the fungus is a clump of hyphae. It can't form any discernible structures. It dies."

"So the fungus is a parasite?"

"We'd have to ask the algae."

●

We passed good months this way, her calling, me listening. She was my favorite sound.

Then the Superbloom took the rest of the ocean in the course of a single night, twenty years ahead of schedule, and K. called me again.

"When I woke up this morning, I thought my satellite feed was broken—the map was just covered." It's hard to process her words.

"…But if it's reached you already, we're long past any way of stopping the spread," she concluded.

I listen to the birdsong through the phone: a kookaburra's alien laughter. Behind it, the wind is high, as it is here. I can see the first storm of summer growing on the horizon.

The kookaburra falls silent. I wipe my eyes with my forearm.

"Is there anything we can do? Maybe if…?" I trail off, unable to even frame the question.

"You should stock some food," she says gently. "If I think of something, I'll… I'll let you know."

It's fully dark now. The vast, pale expanse could almost be the natural ocean, if it weren't for the disturbing stillness of it beneath the starless sky. I feel panic rise, tightening my lungs and heart.

"Oh, and D.? Are you still there?"

I cough, force my voice deeper. "Yeah."

"Don't touch it."

●

The Caldera is the perfect place to light a beacon, and I was once the perfect person to keep it lit. My technical training is in photonics, the art of manipulating and redirecting light. I was one of the first to build lenses from gadolinite, the oily black mineral that makes up the base of the Caldera, though I did it in the comfort of my childhood home on the mainland. But I was losing patience with the frantic pace of manufacturing; I was ready for a quieter life.

By then, I had made some friends in government, and one of them shared my name with the Bureau of Scientific Engagement, a collaboration between government scientists and propagandists. Riding a wave of investment in space ventures, the project aimed to thrill the nation by building a self-powering radio beacon that would send an eternal message to alien worlds. Previous communications to the extrasolar expanse had been ephemeral: a five-minute transmission from the North Pole of spoken greetings in two hundred Earth languages; a gold disk embossed with Da Vinci's naked eight-limbed man and some other things, launched into the sky. The time had come, in the BSE's opinion, to make ourselves known to the universe on a permanent basis.

A simple transmitter would emit a continuous wavelength: a hundred mHz, just energetic enough to escape the atmosphere. My job would be to build and then maintain a lens out of gadolinite thermal glass, a form of passive solar power. The lens would both concentrate the signal into a narrow beam and power itself virtually forever, storing solar energy in a solid-state battery that fed the same monotone signal, even at night.

I was to build the whole thing on-site, on a colonial outpost with no other lucrative resources to offer, nor remaining residents to exploit. The Caldera is an empty-named place, a safe enough distance from real human civilization that the mainland, at least, would have warning, should the worst occur. What the worst might entail, we did not discuss.

●

The day after the Superbloom starts the same as usual, and it's not until I look out the window that I recall what has changed. The Caldera is a narrow island, curled like a fetus against the sea. To my left, the bulk of the island, a great crescent of steaming jungle, pours down into the bay as always. But the basin itself is deathly still, suffocating under the weight of a mat of new life that extends, waveless, to every horizon.

It's hard to look at.

Above the Bloom, on top of the hills on the opposite end of the crescent island, the black, flat-topped needle of the signal tower is barely visible from here. It's been three months since I got it running, and two months since I hauled my personal items to the opposite side of the island from the tower, into one of the last remaining buildings on the island. The tower was starting to make my head buzz.

I check the monitor: the signal is fine. A one-note performance, without even the texture of an ending, communicating the bare minimum of reality. The beam moves like an out-of-control spotlight, the focused radio waves sweeping around the planet as it turns, carving out curly ribbons of space in their near-random search for a receptive target. In the early days of the project, there had been some talk of sending out a message with actual content, even a simple greeting. But then one of our physicists showed that if we stuck to one frequency, the signal could easily reach the nearest galaxy cluster and would likely be detectable at twice that distance. The programming team was furious, but *intergalactic* sounded better than *interplanetary* in the headlines, so the one-note message won out.

●

My contract gives me a year of watch after I finish construction, but already it is impossible to picture life on the mainland. No word has arrived from my supervisors, but that doesn't surprise me. Will I last nine more months here, without supplies, without a plan? I do not dwell on this.

That night, I make my first discovery.

"The Bloom emits light." My words echo on the other end. Does my voice sound different to her because she's listening to its inverted form—across the world, upside down, in broad daylight?

"I thought I was seeing things," she whispers after a moment.

"I see it, too. It's clearer at night, but even in the light it's pulsing. Why?"

"I don't know." Her voice is hushed, hurried, as though someone might be listening. "It wasn't doing this even a week ago, but this Bloom changes so fast. If it were to somehow recruit some new microorganism, something that glows…"

"A third colony member?"

"It's possible. We wouldn't know. But there are hundreds of bioluminescent species."

"Why do they glow?"

"Camouflage. Prey attraction. Signaling to the predators that eat *their* predators."

"Would that look like… a pulse? Rhythmic?"

"No. It's purely responsive."

"Doesn't the pulse remind you of a heartbeat?"

"Yes, of course."

In the green expanse of the bay, a field of little leaflets drinks in the dimmed sun. On the far side, straight across the bay, the black crown of the signal tower looms like a purposeless alien.

"Does the Bloom, or some part of it, *have* a heartbeat?"

"Absolutely not."

●

Later, a call from the department: deliveries will be suspended for the time being, given the circumstances. I do not have to ask what the circumstances are. All around the world, I imagine, human beings are attempting to negotiate with the invader, touching and hacking and plowing, growing more desperate for a response. But the Bloom will not hear them, any more than I would hear a threat spelled out in plant hormones.

I tell him I have enough food for a few months and not to worry about me. There is shouting in the background, but I can't make out the words; the call ends, thankfully, before I get invested. I am sensing already that I shouldn't spend my panic on people I already know. It is easy to forget them; what could I do for them from here?

●

The sky is sickly green in the evening when the light begins to pulse again.

One-two. It is unmistakably a heartbeat, reborn as two flashes of incandescent plant-flesh, and yet no part of the Bloom could possibly have even a vestigial memory of having a heart. I count eighty beats per minute: a healthy resting heart rate for a human.

One-two. The rate does not change. If it's a message, it is insultingly simple. There is no hint of frustration, no pleading, no aggression; just a double-tap of light, repeating endlessly. A beacon reporting back that conditions are normal, stand by. *One-two.* A binary code too flat to be called communication. In Morse code, I recall uselessly, it is just the capital letter *I*, over and over and over, stupidly iterating into the dark.

I am here. Are you?

●

I creep to the edge of the Bloom. From the jetty, I drop a rock into its depths, as I often did when the ocean was still liquid, and watch the surface roll away from the impact in a stunted parody of wave motion. If I close my eyes while doing this and pay attention only to the splash, I will remember that there is still water under there.

I squat, scooping a handful of black sand from the beach and letting it pour from my fingers onto the curling leaves of the colony. No ripple at all. The living matter absorbs the motion, stunts its impact, so it can't be transferred. The motion is born locally, dies locally; sound, spoken prayer, would be stifled the same way.

But the Bloom *is* connected to itself, somehow. The pulse of the lichen at my feet is perfectly in phase with the pulse at the horizon. Light, then, can cross the channels from one end of the Bloom to the other. The Bloom is not a creature, but a culture; light is its language.

I don't know any words in light, but I don't think that would matter, if I could make some kind of deliberate pattern. The intent to speak is its own kind of speech—the astrobiologists taught me that. As long as the signal is clearly *meant* as a message, it is one.

•

"Fine," says K. when she calls back, too early. She woke me up. "Fine. It's sentient."

"I told you. There's no other explanation."

"Hm." I can hear her pacing. "Yes. But that doesn't mean—"

"Why are you so worried? This is a good thing. Maybe we can reason with it."

"Not good. Unprecedented. Bizarre. I can't even philosophically wrap my head around it. The pattern makes intelligent life unmistakable. Why would a living being advertise its existence like that? What takes that kind of stupid risk?"

"You're the one who's studied it. What do you think?"

She exhales. I can hear her brain working. "I think... whatever it is, it doesn't know we're here. Yet. But it's looking."

"I'm going to answer."

"With the beacon? Is it moveable? I thought you couldn't redirect the beam."

"I can do it. I just never had to before."

"Okay. Okay. But D., listen. This is not a conversation with a person. Sentience is not the same thing as a brain. I've been studying this thing. It evolves faster than its components, faster even than some viruses, but it also started pulsing all at once, like a single organism... If this is intelligence, it's clearly distributed—spread out in the body of the Bloom, coordinated, but not centralized. It is *nothing* like us."

"What is it like?"

"God. Fuck. I don't know. An octopus?" She's close to tears. "Who knows what it would do if it recognized another intelligence? And you want to give away your position, before we even know what will happen! What if it takes the signal as a threat? What if it *answers*?"

Her voice is so plaintive, so childish, that I half want to shout at her. *There is no other option!* But I can't say that. She knows.

For a moment I consider telling her I was planning to come see her when my contract was up, but even thinking the words makes me want to howl.

Instead, I tell K. I love her, and then I hang up in a hurry so I don't have to hear her sob.

In the evening, I trek north. I weave among my discarded shipping containers, most twice my height, their steel now coated in the rich green of a kudzu infestation at least a foot deep on every face. The vines are flowering on the southeast side where I approach; I breathe in clouds of grape-like perfume as I pass each cluster of white and purple blossoms.

The place steams with life. Between the blocks and everywhere the vines haven't claimed lies a thick carpet of mosses in varying shades, from pine-green to chartreuse and golden yellow. Already, beneath my boots, the fragile stalks of a bryophyte have been crushed into wet salad.

I need my flashlight to find the ladder on the far side of the tower. I hover on the bottom rung, waiting for the doubts to come; but my wonderful brain is silent, and I hear nothing but the wind through the leaves. The top rung is covered in seagull scat, so I have to haul myself onto the platform beneath the beacon like a sea lion. I turn off my light and recover there for a few moments, with my back against the thin railing, staring upward.

The sky is clear now. The compound lens of the beacon looms over me, its outer rings glittering with reflected stars. The pieces are arranged in concentric circles, like a slice of a giant black onion. Each layer is made of two to thirty segments of gadolinite glass.

It is impossible to tell by sight that the signal is firing. I pass my hand over the opening in the center of the onion slice, and imagine that I can feel it, a sort of metaphysical buzz; but I know I can't actually feel anything, as surely as I know the signal exists. The beam, even concentrated by my lens, is both silent and invisible to me.

I pull myself up with a groan and stretch upward to run my hands along one of the rings. The dark glass is warmer than I remembered. The smaller rings are closely nested and hard to differentiate by starlight, so I work my way inward by feel. Just below the innermost ring, attached to the pole that supports the beacon's weight, there is a latched metal box, unlocked.

The terminal inside is still charged. I power it up and it chirps softly, as though it recognizes me. Black letters appear against the green-grey field: I N P U T ?

My mind is empty. I turn away from the beacon and nearly lose my balance. The railing, rusted from the salt spray, groans but holds steady for now. How is it up to *me* to decide what to say to an alien from my own planet?

It has stopped glowing, I realize as I stare into the sea, so it's possible I've missed my chance, but somehow, inexplicably, I feel that it is actually aware of what I am doing and has simply paused to wait for my answer. *Impossible!* I can almost hear K. say in response.

I picture her on the other side of the world and feel my spine straighten a bit.

I take great, gulping breaths of the briny air. I reprogram the beacon.

I fiddle with latches in the dark. The lens is twice my wingspan and half my weight, but at least the whole thing comes off its mount without so much as a screwdriver. I hoist it onto my shoulder like a parasol and then lower the circular end to the platform, feeling my long trek across the island screaming in my kneecaps. When I stand up, the beam is pointing just below the horizon, its waves colliding with a distant section of the Bloom's vast body.

The Bloom is still as stone. In the silvery light, the world looks primordial, as though made of just-cooled magma, unmarred by soil or water. But I know the Bloom is there and watching me, in its own way; it holds its breath as I hold mine.

We watch each other.

Just where the beam hits, a part of the Bloom begins to rise. But this is an illusion: it is simply luminescing, first there and then all over, the whole field of it suddenly turning white with light—far brighter than before. In seconds I'm forced to cover my eyes with my arm, but it's not enough.

I wake up on the beach a few meters from the tower, my whole body aching from the fall. The world is still flashing around me, so bright I can almost hear the new pattern: the same one I chose moments or hours ago.

Long, short, long. *K*, the Bloom is saying, shouting, singing, to me and to her, and I can feel her amazement radiating straight through the center of the Earth.

Lynne Peskoe-Yang's story "Superbloom" was originally published in Metaphorosis on Friday, 1 January 2021. See magazine.metaphorosis.com

About the author

Lynne Peskoe-Yang is an author and freelance journalist based in New England. Her writing is informed by an abiding passion for ambiguous technologies and the humans that make and wield them, for better or (often) worse.

Scraps

Juliet Kemp

The bell jingled, and Emmeline looked, frowning, at the door through to the front of the shop. She was in the middle of a fitting, and one did not expect interruptions if one was being fitted for charmwear at Emmeline's. When a moment passed and Joe, her apprentice, did not appear around the corner, she smiled at Mme Gantiel.

"My apologies, Madame. Would you excuse me for just a moment?"

At least it was cheerful Mme Gantiel, rather than one of her fussier or more class-conscious clients. She'd never minded any of them, in the years since she'd taken over from Papa, but recently, she'd become more and more irritated by their self-absorption in their own tiny part of this one small city. There was more to the world that that. She sighed, transferred the pins in her hand to the pincushion at her waist, and went through to the shop front.

Charmwear was never ready-to-wear, so Emmeline had no stock on display, and she did not need to advertise to fill her client list. Thus the shop front was tiny, holding only her desk and appointments book, and just now it was almost all taken up by the guard captain who stood there. Outside stood a similarly large lieutenant. Well, that explained Joe's absence.

The guard nodded at her. "Captain Berrith. I need to inspect your premises, miss."

"My premises? What on earth for?"

"I need to inspect your premises, Miss."

She swallowed. "Well, this is a nuisance. I have a client now. Could you wait a few minutes until we finish?"

He nodded amicably, and made no move to wait in the street.

Emmeline got through the remainder of Mme Gantiel's fitting in record time. She was proud to notice that her hands weren't even shaking.

The inspection was anticlimactic. She didn't glance towards the hidden box, and they didn't find it. But they did rifle through every cupboard and drawer in her fitting room and workroom.

"What do you do with leftovers, miss? After you've cut a dress or whatever out?" Captain Berrith demanded abruptly.

Her stomach lurched, but she answered calmly, pasting on a slightly puzzled look.

"Large pieces can sometimes be used in another garment — those are stored here." Filed by charm and then by colour. "I keep a few smaller pieces, in the small boxes there, for trimmings as needed. To cover buttons and so on, you understand. Anything else goes into the bin in the corner," she nodded at it, "and is collected by the municipal dust-truck weekly."

As she was obliged to do; and the dustman was obliged to burn it. Couldn't let the plebia get their hands on charmcloth, not for their own use.

"Is there a problem?" she asked.

"Well now, miss," the lieutenant began chattily, then shut up at a glance from Captain Berrith.

"These labels here are accurate?" Captain Berrith asked, running his finger along the shelf edges. *Warmth, Beauty, Plausibility, Charm* — the charms of her trade. Hardly ones to interest the Guard.

"Of course." *And get your hands off them.*

Five minutes after they finally left, Joe reappeared via the back door.

"We had visitors while you were gone," she said.

"Did we?" he said, not meeting her eyes. She'd known for a while that Joe's spare time was spent in what he might call politicking, and the guard would definitely have called rebellion. She'd not mentioned it. They both had their secrets.

"Visitors looking for charm scraps, if I'm not mistaken. For someone sewing charm scraps."

Joe raised his eyebrows. "Rumour I heard was, they found some Happiness, all sewn together from bits. Some folk reckoned it was found on someone, and they're off to the clink now. Some folk said it was just dropped on the street."

"Do they suspect the Masquerade?" she asked. She hoped, desperately, that it had just been dropped, and no one with it at all.

"Most like," Joe said. "Masquerade gets blamed for everything, right?"

The Masquerade. The most popular rumour about the name was that they wore masks. Which would be foolish; masks drew attention, and the Masquerade preferred secrecy. More likely was that the name was a muddy reflection of the Guisers, the traders from over the mountain who brought charmcloth; the charmcloth that, in barely a decade, had turned a city of many porous layers into a city of two halves divided by an uncrossable chasm. The Masquerade's slogan was 'true equality'. Emmeline wasn't even sure what that would look like any more.

"Mm," she said, staring out of the window at another guard patrol. There were more and more guards, now.

She'd wondered if someone would notice the scraps, sooner or later, despite her efforts to hide them. She hadn't thought about what would happen.

The sensible thing would be to stop. The sensible thing would be to do as she always had before: keep her head down and be grateful for what she had.

"I imagine," she said, "that the Masquerade would love to be able to use charmcloth."

Out of the corner of her eye, she saw Joe stop moving. "Lots of people would love to be able to use charmcloth," he said. "Warmth, for one, this time of year. That bit of Happiness, I'm sure someone would hate to have lost that. If there was any truth in it, I mean."

They looked at each other for a moment. "I wonder," she said, "how one would go about finding the Masquerade. If one were so foolish as to want to."

●

It had begun with Memory, only a couple of moons ago. She didn't handle Memory often. Memory was for small things and keepsakes, a different kind of craft from hers. But Mme Ydrit, newly widowed, wanted a nightgown of Memory, to remember Mr Ydrit as she slept.

"I know it seems ridiculous," she said, dabbing at her eyes with an untidily-hemmed handkerchief of Solace that Emmeline recognised as coming from the funeral house, "but I'm sure you'll understand. You always make me such beautiful things, and I do want this to be beautiful."

As Emmeline sat and cut and sewed, she looked at the piled scraps of shimmering silver Memory, and her fingers slowed, until she put Mme Ydrit's nightgown aside. She picked up the scraps of Memory, and laid them out on her worktable.

She thought of her grandfather, stitching little pieces of cloth together; of a quilt on her childhood bed made with little pieces of Granny's skirt, Grandfather's apron, her aunt's baby blanket. She remembered her father sitting by her bed in the dim evening light, telling over the list of the pieces in a soothing drowsy drone. They'd lived down by the docks then, and Grandfather made workwear and in tough times mended sails. Emmeline used to gaze at the ships coming up and down the river, dreaming of boarding them and going to faraway lands.

Grandfather had taught her to sew, and later, Papa had taught her to tailor. By then they'd moved away from the docks. Papa's burgeoning tailoring business was doing well, and the well-to-do didn't want the smell of the docks in their nostrils when they stood to be measured. Emmeline still thought of the ships, and once she finished her apprenticeship, she had started putting coin aside to go away for her journeyman time. There were other cities, down the river or across the plains; other things to learn.

Then Grandfather had died, and it didn't seem like the right time to leave Papa on his own.

It had been a year, maybe two, after that, when charmcloth had arrived, with the Guisers who had never come over the mountains before. It was expensive stuff, but oh, so much in demand, right from the start. Emmeline had just finished her journeyman time, and it seemed like a golden opportunity to specialise in something that the rich would pay through the nose for twice, first for the cloth and then for the tailoring. She'd had to use up her travelling money for the initial investment, but she'd known it would pay off, in the long run.

Then Papa in his turn had died, and suddenly she was the proprietor of a shop, with a solid reputation with this new material. She still wanted to travel, but she'd had to take an apprentice, Joe, to cover the workload; and then she felt a responsibility to see his training through. He would be done this time next year, though. By then she'd have enough saved to travel, to keep herself for a while, and then to set up somewhere else. Somewhere new. One more year. It could be worse.

It was the year of Papa's death that what had been purely a matter of money became a matter of law: charmcloth (in its limited quantities, one delivery per season) was only for the patria. The patria had barely existed as a separate group before then; an old name, dating back to an older, more divided society that the modern city felt it had (ha!) left behind. Certainly, some had more money than others, but money you could acquire, if you were lucky and worked hard. But once only the patria could use charmcloth, suddenly the city consisted of two halves: those with the charms, and those without. Folk from all parts of society still traded; but how could a trader without Luck compete with one who had it? Who could measure their honesty — or lack of it — against someone wearing an undershirt of Plausibility? Anyone could attend a dance, but lacking Beauty or Charm, your wooing would proceed less smoothly. Even in the army, where, notionally, officers were provided with Death and Destruction regardless of their backgrounds, why, having access to

Strength or Authority beforehand eased your way to that gold braid on your shoulder.

Those with charmcloth found their expectations changing in ways such that those without it came up short, every time, in every way. And those with charmcloth were, more and more, the ones making those decisions.

Folk who couldn't buy it tried to work out how it was made, but without success, and those who tried to follow the Guisers on the way home came back with broken bones, or not at all.

Her grandfather wouldn't have trusted charmcloth, and Emmeline thought, now, that he would have had the right of it. She could still see his fingers clearly, holding scissors or chalk or pins; but the memory of his face was fading.

He'd done a little tailoring, her grandfather, but it was that patchwork quilt that she remembered best of his sewing. She looked down at the pieces of Memory on the table, then, slowly, began to move them around, trying them against one another, comparing the result with her memory of that quilt. She shouldn't use these scraps, of course. She should throw them out with the rest. But, perhaps, just this once... A keepsake, just a private one, for her grandfather's memory.

Her first attempt was sadly ragged, the lines of the charm running this way and that way, wriggling against one another. She sighed, and pulled the stitches out, and tried again. This time, she matched the scraps carefully, trimming edges, fitting the subtle lines of the charm back together. Her eyes prickled and her back ached as she sat into the night, sewing under the flicker of the gaslamp. It was past midnight by the time she was done. It looked right, the lines flowing smoothly; but with Memory you needed something to trigger it. She held the tiny bag open in her palm, took her grandfather's thimble out of her sewing box, and dropped it in.

The memories sprang to life inside her mind, reeling across it like pictures on a string, bright and new. After a few minutes, Emmeline put the bag carefully down, wiping tears from her cheeks. She tucked it inside a drawer. Tomorrow she'd make an outside, and a lining, to sandwich it between. It wouldn't do for the city's premier charm tailor to be caught with illegal cloth.

Her glance fell on the piles of trimmings from her attempts, and she shook her head slightly. Wasteful. Next time... Then she shook her head more sharply. There must not *be* a next time. She couldn't be caught using charmcloth for herself. Prison, public whipping, loss of livelihood...A fine. Her leaving money gone. No. Once was more than enough.

She'd sewn that little bag of Memory in the middle of the autumn. In the next weeks it grew colder, and the nights grew shorter. It didn't affect Emmeline, who would well afford firewood and a thick quilt. Not all her neighbours were as fortunate.

"You seen Granny Zeta today? I had some firewood for her yesterday. Told her it was scrap, but she still wouldn't take it. Too cold to be without firewood, tis."

Emmeline, picking out unbruised apples at the greengrocer, looked up. The speaker was Gareth, a young builder who lived around the corner.

The grocer shook his head. "Food or fuel, and sometimes neither. I hate this time of year."

Had it been that way when she was younger? Not as much, Emmeline was sure. There were more folk struggling, now; while the patria grew ever richer and more comfortable.

Home again with her apples, Emmeline turned over the scraps of Warmth that she'd just cut from the bolt in making Major Arad's new winter cloak. She didn't usually do menswear, but Major Arad was insistent that her cloaks were better than his regular tailor's. This year's cut was wildly fashionable; open across the front, it barely reached the wearer's hips. Made in wool it would leave the wearer freezing; in charmcloth, it didn't matter. Not enough merely to have the advantage; to be fashionable, one had to flaunt it. And what, she wondered savagely, would happen to the Major's old cloak, the one she had made for him only last year? Doubtless it would go in the disposal. The Granny Zetas of the city couldn't be permitted charmcloth of Warmth, even if it was last season's style.

Unbidden, her fingers were arranging the scraps alongside one another, turning them to fit together. She paused, suddenly unsure, then the wind whistled through the crack in the window and her chin went up. She pulled her bag of Memory out, seeking a clearer recollection of the patchwork caps Grandfather used to make from flannel. This, he would have approved of.

She sandwiched the Warmth, patched carefully together, between two layers of plain flannel, and took the cap to Granny Zeta the next morning.

"It's my grandfather's anniversary," she said awkwardly, wanting to make sure the old lady would accept the gift. "He used to make these, and I wanted to remember him, and I thought, maybe…"

Granny Zeta smiled at her, and took the cap. "I remember your grandfather too, dear. Thank you kindly, and I'll burn a candle for him tonight."

She put it on, and her face crinkled in pleasure. "Ooh, now, that is nice and warm. You've your grandfather's gift with a needle as well as his generous heart, dear. My thanks."

Emmeline sat for some time that evening, looking at the basket of scraps and thinking of Granny Zeta. There were too many Granny Zetas. But she could hardly help them all. Sooner or later, she'd be caught. But then — what if no one knew where they came from? There were plenty of charitable organisations, these days. An anonymous gift, a series of anonymous gifts, to a different organisation each time… Surely that way there could be no trouble.

Slowly, she reached for her pile of scraps, and began to pick out more pieces of Warmth. And then after that, maybe some Happiness. People could use that, this time of year. It felt a damn sight more useful than sewing pretty this-and-that for overbred ladies. The pretty this-and-that was putting pennies and pounds into her savings. This — this would keep her busy, until she could leave. Less than a year, now.

She couldn't predict when she'd have scraps left over that she could use, and she couldn't allow them to be taken away every week; so as she tidied up every evening, a handful of pieces went into an old hatbox, hidden under a floorboard she'd prised up. When she had time, she sewed them up, as linings hidden within normal fabric, and dropped them off to one charity or another.

She told herself that it wouldn't go further; but she knew at the back of her mind that she wasn't telling the truth. The guards' visit, only another few weeks after that first cap for Granny Zeta, was only the final stitch in a decision already made. Working on her own she could do a little. Working with the Masquerade she could do more.

●

The trouble was, the charms the Masquerade wanted most were the ones that Emmeline found hardest to come by. Stealth, Patience, Secrecy, and their cousins. Not the stuff of high fashion that she most commonly dealt with, although the similarly-useful Concealment and Deception were both more popular in her work than one might think. She became ever more skilled at using the tiniest of pieces, sewing the scantest of seams. Every time she mastered a slightly more frugal technique, she went back through the scraps bag again, sorting out the tiniest of pieces from previous constructions. Each night another scarf or handkerchief or cap, its outer layers of patchworked flannel and cotton and linen concealing its inner secrets. She didn't give anything directly to Joe; she put each finished item in that hidden box, and she was careful not to see when he took it. After that first conversation the day the guards had visited, neither she nor Joe referred to the matter with word or gesture. She yawned more, in the daytimes; but it was worth it.

A while passed, and one day Joe was sweeping out the workroom, with heavy sighs and sideways glances at her. Emmeline sighed.

"What is it, Joe?" Time off, doubtless.

"Could I have a word? About something private?"

Her eyebrows flew up. "Of course." She glanced around, then beckoned him into the fitting room, which had no windows, and shut the door.

He looked down at his hands. "They wanted me to ask... They need something stronger."

He mimed, briefly, a pistol, aimed at the floor, and Emmeline blinked. Destruction. Death. Charms she'd never worked with, charms that the armorers near the river, closer to the city limits, used.

"I don't..." she started.

"They could — someone could get the makings for you," Joe said, still to his hands.

She swallowed. "It's not that." Her decision solidified as she spoke. "It's not — I won't. Not those." Not killing.

Joe nodded, his shoulders relaxing a bit. "I didn't think so. But they asked me to ask. I hope you don't mind..."

She shook her head, still thinking. She knew, of course, that the Masquerade weren't a bloodless group. She read the papers.

"I won't do that," she said. "But — protection. I could do more of that. If I had the makings."

After that, she started finding bags of extra scraps in the box. They didn't speak of it again, even when the news started talking of illegal charmwear and charmwork; even when the guards announced that charmworkers would have to hand their scraps and leftovers over to be destroyed; even when those bags of scraps began to be weighed against what had come into the shop. Emmeline sewed smaller and smaller. She found ways of secreting the tiniest of pieces away — there was always an error margin in the weighing — and the bags of extras kept appearing in the box, though they were smaller bags and smaller pieces now.

She changed, just a little, the design and style of the clothes she made; she used more thread-heavy stitching, more cutaways, more decorative furbelows that deceived the scales by compensating for the bits she cut out or the seams she sewed a touch more scantly. It was as well that the guards doing the weighing didn't understand tailoring.

And all the while she kept counting her savings. Soon. She'd be able to leave, soon; leave this wretched place behind.

●

The guard captain, standing in the front of Emmeline's shop, looked like a man with beautiful visions of promotion dancing in front of his eyes. Joe, held firmly by a private nearly twice his size, one eye puffing up and blackening, looked sick and scared and trying for defiant.

"It hangs together beautifully," the captain said to Joe. "You're an agent of these revolutionaries, you have access to leftovers, and you've seen your employer doing this kind of work."

"Nonsense," Emmeline said sharply. "He barely has the skill to thread a needle yet. He couldn't possibly have done this. It's excellent work, if not as good as my own."

She gestured at the dismembered handkerchief lying on the table.

"Well, miss, unless you're about to confess yourself, ha, I'm afraid I have to disagree with you," the captain said briskly.

Emmeline stared at him, envisaging herself confessing, being taken away in Joe's place, Joe set free.. Except of course Joe wouldn't be set free. The visions wound onwards. Both of them in chains, under question... She swallowed sickly.

"Well," she said weakly. "I am sure you are wrong, and I must deplore you depriving me of my assistant. I will be along later to check on him, and I will be speaking to my patron."

"You do that, miss," the guard captain said equably.

They dragged Joe out.

"I'm sure this can all be straightened out!" Emmeline called after them, willing her voice not to shake.

●

She waited a nervous half hour before she tied her cap on, hung a shopping bag on her arm, and set off. She'd made a scarf of Discovery last night, and Joe hadn't had a chance to take it this morning. That should help her find the place she needed. She could have used Concealment, too, but there was nothing to be done about that; she had no time to piece together the tiny handful of scraps hidden in the press.

But a woman of her age, drably dressed and carrying a shopping bag; she looked like she belonged here. That would be concealment enough. She walked like she knew where she was going and like it wasn't important at all, and she eyed the guards in the street with the right amount of caution. Wary, because who wasn't wary, down here, of the guard? But with no reason to hide from them.

She knew roughly where Joe spent his spare time. She was banking on finding the centre of the revolution close by. She was banking on there *being* a centre, and someone of authority she could talk to. When she reached the Bull and Cat, she tied the scarf more firmly around her neck, and fixed in her mind what she wanted to find. She concentrated on the feel of the scarf at her neck, and on where her instinct was telling her to go next. Although — if Discovery alone would do the trick, wouldn't the guards have found the people she was looking for long before now?

Well. It was this or nothing. Hand rubbing the corner of the scarf, she turned right from the corner of the pub, then left down an alley, cleaner than you might have expected round here. Left again at the end, then right into a courtyard, past what might be a heap of refuse and might be trying to become compost for the window-boxes growing green leafy vegetables, and up a wooden staircase to the second floor of the middle house. The staircase didn't creak underfoot; it didn't shake. The curtains in the second-floor window were thick enough to block out all but a sliver of light around the edge.

The door swung open before she could knock. Her stomach lurched. A girl of about Joe's age stood just inside, looked her up and down, then stepped back to let her in.

"Thanks, Hira. You'd best be off." The voice came from the far corner of the room, where a woman sat in a threadbare red armchair, her grey hair scraped back behind her ears. She was smoking tobacco wrapped in a twist of black paper, and from the ash scattered around her feet, she'd been there for a while. Emmeline had vaguely expected piles of papers or stacks of weapons, but there was nothing but the woman in the chair, a table with a pot of tea, and a fireplace. A long strip of parchment hung on the wall beside the table, with writing in the script of the city beyond the plains. A souvenir of this woman's travels? Emmeline felt a sharp stab of envy.

"You can call me Sally," the woman said. "And you're Emmeline. The charm patcher with moral scruples. We saw you coming, you know, 's why we let you in." She snorted. "We've got your patches, too, remember. And young folk with good eyesight."

"Joe," Emmeline said. "They've taken Joe."

"Yes," Sally said. "A sad thing, for certain, but nothing to be done."

"Why not?" Emmeline demanded.

"Cost too high. How many would it take to get him out? What would they do when they realised who took him? We can't take that risk for the rest."

"So you're just going to leave him?" Emmeline's stomach churned.

"Joe knew the rules." She looked at Emmeline for a moment, then offered, "He might get away with a flogging."

"And he might not." They'd been cracking down harder, or late.

"Like I say. He knew the risk." She looked at Emmeline. "Just like you choose your risks."

She held Emmeline's gaze for a moment, then looked away, drawing her attention inwards; an obvious dismissal. Emmeline stood for a moment, helpless and frustrated, then clenched her hands and turned to go. There was no help here.

"I'm glad you came, though," Sally said, as Emmeline reached the door.

Emmeline paused. "Yes?"

"Those charm-patches. You've made all the difference for us. I wanted to thank you."

If only that had done Joe any good.

"If you were to need somewhere to go," Sally said. "You know where we are."

"Just not if I were arrested," Emmeline said.

"No," Sally agreed. "Not for that."

Emmeline struggled with her thoughts, on her way back through the streets. She still agreed with the aims of the Masquerade, right enough. One part of the city throwing their wealth around while the rest scraped for pennies, that wasn't right. But the dull side of the mirror, where you abandoned a person for the sake of the cause, well...

It was too hard to swallow.

●

By the time she got back to the workshop, she had half of a plan in mind; and no time to do anything but hope that the rest appeared as she went along.

She worked quickly, cannibalising the row of hangers with completed or half-completed customer orders. She pulled down the gossamer-thin petticoat of Plausibility, designed to fit under Mlle Yara's Solstice ball gown. Emmeline had never managed to work Plausibility into a patch; it tore and frayed easily enough that sewing it straight from the bolt was a challenge. The petticoat would have been long on petite Mlle Yara; on Emmeline it came only to mid-calf, and a couple of rolls of the waistband brought it up enough to hide it under her outer skirt. She held it together with a chain of safety-pins, and kept rifling through the wardrobe.

Major Arad's undershirt of Luck, awaiting its buttons; the only piece of Luck that had come her way in the last couple of years. People were superstitious about Luck; they preferred heirloom garments and keepsakes. It wasn't done to rely on it too much, either. Emmeline had carefully tucked away the few fragments of scraps that she'd come by, but there was no time to do anything with them now. She pulled the big undershirt on and shrugged her blouse back on over it, frowning at the way the undershirt bagged out the blouse. But she would be wearing a coat over it, and she found it hard to believe that the guards at the prison would have an eye for fashion. It would pass.

She tucked a couple of things into her bag, then found herself packing up the roll of her best dressmaker's tools, the ones that she would save if the shop were on fire. She paused, wondering what she was doing. The undershirt shifted against her skin, and she breathed in, slowly, and let her hands do what they would. It would be foolish to carry the purse of her leaving funds through the streets; but she found herself hanging it under her skirts. At the last moment, she thrust the tiny Memory bag, the one that had started it all, into her skirt pocket, then let herself out of the house.

Jimmy the Cart wasn't at his workshop in the next street. She could hear voices raised around the corner. She bit her lip for a moment, then ducked in. When she came out again, an observer, if they looked carefully, might have noticed her moving just a very little stiffly.

The prison was a ten minute walk. She knew the streets were heavily patrolled here, but as she walked, they seemed oddly deserted. She let her feet navigate automatically through twists and turns that her conscious mind wouldn't have taken, pausing for a moment then moving again, feeling the shift of the undershirt as she went.

There was one, young, harried-looking lieutenant on duty at the prison, who peered at her from behind the barred door.

"Go away, miss," he said before she could say anything.

"I told your officer I would be back," she said, calling on her best haughty tones, "and I am. You must let me in to see Joe Bones."

"Miss," the lieutenant said. "I ain't letting anyone in to see anyone. It's late, miss, and you would be best back in your home, miss."

"I have a letter from Lady Wirral for the prisoner," she said, drawing herself even more upright, feeling the petticoat against her legs, "and I must deliver it, or she will want to know why."

There was obvious anguish in the young lieutenant's face. Everyone knew Lady Wirral. She had *opinions* about prisons. Emmeline made nice robust walking-clothes for her to go and harass the prison officers in.

"Let me in right away," she said, "and I won't mention to Lady Wirral — or to your superior officer — that you delayed me."

The lieutenant swallowed — Emmeline wasn't sure who was the bigger threat — then backed away a bit from the barred aperture. With clankings and clatterings, the door creaked open a bare couple of inches.

"There, miss."

Emmeline hoped desperately that he wouldn't ask to inspect the sealed envelope she was brandishing, but her Luck held.

Joe was peering through the barred window of his cell, looking out at the city. He spun round when the lieutenant unlocked the cell door, opened his mouth, then shut it again until they'd been left alone.

"Emmeline..." he started, sounding anxious.

Emmeline was already reaching up under her skirts, uncoiling the length of rope she'd wound round her waist and legs, and the cart-jack she'd strapped onto one leg. There were two matching patches of raw skin, top and bottom, where it had very nearly slipped down.

Joe blinked at her, wide-eyed.

"I assume you didn't want to stay here," Emmeline said.

"But the Masquerade..." Joe started. "People don't *get* let out. It's too risky."

"I'm not here for the Masquerade," Emmeline said briskly. "This is purely a personal endeavour."

"But..."

Emmeline could see, suddenly, the shape of Joe's worry. That, inevitably, the blame would be laid at their door; that the consequences would follow them, would smother the rebellion, exactly the way the group were trying to avoid by abandoning anyone who was caught.

But she couldn't leave Joe here.

She swallowed. "Don't worry," she said. "I'll make sure that doesn't happen. I'll make sure they know where to put the blame. Now, for pity's sake, you need to *go*."

She went to the window, fitted the cart-jack in between the two bars, and began winding, grunting a little with the effort as it began to bite into the bars. After a moment, Joe stepped up and took over. Emmeline shook out her skirts, then squeezed in beside Joe to tie the rope onto another bar.

It took surprisingly little time before there was enough of a gap for skinny Joe to slide through. Emmeline leant out to watch him shinning quickly down the rope. When he was nearly at the bottom, she took a deep breath, squared her shoulders, and marched out of the cell. At the lieutenant's little room, she insisted that he make a record of her visit, with her name and address nice and clear, and whom she had visited. All the while he was writing, her neck prickled with anticipation of a shout, someone realising Joe had gone. The undershirt, despite its softness, prickled against her skin.

She marched out of the door once he was done, head held high; then took to her heels and ran.

●

She fetched up at one of the outer bridges over the river, most of the way to the city limits. It was late; the houses along the riverside were quiet.

The water flowed under the bridge, ripples gilded with moonlight. Flowing out of the city, away past the foot of the mountains and onward to the distant sea that she'd seen only on maps. Her eyes rose upwards to the mountains themselves and to the pass the Guisers came over. How *did* they make the stuff? The world was so much *bigger* than this one small city.

She couldn't go back to the shop, now. She might have protected the Masquerade — she certainly hoped so — but that was the cost of it. What now?

She felt the weight of the purse holding her leaving fund, hanging from her belt. She'd been intending to stay until Joe was through his apprenticeship; but that tie was gone too. She could just leave, finally, like she'd planned. She should have given Joe the key to the shop. There was a lot of charmcloth there, kept safe under lock and key. Someone could use that.

She thought of Granny Zeta, of all the Granny Zetas. She thought of the Masquerade, and whom they sacrificed for what. In her head, she heard Sally — *you know where we are* — and across the other side of her belt from her purse, she felt the weight of her dressmaker's roll. Her tools. She'd been doing good work, here. She'd been helping.

Her hand stole into her pocket, to the little bag that had started everything, feeling the hard lump of the old thimble inside it. But this time the memories of her grandfather that sprang to life weren't of him at home with her. They were of him working in the doorway of the shop and greeting everyone who passed; of how often he invited someone who was struggling to share their dinner; of the hundred little generosities which meant people like Granny Zeta remembering him with such warmth.

She looked, for another longing moment, up at the mountains. Somewhere new. Somewhere with no responsibility save for herself.

Somewhere she'd always know that she'd turned her back and walked away.

She took a deep breath, and turned, and walked back into the city.

Juliet Kemp's story "Scraps" was originally published in Metaphorosis on Friday, 7 April 2017. See magazine.metaphorosis.com

About the author

Juliet Kemp (they/them) is a queer, non-binary, writer. They live in London by the river, with their partners, kid, and dog. The first book of their fantasy series, *The Deep And Shining Dark,* was on the Locus 2018 Recommended Reads list; the fourth and final book, *The City Revealed,* came out in 2023. Their short fiction has appeared in venues including *Uncanny, Analog,* and *Cast of Wonders*. They were short-listed for the WSFA Small Press Award in 2020 and 2023, and had a story in the 2021 Lambda Awards shortlisted anthology *Trans-Galactic Bike Ride*.

When not writing or child-wrangling, Juliet knits, indulges their fountain pen habit, and tries to fit an ever-increasing number of plants into a microscopic back garden. They can be found at julietkemp.com or on Bluesky as @julietk.bsky.social.

We, You, and the Gallery

Alex Penland

We had thought ourselves safe, but then you found us in our little ship. There was a thrilling chase. In our desperation, we flew too fast and crashed, and you crashed too. Now we and you are both stranded on this empty, alien world. We do not know if you have survived. We know that only one of us remains, but we are still *we*, even when most of us are gone.

In your language, we believe, you sometimes say silence is *deafening*, but our experience is incongruous with that. The silence brings horrible clarity. In it, we are aware of the breathing which does not accompany our own, of the footsteps which do not fall around us, of the conversations which do not linger in our periphery. The silence is an illumination of all that we have lost.

We have buried the others by the cavern entrance. It is our hope that their decomposition will bring life to the dust of this barren world. Even near the subterranean spring there is nothing living here. No fish. No insects. No bacteria. Our scanners show a frustrating level of microbial safety.

●

It is there, by the spring, that we first speak to you. Your species needs water as desperately as ours does. Like us, you must have salvaged what you could from the wreckage and taken shelter in the caverns.

We do not know where you have hidden, but it's you who cries out—"Who's there?"—when we cause a thoughtless splash against the silence.

We are momentarily afraid, but we do not see you. The cavern is small; water rushes from one fissure into another. The only other point of entrance is the way from which we came. But for your voice, we seem to be alone.

"Where are you?" we ask. There are several sounds: one of your weapons firing, then the crumbling of rock, then a series of words my translator does not choose to divulge.

We think we understand. There is a phenomenon within caves: the chance alignment of reflective surfaces allows for sound to travel very far and very clearly. This must be the case now. You are not in the same cavern as we are; you might be miles away. You might be on the other side of the wall. There is no way of telling.

We test this by stepping briskly to the side. Your cursing fades to nothingness. When we return to the spot where we stood, your voice returns as well.

"It's a whispering gallery," we say into the anomaly. You stop shooting the walls.

"So you don't know where I am?"

"No."

"Great! So we can negotiate."

We're struck by your audacity. "Negotiate what?"

"Resources. Surrender. I don't know. How many of you are there?"

"We don't think we should say."

"Is that plural pronoun your hive-mind thing or does that mean there's more than one of you?"

We do not answer that.

"Well, assuming you're not alone, you got a resources issue. I got plenty of food, you know. Plus, I think I can get us outta here if you ask nice. You lot surrender and I'll get you a cushy cell 'til the war ends, I promise."

We do not answer that, either.

"Listen, it's better than dying out here, ain't it?"

"It is." We feel very alone. We wish desperately for our company, for the ability to talk this through together, but there is nothing to be done about that. "It is better than dying out here. Why would you bother to rescue us?"

This time you're the silent one.

"You need us alive," we say. "You need help too. We have no proof that you can help us. We have no proof that you will not slaughter us. So no, we do not surrender, and we will not tell you our location."

We step away from the gallery before we hear your reply. There is much to do; we have a ship to scavenge, inventory to document, plans to make. Possibly we have defenses to build. You are correct—we cannot survive here forever—but that does not mean we plan to die here, at either your hands or starvation's.

The room with the gallery is also the most defensible, and there is a nearby chamber that is cold enough for storage. We decide eventually to make this room our base, though during the process of moving supplies we make quite a lot of purposeful noise. You think we are numerous, after all.

Here it is dark and smells of sterile clay. Cool. Humid. The dead rock of the cavern is as much an absence as our silence. We ache for the fresh vegetation of home; the life in the air and the scent of the flowers.

But we cannot mourn. There is work to do.

●

Occasionally we see you. Once, while we deconstruct the refrigeration chamber in the wreckage of the ship, we spot your outline on a distant hill.

That night you say, "I saw one of you on the wreckage," and we reply that yes, you did, and hope you ask no further questions.

Once, when we venture out to scout a location for a distress signal, we find a machine of some sort, gathering sunlight. We steal it. That night you ask, "Did you steal one of my water purifiers?" and we reply that yes, we did.

Then we think it over. Perhaps you do not have the same access to water that we do. Perhaps you were unlucky. We feel a bit guilty. A few days later we return the machine without comment.

"What did you do to it?" you ask. We do not answer.

Once, we hear you crying.

We do not cry, though we have studied the phenomenon in school, so, although it takes a moment, we understand the sound. In your language, the convulsive gasp is a signal of despair. We do not think you meant to share it with us.

"Are you in distress?" we ask. You stop crying, or perhaps you move from the spot. You never respond to the question. We do not ask again.

●

One day we return to the wreckage site and you are standing there, arms crossed, waiting for us. You're male. Human, of course. Not as young as we thought you'd be, nor as well-armed. There's a pistol at your hip—it still smells of gunpowder from your duel with the cavern walls—but your ammunition belt is empty. Its grip is visible from your holster; the clip gauge on the side is blank. If you possess firepower, you possess only the shot in the chamber.

"Every time I see you out here, it's just you."

We are frozen to our location. We meet your eyes.

"You're alone, ain't you? You were lying. No one else survived the crash."

We hardly breathe.

"You had me pretty fooled. I was impressed." You hold out your hand. Are we supposed to shake it? We don't shake it. "I'm Edwin. You got a name?"

"Do your fingertips have names?" we ask. "Do your hands?"

"I call 'em Left and Right, generally. So... no? No name?"

"No name."

"Why do you say *we*?"

"Your hand is still your hand, even if we were to cut it from your body."

You nod. You glance behind yourself, back towards the way we suspect you came. "I'm gonna call you Honeybee."

"What?"

"You're a hive alien. You look like bees. You ever see a bee?"

"We are not a bee."

"I'm not saying you are. It's just a name. I gotta call you something. Like it or not, we're both stuck here."

We aren't opposed to names, really. Our opposition is to *you*, not your customs. Honeybee. Hm. "Are we? Didn't you say you had a way out?"

"Thought I did. Turned out I didn't."

"Hm." We lean next to you against the ship. "Neither do we. What was your plan?"

"Originally I was gonna steal components off your ship, but then you gave me back the water purifier." You sigh. "You ain't gonna surrender. I sure as hell ain't gonna surrender. So what now?"

"You have food, but no water?" we ask.

"Yup."

"We have water, but our food is running out. In our language, we say that it is better to die as a community than to live a longer life alone." By the odd look you give us, we suspect you understand the situational irony. "By this we mean that we risk a shortened life by offering to trust you, but if we rely only on ourself, our expiration date is certain."

You work through that for a moment. "You suggesting we share?"

"Yes. Return here tomorrow. We will bring you water."

"And then what?"

We shrug. "Show us your resources. Show us your ship. We're making the choice to trust you. Trust us in return, and we'll plan our escape together."

You look surprised, and a little wary, but you offer us your hand again. This time we do shake it.

"All right," you say. "Good to meet you, Honeybee."

"Good to meet you, Edwin."

●

This is what you possess: a truly massive cache of rations (roughly half of which are toxic to our biology, which makes division simple), three water purifiers, and half a ship. You do not have the same electrical and engineering knowledge that we do, and we suspect that you would simply have stranded us both if you tried to dismantle our ship to fix your own. You need us more than we need you, we think.

"There are elements we can work with," we say, perusing your technology, "but it's going to take a while. We'll be in a race for time with food."

"And by we, you mean you."

"Unless you can learn engineering on the fly." You laugh. "I have another job for you. As your rations consist of processed bars—"

"Don't give me that judgy tone."

"—*they cannot be farmed*, whereas our rations contain seeds, and likewise will rot sooner. We suggest that you attempt to farm some of our rations while we repair your ship, and that we subsist on your rations in the meantime. Our food grows quickly. It's meant for this exact scenario."

"We're repairing my ship?"

"Ours has been stripped more thoroughly. We believe yours is a more functional base." We replace the panel we were inspecting and stand to meet your eyes. "We are risking quite a lot to help you, Edwin. We understand that humanity is... individualistic..."

"We comprise individuals, yeah."

"And it is out of respect for you, as an individual, that we are trusting you will not make the same collective choice as your species."

You frown.

"Namely, that you will not choose war. That you will treat us, together, as a collective for the time being. Our good will be your good. Your good will be our good. We will become a community, not a pair of individuals at war."

"You know we have communities back home, yeah? I ain't unfamiliar with the concept."

"As far as we can tell, your hives are constantly in swarm."

You pause, then laugh. "Fair point. I won't screw you over. I'll even let you go free. When we get this fixed we head to the nearest neutral world and part ways. On my word, all right?"

We wince. We do not like the idea of landing on a neutral world, especially not alone. They are dangerous and unpredictable in their diversity. "Forgive us, please, but your word means very little. We will trust in cause and effect."

"What?"

"We will see what happens and how you react. We will see how you respond to the situation we have found ourselves in. As time passes, we will learn the mark you choose to leave upon the world. This is the information we need in order to determine the value of your word."

"Again—what?"

"Trust takes time, Edwin. We simply do not know you yet. This is a dangerous decision, but one we are making consciously. Do not attempt to put us at ease with promises we have no way of validating."

You shrug, scratch your neck, survey the desolation of our surroundings. "All right. Guess I can't blame you for that."

●

Time occurs. Days pass, then weeks. You are proving to be an adept farmer, particularly when faced with our fast-growing crops. Our rations are quick and hardy—they can be grown nearly anywhere, and the sweet resin which compacts them doubles as nutrition for whatever soil one can find. Like us, they are less tolerant to heat, but there is a cavern protected from the midday sun that still has some ambient light. We cart in sand from the surface.

The first harvest, one month in, allows us to set aside the remaining ration bars for an emergency supply. The second harvest, two weeks later, allows us to dry fruit for storage. By the third, we have more food than we can eat.

We begin to enjoy our meals together. At first, this is only in shared spaces—the ship, or sometimes outdoors when the weather is bearable.

Over time, however, you introduce us slowly to your space. You reveal that you have inhabited a cave on the far side of the hill. We suspect that you did not survey your surroundings when you crashed, but rather picked a direction to walk in and colonized the first cave you found. It is not nearby. It is not easily defensible. It is well-hidden, to your credit, but only because no tactical mind would choose to hide there.

We do not tell you this. Instead we express our honor when we are allowed to observe the mementos tucked beside your bed, the books piled in corners, the stringed instrument you rescued from the wreckage. It is not clean. The odor of your dirty laundry makes our antennae curl.

Yet you have built furniture: a desk, a lifted bed, storage in unexpected places. It is more confined than our cavern, but you have built an ingenious home in very little space. We are fascinated.

We are also often frustrated, though somehow not by you. When working, we are challenged by the incompatibilities between our two technologies. While hardware is obedient under the pressure of brute force, software is less pliable. Our universal translator is decidedly unhelpful when it comes to programming languages—as are you.

Today, as I swear at the translator, you don't offer to assist; you watch and laugh until we enter a command. The engine roars threateningly, which stops your teasing.

"Are you wasting fuel at me, Honeybee?"

"You can laugh, or you can help."

You're about to respond, but there's a jolt against the side of the ship that has nothing to do with software. You're at the window before we can turn around. The sand on the ground is blowing. The wind's picked up.

In the distance the air has begun to shimmer: heat. Intense, visible heat. You stick your head out the door to observe and burn your hand on the outer wall of the ship. A smell of singed flesh flashes through the bridge. Another untranslatable word—you duck back in.

"Hey, Honeybee, got a fun fact for ya. My life support's down."

"We are aware." We're trying to assess if we've fixed that yet. The translator is currently displaying the code in front of us as a list of various species of snake.

"Did you fix it?"

"We... aren't sure."

"You think we can make it to a cave from here?"

"We aren't sure, Edwin."

"Well, when you gonna know?" We open our mouth to respond. You don't let us say it again. "Right. Come on. We're making a break for the caves. Now."

We look up from the computer. You're holding out a hand, halfway out the door already.

"Come on. I ain't leaving without you."

"Is it close enough? Will we make it?"

"I ain't sure."

●

The storm is at our back. We try to fly you, to move more quickly, but our wings blister when they spread. When the pair of us dive into the caverns we are afraid, for a moment, that they will not provide adequate protection, but you drag us further below the surface and pat out the charring on our clothes. We press ourself against the cool ground and shiver. In your language you would say we are 'gasping for air'. We are not sure that this translates directly to our circulatory system, but the intent behind the words is accurate.

We suspect you are more resilient to heat than we are. You are leaning against the wall, sweating, breathing, staring at the inferno that rages outside.

It becomes slowly apparent to us that you have led us to our cave, not yours. It was the closer of the two dwellings; it was also a tactical mistake, to bring yourself to our territory. The action suggests trust. Behind the dull exhaustion of the heat, we are conflicted.

"Think we've figured out why nothing lives here, Honeybee."

We nod, still fragile from the storm.

"You all right?"

We haul ourself to a sitting position. It seems dangerous to tell you that we are vulnerable to temperatures—we do not know what information will be reported to your superiors. To risk our life is one thing; to put all of us at risk is another. And yet you chose our survival over your advantage.

"Bee, look at me."

But we are weak. We feel a strange, trembling headache, and our body is enervated. When we look at you we do not register your expression. When we fall, we do not register your catching us. The world fades.

●

There is a sound of rushing water.

We have cooled significantly. Before we open our eyes we can feel our hands and feet are submerged, though our body lies on cold stone. We realize what has happened—you have saved our life, at least temporarily. We had overheated; now we have cooled.

We have perhaps cooled too much. We sit up, slowly, battling the lethargy in our joints. Heat makes us weak; cold makes us heavy. Our blood feels like syrup in our veins.

You made a fire some time ago; it has now dwindled into embers. The smoke still trails along the ceiling, leaving chemical traces in the air. You yourself are currently sleeping on my bed, having covered yourself in empty ration canvas to keep in the heat from your warm-blooded body.

Unlike you, Edwin, we do not generate heat well. Our bodies are more vulnerable to environmental conditions. We need warmth. Unthinking, we crawl across the cavern—we do not have the strength to walk—and bury ourself in the bed beside you. When we rest our forehead on your back, you are like a lantern on a cold and unforgiving night. Then you turn in your sleep and wrap your arms around us, and the lantern blossoms into the sun.

●

When we wake again, you have rekindled the fire (we wonder how long you searched for our fire kit, how long it took you to recognize it for what it was) and you are cooking fruit on a griddle. The cavern smells like toasted sugar, tart and syrupy. We lay here quietly, watching the scene.

You do not seem alien to us in this moment. You are humming an alien tune, tapping the matte luster of your fingers on alien knees, but there is a familiarity in the domesticity of cooking. We are reminded of morning meals in the cafeteria hall, of baking and frying-up in our rotations of a dozen-or-so individuals. We are reminded of the easy chemistry between ourselves, of the casual warmth and connection of the collective.

We are momentarily and intensely homesick.

"Hey, Honeybee. You alive over there?"

You've noticed. We nod, reluctant to leave the lingering comfort of the bed. We think our thermoregulation has balanced itself, but this is comfortable, and we are very tired.

"You had me worried."

"We were very lucky you knew how to do first aid." We were, in fact, surprised. You knew to put our hands and feet in the water; if you had placed our body, as human anatomy directs, we would have drowned. "How did you know how to save us?"

"I'm military, Bee. We do get training."

"In human medicine, certainly. We are not human."

"We get alien basics, too. You know we've got some of you lot on our side, right? Defectors. Not everyone loves the hive."

The horror is plain on our face, or perhaps the despair.

"Don't look at me like that! We treat 'em right. If someone wants to be an individual, let 'em."

"We simply cannot imagine the desire." There is a spot near the fire where you have folded a mat for us to sit on, and we sit there now. "Having lost our connection to the hive, we cannot fathom the decision one must make to leave willingly. One would lose everything."

"How can you know that? You don't know their whole situation. You don't know what they've been through."

"We have lost everything, Edwin."

"Ah. Right. Sorry." You pause. "You ain't alone. Uh. Lost my own family to a hive attack."

"Did you?"

"It was years ago, so... You know. War's not... great."

You clear your throat uncomfortably. I change the subject.

"Arrowfruit tastes quite good when paired with redspice."

"What?"

"What you're cooking. Arrowfruit. We believe there is some redspice left in the stores—"

"That's what, the red powder?"

"Purple, actually. The name misleads."

We retrieve the bag, and the pair of us begin to cook together.

●

That first day of the storm, once we have eaten and checked the status of the weather, we take stock together of what we possess.

There are enough rations to get us through quite some time. Together we venture closer to the entrance to check on the crops; their cavern is much warmer than it has been previously, but not so warm as to cause them harm. We have water from the spring. We are not sure how long the storm will last, but our basic needs for survival are met.

Next, comfort. We are in our own territory, but you only have what you've carried in your bag. It is admittedly heavy, but it is always on your person and you tend to carry your tools with you: a small multi-device you call a *pocket knife*, extra rations in case you were to become stuck somewhere for a while, and most importantly a spare set of clothes.

You chuckle at our visible relief. "What, you don't like how I smell?"

"We were taking into consideration that your living quarters smell quite strongly of human body odor."

"It's not like I got a shower in there!"

"And do you have a similar excuse for your ship?" Our antennae curl. "We understand that you have a dulled sense of smell. We can forgive that. We're simply appreciative that we won't have to live with it."

"It ain't that bad."

"Not to you."

You also have a deck of playing cards.

You attempt to teach us the game of *poker*, which does not go particularly well. When you run out of the pebbles you've insisted on gambling with, we offer you some of ours. We receive in turn a lecture on how we are missing the point, to which we reply we have clearly won the game and ask how much of the point we can possibly be missing, and it is at this point that you decide to find a project rather than a game to play.

The phrase in your language is *sore loser.*

You decide to 'spruce up' our living space, starting with the bed. We have been sleeping on a pile of mats, which is quite comfortable, but—

"Listen, if I'm staying here, I ain't sleepin' on the floor. I'm making you a bedframe."

Implicit in this decision is the implication that we will be sharing a bed again. We are not sure how we feel about that assumption. Certainly it was comfortable. Certainly you did not kill us in our sleep, or in our illness, and you had the chance to do so. Your gun lies near the cavern entrance, a single shot still loaded in the chamber.

And yet we wonder whether bed-sharing contains the same implications for you as it does for us—do your people cluster the way we do? Do your people bond together, form lifelong connections? Or are your romances as individualistic and flighty as the rest of your culture? Are you, Edwin, like the rest of your people? Is there even something that can be defined as 'the rest of your people'? Are we simply overthinking things?

"We are not ectothermic," we explain eventually, watching you consolidate supplies and tear apart crates. "We are capable of sleeping alone if you wish to bed down elsewhere."

You shrug. "It's no bother."

"Are you sure?"

" 'Course."

And the matter is settled.

On the second day of the storm, we teach you our games. We spend some time carving a set of horribly unbalanced dice from spare parts of the bed project, then show you how to use them. You enjoy dare-dice best, where we take turns suggesting a task and then roll to see who must perform it.

The game is generally used to allocate horrible chores back home, but we are stuck in a small and mostly-featureless room, and so dares quickly become questions.

We begin to learn about each other.

The weirdest thing you've ever eaten: sawdust, when you were in particularly dire straits on a survivalist training exercise.

The most memorable dream we've ever had: it occurred the night before we began our military training, when we dreamed we were a comet sailing peacefully through the universe. When we awoke, we had a distinct memory of a bright light on a horizon that could not have existed, and a longing for understanding that would never come.

Your childhood dream: you wanted to be a space pirate.

Our favorite color: starlight. Pale and shining flecks against the black.

Your most embarrassing moment: you were a child. Your older sister once called you *Ed-lose*, and it upset you so much you cried and threw up your dinner. You no longer speak with your sister, but you insist that is not the primary reason.

You ask us what we would have done if we had not joined the military, which is confusing. Then it occurs to us that you believe that soldiers are different from ordinary citizens. We find this disheartening. If your citizens are not the same as those who fight, and your people are individuals, how can you truly understand the cost of war?

"Maybe," you say. "But I think if I weren't in the military I'd be something real dull, which, well, I guess some people might want to do that with their lives."

"Why was this the life you chose?" we ask, abandoning the dice. "Why would anyone choose war?"

You're quiet about that for a while, leaning back against the cavern wall. For a little bit the only sounds are those of the subterranean spring and the distant chaos of the storm. We allow you your time to think, observing you instead. We have become familiar with your face, with the softness of your body. Your appearance has begun to bring us comfort, and that is a frightening thing.

We wonder if perhaps others have not abandoned their communities, but simply chosen new ones.

"I didn't really choose it," you admit. "The military's a shit job, so people in shit situations are the ones who sign up. You get a good deal—good money, good education, good place to lay your head. I didn't have any of that when I signed up. I do now. Not sure it's worth the golden chains, though."

"Do you regret it?"

"I did." There's an invisible edge to your answer, somehow. Something clinging behind the words, something which makes our back flutter, which brings a shiver to our fingertips.

We lean forward. "Do you regret it now?"

"You know, Honeybee? I ain't sure."

●

The storm rages on. Days blend together. Time passes.

At night we sleep encircled in the safety of your arms. At first we refuse to talk about this during the day, but then you put your arm around us in a moment of sympathy, and we lean our head on your shoulder, and the physical barrier is broken. What was relegated to sleep becomes common. We sit together. We eat together.

We are no longer alone.

●

We are awoken by a faint and repeated alarm. We roll over, bleary, to ask you if you recognize the signal. You are not there.

We sit up. We are surprised and a little confused.

The situation makes more sense once we realize the noise is coming from the whispering gallery, and once we realize we can no longer hear the storm outside. It is one of your devices, then, and the world outside is safe for passage. You have returned to your cavern to retrieve it. There is nothing suspicious or unexpected about that.

And so we take the time to think.

This bond we've formed with you, whatever it may be— we know it's doomed. We asked you to consider our pair as a community, and while we meant that, it was not intended to be mutual. For us to consider you the same is—

It's dangerous. There is no other word for it. We do not part from our community, and upon leaving we must part from you. You have shown no inclination towards joining our hive; we cannot bear to join your swarm. There is no future in which we stay together.

And yet we lie back down and soak in the warmth you left behind. The echo of footsteps that are not there have grown softer in your presence. The silence is no longer intrusive. We cannot deny the change.

Last night you placed your hand on our chest and asked us where our heartbeat was. When we didn't know what you were talking about, you placed *our* hand on *your* chest in demonstration. We laughed; we told you how we have a dozen small hearts down our abdomen, explained our circular breathing. Wasn't that covered in your training? But you say you only learned the protocol, not the biology.

You placed your hand upon each heart of ours and felt its rhythm. You called us fascinating. You called us beautiful.

Love is a state of neutrality in the hive. We are always perfectly in sync; it is the glue which seals our metaphorical cells, a propolis of the soul. We join sometimes—mostly in twos, sometimes more—but to do so is to entwine two threads within the greater aegis of the soul. Beautiful, yes, divine, but not a source of conflict.

We are accustomed to love, accustomed to connection, and yet somehow entirely unsettled by the feelings you inspire in us. When we speak, we argue as much as we admire; when we fight we are drawn together more than we are repulsed. Everything you are opposes the virtues we were raised on, and yet this only seems to draw us closer.

We asked you, yesterday, what your greatest childhood fear had been. You said: us. The hive. We were the ones who killed your family. (Just as you killed ours. We have forgiven, not forgotten.) But you are no longer afraid.

We are. We are terrified.

We do not want to leave this community.

We do not want to leave you.

●

We have drifted back to sleep again. This time we are awoken by your distant voice, and this time you are not alone.

"Sorry," you say through the gallery echo, "I didn't quite catch that. Can you state your name and ID again?"

"This is Jeffrey Reynolds, ID 809192-9."

"Hey there, Jeff. Good to hear your voice, it's been a hot minute out here."

"We got your distress call, Ed. What happened? We thought you were a goner."

"Oh, nothing too special. Took a dumb chance chasing some..." You hesitate. We know your language. We can hear the habitual use of *bugs* on your lips, and we hear you repress it. "Took a dumb chance on a chase and we both crashed."

"Any bugs get out?"

You hesitate. We understand. You can tell them we all died, and we would be safe. We could leave on the repaired ship and this man could send rescue for you. But we suspect you want us to defect, that you do not want to part ways either. You will want to know what our options are.

"Yeah," you say. "The crash didn't get 'em all. But don't you worry, we're all gettin' on good. Say Jeff, you know how the asylum process works? Think I'd be able to offer my friends here a deal?"

"Sure, probably. Citizenship in exchange for time served against the Hive. Standard." We can hear the disgust in your friend's tone. "Sure happy to turn a blind eye if you squash the bastards before we get there, though. All those legs. Ugh. Freaks me out."

"Well, guess we have differing opinions on that." Your voice has gone cold, polite. "What would asylum look like?"

"Can't say as for sure, man. Tell you what, send me your coordinates and I'll make sure there's a specialist on board, huh? Give 'em a good deal?"

"Certainly." You pause again. "Uh, you know what, Jeff, I gotta go find those coordinates exactly, they're still on my ship. I'll get 'em back to you soon, yeah?"

"You don't have them with you?" Jeff's surprise is warranted. You absolutely have them with you. You are likely looking at them, taped to your cavern wall, right in your eyeline. "Right. Yeah. Sure. You can leave the signal on too and we can track—"

There is an audible click.

"Turned it off," you say. "I can't bear that guy. You catch all that, Honeybee?"

"We did."

We are aware you could have deceived us. We can think of a dozen ways that conversation could be faked, and a dozen reasons why. We think of the round you left in the chamber. The gun is with us now; you did not bring it with you when you went to answer the call.

You are an individual; this does not mean your choices are selfish. You have chosen only once to cause us harm, before you knew us. You have kept us safe a dozen times since. Time has passed, and we have seen the mark you choose to leave upon the world.

We pick up your weapon and turn it over in our hands. It has never been used for violence against us. You are the only thing which has been profaned in such a way.

We say: "We do not wish to join your military."

"I know, Honeybee. Just wanted to know what our options were." You exhale. "I don't want to fight my people either."

"And similarly, you would be required to if you joined us."

"Of course." You're quiet again for a moment, thinking. "Before we make a decision, we should check the ship. See what damage the heat did. See if we have any other choice, you know?"

We stand together in front of the ship.

It's fine.

It's absolutely fine.

Our ship—that is, the hive ship—has melted irreparably. It is a twisted and deformed hunk of metal and wax, a final monument to those of us who died in its crash. Eventually, future storms will smear it across the face of the planet, and it will be gone forever.

But your ship? Your ship is pristine.

"How?" you ask. We are already climbing in through the hatch, assessing. "What did you do to it? It looks better than when we left it—"

"It's not better," we say, "but it appears we did, in fact, fix the life support before the storm hit. The interior was able to protect itself. We had also connected our shields with yours, and that seems to have been a miraculous success, though it's built to withstand far more intense heat on atmospheric interaction."

"Well, that's good."

"In fact," — we peer out from the hatch again — "we think our work is done."

"Done?"

"Done. Complete. The ship is low on fuel, there are a dozen bugs in the software, but we believe a trip to the nearest neutral planet would be viable."

You're staring at us.

"Edwin?"

"So that's it?" you ask.

"What?"

"You're leaving?" There's a panicked shiver to your voice.

"We didn't say that. We said the ship is viable. We..." We leave the words unspoken. We aren't sure what we were going to say, anyway. "There are decisions to be made, that's all."

"Yeah." You glance up at the sky. It's brightening; a brilliant blue after the firestorm.

We hesitate before speaking again. "We do not wish to part ways, Edwin."

You exhale. "No. We don't."

"And yet we don't wish to fight our own people."

"No, we don't."

We sit on the ground, leaning against the ship, looking out at the wasteland that has become something like a home. Your breathing is slow and even; mine is a low hum against a background breeze. Our hands brush accidentally. We exchange a glance of quiet desolation.

"We wonder when you started referring to us as a plural."

You roll your eyes.

"You think of us as a pair."

"Yeah, I do. Don't you?"

We close our eyes, thinking of our past pairings, thinking of the hive. We nod. We think perhaps that the two of us are more a pair than any other person we have loved. It is a dangerous thought.

"Listen," you say, "I don't know how they do this in the hive. I don't know if you just... love free, or only love your queen, or how it works, but humans, when we choose someone else— Well, we got a thousand different ways to fall in love, but where I'm from it's usually just... We pick the other individual we love best, and we make our choices from there."

To be loved best seems impossible. One is not meant to be loved best. One is meant to sacrificed for all, not sacrificed for. The image of the pair of us in our patchwork ship, running from our people, hiding out in the wild diversity of the neutral planets—it surfaces in our mind and we cannot dislodge it.

We imagine what it would be like, to travel the stars and trust only in each other. We imagine love rife with conflict and passion. We imagine life, free and forlorn but never lonely.

Never lonely. Not with you.

We cannot bear to open our eyes, to see the look upon your face. Perhaps it is not as desperately fond as your voice; perhaps there is not the same helpless affection. Perhaps you are lying. We could not survive it, if you were lying. We have changed too much by loving you to be the person that we were.

"And sometimes that individual changes, Honeybee, I won't lie about that. But I don't know you as the collective, right? I know you as Honeybee. And Bee, I love you best. Easily. I love you best."

We open our eyes. You are not lying. We reach out to clean the tears from your cheek. Our hand is unsteady.

"I can't fight 'em," you say, "but I can't go back, either. If we don't want to split up, if you'll have me..."

"This is our collective," we whisper. "Us."

We have buried the others by the cavern entrance. Our hive seems very far away, and you are close, and you are also fascinating, and you are also beautiful.

"Us," you say.

It is dangerous, and perhaps it is ill-advised, but you never send the coordinates to your superior. Instead, we make our preparations. You harvest the last of our crops: a bit dry, a bit small, but survivors of the storm. We gather a list of neutral planets—an eclectic bouquet of utopias and university worlds, of war-torn dust-traps and regressed historical inaccuracies, of oceans and jungles and constructed habitats. They are unpredictable, but so are you. Perhaps unpredictable does not always indicate danger.

Our first task is to repair our ship beyond a state of limping; after that, we will take to the void. We will have our choice of worlds; we will have our choice of stars.

When the time comes, we chart our course and leave.

We leave together.

●

On an abandoned, uninhabitable planet, there are several shallow graves. There is, for now, the wreckage of a single spaceship, slowly deteriorating in a harsh and unforgiving climate. In the myriad caves below the surface, there are wild fruits which drink from natural aquifers. They can be found safe in the shade, growing wherever the last traces of light will touch them.

There is a cavern. In it are the scattered traces of habitation; a charred fire pit, broken boards, a bed which was gratefully abandoned. On the wall, we have carved one message in two languages. The engravings are side by side.

We have written:

"In this place, violence was supplanted by love. May the universe share our same conclusion."

Below our message, you have fired a single shot into the wall.

Alex Penland's story "We, You, and the Gallery" was originally published in Metaphorosis on Friday, 20 January 2023. See magazine.metaphorosis.com

About the author

Alex Penland is a former museum kid. They spent their childhood running rampant through the Smithsonian museums, which kicked off an early career as a child adventurer. Alex has worked in the field with NASA scientists, linguists, and acclaimed photographers. Now a Pushcart-nominated author, Alex currently lives in Scotland while studying for a PhD in Creative Writing at the University of Edinburgh. They still run rampant, but they've breached the Smithsonian's containment.

www.AlexPenland.com, @AlexPenname

Visions for the Independent City of New York

Cidney Mayes

Addie Bell was six years old when she first held colored drawing pencils between her uncoordinated fingers and made marks on a crumbling map of the old, flooded tunnels beneath the city. It was a typical pastime for a child of her age, but looked different depending on what district of the Independent City of New York the child found themself living in. If Addie had resided in the Cloud District, she would have colored with a stylus on a tablet, swiping in a palette of pixels to drop red into the waiting outline of an apple on her device. Her street would have been clean, her clothes pristine, and the top of her house would have reached like a golden chapel into the sky. If she had lived in the Mids, Addie would have sat in a clump of other children her age, sharing supplies, and fighting over who would get to use their orange pencil to color in the sweet fruit on their alphabet worksheet. Her father would have had a blue-collar job and kept things in the Cloud District running smoothly. He would have been compensated well for his services. Instead, Addie Bell was one of the few children in the Deep, the level of the city that sat closest to the polluted water, to own such a nicety as colored pencils and thought herself very lucky to have such a treasure.

Addie's father, Charlie, was a weathered man with gnarled, arthritic hands who walked the dank streets collecting all manner of items. An accident on an oil rig had robbed him of good posture, unable to perform the necessary heavy lifting out at sea, so he walked the streets and shores looking for things to sell, objects dropped by those who lived above or washed up on the street banks with the tide. Items that would fetch a good price with the junkman were quickly sold, but occasionally he would bring home a gift to his daughter. It was just the two of them who lived in a city-appointed, wooden shack that could not keep out the damp. When he saw the pencils on a grimy street corner, fallen through a grate in the scaffolding above that held the rest of the city aloft, he pocketed them.

His daughter's rise to fame, and subsequent tragic fall, was not something he anticipated when he handed her the mildewed, tattered box of half-used drawing pencils.

Addie was fascinated with her new colors. Boxes, scraps of paper, and even the walls of their shack became her canvas, filled with faintly drawn shapes and lines. She knew that it would be very hard for her father to find more of the magic pencils, so she used them lightly, delicately, leaving whispers of luminous color one might miss unless they looked carefully.

The day after her father had given her the pencils, Addie went with her neighbor, Mrs. Martinez, while her father went off to pick through flotsam. Together, Addie and Mrs. Martinez walked for half an hour up the winding, unsteady steps to the lower Mids to take their usual spot. While Mrs. Martinez, a short woman with ink-black hair and a kind face, thrust her wooden cup into the path of passersby, pleading for alms, Addie entertained herself by drawing on the cracked concrete, relishing the soft scratch of her pencil against the pebbly surface. Mrs. Martinez's benefactors were quick to give Addie a bit of their change, too, amused and maybe a little wistful that she knew nothing yet of life's hardships and cruelty. Addie accepted the coins shyly, placing them with a muted *clink* into her dress pocket.

She dutifully gave the coins to her father that night. She didn't need them. She had her magic pencils. Besides, her father used the money to buy them something good to eat. Slices of not-too moldy bread and pale cheese, which they toasted over their stove. Addie drew a picture of herself and her father, eating their cheesy toasts together, which he accepted with wet eyes and pinned to the wall of their shack.

●

Everything changed the day a city official, clothed in white and carrying a tablet that glowed blue, meandered down the street. He stopped occasionally, making notes on his screen, and commiserating with his assistant about the poor conditions of the Lower Mids. Addie watched out of the corner of her eye and noted that the hem of his pristine robe was smeared with dirt. He mumbled to his assistant, something about 'real change this term'. He stopped in front of Addie's spot and cocked his head, staring at her with the curiosity of a cat watching a fish floundering in the shallows.

Addie kept her eyes fixed on her work. She drew faces of people on the street with surety, tiny birds who rummaged through the trash bin with realistic detail, and the market streets of the Mids with captivating perspective. Her drawings had a strange, bright quality due to her odd color choices. Addie felt the hair on the back of her neck prickle as the man watched her. Finally, he cleared his throat, and asked, "Child, what is your name?"

"Addie Bell," she replied, not looking up from her work. People around them grew quiet. Mrs. Martinez clutched her wooden cup and took a few steps closer to her charge.

The city official, more astute than his peers who had never left their borough in the skies, sensed the uneasiness at his presence. The citizens were wary of his pointed interaction. "Well, Addie Bell, might I commission you to draw something for me?" He held a silver coin between two fingers. It caught the light, and the small crowd grew larger.

Addie looked up from her work then, sensing the shift in the air. Her face pinched in confusion. She had seen men in pristine, pale clothing walking in the streets every once in a great while, but never had any of them spoken to her. Nor had she ever seen a silver coin before. "I only trade for 3 coppers," she said nervously.

The crowd tittered as the city official flashed a toothy smile. Addie's cheeks flushed; her stomach flipped. She felt suddenly self-conscious. Everyone was looking at her.

"I see. This is worth two hundred coppers. If you draw what I ask for, you are welcome to keep the extra." He kept the smile plastered on his face as his assistant withdrew a smaller tablet and held it in front of her, capturing the interaction on video.

Addie looked to Mrs. Martinez for confirmation of this sum, who gave her a tight nod. "Okay. What would you like me to draw?"

"Have you ever seen the city from a distance away, where all the buildings can be seen together, reaching into the sky?"

Addie shook her head as her eyes pricked with tears. She didn't understand what the man wanted, and everyone was still staring. All she knew how to draw was what she saw, and she had no idea how to draw what he wanted.

"Let me show you." The city official swiped his fingers around his tablet and flipped it around for her to see the photo of the city's skyline.

Addie stared at the picture for thirty seconds, taking in the shapes and details of the buildings that stacked on top of one another, clawing for purchase, trying to escape the rising sea beneath them. "Okay," she said, once she had memorized all she needed to. She spread a clean sheet of paper on the concrete and began to draw, now oblivious to the swell of people around her. Addie grabbed colored pencils, seemingly at random, as the buzz from the crowd fell into the background. She used her whole arm to draw wide swaths of color, painting the sky in a frenzied rainbow, then placed the buildings against it, exactly as she had seen in the photo.

When she was done, she stood and placed her hands on her hips, scrutinizing her work. Satisfied, she handed the drawing to the city official as his assistant took a photo of the exchange. Everyone clapped politely. The city official handed the silver coin to Addie, who thought it felt very heavy, and left with his drawing. The crowd dispersed, and Addie and Mrs. Martinez bought a hearty dinner to bring home, as well as a sealed box of brand-new colored pencils which Addie clutched tightly to her chest.

The video, artfully edited by the official's press team, went viral the next day. The drawing was posted to the city official's website with the tagline *a vision of what the Independent City of New York could be.* Cloud District citizens, as well as Upper Mids, loved it. The comments poured into all social channels, hashtags trended, and approval ratings went up, up, up.

Addie was unaware that anything had changed. The next day, she and Mrs. Martinez returned to their street corner and went about their business as usual. They did not know that the city official was very astute and knew just how to keep the buzz going. He made some calls and secured for Addie Bell a scholarship to a prestigious STEAM Academy where science, technology, engineering, art, and mathematics students studied to become the next generation of city leaders.

More men wearing cloud-white uniforms appeared that afternoon, stepping out of a black car. Addie felt her stomach twist into knots as they approached. Mrs. Martinez stepped in front of her, blocking her from their view. It took some convincing for Mrs. Martinez to move aside and let them talk to the young girl. They asked where her father was, and when she told him, one of the men scrunched up his nose like he'd gotten too close to the Deep's standing water. With Addie leading them, they descended rickety stairs to the banks of the Deep.

Her father stood, arms crossed and shabby clothes hanging from his thin frame, as the official's men showed him a piece of paper with a shiny seal. They spoke of moving, of government allowances, of giving Addie *opportunity.* Addie's father stood as still as stone, distrustful. He believed it was all a sham until they showed him the viral video, and asked Addie herself. "Wouldn't you like to go to school? To take some art classes?"

Addie's eyes grew wide. She nodded, unable to speak. Mrs. Martinez often spoke of school. It sounded like a wonderful place.

Seeing Addie's face, her father finally set down his collection bucket, grabbed his daughter's hand, and followed the men. Mrs. Martinez and their neighbors watched them go, with smiles that did not quite reach their eyes.

Another video aired on the city broadcast. It was a compilation of quick cuts set against an uplifting song, showing Addie accepting her scholarship, moving into a house on the outskirts of the Cloud District with her father, and walking past the gates of the STEAM Academy. Her life, compressed into a forty-second press piece, could not convey the unbridled joy she felt as she stepped into her first art class, how her heart fluttered against her ribs, how her fingers itched to draw.

In the Academy, students sat in a ring, their heads bowed like acolytes before their easels. Each flicked their eyes towards the center of their circle, observing a bowl of fresh fruit set before them. A white-robed instructor sat Addie before an easel and told her to draw. The next two hours flew by in a blur of color and shape. Addie had never known such peace, to sit and draw undisturbed, listening to gentle music.

At the end of the class, the work was critiqued. Addie listened as students commented on one another's shading techniques, use of color, or perspective. Addie's drawing was last. It left the class speechless. She did not simply draw the fruit and the table on which it sat like everyone else. She drew her view of the whole room, including the instructor as he paced between easels, the students at worship before their own art, the sweeping pillars that held the ceiling aloft, in her signature display of churning color.

Addie twisted her hands, nervous at their silence. Tears stung the corners of her eyes as her fear and shame grew. Her art did not look like everyone else's.

"It is extraordinary," the instructor finally declared, and students began hounding Addie with questions. They clapped her on the back, praised her composition, and marveled at her color palette. Addie smiled so wide that her cheeks began to hurt and felt as if her chest could burst from happiness.

After that, people began to call Addie Bell *singularly talented, visionary*, and *genius*. A month went by, then two, and Addie settled into her new life. She and her father took to spending their weekends in the park, taking picnics of fresh fruit and bread. Addie like to draw her father sitting in the grass, running his hands through it, marveling at its softness, head tipped to welcome the sun on his skin. In the Deep he'd always been hunched, plagued with coughing spasms. A visit to the doctor had finally cleared the ailment in his chest, and he now breathed much more easily. While Addie went to school, he got a job in the Mids sorting scrap metal in a factory. It wasn't glamorous work, but he made a decent wage and was home in the early evening to share supper with his daughter and listen to her talk excitedly about her day.

As she grew up, Addie became the most celebrated artist in her school. Requests for her artwork poured into the Academy from Cloud District citizens, for everyone with taste wanted a Bell original for their homes. Her instructors encouraged her to examine the world around her, noting the line, shape, and shadow of her environment. Addie drew and painted, observing her subjects closely. And the more she saw, the angrier she became.

It started with small things, trivial points of friction with her classmates. The other students who grew up in the sun and sky knew nothing of the damp that swallowed those who lived below them in the Deep. They teased her for being an outsider, then grew jealous when she stole all the attention of her art teachers. She did find friends, and enjoyed spending time with them, but they could never understand where she had come from. When she tried to tell them what it was like growing up in the Deep, she was met with uncomfortable silence. Such things were not talked about. The news did not even mention any happening south of the Mids. "Well, you live here now," they would say, and the conversation quickly moved on to shopping and crushes.

Her father did not like to linger on the past, either. Addie could not bear the pain in his eyes when she tried to bring it up. So, the picture in her mind of the Deep grew faded and fuzzy, time softening the harshness of her memory. But she always thought fondly of Mrs. Martinez and wondered how she was doing. It did not seem right to bury the past so easily, so she kept the dulled shards of her memories, the jabs from her classmates, their lack of understanding, pressed tight against her ribs where they pricked her heart when she lay in bed, trying to find sleep.

On the day of her sixteenth birthday, the dulled shards of her pain were sharpened to razor points when she saw the news. The broadcast played on the screen in her room as she dressed for school. There was no way to change the channel. The broadcasts came at scheduled intervals, morning and night, regardless of if they were wanted or not. The reports reminded them all how lucky they were, and the dangers of what happened when one strayed too far from the confines of the Cloud District. This morning, the broadcast was a tale of the latter. A report on a crackdown of panhandling in the lower Mids, an effort for city-wide improvement.

Addie watched in disbelief, hairbrush halfway through her tresses, as Mrs. Martinez flashed across the screen. She, and a few other faces she recognized, were moved off their street corner by Cloud guards. The old woman's hair was streaked with silver, the lines of her face deep with dismay, her back hunched, but there was no mistaking her. Time had not been as kind to her as it had to Addie.

With trembling hands, Addie tied her hair into its neat twist. She hugged her father goodbye, slung her bag over her shoulder, and marched to school. Her thoughts were in tangles. At the beautiful gates where she had nearly wept with joy upon first seeing them, she felt her cheeks flush and acid creep up her throat. Her feet were cemented to the sidewalk. The sight of Mrs. Martinez's face had rattled something deep within her, and Addie could not make herself go inside. Instead, she turned on her heel and began the very long walk out of the Clouds.

Addie strode past the towering, gilded homes to the first flight of stairs made of cement and iron. Down she went, minutes turning to hours, descending to the Mids. The smell of standing water filtered up from the Deep even here. It stung her nose and sharpened those memories that had gone as soft and blurry as blended pastels. Her shoes were dirty and stained by the time she reached the corner where she'd spent her days drawing on the rough concrete. Mrs. Martinez was nowhere to be found. There were very few people around and the street was oddly quiet, given that it was midday. Addie hadn't really expected her to be here. She took a long breath through her nose, adjusted her school bag, and took the rickety stairs back down to the Deep, ignoring the strange looks from passersby.

The shack was smaller than she remembered. Addie rapped on the rough wooden door with her knuckles, and a faint voice called through it. "Who's there?"

Addie spoke past the lump in her throat. "It's Addie, Mrs. Martinez. Addie Bell."

The door opened a crack. Only Mrs. Martinez's wide eyes were visible. "Oh, mija, it's really you. Come in, quick."

Addie stepped inside the shack and took the offered seat on a three-legged stool. Mrs. Martinez sat on her bed with a groan. "Mija, what are you doing here? Don't you have school? A smart girl like you shouldn't be missing your classes."

"I came to see how you were doing." Addie decided not to tell her that the reason for her visit was because she had seen her on the broadcast, and that she wanted to relieve herself of the invisible guilt that she carried with her. She had thought that seeing Mrs. Martinez would make her feel better. It only made her chest ache.

Mrs. Martinez's eyes darted to the door. "That's very sweet, but I think you should go back home." She inhaled a wet, raspy breath and coughed, her body shaking under the attack.

Addie stood, alarmed. She sounded worse than her father ever had. "You should see a doctor," she said, once the coughing had subsided.

"No doctor will see me," Mrs. Martinez croaked.

"Why not?"

"I don't have insurance."

Addie narrowed her eyes. "What's insurance? You're sick. Papa saw a doctor and ..." Addie stopped at the sad look that passed across her former caretaker's face. Her cheeks burned, mortified. Of course, her father had only seen a doctor when they moved into their Cloud house. "I'm sorry," she said softly.

"It's okay. I'm glad you came to see me. I've missed you, but you really should be in school."

Addie stood and gathered her bag. "You're right. I'm happy I got to see you. Bye, Mrs. Martinez." She gave the old woman a careful hug and left. Instead of heading towards the shaky stairway, she walked along the damp, grimy streets of the Deep, stopping when she reached the sickly lapping of the water's edge. Had it always been this far up the street?

She stood, gazing out past the gloom of the rusty beams that held the city aloft. The water sloshed in and out, reeking of sewage and decay. A dead seagull, wings akimbo, floated nearby.

Whispers of dissent had been bubbling up from the Deep for some time. She had overheard her classmates, the children of government officials, share stories in hushed voices. They spoke of strikes, protests, retaliation. The ember of anger that had ignited in her chest this morning turned into a roaring flame. The sea was eroding homes, eating away at their crumbling foundations, yet the Mids did not welcome the people who lived in the Deep into their level of the city. Addie could not imagine the Clouds ever doing anything to help.

She looked at her shoes, stained from her trek. Shame made her eyes prick with tears. She'd been so blind; dazzled by the sparkling life she'd been given. Why had she been chosen, out of all the people here, to move up to the Clouds? Addie felt, suddenly, that she did not deserve it.

That night at home as she lay in bed, unable to sleep, she searched for her own name on her tablet. She found a video that had aired after her first art class. A reporter had taken a short clip of Addie with her still-life drawing, the one she'd been so proud of on her first day. When asked about the nature of her composition, she replied that she'd drawn what she saw. She scrolled and found the video from the city official, the one with the tagline, *a vision of what New York could be.*

Addie pushed herself out of bed and hastily cleared her worktable. She grabbed her colored pencils and began to draw a copy of her own artwork. She drew it nearly identical to the original, with swirling colors and the city skyline. Only this time, she added a slashing line of blue: the ocean rising to swallow the city, bodies floating in the water. She scrawled *a vision of what New York WILL be* across it in jarring red.

By the time she was done, the sun was just beginning to rise. Addie readied herself for school, ignoring the broadcast that played yet another cautionary tale. She placed her newest piece into her portfolio, tucking it safely between other drawings. Addie hugged her father a little tighter than usual as she said goodbye.

While everyone else was in their classes, Addie stole away to the workroom. She made dozens of copies of her newest piece, printing bundles of flyers which she shoved into her bag. Lastly, she made a large banner, wider than her arms and half as tall as she was. Perspiration beaded on her brow as the laser printer did its work, rolling out her print one inch at a time. It finished just as morning classes were dismissed. Her heart pounded in her ears as she rolled up the giant banner and marched back out the school gates.

She walked, head held high, straight to the heart of the Cloud District. At every corner, she tossed a few flyers from her bag, marring the pristine streets. She moved quickly, not stopping to hear the shocked murmurs at her behavior, or the fearful whispers of rebellion. A little drone began to follow her once she was three blocks away from her destination. She broke into a run, anxiety making her swift.

On the steps of the capital, Addie dropped her school bag and rolled out her banner. The drone had caught up with her and was now beeping shrill commands. Heavy footsteps sounded on the marble steps, but Addie did not look up from her work. She pushed the paper until it unfurled across the stairs. She stood, hands on her hips, studying her work. She could not hear the shouts above the sound of her own pounding heart, but she felt hands grab her roughly at the elbows. She was steered into a car that hovered off the street by Cloud guards, their faces obscured by helmets.

Addie did not feel scared until they escorted her to a windowless, white room that smelled of antiseptic. Her stomach clenched in fear as they pinched her arm with a needle that put her to sleep, and set about dissecting what had given this girl from the Deep the audacity and to paint the world in such colors.

Addie Bell's fall from grace was a brief news headline on the evening broadcast. Too many people had seen the flyers for the incident to not be addressed. It made for a wonderful cautionary tale. Clouds sneered at their screens and removed their Bell originals from their walls in shame, for the little girl from the Deep had no real talent at all. It was, in fact, a horrible anomaly of her vision that distorted her way of viewing the world. For Addie Bell was colorblind and did not perceive the world as those with all their proper eye cones did. She had been picking colors blindly, scribbling nonsense onto her canvases. There was no real *vision* there at all. And her vulgar art did not paint the whole picture, the effort the city was making to stem the rising seas, to help clean up the streets of the lower districts. The Clouds washed their hands of her and went about their lives.

Addie was questioned. The government wanted to know whom she was working with, who had given her orders to destroy her own art. Her answers were simple, and honest. After a few hours of questioning, when they had given up trying to extract names of other dissenters from her, they left her alone in a cell.

Her father watched the nighttime broadcast in stunned disbelief. He couldn't believe that his sweet, gentle daughter had done something so rash. He pressed his gnarled fingers to his mouth as images of her face flashed across the screen. He had no idea the rage she had carried inside her. His own anger had burned down to ashes long ago. He shrugged back into his jacket and walked under the golden glow of streetlamps to city hall.

No one could tell him where his daughter was. There was no record of her or where she had gone. He was turned away politely the first three times. On the fourth day, armed guards escorted him down the pristine marble steps where Addie had unfurled her banner, forbidding him from asking again.

In a last effort, he traipsed back down to the Deep, as Addie had done a week prior. He knocked on Mrs. Martinez's splintered door, and was welcomed in. She gasped wetly for breath. Her skin had the telltale gray tinge of lung sickness. When he told her of what had happened to Addie, fat tears slid down her cheeks.

"But you should be proud," she said as she dried her face. "She's a very brave girl."

He wanted to feel pride. Instead, he felt hollow. He thanked Mrs. Martinez for her time and began his long trek home, heart aching. Addie had given him something he could not give her in return: safety, and a place among the Clouds.

After the first few weeks, Addie lost track of how long she'd spent in the prison. She wondered if it had done any good, spreading her message through the streets. She hoped her father could forgive her, even if he never understood why she'd done it. Over time, her face paled, regaining the ghostly pallor of her girlhood. Her days dragged on in monotony, devoid of sun, art, and companionship. Sometimes, Addie found her fingers curling delicately, as if embracing one of her pencils, the habit hard to shake. At night, she fell asleep with a soft smile upon her lips and dreamed of a sky stained with a kaleidoscope of color.

Cidney Mayes's story "Visions for the Independent City of New York" was originally published in Metaphorosis on Friday, 1 December 2023. See magazine.metaphorosis.com

About the author

Cidney Mayes is a middle school librarian from Portland, Maine with a passion for anything magical. She is a book reviewer of children's and young adult novels, and has been an educator since 2015. Her recent published works include short fiction in West Avenue Publishing's *A Coven of Witches* anthology, *Metaphorosis* magazine, and *Carmina* magazine. When not writing, you can find her giving tarot readings, walking in the woods, or playing board games with her husband and friends.

Sudden Oak Death

J. Tynan Burke

Arboreal silhouettes filled the unilluminated park around Dr. Kort Zantoosian. Behind the foliage, the milky haze of Saturn's E ring shone through an astroglass dome. But Kort saw none of this, for he was floating inside the canopy of his favorite tree, its branching tendrils surrounding him in a near-perfect sphere. Of all the trees he'd grown in the park, this Zantoosian black oak, which he'd nicknamed the Orb, was his favorite. It was, he thought, just a great, really very good tree. Words failed him when he drank.

Kort tapped a command into his wrist tablet, and air jets from his belt hissed him into a lazy somersault. As he spun, he drank from the pouch of whiskey he'd brought. Sometimes it felt pretty great to be Kort Zantoosian; better, he often worried, than he deserved.

In the shelter of the Orb, he could let go of his worries, most of which concerned his duties as Head of Arboriculture at New Lahej Orbital Habitation Park. No more did he fret over the typo he'd discovered on a requisition form from the previous week. Kort didn't even think about the park's mediocre review in the latest *Lonely Planet: Saturn*. He just admired his handiwork.

Creating this species of oak had been one of his rare strokes of youthful genius. He probably could've parlayed it into an associate professorship somewhere, but was that any way to live? Besides, it turned out he had a knack for systems engineering. These trees were a perfect synergy of biological research, his first love; and the slow grind of forestry, his true talent and a sometimes-adequate replacement. His research had gotten him hired, but it was his engineering chops that had made him, and the park, semi-famous. A beautiful space, filled with artfully-crafted exemplars of his eponymous species of oak — *that* was pure Kort Zantoosian.

This simple confidence lasted until he noticed a lump bulging on a branch. He ordered his belt thrusters to bring him closer and turned on his jumpsuit's lamp. After a drunken minute, he identified the crinkled lump as a gall. He hadn't seen one in years. Habitations tended not to have insects at all, not to mention ones that laid eggs in plants. How had a bug gotten past their defenses?

Kort's easily frightened self-regard vanished, replaced with a familiar dejection. He cursed. Maybe *Lonely Planet* had been right, and the park really was only "recommended on Free First Fridays".

A bleep from his wrist tablet reminded him that he had somewhere to be. Aided by the alcohol, he shook off his rumination. The gall would still be there in the morning. At his instruction, his thrusters carried him out of the oak. His mood lifted as he flew past terraces of curling roses, stands of yellowing aspen, and a three-dimensional hedge maze. The thrusters brought him to a rest area by the dome wall. With one arm through a grab hoop, Kort drank from his pouch of whiskey and waited.

The E ring was a vast cloud of mineral water that spewed from Enceladus. The moon would spend the rest of its existence ensconced in this fog, but New Lahej, which orbited Enceladus's poles, broke free at the height of its trajectory. Kort watched as the ring plane fell below him at thousands of kilometers per hour, becoming a featureless gray sea that stretched to the horizon. At the same time, the dawn terminator crested over Saturn's dark bulk, revealing the planet before him. Kort sipped from his pouch and stared, like a child riding a space elevator for the first time. Planetrise — this monthly conjunction — never got old. But humans did, Kort had learned, and at local midnight it was past his usual bedtime; after thirty minutes, he floated out of the park dome to the axial monorail, which he rode to the aft habitation discs.

The next morning, he bought a pack of hangover nanobots on the way to the lab; he'd outgrown the goals of his old grad-student self, but not the drinking habits. Perhaps he still had some of the old modes of thought, too: being responsible for solving problems at scale could be such *drudgery*. But duty called, even if, as seemed likely, this was the fault of the pest-control people, not him. At least getting to the bottom of this would be good for the oaks.

He convened a crisis-management team, ordering them to search the park for bugs. He would lead the search for more galls himself, as was his professional responsibility. This would also let him humor a psychological dysfunction which told him the gall represented a personal failing. Still, the task required *some* delegation, which went to Iphie and Dewen, his hand-picked interns.

Curiously, the team didn't find a single bug. The gall was even more curious. It was warm to the touch, getting warmer, and apparently alone in the park. He couldn't say much more with certainty. The Enceladan Authority had never sent the DNA sequencer they'd promised, so he'd have to do a visual identification of the creature inside. He spent the coming days waiting for it to grow just large enough for a confident identification. The gnawing apprehension made his neck itch, and he found unaccustomed respite in his routine late-summer tasks.

Eleven mornings later, Kort was floating before the gall, inside the Orb's sphere of branches. He was flanked by Iphie and Dewen, and not a few camera drones. Lit up by floodlights, and carrying an ionic multitool, he was reminded that an arcane term for 'arborist' was 'tree surgeon.' He half-smiled, then slipped back into his usual grim mask. Nothing here was amusing.

When he cut one side off the gall, a cloud of dust escaped and spread steadily outwards. Kort released a vacuum drone from his toolbelt and squinted at the deformity; the inside of the gall was scaled with burns, but otherwise empty. Pushing back from the branch with a groan, he closed his eyes and held the multitool out to Iphie. "Did I set this to something stupid?"

She turned it in her hands. "Why'd you dial it to 'vaporize', boss?"

Kort swallowed. Dewen shook his head and plucked the tool away. "Let's cut Dr. Z a break. Multitool's set to 'incise', doc." He placed it in Kort's still-waiting palm.

Kort holstered it with a sniff. He just knew he'd screwed this up, and doomed the park, or at least the Orb — though he couldn't articulate *how*. "Can you two clean this up? Start analyzing the dust and make sure this thing's really empty." He jetted away before anybody saw that his eyes had started to water; right before he exited the Orb, he spun around. "Be back in a few hours." He didn't mention that he'd be getting a Monte Cristo and a Bloody Mary at his favorite greasy spoon over in the habitation discs.

"Hell of a time for one of Iphigenia Halikas's famous jokes," he heard Dewen say. Iphie giggled.

Later, smelling of fry-oil and tomato, Kort joined them in the lab, where they summarized their findings. The dust was ashes, the interior of the gall was uniformly charred, and it was indeed empty. None of the three had heard of anything like it, a problem the park's database seemed to share. *A second-rate library for a second-rate arboriculture department*, Kort thought with a frown, at an "*okay to miss if you aren't already in New Lahej*" park — a downgrade from their peak a few years ago. It was still a better review than the ones before he'd joined; that cheered him up some days, though this was not one of them.

Any number of things could explain the gall. Most likely, a bug had hitched a ride inside somebody's clothes, and Kort's tool had simply malfunctioned. Unless it recurred, well, *shit happens*. Besides, Kort couldn't linger on low-priority unsolved mysteries: it was time to begin the preparations for leaf-fall. People visited by the thousands every year for that magical season, when the leaves changed colors and detached, turning the dome into a botanical snow-globe. It was the one thing *Lonely Planet* had found to compliment without reservation. Given the park's funding realities, leaf-fall was also more important than ever. So Kort's arboriculture department focused their energies on beautification, and interventions that would stretch the season.

On evenings and weekends, Kort practiced classic video games for an upcoming tournament, spitting curses at his ancient and buggy haptic bodysuit. Once, at an invitation from Iphie and Dewen, he attended a showing of *Titanian Tulips*, an inaccurate rom-com set during the first successful terraforming.

One afternoon, while Kort was fiddling with the aspens' hydroponics tanks, Iphie approached looking nervous. There were more galls, she told him, with a strained expression. She'd found them in the Zantoosian black oak at the park's entrance. "Let me know how I can help," she added.

Kort rested his hand on the case surrounding the root bulb, harder than he needed to. He had written off his earlier fears as depressive false prophecy; it was never a good day when those were actually confirmed. "I see." Feeling his mind dissociate from the issue, he looked off to the wall of haze outside the astroglass. "Thanks."

Iphie pulled herself along a tree trunk and reoriented herself to be level with Kort. The movement released a drift of cherry-red leaves from what was now over her head.

Kort's mind clutched at the distraction. "The aspens are a little early," he said, pointing at the leaves. "I'm just about to add fescue extract to their water; there was a paper in *Astroarboricultural Digest* ..."

Iphie put on the half-smile she used to humor people. "Is that Brenndan Gwilt's study?"

Kort blinked twice. "Your faculty mentor, isn't he? Small worlds." Sometimes he forgot Iphie had come recommended by a researcher more eminent than he'd ever be. He poked idly at some pipettes.

Iphie nodded at the water-treatment setup. "I can probably handle this, if you want to go look at the —"

Kort snapped back to reality. "The galls. Yes." A stomachache began to stir in his belly. "If you could take over on the aspens ..." He looked down and tapped something into his wrist tablet. "You have my notes."

"Won't let you down, boss." Iphie pulled herself to the workstation. *I can trust a protege of Gwilt's to feed a plant and fix the plumbing,* Kort thought, using the derogatory terms he'd heard for arboriculture in the academy. Stomach tightening further, he blew out a deep breath and hauled himself away with a nearby grab hoop.

While he jetted to the tree he called the Corona, Kort tried to keep his mind blank, but rumination struck when he reached the canopy. He'd known the Corona's broad halo of branches for almost two decades, from when he'd planted it at the entrance to dazzle spacefarers. He knew every twist and turn of its fractal limbs; like the other oaks, shaping it had been a painstaking, years-long process.

Inspecting the perfectly proportioned branches was almost enjoyable, except for his ratcheting nerves. When he found the first gall, the tension became otherworldly. Lizard-brain panic gripped him; he was in free-fall, towards every surface at once. He cast around for something to orient himself with. Only the gall could hold his attention. Looking at it made him feel helpless, but that was preferable to the feeling of imminent death. So he stared at the gall, willing the canopy to be 'down'. Eventually perception came around.

The galls were like crumbs in a kitchen: with each one he saw, three more revealed themselves. Then nine more. The exponential proliferation was as stunning as a broken nose. He felt, for lack of a better term, weightless.

Where had all these galls come from? It would've taken a whole swarm of insects to lay this many eggs. Surely the park staff, still on high alert, would have detected that. And why were they only affecting Zantoosian black oaks? The trees were mostly the same age; was this a genetic flaw? Would they soon all become disfigured? Kort's face began to twitch. Perhaps he shouldn't have created the species; perhaps oak trees were *supposed* to turn to spindly knots in microgravity. All he'd done was paste in the allometry genes from an ancient shrub called Kepler Kudzu. All it was supposed to pass on was its beautiful form in microgravity. He'd had an AI read every source on it he could find; it was a hardy plant, with no records of disease, and no predators.

Kort pawed through the branches until he accidentally crushed a gall in his fist, mashing something hot into his hand. He yelped and shook it away; half-singed chips of wood dislodged from his palm. He stared at the stippled wound, not quite a burn. Face twisted in disgust, he released a vacuum drone, then ran away to the lab, where he could have his nervous breakdown in peace.

He locked the hatch behind him. The disinfectant he sprayed on his palm burned, but was not the reason tears welled in his eyes. While he slapped on a bandage to keep himself from scratching, he did breathing exercises. Zantoosian black oaks were his legacy, from a time when he made things, instead of just doing them. And now the whole species was a potential fire hazard.

●

Once he'd calmed down, he arranged for a meeting with the park's administrative director, Helen Ramsey.

Helen suggested removing all the oaks from the park. It was a polite way of saying Kort should space them. She reflected aloud on the wisdom of keeping smoldering wood sitting around a space station.

Kort countered that 'smoldering' was an exaggeration — they were barely sixty degrees, about the same as a hot water pipe. He suggested that they could identify galls with infrared imaging and remove them manually. This was no time to be eliminating signature attractions; the Orb was even in their logo. Besides, orbitals dealt in this level of risk for anything worth doing, from cooking to electricity generation.

Helen showed her palms and shrugged. As long as it wasn't spreading, she said. Kort was the expert. "And remember," she concluded, "dead people don't buy concessions."

Kort bit off a sarcastic reply. Detecting this, Helen gave a sympathetic smile. Having worked alongside him for years, she could read his emotional state better than he cared to admit.

●

Kort tasked the interns with finding and lancing the rest of the galls. This left Kort to study their source alone, as he liked it. The others might lead him down the wrong path. Also, as he happily told himself during his plentiful moments of darkness, the whole thing was his fault, and his alone to fix. If it was a genetic malfunction, then his academic research was to blame; if he couldn't solve the problem with more research, it would be final proof that he was a failure as a scientist.

Every research path Kort pursued hit a dead end. He began to feel like a cactus in a drought, sinking a taproot ever deeper in search of water that just wasn't there. His nightly video game practice sessions grew shorter, punctuated with ever-fiercer blasphemies. He lost his hairbrush and neglected to buy a new one; his hair came to resemble the oak by the park's entrance. After three days of this, Helen invited him to dinner.

He was familiar with this sort of invitation. She was worried about him. Her semi-managerial status over him always made such things awkward; they'd built out the park together, and he considered her a friend, but they were not peers. Kort spent the hour before fretting over nothing and everything.

The two ate at a Titanian-fusion restaurant inside one of the spinning habitation discs. Their table featured a tablet showing a stabilized view from outside. Unfortunately, at that point in New Lahej's orbit, said view was of impenetrable gloom.

Once they'd ordered, Kort poured himself a second glass of wine. "Let's get this out of the way — what's on your mind?"

Helen gestured at his hair and rumpled shirt. "You've looked like it's laundry day for half a week. I wanted to check in."

Kort had assumed as much, so his nonchalance was reasonably convincing. He took a sip of wine, a passable Titanian burgundy, which was staining his lips red. "Nothing to be concerned about. I've been working harder than ever."

"You know how you get. Take care of yourself." Helen retrieved some beansprouts from a communal dish. "Which brings me to my second point. Let's bring in some help. An expert."

Kort's hand stopped on its way to the vinegar. "I am an expert."

"You know what I mean. A specialist."

"In what?" Kort grabbed the vinegar and gave what he hoped was a genial laugh. "Mysterious tree fevers?"

After a thoughtful bite of tofu, Helen said, "There's a researcher down below who's interested. Brenndan Gwilt, at Shahrazad."

"You don't say," Kort muttered, mouth as small as he felt. A *real* research scientist coming in to fix his problems. And his intern's mentor, to boot. Moments like this made him wonder if he served any actual function.

He remembered he had food, and tucked into his jook. His blood pressure lowered after a moment. Helen was only doing what was best for the park. "As long as he brings a research capsule."

Helen let out a held breath and took a generous drink of wine. "You can tell him yourself. I scheduled you a holo at eleven tomorrow."

After dinner, they parted ways at the lift; Kort's cabin was in a different disc, and he'd need to get there via the axial monorail. "Remember, we're all on your team," Helen said. "And you're never alone on a team. Eleven tomorrow." She waved goodbye and walked off, slippers thwapping on the tile floor.

What Helen had left unsaid — that *he* needed to be a team player too — was not lost on him. He trudged back to his cabin, where he turned on the vanity lights around his bathroom mirror. He hadn't done so in ages; a few of the LEDs had gone out, apparently. He leaned in and inspected his face in the uneven light. The wine stains on his lips would pass, but restless nights had brought out the creases on his forehead and around his mouth. At least he could address his unkempt hair, which was grayer in the mirror than it was in his self-image. He plucked a barrette from a drawer and pulled the frizzy poof back into a bun. After correcting his posture, he marched to an all-night market, where he bought replacement LEDs and a hairbrush.

In the lab the next morning, he didn't look any younger, but at least he looked like somebody who'd come to terms with the fact. It would have to be good enough for his first holo with Brenndan Gwilt, whom he finally got on-screen after lunch. Like many Enceladans, Brenndan was jet-black; he also had gray stubble so disorderly, it dispelled Kort's concerns about his own appearance. The two men exchanged pleasantries and gossiped about the interns before getting to business.

"So you're having trouble with your famous trees," Brenndan said. He pecked at his wrist tablet. "Explosive tumors or something."

"Or something," Kort agreed. "And here you are, a specialist in arboreal disease." He'd prepared for the conversation all morning, but even so his gut was a chilly hollow. "Director Ramsey said you wanted to come help."

Brenndan nodded. "I'd love to see it in person. Shahrazad will foot the bill."

Kort resisted scratching under his collar. Instead, he barreled through his anxiety. While he did fear the outside expert's judgment, letting that wreck the park would be awfully self-destructive, even by his standards. "And we'd love the help," he said through a scratchy throat. "Do you have access to a research capsule?"

"Good idea." Brenndan held up a finger. With his other hand, he navigated a touchscreen. "Alright, I'm next on the list." He leaned closer to the display and squinted. "I can be there in under a week."

Kort pasted on a smile and said that sounded great. They spoke little after that, to Kort's relief; Brenndan had affairs to wrap up.

●

Three days later, an eruption at Enceladus's south pole damaged the comms rig of Brenndan's spaceliner. The passengers were fine, but the vehicle had no bandwidth for nonessential communications.

"Does it even matter when he gets here, anymore?" Kort said. He was floating, agitated, before the trunk of the Corona. "*Look* at this!"

"Doesn't look great, boss," Iphie said. She and Dewen were floating opposite Kort.

" 'Doesn't look —' " Kort hissed. He bashed the trunk with the bottom of his fist. Brown leaves rustled and drifted away from the canopy. Next to his hand, cankers sunk into the bark drooled maroon ichor, which formed hardened globules. "Watch this." He produced an ionic multitool, checked twice that it was set to 'incise,' and shaved off the bark around one of the cankers. Faint steam wafted from the exposed phloem, which should have been tan, but was oddly pink. "We've got a tree cooking itself alive here." A waiting vacuum drone sucked up the detritus.

"If it weren't hot, I'd guess Sudden Oak Death," Dewen said, his expression eager as always.

Kort waved it off. "Had the same thought. Sudden Oak Death doesn't produce galls." He huffed. "And our epidemiologist booked the *one spaceliner company*" — here he thumped a hydroponic casing — "too *cheap* to use proper comms shielding!"

Dewen held up his palms. "I'm sure the school was the cheapskate there, Dr. Z. Even when they pay for your conference ticket and hotel, they make you fly coach."

"Yeah." How did Dewen know that? Were they already sending him to expensive *conferences*? Kort hadn't received that honor until he was several years older. He sighed and rode his thrusters away from anything thumpable. "So we're on our own for two more days."

"There's worse company," Iphie said with a wide shrug. "If you're worried about *esprit de corps*, you can always take us out to dinner and bill the park."

Kort laughed. The interns were smart, but that flash of youthful audacity reminded him that he was the seasoned adult. His anger gave way to embarrassment; he needed to take charge. He turned towards the lab and pointed a finger forward. "Once more unto the breach," he said, flying away.

"Huh?" he heard Dewen say behind him.

Infrared imaging showed that only a third of the Corona was infected, but that third was nearing fatal temperatures. Together, they excised this portion, then rehoused it as a cutting. On the starboard face of the dome, there was an empty capsule they usually used for quarantine; they moved the new cutting inside. A further infrared scan identified another infected tree, a spiral-shaped oak nicknamed the Screw. They quarantined that one, too. Iphie programmed the capsule to vent its contents if the temperature went above 'scalding'.

That night they ate dandan noodles at a Sichuan restaurant in the discs. Kort did his best impression of a responsible adult, even managing some pleasant small talk. His eyes went wide when he learned that not only had the interns never been to China, they'd never even been to Earth. He supposed he should've guessed as much by their résumés. Still, it was something different to hear it from their own mouths. He seamlessly transitioned from feeling grown-up to feeling old.

The next morning, as New Lahej cleared the E ring's mists to reveal a waning Saturn, they found fifty-one galls on the Orb. Kort lanced each with cautious fury. *No sores or ichor, at least*, he thought as he worked the cryo-needle. *Not yet.* But a different oak, the Handlebar, was less fortunate, and was moved to the now-overcrowded quarantine capsule. To make matters worse, the capsule had developed something of a crowd; facilities had to push back the guests and put up screens. Kort hoped Helen wouldn't chew him out for not doing it sooner.

Four hours later, the capsule pushed an alert to their wrist tablets: it was approaching the venting threshold. They hurried over, slipped between the screens, and crowded around a readout. It showed that the Screw was nearing seventy degrees. The interns helped Kort float the other trees out, but he insisted on performing the final task himself. With one hand pressed to the astroglass, he tapped the command into the capsule's controls, and watched the Screw twirl off into the vacuum, where it would someday join Saturn's rings. He'd designed the tree to look like Da Vinci's flying machine; he imagined that old Leo would have found it a fitting death.

Kort shoved off from the astroglass with a finger. Not bothering to hide his tears, he drifted backwards a moment, then turned to Iphie and Dewen. "We aren't totally fucked yet," he said. With a hypomanic smile, he added, "If there's one thing I've learned, it's that you aren't actually in trouble until there's been paperwork."

Brenndan wouldn't arrive until the next morning, but there was still plenty Kort could do. He convened the crisis-management team again. Feeling a creeping dread much stronger than his usual existential angst, Kort asked them to search every plant in the park for symptoms of the disease. The results confirmed his fears: the weeping cankers were no longer limited to Zantoosian black oaks. The other plants didn't show elevated temperatures, and had less severe symptoms, but this gave him little solace. It was a well-known pattern in epidemiology: the creature could only incubate in one species — hence the oaks' monopoly on galls — but had a later stage with less discriminate effects.

●

An hour later, Kort was floating outside Helen's hatch, examining her nameplate. It was lightly oxidized and could've used a good scouring. But he was distracting himself; he rapped on the hatch, and was called in. He squared his shoulders to feel courageous, and pulled himself over to a handhold at her workstation. She seemed unsurprised to see him.

"Would this have anything to do with that crowd gathering around the entrance?" she said, tipping her head at the window, which overlooked the middle ring of the park.

"Ahha ha," Kort said, flat-footed. He cleared his throat, let out a sigh as defeated as he felt, and filled her in.

"Dr. Gwilt is almost here, right?" Helen said. "Let's see if he can figure it out." She took a measured sip from a pouch of coffee.

"Exactly what I was going to suggest," Kort said. They were on the same page, which usually presaged outcomes he could live with. He relaxed his grip on the handhold.

Helen kicked off her workstation and flew over to her window. Kort followed, and they gazed out at the flora and fauna they managed together. "People really do love this park we've built, Dr. Zantoosian. Even that family" — she pointed — "trapped in the hedge maze." She sipped her coffee again. "If your expert can't fix it, you *will* be spacing the oak trees. I'm sorry to be so pointed, but I need to be absolutely clear."

Kort swallowed at hearing it, though he'd assumed it was coming. "Absolutely," he said.

Helen nodded. "Great." She pushed off the window and settled into her workstation. "I've got to get back to this. Have facilities do something about that crowd, would you?"

"I'll ask them to put fire-suppression drones around all the oaks, too." He thanked her, and rode his thrusters out of her office. The meeting had gone so non-terribly, he almost smiled.

The remainder of the day passed in tense boredom. Only one thing really happened: they had to jettison the Handlebar after it reached the flash point. A sad moment, but not nearly as emotional as the death of the Screw. Like any creator, Kort did not love all his creations equally.

●

A sliver of Saturn loomed waxing in the sky when Brenndan's ship arrived the next morning. Near the battered spaceliner, Kort and Iphie waited in front of a shuttle. The scientist emerged from a hatch, two bags floating behind him on a sledge. Over on the starboard side of the ship, the spaceliner crew was removing the research capsule. Kort stared at the cylinder full of first-class equipment. His tongue went slightly dry. He hadn't had access to this caliber of tools since the rose rot crisis six years earlier. It was too bad he only got to play with the expensive toys during catastrophes.

Brenndan waved an arm. "Ms. Halikas, Dr. Zantoosian! Where should I have them put this thing?" He pointed over his shoulder at the capsule.

Kort focused on the green-and-white module, the better to not think about how chipper this interloper was. "Have them tie it down here, facilities will do the rest."

The three secured Brenndan's bags to their monorail car and traveled down the station's axial shaft. Strapped into the drab polymer seats, Iphie and Brenndan shot the breeze, while Kort, unable to think of something nice to say, fussed with his belt. At the habitation disc nearest the park, they rode a lift outwards, and showed Brenndan to the hotel Shahrazad had booked.

They toured the park an hour later, and Kort's inner critic was loud. When Brenndan said, "I'd never have thought aspens could be so lovely," Kort was sure he was just being charitable, and said something self-effacing. When Brenndan asked, "Have you tried centripetal drip irrigation?" Kort took it as proof of his disdain. He mounted a defense of their hydroponics, which he didn't even like. When they reached the Orb, and Brenndan said, "And this must be the tree from your logo," Kort heard faint praise indeed, and was unable to suppress a glare, after which Brenndan stopped commenting on much of anything. So it went: Kort was skittish and irritable all through the day. The team made little progress, even with the research capsule's sophisticated databases and equipment.

Before bed, Kort took a rare trip to the gym to wallop a punching bag. He wondered if his jaw would ever unclench. Did Brenndan think he was there to help with the *irrigation system*? So what if they couldn't afford anything fancy? After the gym, he tried to unwind with a glass of whiskey and a bad true-crime holo. What a waste of a day. Brenndan had been nothing but condescending. How were they supposed to save the oaks with that sort of dynamic? Kort might as well go space them right now.

Well when you put it like that, he thought, *who really has the problem?* He sighed and tried to enjoy the rest of his show. He'd do better tomorrow at focusing on the well-being of the trees. Or at least try.

●

The next morning, while he was still eating breakfast, Kort got a message from Helen asking him to stop by her office. A good breakfast being essential to his mood, he finished eating, then hopped right into the shower and hurried over. When he saw that Brenndan and the interns were already present, his cheeks went hot with anger and embarrassment. Why had they been meeting without him? Even if they had a good reason, it was still half-humiliating.

Helen gestured Kort to grab a handhold by her workstation. When he was settled, she saw the pained expression he was failing to hide. "I messaged you as soon as they filled me in," she said.

And why did they fill you *in first?* Kort thought. *Is this Brenndan's doing?* But maybe there was a perfectly reasonable explanation. He just had to not freak out until he knew for sure. Easier said than done, of course. His jaw clenched.

"There've been... developments, doc," Dewen said, with an apologetic wince. "Iphie and I got here early. You weren't around, so we talked to Director Ramsey."

"And I've only been here a few minutes," Brenndan said, showing his palms.

The interns had tried tiptoeing around him, Kort realized. Had he been *that* bad lately? It wouldn't do to stay mad — they were basically children — but he barely avoided rolling his eyes in the ensuing burst of exasperation. "Okay, Dewen, and?"

"It's the Orb," Dewen said. "Cankers. We have to quarantine it."

The outrage drained out of Kort; his muscles deadened. He just nodded.

Dewen continued: the cankers had made it to the aspens. And there'd been a mass wilting of rosebushes. And, and. *My world is falling apart*, Kort thought.

"Dr. Gwilt was just telling me his general strategy for handling outbreaks," Helen said.

"Eliminate the disease vectors, basically," Brenndan said. "Think of *Toxoplasma gondii*: it can only reproduce inside cats, but still infects other mammals. Chase off the cats, and it soon goes away."

"Vectors? You mean the galls," Kort said, even as he knew it wasn't the answer.

"More broadly," Brenndan said, "the *oaks*. Unfortunately. Get rid of them and it should run its course."

With a grunt, Kort got himself to nod, a feat much more heroic than it looked. His toes tingled as his panic rose. Why couldn't they have been *wrong*? His proudest accomplishment was literally dying in front of him — and helping it along was *the right thing to do*.

Well, of course it was the right thing to do. Any idiot could see that. Why was he too bullheaded to accept it? Not for the first time, Kort hated himself for being so vain. How little must others think of him, if even interns felt the need to go over his head? He searched their faces for spite or pity, and though Brenndan was studiously aloof, the people who knew him wore expressions of empathy. Helen even flashed a supportive smile.

Time to give in. Kort took a few deep breaths, willing his panic to turn to resignation. It was a not-entirely-healthy coping mechanism he'd developed over the years, one which got plenty of use. "I'll grant that leaf-fall would be... largely unaffected," he said, curling up imperceptibly. "There's much more to the park than the Zantoosians."

"Indeed," Helen said.

But Kort still couldn't avoid the bargaining stage of his grief. "Give us one more day," he said. "We only just got the research capsule, and the situation isn't likely to escalate."

Helen turned to Brenndan. "Do you agree?"

"Dr. Zantoosian is correct on both counts," Brenndan said.

"I'll see you here tomorrow morning, then," Helen said, tapping something into her workstation.

While he and Brenndan jetted down to the research capsule, Kort tried not to slouch. He'd bought himself hope to hang onto — thin though it may have been — and he would hold his head high and do his best. This would require effective collaboration; he was lucky his pride was still dead from the meeting. After a few false starts, he said, "I'm sorry I've been... tense, lately."

Brenndan passed a twirl of fern trees and turned to face Kort. Kort supposed he deserved the scientist's guarded expression.

"Accepted," Brenndan said with a professorial nod. A thoughtful pause, then, "I can't say I envy your position. But I'm here to help."

The fern trees receded behind them. Kort sniffed. "I'm very defensive of my operation, is all."

"Honestly, that's a flaw that I share." The research capsule's pitted hatch swung open at a command from

Brenndan's wrist tablet. "You can ask Ms. Halikas how hard it was to secure my mentorship."

Kort followed him inside. The lights came on; every surface was as irritatingly white as Enceladus's crust. "She seems to think highly of you," Kort said.

"And I her." Brenndan clambered through the room, powering up the machines. "But a year ago, I only looked at her application because they told me I had to take on an undergrad."

Kort was surprised to find such a kindred spirit in the academy. "Well, it's good for both of us that you did." He gestured around the capsule. "Shall we?"

"Let's." Brenndan turned a dial with a satisfying click, and the atomic force microscope began a warm hum. He thrust a packet of slides at Kort. "Femtoslices of a young gall. The freeze-drier just spit them out. Coffee?"

Two pouches of coffee and three packets of slides later, Kort pulled back from the eyepiece, blinked, and checked it again. He wasn't hallucinating: there was something foreign growing in the intercellular spaces of the gall... rather, there were the outlines of something, almost as if the something itself were...

"Invisible? You're mad," Brenndan said when Kort told him. "This machine can see *atoms*. Nothing's *that* invisible." He looked into the microscope and fiddled with the controls. "Hm."

"Hm?"

Brenndan tried another slide. "Hm."

They brainstormed experiments, and performed the ones time allowed. It seemed that the growths were detectable only by their effects on other things. Stumped, and short on other ideas, Kort and Brenndan each wrote a query script for the database AI, instructions to search its massive archives for similar cases. Then they left the capsule in a daze, their eyes ill-adjusted to the park's evening light. Brenndan began to jet away.

"Wait," Kort said.

Brenndan hissed to a stop and turned. "Yes?"

"There's 'planetrise' tonight at midnight," Kort said. "New Lahej will exit the ring right when Saturn's dawn terminator begins to sweep by. Definitely not something you get to see from down on Enceladus. You poor bastards are stuck in the ring." Kort spread his arms to indicate the park. "And I've got the keys to the best view in town."

Brenndan rubbed the stubble on his cheek. "What the hell — sure. Nothing else to do but wait for those queries to run. Let's see if you can impress this 'poor bastard'."

Kort let out an embarrassed chuckle. "I'll supply the whiskey. See you at — eleven?"

"Looking forward." Brenndan tapped his tablet, and his thrusters carried him backwards towards the exit.

●

Back in his cabin, Kort decanted his finest Titanian whiskey into pouches. He seemed to have reached the acceptance stage of grieving; he wanted only to see his trees off in style. At eleven, he met Brenndan in the axial shaft, and they entered the park. Brenndan got lost almost immediately and called out. Kort hadn't brought somebody else here after hours for ages; he'd forgotten to turn on the lights, which he dialed up to 'dusk'. The dome was now paused in twilight, a tapestry of dark greens and consuming shadows.

They toasted while floating before the remaining two-thirds of the Corona, long might it live. The alcohol landed hard, and once more Kort's problems slipped from his mind. They drank with relish; soon they were in the meadow, jetting after a sports drone, at a speed just this side of reckless. Shortly before midnight, they alighted at a rest area at the front of the dome, panting.

Kort killed the lights, and all was dark. "Here you go," he croaked, thrusting his arm at the astroglass.

New Lahej broke free of the ring, leaving a brief hole in the saltwater cloud. Brenndan stared as the sunlight spread across ammoniac Saturn. Both men sipped their whiskeys. Finally, Brenndan turned away and said, "You weren't kidd —"

An alert from his wrist tablet interrupted him. Brenndan shook his arm like something had bitten him, then laughed at himself and lifted it to read. "Database AI," he said. "Found something. C'mon." He tried to shake himself sober, and turned this way and that. "Um."

Kort's heart began to pound. Had they found a solution? He turned on the lights, programmed the destination into his wrist tablet, and waved Brenndan to follow. It took all his restraint not to rush there like a maniac.

In the capsule, they jockeyed for space around the AI readout. "You've got to be shitting me," Kort said, following it with a belly laugh and a somersault. The AI had found an ancient document buried deep in the research capsule's database. It told of an ailment, much like this one, which had afflicted Kepler Kudzu back when it was still being cultivated. As that plant was the source of several key genes for the Zantoosian black oak, this was a major breakthrough.

Kort cackled. "It found these documents *where*?"

Brenndan tapped the screen. "Newly digitized." He leaned in and squinted. "In some language called 'Esperanto'."

"No wonder I never found it."

"I don't know how people found *anything* before AI's," Brenndan said.

Kort snorted. "You'd need a whole... *mountain*... of interns!" He mimed throwing a pile of documents. "The hell do we do with this?"

"Are you good to script?"

"Not like this." Kort blew out a deep breath. His face brightened then, and he pointed at Brenndan. "But we have teammates who *can*."

●

New Lahej was still well outside of the ring when Iphie and Dewen rang from the park's entrance.

Jetting backwards so he could use wild gestures, Kort explained their summons with a massive grin. He and Brenndan had found the key insight, but the two men were far too drunk to write the next research script, which would have to deal with the document's arcane hypertext encoding. Could Iphie and Dewen? Please?

"You got it, boss," Iphie said with a bad salute. Dewen, for his part, tried not to look as annoyed as he obviously felt.

The interns unearthed more actionable information. This *lumo viruson* — light virus — was, to the ancient scientists, a scourge made of hungry energy; the affected Kepler Kudzu glowed. The writers hadn't hidden that they assumed an extraterrestrial origin. They'd also declined to publish their findings: in those early days of space exploration, such a claim was the fastest way to destroy one's reputation. And the cure? In retrospect it was obvious. Their predecessors had identified a narrow temperature range that eliminated whatever caused the *lumo viruson* infection without also killing the woody tissue of its host. Surely the same would be true for Zantoosian black oaks.

Rather than treating the entire habitat, as the ancients had, they could move the oaks into the quarantine capsule and leave the rest of the park untouched. It was a gentler version of Brenndan's 'eliminate the vectors' plan — one which, Brenndan noted, was only possible due to the portability inherent in Kort's hydroponics architecture.

Over a breakfast of hangover nanobots, Kort and Brenndan decided that the director would be more sympathetic to their plan if Brenndan pitched it. Helen regarded him skeptically as he did so in her office.

Leaf-fall could proceed according to schedule, Brenndan suggested; he would take two infected trees to Shahrazad University on Enceladus, where they could be studied with proper containment. Of the remaining trees, the worst cases would be destroyed, and the healthiest would be cured.

Kort interjected to say that this latter group included the Orb.

Helen said that was good; they'd all grown very fond of that tree. So where, she asked, did this *lumo viruson* come from? Would it come back?

Brenndan recited a spiel, obviously not for the first time, about the history of epidemiology. The theory often came after the cure; some questions could only be answered with methodical investigation, and a crisis was no time for that.

With a sharp nod, Helen said they had a deal, then dismissed everybody but Kort.

"Good work," she said, rolling out stiff neck muscles.

Kort tried not to sound self-conscious. "Team effort. But thank you."

She leaned forward. "Why don't you take a sabbatical, Kort?"

"Oh?" Kort froze. Surely that wasn't a euphemism.

"I'm just guessing, but there's a university that could probably use an expert in managing populations of Zantoosian black oaks." She chuckled. "Assuming that fire for research you used to talk about is still around."

Perhaps humor would let him hide his swelling relief. "You don't say." He pretended to check his wrist tablet. "You'll have to introduce me."

Helen reached out and grasped his shoulder. Holding his eyes, she said, "Are you okay, Kort?"

For once Kort didn't try to wriggle away from another's sympathy. Instead he bowed his head and closed his eyes. The park he believed in was safe, and he had the opportunity now to scratch his research itch. Truly, he *was* okay; if he was being honest, he felt almost giddy. But what should he do with such an unfamiliar feeling? Flee? Weigh the wreckage of the last season, and dwell on losses still to come? Or be refreshed in it, learn to find it again?

He pushed back from her finally and regarded the park from her window. The air held more leaves than it had yesterday, as it would again tomorrow. "Yes, actually. I think I'll take you up on that." Managing a cautious smile, he added, "If you're worried I'll be upset about losing the oaks, don't be — I can always grow more." He wasn't so old that he didn't have time for that; he had a hunch that what he valued would always find its way back into his life.

J. Tynan Burke's story "Sudden Oak Death" was originally published in the anthology Reading 5X5 x2 on 1 August 2020. See books.metaphorosis.com

About the author

 J. Tynan Burke is a software engineer and writer. Lately, he's been working on the script and code for a cosmic horror video game. He lives in Denver with his husband, their enormous cat Samwise, and their tiny cat Momo. His dream is to one day be an old man futzing around in the garden. You can find more about his writing at www.tynanburke.com, and find him on Bluesky @thearchduke.bsky.social.

Shadows on Glass

Jamie Lackey

Theodora Rhodes stood in the doorway and stared out at the field. The corn was chest-high and green, growing in neat rows.

It seemed impossible that the war had left a single thing untouched. And yet, here she was, familiar boards creaking under her bare feet, familiar smell of hotcakes and burnt coffee wafting from the kitchen. And in front of her, corn swayed in the summer morning breeze, just like it always had. If she closed her eyes, she could almost hear her brothers shouting at each other.

But she could also almost hear injured soldiers moaning and horses screaming, and see the purple haze of magic staining the western sky. She shuddered and opened her eyes.

The war was over, and her home was still here. And the memories would fade, with time.

She leaned against the doorframe and winced as the stump of her left arm caught against the rough wood. She scowled down at the thick bandages wrapped around the stub of her elbow joint. The constant pain had faded to a dull ache, but the ghosts of sensation remained.

Last night, she had reached out both hands to take her dinner plate. Her father had been unable to meet her eyes ever since.

"Teddy, come on in here. The food's ready."

Her father had set two places at the too-large table, and she sat in what had been her brother Toby's chair, next to their father's place at the head of the table.

None of the boys had come home from the war. Teddy imagined their bones bleaching in a field, and wondered if corn grew around their scattered remains.

"I hear there's a man in town selling prosthetics," her father said.

Teddy had to put her fork down to pick up her coffee. "Doc says I'm not ready for a prosthetic yet."

"You ought to go take a look anyway. It'd be good for you to get out of the house. He's set up at the old Methodist church."

After breakfast, Teddy stacked plates and carried them to the sink, but her father waved any further help away. "Get on with you."

She struggled out of the clothes that she'd managed to get herself into—a pair of Danny's old trousers and her mother's old sleeping shirt—and tried to make herself presentable.

All of her old things had too many buttons. She managed to fasten a skirt, but it slid right off of her hips. She ignored her growing frustration. She'd never have two hands again, and getting angry about it accomplished nothing.

Resigned, she pulled on her uniform. The hems on the pant legs were worn through, and the bloodstains refused to wash out, but the left sleeve was already tied up, and it was the only thing that fit. The nurses had replaced all of the buttons with snaps, so she could get into and out of it herself. Even now, the uniform felt right. Even now, when all that it stood for was defeat and ashes. There was nothing she could do about her hair—it was growing out around her face, uneven and split at the ends, too short to braid even if she'd had the use of both hands. She supposed a hook could be useful. She wondered what options the vendor would have.

She had a bit of money—the Western government had offered to handle all the back pay that was owed to the defeated Eastern soldiers. Maybe it was time to invest in a new wardrobe—she could head to the store after she stopped in at the church.

It felt good to be dressed, to get out of the house. The sun was warm on her face, the path familiar under her feet.

She pushed the church door open and froze.

The prosthetic vendor was a Western dandy, pale-haired and wire thin. His wares glowed with an eerie purple light. Teddy's stomach turned. This dark magic was what they'd been fighting against—what her brothers had died in vain trying to destroy.

The dandy hit her with a charming smile that looked out of place on his narrow face. "Good morning, miss. You must be the Rhodes girl."

He, and his wares, made her skin crawl. She chastised herself for being irrational and reminded herself that the war was over, but took a step back as he approached. "Look now, I don't know who told you what, but I'm not interested."

She stepped back again, but he grabbed her shoulder before she could escape. His hand was cold and soft. "Now, now," he said in a hearty, earnest tone. "Let's not be hasty. My prices are very reasonable, and you can't really want to be a cripple for the rest of your life. I know that's not what your father wants for you."

She shrugged his hand away. Anger and shame and bruised pride mixed uneasily in Teddy's belly. When had he talked to her father? "I'd be happy to explain just what I'd like you to do with yourself, but that's not a discussion for polite company."

He stepped close—too close, and Teddy almost choked on the the lightning-strike scent of magic that clung to his skin—and lowered his voice. "Do you really intend to let fear and ignorance destroy what is left of your life? What are you going to do with yourself, Miss Rhodes? The back pay that my government is so generously providing won't last forever. How will you support yourself? With one hand, you're a burden on your poor father. With two, you'd be able to help him, to support him in his twilight years. Maybe even get yourself a husband to help with the farm. I know it's hard to believe, but I'm here as a friend."

"You don't know anything about me," Teddy snapped. "Don't pretend that you do." She turned away and let the church door fall closed behind her, then headed back home. She didn't have it in her to try to do any shopping today.

How could her father have sent her here? What had he said to the dandy that made him so determined to strap one of his abominations to her arm?

Her father tried to hide his disappointment when he saw her still-empty sleeve. Teddy tried to hide everything she was feeling, too.

●

Her father invited the dandy for dinner that night. "Teddy, I believe you met Mr. Duncan."

"In passing," she said. Her fingers itched for her repeater, but it was gone, surrendered on the battlefield along with her pride, in exchange for her life.

Her father served bland stew and hard biscuits, and had the dandy sit in her mother's chair.

Her father looked tired. And old.

Teddy dunked a biscuit in the stew and watched it closely. It was hard to look at either man's face.

Her father leaned forward. "Mr. Duncan was telling me about a new model of prosthetic—"

"No," Teddy said.

"But Teddy—"

She slammed her single fist against the table. "I said no, Dad. Absolutely not. I will not attach myself to one of his monstrosities."

"I am offering a significant discount to all veterans, on either side," Mr. Duncan said.

"So the cost would be something other than my soul?"

"As I said, my prices are reasonable. You can have a state-of-the-art prosthetic for the cost of a single memory. You won't get that deal from anyone else."

"I'm not interested," Teddy said.

But Mr. Duncan reached across the table and placed one hand on her wrist. The touch was gentle, but his eyes burned into hers.

The smell of blood and cordite, the sound of ragged screams and hopeless moans. The doctor's face looming over her, exhausted and pale. The taste of harsh whisky, the cold, ragged edge of the saw pressing into ruined flesh. The endless rasping against bone before the darkness came.

Teddy jerked away, and she was in her father's kitchen again. Her biscuit had dissolved in her stew.

"It's not one you'll miss," Mr. Duncan said. "Or you can choose another. It can be any memory, willingly given."

"Please, at least think about it, Teddy." Her father took her one hand between his. "I just want to know that you can take care of yourself."

Teddy stood up, shaking with her bottled rage. "I already know that I can take care of myself, Dad. I was a soldier, and I know what I'm capable of. I learned it over and over again, these past five years. And I'd rather have no hands at all than make the very thing I fought against a part of myself."

She stormed out of the dining room. She'd never bothered to unpack her kit, so there was no need to take time to toss necessities into a bag. She grabbed her cash and slung her rucksack onto her shoulder.

Her father stood in the doorway. "What are you doing?"

"Leaving. Don't worry about me. I'll be fine. But I can't stay here, not after this."

"I don't understand."

"That's because you haven't seen what their magic can do, and what it costs. Their factories will keep churning out products—there's nothing I can do to stop that now—but I will never, ever use one."

More memories flooded her mind, of purple-tinged mist creeping over a hillside, of fallen men getting back up, their eyes and fingernails and gaping wounds glowing that same purple, turning and shambling back toward their own line. Of rain that ate through tents and blankets and flesh, of cannons that shot jagged purple lighting that cut men down like a scythe through wheat.

"Some of our methods have been regrettable, but that doesn't make everything we touch evil," Mr. Duncan said. His earnest tone grated on her nerves. "We were at war.

There were atrocities committed by both sides. This technology proves that we can harness our magic for the good of mankind."

"I hope you're right," Teddy said. "I really do. But I'm going."

Her father didn't move. "Please don't. You're all I have left."

"I thought I was a burden," Teddy snapped.

"I never said that. I just want what's best for you."

"But you can't trust me to know it for myself?"

Her father sagged. "I'm sorry. Please, just—just stay, Theodora."

Mr. Duncan held out his hand. "My offer stands, Miss Rhodes. If you ever change your mind—"

"I don't think that's likely, son," her father said, his voice still tinged with regret. "And I know myself that my cooking isn't anything to stick around for, so you'd best be going."

Mr. Duncan tipped his hat to them. "As you wish. Goodbye, Mr. Rhodes. Miss Rhodes. I do wish you well."

They stood on the porch and watched him go. "I do believe that he meant every word," Teddy said. "And it might even be true. But I can't use their magic. Can't make it a part of myself. I—I just can't."

"I don't understand, but it's your life, your arm. Your choice. I'm sorry I pushed you. Will you stay?"

Teddy closed her eyes at the pain in his voice. "Yeah. I'll stay."

●

Teddy stared out at the corn. It was taller than her, now. She wondered if the fields her unit had watered with blood had higher or lower crop yields than normal, this year.

Or if blood didn't change a thing.

"I was thinking of trying to plant a rose garden," her father said, handing her a cup of coffee. "Your mother always wanted one."

"Would they be able to survive the winter?"

He shrugged. "I dunno, we never tried it. Come on in, food's ready."

Teddy followed him, then poked at what she could only assume was meant to be oatmeal. "Dad, let me cook. Even one-handed, I think I can manage better than this."

"Are you sure?"

"Yes."

He grinned at her. "Thank the Lord. I was starting to worry that we'd starve."

Teddy's arm healed, and she got a simple prosthetic with a hook. In her first week with it, she shredded four shirts and a skirt, and she dropped two plates. She kept practicing.

One of the town boys who'd lost a leg got a fancy Western prosthetic, and could walk—even run, Teddy heard—like he was whole. Teddy told herself that it wasn't her place to judge.

He didn't meet her eyes when they crossed paths, but he muttered, "I figured that we couldn't beat them, so...." He trailed off and shrugged.

"Having that thing attached to me would give me nightmares," Teddy said. "I was at Tikamat."

"Our unit never saw any purple action."

"Count yourself lucky."

"I do, Miss Rhodes. Believe me, I do."

"What memory did you give them?"

"A week in hospital, after I lost the leg. I was feverish, almost died."

"Do you miss it?"

"The memory?"

Teddy nodded.

"You know, I do. You wouldn't think so—I know it was a bad week, even not recalling it. But the empty space—well, it feels a bit like my leg did, before."

●

The next Westerner to come into town was different. His fine brown suit was worn through at the knees and elbows, and he didn't smile. He drove his cart to the farm and stopped. He hopped down, hat in hand. "I hear you were in the war, miss."

"That's right. I'm Theodora Rhodes." She held out her hand, and he shook it. He had a nice, firm grip.

"Name's Tim Brady. I was a photographer during the war. I worked on the front lines, and I'm looking to sell some pictures. I've got them on glass plate." He patted the wagon.

"Do you still have your camera?"

He shook his head. "It was government property. I couldn't have kept it fueled on my own, anyway. I've got no gift for memory-taking."

"Did they turn you out after the war was done?" Teddy asked as she glanced through a stack of glass plates. Nightmare images stared back. Ghostly outlines of dead men, charred fields, smoking houses. Piles of corpses frozen to the ground, a horse melted by the deadly rain, a nurse tossing an amputated arm into a pile of discarded body parts.

"Not exactly." Mr. Brady's tone hinted at a longer story, but didn't invite more questions.

The last one in the stack was a blurry shot of a horde of purple shamblers. Teddy shuddered. "I can see why you're having trouble selling these."

He pointed at another section. "These tend to be my better sellers. They're more scenic shots of places before the battles started. I'd be happy to trade a few for a place to stay and something to eat."

"Did you take portraits?"

"I did."

"Ever join up with the 17th regiment?"

He shook his head. "No, sorry."

Teddy shrugged. "That's the unit my brothers were with. Anyway, come on in, I've got dinner on the table, and I should be able to scrounge up an unbroken plate for you."

"Thanks, Miss Rhodes. I'll see to my mule first, if you don't mind."

"That's fine, Mr. Brady. Come on in whenever you're done."

Dinner wasn't fancy, but it was hot and filling and a far sight better than anything on the lines. Mr. Brady tucked in with enthusiasm.

"You've arrived at an opportune time, if you're looking for a bit of work," Teddy's father said. "I could use some help bringing in the harvest. Can't pay, but you'd be welcome to stay here till we're done."

"That's mighty kind of you, Mr. Rhodes. I'm much obliged."

He had a nice smile. Small and tired, but nice.

Days slipped by. "That Brady's a hard worker," her father said one morning, while Mr. Brady was out seeing to his mule. "We'll have the harvest in pretty soon, now."

"That's good news. Do you think the weather will hold?"

"I think so."

"Good."

"Teddy, I know you never gave much thought to marriage, but with the boys gone, we're gonna need help around here, and we can't afford a hired hand."

With a fancy Western prosthetic, she would have been able to help him herself. "I understand, Dad."

"I think he's a good man."

If Mr. Brady hadn't come, it would have been one of the boys from town. But that didn't mean he was wrong. "I think so, too."

●

The next morning, Teddy got dressed and followed her father and Mr. Brady out into the field.

"I thought I'd try to help today," she said. She was getting used to the hook, and her body was still accustomed to long, physically active days.

"Another set of hands is always welcome," her father said.

Teddy waited for him to wince at the phrase, to apologize. Instead he just smiled at her, then turned back to the corn.

She steadied the cornstalk with her hook and snapped the ripe ear off with her hand.

It had been easier with two good hands. Still, she grinned as she tossed the corn into the wagon.

As they walked in that evening, her father nudged her shoulder with his own. "I guess you showed me," he said, his voice soft.

"What do you mean?"

"That you don't need anyone to take care of you."

●

Teddy sat on the porch after dinner, trying to mend one of her torn skirts, but mostly staring out at the piles of cornstalks in the harvested field. Mr. Brady wandered out and stared up at the sky. "Do you have nightmares, Miss Rhodes?" he asked.

"Of course I do."

"Yeah. Me too."

She liked the lines of his face, liked that they didn't need to talk about the nightmares to understand each other.

But mostly, she liked that she could like him without needing him. She wondered what it was that he needed. "Why are you here?" she asked. "Why aren't you back West, taking pictures for the government? I'm sure they'd take those plates off your hands, too."

"I'm sure they would. And they'd print the ones that serve them and dispose of the rest."

"Is that why you left?" Teddy asked. "Because you didn't want them to destroy your pictures?"

"Destroying the evidence doesn't make it any more or less real. They can't change what happened. But they can change the story."

"A few pictures isn't going to change that," Teddy said, thinking of the boy in town with his fancy prosthetic.

Mr. Brady shrugged. "Maybe it's a good thing. We all have to move forward together, now. Western magic is the way of the future. The past is done, and should be buried along with the dead. But I'm not ready to let it go. The things in those pictures—they're real. They happened."

"So, what do you plan to do? Travel around, selling off plates one at a time?"

He shrugged again. "No one wants them, Miss Rhodes. No one but the one group that I don't want to sell them to."

Teddy set her mending aside. "So don't sell them."

"I can't cart them around forever—they're not exactly sturdy."

"Don't do that either."

"What are you suggesting, Miss Rhodes?"

"You can call me Teddy."

"Your father calls you Teddy."

"My brothers did, too."

"Can I call you Theodora, instead?"

"If you'd like."

"You'll have to call me Tim, then."

"Or Timothy?" Teddy said, giving him a small smile.

"Sure." He smiled back. "So, what exactly are you suggesting, Theodora?"

"Stay. Stay here, with us. Help on the farm. We can build a greenhouse so that we can grow roses."

He was silent for a long moment. "You want to use the glass plates to build a greenhouse?"

"Yes."

"The sun will bleach them to nothing, eventually."

"That's the way it is, with time."

"I'd want to save some of them," he said. "At least a few."

"Of course."

He held his hand out to her, and she took it. "I've always liked roses."

"So did my mother. But I worry that the winters would be too harsh."

"Okay."

"Okay?"

"I'll stay with you, Theodora. And I'll build your greenhouse, and let the sun bleach my photographs."

Teddy squeezed his hand.

"Maybe they will." His hand was warm, and chapped from working in the fields.

Teddy laced her fingers through his, and they watched the stars come out together.

●

Jamie Lackey's story "Shadows on Glass" was originally published in Metaphorosis on Friday, 4 August 2017. See magazine.metaphorosis.com

About the author

Jamie Lackey lives in Pittsburgh with her husband and their cat. In addition to writing, she spends her time reading, playing tabletop RPGs, baking, watching anime, and hiking.

www.jamielackey.com, @AnyaSelena

Notes from the Laocoön Program

Phoenix Alexander

The orbital module fails to detach and we ignite in the full-mouth kiss of the planet's atmosphere, spinning with a velocity that pushes us to the black brink of unconsciousness. G-force grinds us into seats molded for our forms. There is the view through the porthole in my periphery — of jittering flame and cartwheeling stars and the glowing edges of unfamiliar continents — and the interior of the capsule in front of me. My vision breaks, the views looping into kaleidoscopic fragments.

I do not panic. I trust in my training. Anything can be controlled: my breath as my body is buffeted by forces huge and inhuman, and the focus of my vision as it lightens with the threat of unconsciousness.

The combined mass of the disintegrating orbital module and our descent module is too much for our parachute to bear. I am calm as it shreds in the force of re-entry, incendiary rags streaking the black beyond the porthole. Sparks fall inside the module, too; orange nodes of slag burrow into my legs. There is a hot meat smell, but I feel no pain.

The planet's surface comes rushing up, patches of harsh white vegetation rippling across its surface and I see something move beneath the earth, as if the chalky ground were a skin over something far more alive, and vast. For a moment there is the nightmarish impression of skin pulled taut over a face the span of an entire world. I am drunk with adrenaline — and I *brace*.

The successful firing of the landing rockets is a small mercy. The capsule finally hits the planet's surface and my spine, elongated after months of weightlessness and beaten by the tumbling violence of our descent, breaks. There is pain — and then pride as I identify which vertebrae have shattered (they are somewhere in my cervical spine, perhaps C3 and C4, where my neck meets my shoulders). Beyond the porthole: fire.

●

The memory is of a hot and starry night on a date on which something is celebrated, I forget what, because in this memory you are the most important. And in this memory I clutch in my hand a little burning thing. Nothing loud or dangerous, just a sparkler, flaring fire as I draw words in the air: words I will never say to you but that I pray you can make out.

Kiss me, Brian Lowe, I write, laughingly. You always hated your name for being too dull. To me it is miraculous. *Kiss me.* The words hang in afterglow between us and then disappear. You are bolder than I, living a happiness that I envy. Entirely comfortable in your skin. Yours was a happy childhood, free of the scandal of your mother deciding to love women when you were in high school. *You* were not bullied by children as cruel and judgmental as their parents — though not as cruel and judgmental as my father, who tried to 'beat the queer' out of my mother until, one day, she simply left.

You would never call yourself that, would never define yourself by your most intimate desires. You are just *you*. You, laughing, the beautiful contours of your face lit by the sparkler as you dodge backwards.

"Stop it, you'll set my coat on fire," you smile, grabbing my wrist. The moment is a gentle kind of control and your breath is warm.

So I stop writing the words, and I don't say them. I have the feeling of a moment passing. Of some kind of threshold being crossed, an alarm in my mind blaring to announce that *time is up*, and I don't know why I felt that and I am full with regret.

I say this to you instead: I am moving to California for Test Pilot School and I am asking Alice to marry me. Because I can't tell you that I am my mother's son, as shameful and perverse as she. I won't label myself as she did, though, giving ammunition to those who would spit out the word like shrapnel, like my father, weaponizing a private act until it signified something as far from intimacy as it can be... I just love you, and I don't know what that means or how I would live it, but I love you anyway. I don't say any of that.

Anything can be controlled.

Your face tells me everything I need to know in that instant and I see the lie reflected back to me. You withdraw your hand and my skin feels the loss immediately.

The horrible thing is that, still, you never looked so beautiful. I do not know if the sparks in your eyes are your own or from the sparkler I hold like a white flag, still burning, between us.

●

I must have lost consciousness briefly. My eyes peel open to smoke roiling across the surface of my vizor and Mikhail yelling in my earpiece. The capsule has landed us on our backs and, amazingly, the thing is in one piece. I look up at the million blinking buttons of the control panels: all red, all furious. There is a line on the computer command transcript that indicates a control override on the orbital module, but I issued no such thing. I *would* not. There must be a mistake. I close my eyes, seeing nothing but pulsing black. The black begins to glow orange and I open them again. Flames have now spread to a conflagration in the view beyond the porthole to my right. The planet's surface beyond is an unlikely plain of tiny, white-headed flowers with fat stamens, and squat pills for leaves. We have burned a great black patch through them and streaked the earth with the violence of our landing. To my left: my companion, Mikhail, fumbling at the harnesses with an uncharacteristic clumsiness that is the only sign of his discomfort.

I attempt to shift in my seat. Nothing happens. My limbs do not work.

"Mikhail," I say. My voice is a poor, croaking thing. "My back is broken." I don't know if he hears me so I say it again. "My back is broken."

I see Mikhail's eyes narrowing through his visor and I know it is bad. He unclips and peels the belts from my torso, crusts of melted polymer falling like confetti upon my shoulders. He says something and my ears ring, the sounds taking sluggish moments to coalesce into something intelligible.

"Don't move. I need to look outside."

I see his lips move and make out the word *outside* and hear it in comically slowed syllables (*ah-ooh-tsai-duh*). I visualize him stepping onto a planet of flame, a little David in the face of a fiery Goliath the size of a world. Perhaps it is the endorphins, the adrenaline making me feel invincible even as my insides clatter nausea.

I speak to him to control it.

"Sounds good. Check where the fire is."

Mikhail climbs over me towards the entry hatch above my head. I peer into the polycarbonate bowl of his visor as he passes. I want to raise my hand, folding the fingers until just the thumb sticks up: the classic gesture — just to do *something.* I cannot. So I give him a smile instead. Bravery in the face of the infinite unknown. He returns the gesture, pulls at the hatch above my head, and crawls out into a new world.

●

"You have a slightly erratic psychometric profile," they tell me.

I ask them to explain, precisely, how my psychometric profile is 'slightly erratic.'

The Chief of Operations answers. He is a powerfully built and diplomatic man who has completed three spacewalks in his career — yet who is still, as far as I'm concerned, prone to lapses of appalling stupidity.

"Well... if you're asking. You never admit your errors. You blame everything and everyone else: your colleagues, the engineers, the computers, equipment. You have bouts of rage — usually directed to female staffers. You —"

"Enough."

The Deputy CO silences him and the two exchange glances while I stand very still, crushing my lips together, because to move them at all would probably cost me my career.

A lesser man would have snapped.

A lesser man — yes, you — would have smashed both of their smug faces in, and the smug faces of everyone on the damn committee, sitting at the table like morons.

"The fact of the matter is," the CO is saying, looking back to me with something of a smile on his face, "that despite these... judgments, you are the perfect individual for the mission."

I leave confused: insulted, prideful. Staccato footsteps follow me down the corridor and when I turn, the Deputy CO is on my arm, her face so close I can see my reflection in the water of her eyes.

"Huxley," she whispers. "You don't have to accept this mission. I'm just saying. You can walk away."

I remove my arm from hers.

"Why would I?"

"You wouldn't be the first. There would be no shame."

"I'm not like other people. I'm not afraid."

She looks at me as if to say *you are exactly like other people* and I snap my head away before I do something I regret. Her voice wheedles behind me:

"Just... know that you don't have to say yes to this."

What does she know? Hasn't my whole life been leading up to this? All of my hard work, my training, my discipline?

Of course I say yes.

●

I am still, packed in my chair with the interior of the capsule crushed around me. My knees should be throbbing with pain, crushed almost up to my chin. My bones should hurt and my skin should ache and burn but instead there is nothing.

I am not worried.

I am only a little lonely at the sight of Mikhail's empty chair right next to me. Our in-suit comms work, at least, and he speaks to me breathlessly through my earpiece in lilting English.

"How are you doing in the gravity?" I croak. I wet my lips with sips of water, the straw curling over my shoulder into my suit.

"Ok."

There is the harsh sound of Mikhail's breathing as he stops speaking. I watch from the porthole. I see him straining with each step, padding through the grass around the capsule, and I lose sight of him for several minutes. Then he comes hobbling back into view.

"The capsule is ok. Not going to burn. But... "

His voice trails off. Instead there is his breath, and another breath, and another, each heavier than the last.

The breaths quicken.

"Good," I reply. I take another sip of water, swallowing hard. "But what?"

I watch him stop and force himself to stand at full height, looking around him in all directions. The sky is a rusty haze above him. Pale clouds of ammonia ice string the air like entrails. His heart rate accelerates in my earpiece along with his breathing, our spacesuits sharing biometric readings.

"What? What do you see?" I ask him.

"We — there must be some mistake," he says.

"We don't make mistakes."

"This is not the planet we were trained for."

"You're wrong." I say immediately. "Its mass and radius are what we expected. Same for the surface gravity. The atmosphere is —"

"*Listen*, Huxley. Someone has made a mistake."

Ice-cold agony needles between my shoulder blades and burrows into the base of my skull. The pain is so great my vision greys.

"What do you mean, there must be some mistake?" I manage to say.

"This is not the planet."

"Have you contacted Mission Control?"

He nods. "Nothing. The line is broken or something."

The image of the command code overriding the orbital module rolls green in front of my vision, and with it the awful possibility that *they know about this*. The pain softens, as if something warm has nested in the base of my skull. I do not tell Mikhail. His panic would be the end of us.

I watch him kneel (the movement quick, the planet eager to bring him to its surface) and pull an instrument out of his suit, sinking the needle into the soil. "Calcium, silicon, and iron make up the highest percentage of minerals..."

His head suddenly cranes to the right. He has seen something behind him — something I cannot, no matter how fiercely I squint.

"Mikhail? Mikhail, what is it?"

He freezes, stuck in a crouch.

"Huxley."

"Yes."

"I think I see something."

"What do you see?"

The radio crackles and his words break, infuriatingly. "... someone... hell..."

More harsh breaths, more heartbeats. I do not want to know him so intimately. His pale suited body stretches, then stiffens, caught between rising and — what? Crawling? Away or towards the capsule? He is a good man but an idiot, a coward, indecisive at the worst moments.

I lose my temper.

"Be a man and tell me what you fucking *see*," I roar even though it shreds my throat. The tip of the straw hits my lips. *Fuck it.* I snap at it with my teeth: the only movement I am capable of. I admit: here I lose a little control.

"What do you see? What do you fucking *see*? No, no, don't come in, don't…"

Then he is gone from my view, and there is the sound of the hatch being hauled open behind me and he clambers over my body and falls into his seat, babbling in Russian and hammering at the displays.

"Чужеродная форма жизни обнаружена… Слушаю… Чужеродная форма жизни обнаружена, отвечайте пожалуйста…" There is no answer, from anything, from any quarter. Mission Control is silent.

"Careful!" I shout to him as he jostles me. I know it because I can see my body moving but I feel *nothing at all*, not the impacts, nor the weight of his body.

I have to slow my breathing because I know I will lose consciousness; the panic will send me down. One of us has to be strong.

He falls into his seat, hammering at the controls and at the comms panel on the gauntlet of his suit until, eventually, he calms. I look back out of the porthole. The flowers billow in a deepsea waltz, white dust tumbling in the wake of Misha's footsteps. I can see nothing beyond.

You can't blame me for being angry.

You would be probably dead by now.

●

I ring my wife and tell her the news. The insults from the CO, the Deputy urging me not to take the mission — the disrespect shown — got to me, I must confess. The moment I dreamed about since childhood sours and seems banal, strangely predetermined, as I tell it to my wife. Perhaps it is because it is her I am telling it to and not you.

"Just let it go," she says. "Focus on the positives. My God, Hux! You're going to *space*."

She is cheerful. Suspiciously so.

"Are you sure you're ok with that? You aren't going to miss me too much?"

There is a pause on the end of the line.

"Sure," she says finally.

"You don't sound convincing."

"What do you want me to say, Hux?"

"I — never mind. Bye."

I hang up.

I make another call.

Your voice is sleepy, as if you were sunbathing, sunblinded. I try not to visualize your body.

"Hey, Brian."

"Oh! Huxley..."

I tell you about the mission and the comments from the Deputy.

"Don't worry about it," you say. I can hear that you are beaming and I smile, too. "You're the coolest, calmest man I know."

"I thought so too."

"How is Alice?"

"Oh, she's fine."

"Good. Is her writing coming along well?"

I realize I don't know how to answer him. Instead another question tumbles out of my mouth before I can stop it.

"Are you seeing anyone?"

There is a pause that breaks my heart, because I know the kind of answer that is coming. "Well... yes, actually."

Of course, of course you are. That's what people do. My fingers lock on the receiver.

"Oh? What's her name?"

You laugh again, slightly unsure this time. The sound is cruel to me. I am not smiling anymore.

"Jaeyoung. His name is Jaeyoung."

Part of me is stunned, truly, for the first time in my life. Another part is not surprised at all and accepts this like a death. This: the loss that was traced in the air that night with the fireworks, when I was too afraid to say how I wanted my life to be. With you.

I want to say a million, an infinite number of things, each word a red jewel of something — what? Anger. There is only anger. Anger, anger, anger, pulsing in syllabic form and ready to fall like a meteor.

I hang up.

●

Mikhail is asleep in his seat next to me.

I am glad for his presence. I do not know the time; I cannot see my watch. It has been perhaps two hours or ten since we crashed.

I go over the launch, scouring my mind to find what could have happened. We checked and tripled checked the mechanisms every step of the way; I could not have made a mistake. My fingers found the keys by rote, the checklist running like a biometric display before my eyes. Everything was working perfectly. We ran simulation after simulation and it all worked, everything worked, nothing predicted this.

Someone did this to us deliberately. We were sabotaged.

The Deputy CO. It must have been her. That bitch! That's why she tried to warn me... but why? Why?

I try and move the fingers of my left hand. Nothing.

I try and move the fingers of my right hand.

Come on

Fucking come on —

My index finger twitches. Sweat falls into my eye. I try harder. This time it moves more. The fingers almost — almost — curl a little, as if around a beer can.

I stop trying. My breath comes in gasps and the sound frightens me. It sounds like something else: less than human. Sweat pours into my eyes and between my lips. I can't touch any of the buttons or dials inches from my face to call Mission Control, my wife, anyone. I can't do anything.

A scream rises. I clamp my teeth shut.

I am not screaming in front of Mikhail.

I am not screaming in front of *anyone.*

So I wait for the moment to pass.

Something moves before my eyes.

In the quartz glass disc of the porthole, in the flowerlands beyond, under a dim sky where the stars shine brilliantly: the plants have changed. The petals of the flowers seem to have withdrawn, or closed. I squint, but the distance is just too great to see clearly, and my eyes sting from the sweat. I look out into a forest of gently undulating pearl-white fronds that move, awfully, rising up from the ground like hairs on aroused skin.

"Mikhail," I say.

He snores and whimpers into his helmet.

The fronds move, blown by a wind I cannot fathom, and turn to gesture in the direction of — us. I feel observed.

"Don't you dare," I whisper. I want to make fists with my hands. "The fuck... the fuck is this?"

Yes, I am losing my cool. You always thought I wasn't aggressive, but you're wrong, Brian, you're so wrong. You helped me control it. I never got angry in front of you. But you are not here. You aren't here, supine, broken-backed, on a foreign planet and watched by things like snakes, half-alive, looking at you with pearly tips with no eyes but *you know they are watching anyway* —

You would be screaming by now. I know you would.

Mikhail speaks next to me and I cry out.

"Huxley," sleep-thick he speaks, "why are you crying?"

Then he looks out of the porthole beyond me and shouts in horror.

"Go out there. Go out there and kill them," I yell.

Instead he fumbles for the controls. Speaking to Mission Control, reporting these things in frantic Russian that cannot be true ("Nine meters — no, ten, eleven, ah, I think they are alive, yes... please send help, please help us...")

The comm is silent. There is no one there.

While I shout and curse at him Mikhail turns away, crushing himself even further into his seat, and simply stops looking.

"What kind of a miserable fucking coward..." Rage saves me. I curse him instead of screaming my fear. At some point exhaustion shreds my voice so I, too, close my eyes.

White limbs wave endlessly in the black in front of me and I think I hear a voice from the comm, the CO's voice — "... satisfactory... independent variable..." — and I think, *What on earth can be satisfying about a forest of fronds glowing and growing and watching, without even orbs for eyes?*

●

They tap instruments against the wet membranes of our eyeballs, testing the pressure. We run on treadmills at the bottom of an Olympic-sized swimming pool meant to simulate exercising in zero-g; the pressure makes my limbs iron and my breath come hard through my oxygen mask. They attach other masks to our faces and pump increasing levels of CO2 into our respiratory systems: 2 mil, 3 mil, 4mil. We are sat next to one another in doctor's chairs, me and Mikhail, and he whimpers with terror as the mask is pulled over his head, whereas I take it with a grim smile. I would take anything this way. To serve the greater good.

Could you say that? You, who gave into your baser desires and who even now are probably growing fat and complacent in an unremarkable job in an unremarkable house with an unremarkable man — a *man*! Jaeyoung. The word circles in my head as the CO2 levels pump up to 5mil. Mikhail starts coughing beside me, eyes streaming. I hit the arms of the chair with my fists.

"Who the fuck is Jaeyoung anyway?"

The orderly looks at me.

"Pardon?"

I rip off my mask.

"Mind your fucking business," I reply.

They hold mock funerals for us, as they do for all astronauts. Afterwards the psychologists ask me questions that I have never heard an astronaut asked before.

"Do you believe in the dignity of non-human life?"

"No."

"What aspect of death frightens you more: physical injury or the concept of the oblivion of consciousness?"

"Neither."

"Which is the stronger force: love or fear?"

I do not answer — I cannot answer that — because to me there is no real difference. But I do not tell them that.

●

I wake up to Mikhail crying.

At first I think it is something calling outside — but I know that is impossible, because all my senses are filtered through my suit and come with an underwater muteness, or with a tinny crackle of the comm, or they don't come at all. My eyes open and there it is: the round porthole a meter in diameter, my entire world coming through this circle. The flowers are still there, fat and stupid. The terrain rolls like a crumpled bedspread. As my eyes focus, I see odd patches where the flowers have been crushed — as if something has dragged its belly across the ground in a meandering path, or a line of animals has trampled them. The paths disappear into the distance in a crazed path.

My lips work for the straw. The flesh of them feels cracked.

"What is it, Mikhail?"

At first I don't understand what he says. Then I do.

"I have been tasted... something tasted me..."

"What are you talking about?"

"I woke and something was pushing my back like, like a knife in different places and my suit is..."

His voice trails off. I can tell by the direction of his voice that he was — is? — looking at his seat. I see his dim form hunched in my periphery. I try to move my head a fraction and am stunned by the agony.

"Чёрт!" he curses. Again and again.

"What? What? What is it? I can't fucking move..."

"The *seat*!" he shrieks. "Full of holes! There is something beneath the capsule, there must be something beneath the capsule in the ground..."

The image of that titanic face returns: gaping its mouth as we fell, streaming fire, pushing up against the surface of the planet to take us, sending tendrils up to taste...

Without warning, he squeezes over me again. I can't feel the mass of his body, but he knocks my knees and legs and I shout to him "*Stop, fucking STOP*," because he could be doing more damage to me but he is over and out of the hatch again, shoving it open. And he is outside.

"Mikhail, stop..."

I hear the impact of the hatch rolling to behind my head, sealing me in. I do not scream. You'd be proud of me, Brian — I don't scream. Out loud, at least. I want to move. I want to move my fingers and toes and pull myself out and run to you, thousands of miles away, on the planet I call home. I want to hold you in my arms and feel the warmth of your body and tell you I forgive you for Jaeyoung, and ask for *your* forgiveness in return for betraying you with my sham of a marriage, of a life.

But I cannot move. And so I watch Mikhail stagger over the terrain through that goddamned porthole, bent double under the weight of his own body, his breathing and heartrate alarms in my ears. And something else: a warning tone, electronic this time. A red, glowing visualization of his skeletal structure pops up in the inside of my vizor. And a numerical reading, negative 2, that I do not at first believe. Our suits perform scans of our bodies every 24 hours, sweeping us with minute levels of radiation — and his bone density reading is almost equivalent to someone suffering from osteoporosis.

Impossible.

The suit must have been damaged. I look from the display to the pitiful sight of him clambering over distant dunes outside, headed for God-knows-where.

Nothing makes any sense.

"Mikhail. Your bones..." I share the visual feed with him, although no doubt he has already been alerted by his own suit.

"*Tasting!*" he shrieks. "*Tasting!*"

I remember the cold finger of pain and the wending warmth at the bottom of my skull and wonder, too, if I have been tasted: if tendrils have pushed up from this planet, somehow burrowed through the combined layers of metal and insulating material that make up the outside of the capsule and pushed into my body, tearing the fibers of my suit and tasting, taking mass...

There is movement again outside. Not Mikhail, and visible through the ground-hugging carpet of white dust he leaves in his wake. A head peers up over a mound of terrain in front of him.

A human head.

And another. And another.

They move as one over the hill and come for him.

Dust kicks up in a cascade as he turns to run — but the gravity is crushing, and the creatures, backs bent in parabolas, haul themselves with horrible speed. I can see the muscles of their arms from where I lie here: they are like elderly men and women curled by age, palely human, hideous. Their eyes are big, bulging from their sockets, their heads downturned and necks craning down to the ground. Their backs are the highest parts of their bodies. The spines curve and push upward like the hulls of capsized ships. Their pupils are quick and agile, moving in their broad and horrible homogenous faces. They shamble in pursuit of Mikhail, faster than they have any reason to be. I hear their shrieks and cackles over the comm. They seem to be enjoying this.

They seem — happy.

There is screaming and screaming. I cannot see beyond the pillar of white dust that rises in the distance: the only signifier of Mikhail. Rocks clatter (or is it teeth?) and a final scream arcs up, high and womanish, before the comm goes quiet. I stop screaming as he does. I listen. His heartbeat is audible — accelerating to almost 200 beats per minute — and accelerating further. Then all readings go dark.

They must have torn him from his suit.

My heartbeat is my own.

I bring up the display of my own biometrics in the corner of my visor and find that my bone density is at negative 3 (how can that be possible? How?)

Now that I think about it: why on earth would our suits measure bone density? Why didn't I ask?

...I have been tasted. I have been taken from.

I am alone, on my back, with the planet drinking from my spine, betrayed by those I thought I could trust. They have killed Mikhail. They will not kill me.

When the dust settles I see his spacesuit, torn in two pieces, lying among the flowers.

Perhaps there is no use but I speak into my helmet, hoping someone will answer, hoping for a human voice in my earpiece. "We are being attacked. We are dying. I do not understand what is happening..." I think of you and I start to cry and I ask for help. I beg. It is easy: as easy as I was terrified it would be. For the anger to quench and the awful weakness inside to speak its truth, raw and shameful. "Please help us. Please help me. Please. Please. Please."

Someone clears their throat — I hold my breath for an answer — and there is an intake of breath (a woman, the Deputy CO? Will she be kind to me again?) but there is nothing, no answer.

"I know you're listening. I know you're *fucking* listening..." I can't breathe. My chest rises and falls too fast and what I think is my screaming is the breath trying to come and not coming. I fall blackly into unconsciousness.

It is the final meal with my family and friends before we leave for Star City. You are not there. I regret that now. Isn't that funny? Regret always comes too late. I don't think we are capable of regretting anything as long as there is a chance of turning things back, of changing them at any moment. Or so we delude ourselves. And then the chance is gone, and there it is: regret. The most useless of things.

So we eat, and you aren't there.

There is Mikhail and his wife Isabella, and an Italian astronaut whose name I forget, and my wife and her sister, and her sister's husband and their children. And Mikhail's friends, two men, and their wives, and their five children between them. We toast in our various languages, the adults laughing over vodka while the children crawl and clamor around our legs.

"I tell you," Isabella beams at me. "You're lucky you don't have kids. It's hard, leaving them behind."

I smile and think of you and drink.

"Isn't it funny," my wife says, pink-faced tipsy, "that they aren't letting our husbands dock on the Space Station? Just a shuttle up there, strapped in for the journey, and then shot back out to this very, secret planet on this very, secret mission."

Isabella hiccups. "I heard that the planet is changing location. Can you believe? The thing is *moving*? Planets don't do that."

"Well..." My tongue feels thick and my head hurts. I wonder how much I should bother to explain to these women. "We discovered it about 20 million miles from Venus. It has an erratic orbit — which planets undoubtedly *do* have, and..."

A child grabs my trouser ankle and I yelp, almost spilling my wine. Isabella is no longer listening — perhaps she never was — and leans into my wife, who catches my eye across the table. I see pure wickedness in her as she speaks. "I mean, honestly, Hux would probably smash something vital the moment something pisses him off. Months of precious scientific research ruined because my husband can't keep his temper."

Isabella claps her hands.

"Yes, and my poor Misha would wet his suit when something goes wrong — can you imagine? Putting poor Hux through a faceful of his zero-g piss..."

The women laugh. Mikhail, to my disgust, grins like a fool next to his wife.

"It's ok, I'll just piss on him in the capsule," he gestures to me.

Poor Hux.

"What exactly *is* your mission?" one of Mikhail's friends asks. Mikhail shrugs, laughing like everyone else.

"Data collection, assessment of habitable environment, you know."

The friend laughs, the sound foolish. The man's lips and teeth are reddened from wine. "I don't know, actually. But it's ok. I get it."

Poor. Hux.

I stand up. This is intolerable.

"Here we go," my wife says, leaning back in her seat.

"Yeah, here we go. I'll tell you what our mission is. It's advancing the progress of fucking mankind. How is the writing coming along, darling? Sold anything yet?"

The laughter stops abruptly.

"You know," Isabella interjects. She is not smiling anymore. Her glare is sober. "I always wondered why you married him, Alice. What do you get out of it?"

"What does she get?" I can't let her answer. "This house? An income? Freedom to write those shitty romance stories that no-one wants to publish, let alone read?"

I regret the words as soon as they come out but it's too late, far too late. A child cackles from underneath the table.

Alice is unfazed and raises a glass to me. How I wish it were you there, raising a toast to me. About to say something kind. Not this. Not whatever is coming.

"Nicely put, *darling*. To the progress of mankind."

Somehow that is worse than an insult. She did not lose control; she won.

She drinks, her eyes not leaving mine over the rim of the glass. Toddlers rough away, trampling food into the carpet around the ankles of the adults. You are not here.

●

I hear nothing further from Mikhail. I can see no sign of him outside, nor the ghastly creatures that took him. My comm picks up nothing. I roar and howl into it, screaming for Mission Control, screaming for *someone* to come and get us.

"Mikhail is dead, Mikhail is dead," I tell them over and over and over, and then, I think it is the nighttime, but who the fuck knows on this piece of shit planet with no day or night sky but that endless, star-pricked, white-blue? I hear someone clearing their throat again over the comm and I go to scream louder — but then I am tasted again. Indisputably.

The whole capsule moves. Something is pushing up from the earth and into my bones. Through insulator fabric, through metal, through glass that has withstood the fire of a planet's atmosphere. The view in the porthole shifts to that sky again, and the flowers... the flowers rise with me.

I think I make noises of terror. I don't know. I watch as the white eyeless tendrils push up through the seat next to me and the console panels crack and break and the worst thing is that they are alive, they are sentient, and I know they are hungry for a body I thought was mine and mine only.

I look out of the porthole and the planet has grown a million tendrils, a million limbs, and the flowers aren't flowers at all, and among and within the glowing forest I see the humanlike creatures that attacked Mikhail and Mikhail himself — is that him? Naked and bent, loping over the ground with an expression of such happiness as I have never seen on a human face!

The capsule jolts in the air and my head moves.

I can move! I can move! I can...

I look down my body for the first time since our landing. The tendrils have pushed through my arms and legs and out of the tops of my knees. Two heads, eyeless, featureless, white and glistening, nod from each patella, inches from my eyes. *How awful it is to have one's body violated:* I think I should feel that. Yet I feel nothing at all.

●

What did she see in me? Why did she marry me?

The sex wasn't there from the outset, but she didn't seem to mind.

I asked her once, in the early days, when I felt bad for not taking her like a lover as often as I felt I should.

"It's okay. I don't mind. I'm not much interested in sex anyway. I just like your company."

Why did I forget that?

She liked my company.

But I always felt hated. I always felt that hatred came from her, but perhaps it was always from me.

I hope she didn't hate me.

I know she didn't. If I am honest. I have not been honest for a long time. Perhaps for my whole life.

My father never believed in our marriage. I think he always knew. The cocked eyebrows when I embraced Alice in his presence, the wry smile.

"How is your friend Brian?" "When are you gonna make me a grandad, Hux?"

I avoided his questions every time. Laughing them away the way men tell a joke to hide something raw.

I wonder what my mother would have said.

Why was I afraid? Why couldn't I be kind to the friend that Alice was, if nothing else? Why not kindness?

I have made a ruin of my life and for nothing at all, for a feeling that I am unloved and must stay that way forever. Perhaps the measure of life is how kind we are.

And I have not been kind.

I must have lost consciousness, because I wake and the capsule is on the ground and my body is whole. The flowers nod outside. The stars shine. The ground is white dust rolling between them and there is Mikhail's suit, torn in two pieces still.

There is a voice.

"Huxley. Huxley Davis. Hux."

It is a voice I have heard before.

"Brian?"

The name is clarity. I feel light, as if I will blow away in the easiest cosmic wind.

"Not Brian." A name I recognize. A woman. The Deputy Chief of Operations. This time her voice is not unkind, not mocking. Her words come quick and breathless and sibilant but not unkind. The opposite of that. "I shouldn't be calling you but I... this is cruelty. I can't be long. Listen to me. You were supposed to fail. You all were. That is why you were chosen. There is a creature living under the planet's surface... the planet *is* a creature. A creature like nothing we've ever seen before, and one that feeds on human matter. You weren't supposed to come back. You weren't supposed to survive — because you couldn't. You have too many weaknesses. That was the point. Do you see? That was *always* the point. We wanted to see the effects it would have on the weakest of us. What it wanted. What it *still* wants."

A tear rolls down my cheek and all I can think of is your face. I see the sparkler. I see fire.

"Calcium," I whisper. Bone-white light films my eyes. The creatures, brilliant men and women wrecked with the symptoms of osteoporosis and rollicking as happy and content as idiots across the surface of this monstrous world. "That's all it wants. Calcium. I'm an astronaut. I..."

The weakest of us.

I know she is right. I know.

The mission is not so heinous, really.

Dulce et decorum est, pro scientia mori. "Why didn't you just tell me? I would have died for this mission. My body... everything. I don't care. I don't have much to live for. I would have come here willingly."

There is silence on the comm. Something like weeping.

"...There is a letter for you. From Brian Lowe. Your wife sent it to us here. Would you like me to read it to you?"

I can move my hands. Slowly, and the fingers are curled and the elbows don't move. The creature in the planet has taken calcium from me. It's alright. It is a good price to pay. I think of Mikhail's face and the happiness there. I think of what is on Earth. And I think of the voice here, in my ear, about to read your words to me.

"Yes." I don't know if I say it out loud or just wish it, or just dream it, but there you are: in a woman's voice, over dark space, thousands of miles away, but there you are, there you are, there you are.

●

Dear Hux,

I know you probably don't want to hear from me but I had to write.

I never blamed you. I want you to know that. I *never* blamed you.

But I needed you to be a little braver for me. I couldn't wait for you anymore. God, it hurts to write that, but it is true. Do you hate *me* for that? I think of that and I am ashamed. I can't sleep at night sometimes. Maybe I should've waited just a little bit longer, until you felt safer. Maybe I should have pushed you harder when you told me you were marrying Alice. Maybe I shouldn't have been so afraid. But now you have your life, and are doing amazing things, and I am here on Earth trying to make the best of things too.

There is so much I want to say to you. But I'll stick to the most important because I never was good with words.

Huxley Davis: I want you to know that you are my one great love.

Yours forever,

Brian

●

The afterbreaths of tears on the comm. Then the Deputy says: "… he drew a sparkler at the bottom of the letter. It's in blue pen — the stick part — and lines scratch out of it in red pen so you can imagine the sparks. I wanted you to know that. … Hux? Huxley, are you there? Huxley?"

●

I can move again.

The thing has stitched my nerve endings together with the flowers-that-are-not-flowers, with the fibers that have taken my calcium like alveoli taking oxygen: just a process that happens, without malice, to keep an organism alive. It is alright. Everything is alright. Turning in my seat, sleepily, like an ancient thing coming to life, I push out of my harness. With newborn hands I remove my helmet. The effort makes me sweat, because my fingers are curled and the muscles of my forearms are thin and taut. I press my face to the glass of the porthole. That damn porthole. I do not curse it now. I was a child looking out of it. I am not that anymore.

White-red light makes dazzling lines across my vision and I imagine you out there, you like you were that night all those years ago: young, bearded, beautiful, holding that sparkler out to me. This is it: this is the second chance.

Will you come with me? I imagine your voice saying to me.

Yes, my love. This time there is no hesitation, no fear. None in the slightest. None at all. *Yes.*

Well come on then.

I remove my suit and undergarments and crawl out of the capsule to emerge, naked and blinking, in starlight. My back is bent and my limbs extend rigid under me but I have never felt stronger. The air is as sweet and as new as I imagined air on a new world would be.

You are not outside, but the others are, and Misha crawls forward and touches my arm. He looks delighted, delighted, happier than a man has any right to be.

"Let's go, let's run," he says. Nodding. His chin tucks into his chest.

I raise a knuckle to a horizon distant and flower-filled. A million heads nod, making promises. The planet settles beneath us. Everything answers: *yes.*

I am doing this for you, because I know something the Deputy doesn't. I know what this planet wants, because I want it too.

It wants to not be alone. To take a living person into its most intimate core. To take many people, a million lovers and make them happy, but make them *stay.* It doesn't matter if we are the weakest humankind has to offer. Even the weak deserve a chance to be remade whole.

I'm not afraid now! I'm brave because of you. I see that now. Your love has done that.

Watch me!

Breaking into a run with the group who coax me on, because the gravity is stronger here, but do you think a planet's core can keep me from moving?

Watch me run!

Faster now, howling all my regrets to the windless air (my wife, my mother, my father, I am sorry) and the children I never had and the friends I pushed away and my family who don't matter anymore because *you* are here in my heart, just over that rise of earth, beyond the starlit horizon. My second chance, my angel, my family, my savior.

Watch me, loping life over the planet of a million flowers, breathless blesses from my lips dedicating each and every one of them — to you.

Phoenix Alexander's story "Notes from the Laocoön Program" was originally published in Metaphorosis on Friday, 27 December 2019. See magazine.metaphorosis.com

About the author

Phoenix Alexander is the Jay Kay and Doris Klein Librarian for Science Fiction and Fantasy at the University of California, Riverside, where he curates the Eaton Collection: one of the world's largest repositories of science fiction, fantasy, and horror.

Phoenix is a queer, Greek-Cypriot author of science fiction himself. His work has appeared in *The Magazine of Fantasy and Science Fiction, Escape Pod, Beneath Ceaseless Skies,* and *Science Fiction Studies*, among others. He is a full member of the Science Fiction Writers Association (SFWA), and served as a judge for the Arthur C. Clarke Award for 2021 and 2022. He is represented by Angeline Rodriguez at WME Books.

The Diamond Noose

Ramez Yoakeim

From the smug grins everyone flashed me as soon as I walked into the precinct, I knew I was in for a nasty surprise. I hadn't even reached my desk when the lieutenant called me into her glass-bowl office and handed me a new assignment: liaison to the Angels' Embassy.

I didn't care for Angels. They looked down on us from their palaces in the sky, pretending to help us survive our broken world while ensuring we'd never learn to do it on our own. Some said it was the Angels who set off the nuclear catastrophe that nearly wiped out life on Earth.

"Wouldn't this suit a more senior officer?" Or one more junior. Anyone else, really.

The lieutenant jabbed a paper on her desk. "Laila Aboud, requested by name."

A shiver zapped up my spine. The Angels had hidden eyes in the sky, seeing everywhere, knowing all. They had tentacles in every government, in every department, their shadow behind every throne. How had I managed to attract their attention? "Why me?"

She shrugged. "Ask the Angels when you see them. Do we have a problem here?"

I found myself wondering whose idea it had been to call them *Angels*.

"No, ma'am."

Like I had a choice. This job came with a warm bed and three squares, a firearm, and badge that opened doors and dropped eyes. I'd never walk away, no matter what they asked, any more than she would.

●

After all that, the work was surprisingly mundane. Waiting on my desk every morning was a stack of *requests* from the Angels Embassy: locate knickknacks stolen from the occasional visiting Angel, or quietly deem accidental the death of a prostitute in the company of another, or round up a bunch of uniforms to form a street cordon for visiting off-world dignitaries. Until I arrived at my desk one day to find a single message *requesting* my attendance at the embassy, and my heart dropped to my knees. I wanted to get away from Angels, not get closer.

The embassy occupied an old courthouse downtown. In the frigid gloom under Earth's thick cloud cover, the impeccably restored edifice dwarfed the line of scraggly humanity wrapped around its foundations like a snake about invincible prey.

However the Angels put it, the Transmigration they dangled before those queueing had nothing to do with benevolence. They preyed on our best and brightest, siphoning away those who might help us to break free of our dependence on their conditional aid. Could one of those queuing learn the secrets of fusion one day, or perfect anti-radiation medicines, or discover how to grow crops in poisoned soil, or put an end to the Angels plunder of our water and minerals, or lead us in overthrowing the tyrants they installed to rule us? Not when those with potential got spirited away to the sky.

The queuing adults eyed me warily as I made my way to the uniform separating the line's head from its tail, barring the serpent from becoming an ouroboros. He glanced at my badge and waved me through. Inside, I handed the private security guard my sidearm. "I had no idea they started queueing this early."

"Some never leave." The guard saw me roll my eyes and grinned, his words chasing me to the elevator. "Sometimes, a dream is all that keeps us alive, officer."

A fool's dream of an easy life concerned only with pleasure. Then again, had my lot in life been harsher, perhaps I'd have queued with them.

I wasn't prepared for the mechanical giant waiting for me when the elevator's doors parted. Spindly inside the exoskeleton that afforded her mobility in Earth's gravity, Inspector Geraldine Hoff's skin was as pale as mine was brown, as if we'd been birthed from opposite ends of a monochromatic palette. Her hairless scalp, elongated sloping forehead, and large inky eyes cast as much doubt on our alleged common ancestry as the missing wings myth had it Angels grew to fly around their low-gravity palaces.

While the building's exterior and entrance remained largely faithful to its original layout, the interior bore no resemblance to anything I'd ever seen before. Hoff led me from the lift to a flat-floored ovoid space uniformly lit by the walls themselves. With a whirring flick of her hand, Hoff gestured me towards a blob that oozed up on command and reformed into a stool.

She briefed me on a missing Angel. *The Conjurer* was the nom-de-plume of an artist who composed dreams as a form of entertainment. These visions eschewed euphoric sex or heroic triumph—the sort that'd exhilarate us dirt dwellers—instead, they explored the darker side of the human psyche, torments that Angels no longer experienced. "Any questions?"

I didn't have to ask what the Conjurer was doing on the surface. Where else would he find the human trauma to mine for his *art*? "How does an Angel get lost? No offense, but you stand out down here."

"More reason to suspect something happened to this *Angel*, wouldn't you say?" Hoff bristled at the common moniker. I'd had no idea they considered it pejorative. In their shoes, I'd have been flattered. Would they have preferred us to call them *demons*?

"What exactly do you think I can do that your fancy gizmos can't?"

"Retracing the Conjurer's steps means going places we don't often venture. My bosses, and yours, want a local along to deal with the natives. *No offense.*"

It would've also been politically unpalatable for my bosses to have an undoubtedly armed Angel terrorizing the populace without at least the veneer of local authority, and it didn't hurt to have me around to take the blame when things went awry.

"A chaperone, basically."

Hoff smiled thinly. "Think of it as an opportunity to demonstrate your usefulness."

I didn't know how to respond to *that*.

●

Mildly acidic drizzle scattered off Hoff's flying egg onto the corroded tin roofs of the lean-tos below. Despite the webbing securing me to the seat, my inner ear kept insisting I was falling towards the transparent shell. White-knuckled, I hung onto the seat and fought off motion sickness, only half-listening to Hoff.

After one particularly sharp banking turn, Hoff glanced at me. "You're turning a worrying shade of green."

I clamped my jaws shut against the rising bile and inflated my lungs with the egg's sweet clean air. "I'm fine."

She pursed her lips and returned her attention to the scarred Earth slipping by below. With little light penetrating the thick, ash-laden clouds, we would all have perished long ago, had it not been for the Angels' magic-like power generation, foodstuffs, and medicines. That their largesse came with strings attached surprised no one. That those strings soon formed a noose that held us hostage to their demands *shouldn't* have surprised anyone.

To shift my focus away from the vertiginous view, I turned to Hoff. "Did the Conjurer stray far during his visits?"

Hoff hesitated. "Sightseeing, entertainment. Nothing out of the ordinary."

She meant poverty safaris and brothels. There was little else for Angels on the surface.

"Could he have gotten lost?" How would the mobs treat a lost Angel? I liked to think some would be hospitable, but I feared that others wouldn't be, and I couldn't bring myself to condemn either.

Hoff shook her head. "He knew his way around." She seemed on the verge of saying more but didn't.

Changing tack, I teased her, "Did you know most people think y'all have wings?"

"Wings?" Hoff frowned back at my smile. "We ..." she paused, searching for words, "change bodies like you might clothes. Not as often, but subject to similar whims of fashion and taste. Body parts, like wings or extra eyes or gills and fins, come and go, and are sometimes taken to extremes. Many of my friends forgo bodies entirely to live in the Abstract."

"And that is?"

"Never mind, it's hard to explain." I couldn't tell whether she was boasting or embarrassed.

The egg lurched briefly and I gasped.

Hoff gave me a sidelong glance. "Your file didn't say anything about fear of flying."

I realized I was still holding onto the seat. "I've never flown before, give me time." I tried to let go, but couldn't quite bring myself to do it. "What else did my file say?"

"That you're insubordinate, pigheaded, and cantankerous."

"They could spell *cantankerous*?"

Hoff laughed, and I found myself laughing along, for a moment oblivious to the gulf separating us.

"But it also said you have the highest clearance rate of any officer in your department."

They *had* asked for me by name. I still didn't quite know what to make of that and pushed it aside to ruminate over later.

"Quite the accomplishment, considering how young you are," Hoff added.

I'd never thought of thirty-two as young. Angels were rumored to be immortal, but I put little stock in such claims. If only half of those rumors were true, it would have made them veritable gods. "How old are *you*?"

She smiled coyly and waved away my question. "Longevity's overrated."

"I'd happily part with an arm and both legs to see my fiftieth birthday." With life expectancy in the mid-forties, I found the idea of anyone living to a hundred obscene, let alone longer. How did Angel offspring feel about parents who lingered? Was overpopulation as much of a problem in orbit as it was on the surface?

Hoff stared wistfully into the distance, seeing something in the murky gloom I couldn't. "When life is short, your choices are consequential. Which path you take in life matters more because you only ever get to make a few choices. Live long enough and you end up exploring every path in turn, chasing every dream. What good is success if it's only a matter of time?"

I could tell she sincerely meant it, almost as if she envied me my short miserable life. How easy it was for those well fed to bursting to preach the virtues of restraint to the starving.

●

Hoff pitched the egg down, drawing my eyes to an expanse of pockmarked, corrugated metal roofs below. Having never seen the area from above before, it took me a moment to recognize where we were. "We can't land here."

"It's the Conjurer's first stop after leaving the embassy. The first deviation from his usual itinerary."

"You don't understand. This is Serpent Head's territory. If we land uninvited, he's as likely to feed us to his dogs as answer our questions."

"I'd like to see him try."

"I wouldn't!" Though I'd count it progress to be rid of him and his flunkies, innocent bystanders were bound to get caught in any confrontation, and for what? To satisfy Hoff's desire to appear tough and powerful? Who was she trying to impress? "You wanted a local to deal with the natives, and this local is telling you to stay the hell away from these natives."

Hoff ignored me and took the egg lower. "I'll land there." She nodded at a stone-paved plaza festooned with tattered bunting and lit with dim, oil-burning lanterns.

By the time the egg touched down, everyone had scattered, leaving the market eerily quiet, aside from the hissing of swaying lamps and the incessant strumming of caustic drizzle on improvised awnings.

"Good luck finding anyone who'll talk to us now," I muttered, steeling myself against the sour miasma wafting through the egg's open hatch.

Hoff gracefully eased the considerable bulk of her exoskeleton out into the open, oblivious to the stench. "They're bound to come out eventually."

"That's not how it works down here, how *we* work," I fumed. Why have me along if she wasn't going to listen to anything I said? "You can't just blunder your way to your missing Conjurer with this confidence act, no matter how convincing."

She cast her eyes down, looking slightly abashed, and I felt a little guilty for my outburst.

I set to scanning the deserted clearing, when a boy bolted from a cart he might have been napping under, towards a dark alley and right into my arms. About ten or twelve, though so thin it was impossible to say for sure, the boy squirmed in my grip, eyes wide with fear.

"Let go, pig," he demanded, his bass rumble at odds with his small frame.

"Settle. I'm not going to hurt you," I said. "There's a half-dinar in it for you if you answer my questions."

The boy stopped bucking and regarded me with wide, greedy eyes. "Ten dinars."

It was a familiar routine. "You don't even know what I'm going to ask you."

Suddenly, floodlights lit the clearing—an extravagant display for a planet starved of power. Reflexively, I let go of the boy's scruff and shielded my eyes. His bare feet barely left a mark on the frozen slush as he ran away.

"Kadir's a good lad. He'd never betray his kin for anything less than *five* dinars." A short, plump man swaggered into view. A tattoo of a snake head in faded indigo and crimson ink covered the left side of his temple, its lean body running down his cheek, under the thicket of a rampant salt-and-pepper beard, and reappearing down the side of his bullneck before disappearing again under his coat's collar. "Are you lost, sweetheart?" Serpent Head asked mockingly. Under the blue-white glare, his shaved head shone like oiled mahogany.

From Hoff's exoskeleton an aura swelled, glowing an ominous red-tinged orange.

Serpent Head regarded her contemptuously. "It's true we have little to live for down here, but believe me, we don't die cheaply." A racket of cocking rifles followed.

"Stop!" I raised my arms. "We didn't come here looking for trouble."

"Trouble?" Serpent Head thundered with practiced menace. "What trouble would that be, sweetheart?"

Hoff covered the distance separating us in a wink. "Call her *sweetheart* one more time and I'll dispatch you like the vermin you are."

Serpent Head matched her advance, his stomping army in lockstep. Instinctively, I stepped in-between. "Enough," I infused my voice with every command authority trick I'd learned walking the beat. "We're only here for information," I continued in a measured tone. "An Angel stopped here a few days ago."

I nodded to Hoff, who asked. "What did he want?"

Serpent Head alternated his focus between my eyes as if one would betray the other. "What's in it for me?"

As soon as he'd finished speaking, Hoff pulled out a small silver box and threw it at him. He grabbed it midair and turned it in his hand, examining it. "What the hell is this?"

"Enough pills to offset five-hundred Sieverts," Hoff said.

I glowered at her. Unlike a coin tossed to a street urchin, bribing Serpent Head with a small fortune in medicine only created a bigger problem. Not that it'd matter to the Angels, not when they had us to clean up their messes.

Serpent Head nodded approvingly at the box. "Your Angel wanted a sedative and—funnily enough—anti-radiation pills. For another one of these," he shook the pills in their container, "I'll tell you where he went next."

"No need." Hoff's forcefield deflated, cooling to a muted indigo-blue as she walked back to the egg, winking out entirely once inside. I scrambled after her. The moment the hatch sealed, the egg shot upwards, pinning me to my seat.

"I could have gotten him to tell us where your Conjurer went next," I grumbled.

"That, I already know."

"Were you planning on telling me?" How could she not understand that to help her, I had to know what I was helping with. Keeping her cards so close to her chest was hurting more than my feelings, it was handicapping our chances of finding the Conjurer. Any investigator worth their salt would've known that. What did Hoff actually do for work up there, parking enforcement?

She saw me glowering and relented. "He went to a bordello, then disappeared without a trace."

So much for Angels eyes seeing everything, knowing all. If an Angel could evade their all seeing eyes, could we too?

●

One moment, we were drowning in a murky ashen sea, and the next, we burst into an inverted, indigo-hemmed, blue ocean. Against that dazzling expanse, the Angels' crystal palaces glinted like a glittering diamond necklace girding the Earth, an achingly beautiful noose. Despite the blinding brightness, I couldn't turn away, until my eyes watered and reflexively gummed shut. Hoff noticed and polarized the shell into near opacity. "Is this better?"

I watched the fading kaleidoscopic afterimage on the inside of my eyelids, my gratitude for her thoughtfulness warring with resentment. When again would I get a chance to see sunshine, however blinding? For centuries, our leaders had promised a day when the clouds would finally part. Meanwhile, *when-the-sun-shines* had come to mean *never*. "Thank you."

As I reopened my eyes, blinking away the moisture pooling on my lashes, a nagging feeling I had since we took off from the marketplace coalesced into a question. "Why did the Conjurer buy radiation pills on the black market? Unlike yours, the local ones are useless as currency."

"Currency?" Hoff scolded. "Is that the gratitude we get for helping you survive?"

"You want *our* gratitude for exploiting us?" I responded in kind. "Everything you do, you do for yourselves. Every time you bribe someone like Serpent Head, you strengthen his hand and ensure generations of Kadirs never rise to challenge your interests."

"If you're going to blame us for Serpent Head, you have to ask yourself this: Why would we bother sabotaging your endeavors when you do such a fine job of it on your own? Everything you accuse us of, Laila, you are yourself complicit in."

I smarted from the truth.

Hoff broke the silence that ensued. "Must we quarrel about things that have nothing to do with the two of us? I don't blame you for every fault of your people. Why blame me for mine?"

"Because you have a say. You get to vote on the decisions your people make. *You* decide what's right and what's not. I don't. I live and die by the edicts of the tyrants you installed as our rulers. How our troubles started may not have been your fault, but we're still in a mess, centuries later, because it serves your interests. You use us, Geraldine."

"Can't we leave politics to the politicians?"

"Why am I here, Geraldine? And don't give me this bullshit about locals and natives. You don't listen to anything I say anyway. There's nothing I've done you couldn't have done on your own."

"You're wrong, Laila." Hoff paused and regarded me diffidently, before continuing. "Back home, there are no hardships, no risks. We've forgotten pain, fear, hunger. When we set out to rid ourselves of human weakness, we ended up discarding our instincts instead. You effortlessly saw through my bravado in the face of the first hitch we faced. I'm overwhelmed by your world and woefully unprepared for it. I can't finish this on my own."

She'd called me by my first name twice now. A sincere familiarity, or another manipulation? I couldn't tell. Then I realized that I too had called her by her first name. Was I trying to manipulate her in return, or had I simply forgotten she was an Angel?

"Then tell me why the Conjurer needed anti-radiation pills, when his aura would've protected him as yours protects you," I paused for a response, but Hoff only shrugged. "You said your people choose their bodies. Could he have chosen a body that is susceptible to radiation?"

Hoff's eyes glazed over for a heartbeat or two. "It's not. His current corpus is an older model than mine, but similarly immune to radiation. Curiously, though, he hasn't upgraded his for nearly twenty years."

"The same period he's been visiting the surface, give or take?"

Hoff turned towards me so fast, I recoiled, driving my head deeper into the headrest. "How did you know that?"

"My guess is, the Conjurer wasn't born an Angel."

"No one is born—" Hoff stopped mid-sentence. "—into Transenlightenment."

"You don't have kids?" I'd never even heard a rumor about that. I wouldn't have believed it had anyone else told me. How could a people survive without having offspring? "Why not?"

Hoff shook her head. "You first. How did you work all this out?"

"If the Conjurer didn't need the pills, then they had to be for one of us, for someone he knew. Had he sourced them the way you had, you'd have a record of it. Maybe he wouldn't have been able to explain why he needed them or for whom." I paused, giving Hoff another opportunity to tell me I was wrong. She said nothing. "Circumventing obstacles and challenging limits is something we have to do, dozens of times every day, just to survive. But you just said those sorts of instincts are lost to you, which would make the Conjurer a more recent Angel. One who hadn't yet shed his hard-won survival instincts. One who still has people here he cares enough about to risk doing business with the likes of Serpent Head. Who is it? After twenty years, his parents are likely dead. A lover then, or a child?"

Hoff's response was slow coming. "I don't know."

I snorted and turned away from her, shaking my head.

"We don't keep those sorts of records. We never had to," she added heatedly. After a pause, she drew in a deep breath before continuing. "To answer your earlier question, the longevity treatments preclude pregnancy. We could have found ways around that, but at some point we decided we didn't want to, and however long we live, we too die. So, we invite the deserving among you to join us. We expect and accept a measure of nostalgia for their former lives, until new possibilities sets them free of their past. Why would we need records of their old lives?"

I thought of the coiling queue outside the embassy and shivered. Did those queuing know the price of becoming an Angel was to give up everyone they'd ever loved? "You expect a spouse to forget their mate, a parent to abandon their children, a friend and neighbor to forswear their community after a *measure of nostalgia*?"

She shrugged. "I don't remember what family I once had, or even if I had one."

Where did she think she'd come from, a seed pod? All humans had families, born or found, small or sprawling, loving or venom-filled. They might not like them or want them, but they had them. Whom had the Conjurer left behind twenty years ago? How long had it taken Hoff to forgot those she'd abandoned? "Geraldine, why are you searching for the Conjurer? The truth, please."

"He took something he shouldn't have."

I waited for her to elaborate, but that was all she would say.

●

After Serpent Head's hostile reception, Madam Sparrow's solicitous guards seemed downright hospitable. They ushered us through the darkened brothel to their mistress's alcove in the back where she fussed over a young woman's makeup.

Madam Sparrow watched our approach with naked appraisal. A firm hand to the small of the back propelled the young woman towards us. Midstride, her heel caught on the tail of her two-sizes too-long dress and she tripped. Hoff caught her before she face-planted, and helped her back to her feet. "How old are you, child?"

Madam Sparrow leered at Hoff, answering before the young woman could, "Old enough. You could be her first."

Hoff wrinkled her nose. "Revolting. Inhuman."

I bridled at Hoff's patronizing self-righteousness, especially coming from someone who'd remorselessly sacrificed her family, even their memory. "At least she's warm, well-fed, and has somewhere dry to lay her head at night. So long as no one's forcing her, I have no quarrel with her choices." I turned to Madam Sparrow. "We're not customers. We're looking for an Angel who visited your establishment a few days ago."

"I have no idea who you're talking about." Up close, grey roots peeked from under the edges of Madam Sparrow's platinum-blonde wig.

"I can think of a few ways to jog your memory, none of them good for business."

Madam Sparrow glowered at me, but eventually her rounded shoulders slumped, the fire in her eyes replaced by a heavy weariness that could flatten mountains. "I don't know where he went, alright? Years ago, before he left to become an Angel, he brought his woman here. Paid well for her upkeep too, and she doted on the girls like the children they never had. Every few weeks, he'd visit for a day or two. This time, he took her and left."

Hoff shook her head. "No, he didn't. He entered through your front door and never left."

Madam Sparrow bobbed her head coyly. "Not by the front door, no."

●

Hoff had to fold her frame at the waist to fit into the back door's antechamber. Behind the raised hem of a faded wall tapestry, the tunnel's mouth was pitch black. Narrow and low-ceilinged, it swallowed my pocket torch's beam, dispersing it without illuminating its confines.

"Where does it lead?" Hoff asked Madam Sparrow.

"The woods, an hour on foot south of town."

The hairs on my nape bristled. "The haunted woods?"

Hoff sighed audibly. "It's not haunted."

Madam Sparrow put her hands on her hips. "Haunted or not, some *very* important clients rely on this tunnel's discretion," she cautioned, her emphasis leaving me in no doubt she meant Angels. "Compromise it at your peril." With a huff, she turned and left.

"The woods are only mildly radioactive, but that's enough to turn them into a blind spot for our orbital sensors. I should have thought of that when we couldn't locate him." Hoff peered into the tunnel. "Did you want to go first or should I?"

"After you, but it's quite narrow. You might get stuck."

"The injury to my dignity would be far worse, if we were to fail."

We emerged from the side of a low hill into a dense thicket of dead poplars lumbering side by side like funereal guards. Their naked branches sagged under the accumulated snow. A burden which the chilling wind forced them to shed periodically, obscuring whatever tracks our quarry might have left.

Hoff deposited a blue pill in my hand. "Take this."

My eyes fixed on the tiny pill. "Trust is a two way street, Geraldine." Somehow, unconsciously, Angel Inspector Geraldine Hoff had become merely Hoff, my partner, and my partner Hoff had morphed into my friend, Geraldine. I expected commensurately more from her. "I've trusted you plenty so far. I got into your flying egg having never flown before, jumped between you and Serpent Head to stave off disaster, and threatened Sparrow to find your Conjurer. Now's your turn."

"There're things you don't need to know. But I never deceived you."

"In a true partnership, you don't get to decide what I need to know. That's something you do with an underling. Prove to me I'm not just a useful dirt dweller to use and discard."

Hoff held my stare unblinkingly for a few heartbeats before relenting. "What do you want to know?"

I closed my fingers around the pill to steady my shaking hand. "What did the Conjurer steal?"

"It's not what you think," Hoff said quietly, her voice barely audible over the wind whistling through dead branches. "The nanites he stole protect the newly transmigrated from the perils of life in orbit—cellular damage caused by cosmic radiation, bone loss, cardiovascular irregularities—until they're ready for new bodies immune to those problems."

I popped the pill into my mouth and swallowed. It left a bitter aftertaste. "What else are you not telling me?"

Hoff ignored me and marched off into the faintly luminescent forest in a cloud of mechanical noises.

●

We searched the forest on foot, our progress punctuated by the wheezing and whistling wind, the concert of Hoff's exoskeleton, and the crunches and squishes of rotting debris and frozen twigs in the snow-covered underbrush.

Hoff peered into the darkness, seeing what no human eye could. Midstride, she grabbed my arm and whispered, "Thermal gradient ahead."

A hundred meters later, we glimpsed a log cabin nestled in a copse of dead cedars. Its roof sagged under accumulated snow and a muted orange glow spilled from between the planks of its boarded windows.

"He's here, the Conjurer. This close, I can detect his exoskeleton," Hoff said. "Please wait here. I don't know if he's armed, and I can't neutralize him and protect you at the same time." She didn't wait for me to respond, and started trudging through the snow towards the cabin's back door.

Every time I thought I'd peeled back her last façade, Hoff surprised me with another shell inside. Secrets within secrets, manipulations masquerading as truths. Whether there was someone I'd recognize as human at the core of that matryoshka doll, I didn't know, but I was done trusting. I had to see for myself.

The moment Hoff moved out of sight, I set off towards the front of the cabin and didn't stop until I'd mounted the low-rise porch's warped wooden steps and peeked inside. The cabin was dark beyond a circle of light shed by a flameless lantern of an unfamiliar design set on the floor. Facing it was an Angel in an exoskeleton, not unlike Hoff's, sitting on his haunches by a pile of soiled rags. The door creaked when I pushed it open and the Conjurer looked up at me.

I'd seen that all-too-human vacant gaze of despair before. In the eyes of a mother cradling the lifeless body of her starved infant, or a child staring uncomprehending at the remains of his parents on a pyre. Crying tearlessly and swaying gently to a morose tune only the bereaved could hear, an insistent yet futile attempt at self-soothing.

The Conjurer's blood-smeared fingers trembled, every flutter amplified by his exoskeleton. As I approached, the mess on the floor resolved to a vague human outline that had somehow been turned inside out. The stench caught in my throat like a punch to the gut. I bent to the side and retched.

He muttered something, repeating it at the threshold of audibility. I wiped my mouth on the back of my cold hand and leaned closer as Hoff walked in through the back door.

Dazed, the Conjurer moaned endlessly, "I killed her. I killed her."

I sat on the porch steps, lost in thought and breathing hard to purge the stench from my nose. The more I thought about it, the more I realized it was the Conjurer's raw grief that unmoored me. It was all too human. Was it only the newly transmigrated who retained these shadows of their former self? How long before even those echoes faded? Did Hoff feel anything at all anymore, and if not, was she still human?

When the porch floorboards creaked behind me, I summoned my composure with hurried gulps of frigid air, brushed the freezing moisture off my cheeks, and looked up to find Hoff standing over me. "What'll become of him?"

"He stole restricted technology and inflicted great harm with it. That love motivated him won't excuse his transgression."

"He couldn't have known it'd kill her." I felt sure any punishment the Angels had in store would pale next to his loss.

Hoff bobbed her head, the gesture both oppressively familiar and discomfiting in its otherness. "The nanites are lethal when administered under gravity. Instead of healing her ills, they unraveled her body at a molecular level. They were never meant for surface dwellers. He should've known better."

I nodded, not because I agreed, but because I could imagine how he felt. He hadn't wanted the wife the Angels had rejected to die alone. He either hadn't known the nanites would be lethal on the surface or hadn't believed it. Who could blame him, after a life filled of Angel half-truths and outright lies? I figured becoming an Angel himself wasn't enough to erase that ingrained suspicion we all shared of our sky-dwelling exploiters and benefactors.

I pulled myself up and brushed the snow off my clothes, puzzled at how dry and warm Hoff appeared inside her protective cage.

We both stood staring into the darkness, taking in both the darkness we faced and that behind us. Hoff broke the spell, speaking softly, barely louder than the whistling wind and shivering branches. "Wish we'd met under better circumstances. Still, we make quite the team, you and I."

I smiled a little at that, having no idea what other circumstance she imagined would have brought an Angel and someone like me together. "Until the next time one of yours goes missing, then."

"It doesn't have to be. *Inspector Laila Aboud* has a certain ring to it, don't you think?"

I groaned. "Please tell me all of this wasn't just a recruitment test."

Geraldine shook her head, the exoskeleton straining like a laden truck attempting a steep hill. She reached out an arm and the exoskeleton peeled back, blooming around her hands. Her skin was warm and soft against my frigid hands. "Must you suspect every motive, distrust everyone?"

"Occupational hazard, I'm afraid." *Not to mention your duplicitous manipulations*, I thought to myself, but held my tongue.

"Well? Would you like to become an *Angel*?" Hoff said, as if proposing, hastening to add with a slight nod towards the cabin, "The proper way."

"It's a big leap to leave everyone and everything I know behind."

Hoff bobbed her head. "It's not obligatory. In time, your priorities will change. Your past will fade into the deepest recesses of your memory, until it's beyond recall. It works out for the best in the end."

"It didn't for the Conjurer."

"And see where it led him."

I shook my head. Angels were a cautionary tale, not a model to emulate. No matter how hard they tried, they'd never be truly human again. *We* had to survive if there were to be humans walking the Earth in another thousand years.

Hoff smirked a little. "You're telling me you've never thought about it?"

Gently, I reclaimed my hands from Geraldine's and shoved them into my pockets. "I don't think there's anyone who hasn't, but fantasizing with my feet planted firmly on the ground is not the same as throwing it all away to chase the unknown." I was sorely tempted to say yes, if for no other reason than for a chance to see that diamond noose again, to revel in its brilliance before, left unchecked, it choked the life out of our species.

"You won't regret it, trust me."

Hoff's palpable excitement left me unsure how she'd react if I flatly declined. "Could I think about it?"

Despite the puzzled surprise etched on her face, Hoff's smile lingered. "Take as long as you need."

I nodded and looked away, my eyes drawn upwards to the starless darkness enveloping the Earth. I knew I'd never belong up there, any more than the Conjurer had. I belonged to the earth. To those used and forgotten. I didn't count myself one of Earth's best or brightest; I'd never be a fusion physicist or a horticulturist, or even a revolutionary, but perhaps, when the time came, I could do my small part.

Ramez Yoakeim's story "The Diamond Noose" was originally published in Metaphorosis on Friday, 5 May 2023. See magazine.metaphorosis.com

About the author

Born in Egypt, raised in Australia, and now living with his husband in the United States, Ramez Yoakeim spent his whole life adapting. A one-time engineer and educator, Ramez writes mostly about hope, including "More Than Trinkets", named one of Tor.com's Must-Read Speculative Short Fiction. In addition to *Metaphorosis*, you'll find more of his stories in Flame Tree Press and Erewhon Books anthologies, podcasts from StarShipSofa, and online in *Translunar Travelers Lounge, UtopiaSF, Sci Phi Journal, Anathema, Andromeda Spaceways*, and others. Discover more on his website, yoakeim.com, and BlueSky yoakeim.bsky.social.

The Snow Queen's Daughter

Sean R. Robinson

I extended my hand out the window, reaching as my mother had taught me since I was old enough to understand her words. Palm up, an invitation to the distant skies.

The steppe ended in the distance, the horizon shattered by snow-choked mountains. From my window, I could see the clouds roiling white, the azurite sky behind it a challenge.

Not a challenge, I reminded myself. I could hear my mother's voice in my ears. *Never a challenge. A welcome. Welcome the cold. Welcome the snow, Daughter.*

I waited, palm up in invitation until my arm grew sore. Until even my cold-hardened face was uncomfortable. And when my attention drifted to the desk beside me, I gave up, cursing. I didn't want to welcome the cold, didn't want to turn the weather.

I wasn't a magician, and no matter how much my mother wished otherwise. I wanted to be a scientist.

●

My mother's house was, of necessity, a place of cold wars. I carried the newest declaration in my hand as I went to find her, ignoring my ever-disappointing lessons in magic. I had read the paper a hundred times, trying to gather my wits for my mother's frigid regard.

Her palace was a wonder of ice, wrought into walls and doorways, galleries, and apartments. Each morning, she would sit in her apiary, a tray beside her, cups of white bone china ready for her morning tea. My mother had always preferred Jasmine tea as her snow-bees danced around her. I preferred Gunpowder Black.

Today, she sat in her snow-wicker chair, a leopard curled around her feet. She wore white damask, a bear fur shrug across her shoulders. Mother sipped her tea and listened as the snow-bees told her of the sights they'd seen in their travels. They danced for her, and she understood— she was their queen.

There was a looking glass behind her, hairline cracks breaking the reflection into a thousand pieces. I watched as Mother sent a snow-bee into the distance. There would be a blizzard somewhere in the world.

I knew she was disappointed that her only child did not have wings like snowflakes and eyes like dark winter. I had never been small enough to dance on her fingertips and proclaim the wonders I'd seen. I had settled for essays and letters and books of dark leather.

She was magic and I—no matter how much I tried— was not.

I unfolded the paper that had arrived by post that morning. I read it again. Mother did not look at me as the bee-swarm grew thicker. One or two landed on my hands, but I brushed them away. I had learned to hate my snow- winged siblings.

"I've been accepted to University," I said. There could be no preliminaries for that conversation; no warnings or advisories.

She did not speak.

"In Copenhagen," I added. "I'm to take a degree in Boreal Alpinology."

It was my concession to her. If I could not be magic, I could be snow. She loved the snow.

My mother did not speak for a while longer. She sipped her pale tea and watched her bees. I was the dark- haired daughter she had borne and that was the latest in a long line of disappointments. I did not care for her gentle teas, her precious insects, or the bluster of winter through the fjords.

We were too different, and we were both tired of pretending we were not.

"Why?"

I sighed. "I will study the movement of snowstorms. The growing and shrinking of glaciers. I will learn why the Aurora glows."

There were only so many words to make her understand.

A single pale brow rose on her face. "Why not simply ask them?"

Because that was magic.

She had tried to teach me to love the blizzards that hunted the palace grounds, and the squalls that danced through her many galleries. I could not love her snow-choked rose gardens any more than she could understand why I read the diaries of Meta Brevoort and Lucy Walker.

"Because," I said. There was no answer my perfect, icy, mother would understand. "Because it will be a place where I am not a pale copy of you. I have failed miserably at frost-craft, so perhaps I will learn something worth knowing."

"No," my mother said. "You will learn here. You have not been a diligent daughter."

I knocked her teacup from where it sat. It shattered on the floor

"When will you let me live my life, Mother? How long will you keep me trapped behind the drifts? I am not you. I will not have a Storyteller come over the hills, break my heart, and leave me with child. Perhaps in Copenhagen I might be free."

And perhaps I was as much like my father as I was unlike my mother. That, I left unspoken.

The Snow Queen stood and her ice swarm erupted out into the air. She did not look back as she left the apiary. The wind that blew off her skin carried her voice back to me. It held a bitter edge.

"You think that I am a queen from a Fairy Tale. Fairy Tales are never true, Daughter."

The silence that followed was bitter cold.

"You will take a sledge south before the spring, then," the wind said. "And when you have learned to be warm, perhaps you will come home to learn that there is more to winter than the cold."

I nodded, heart in my throat. She would spend the rest of her day maintaining her frozen kingdom, attended by her bitter-wind courtiers.

"I hope you are happy, Ylsa. I hope you find what you seek," the wind said in a quiet, final breath.

"I'm sorry," I said, but my mother had always been too far away. I could name what I sought: my place.

My leave-taking was quiet. Mother's snow-bees whirled around the sledge as I hitched up the bears. They were restless; the air had begun to smell of spring. Mother did not wish me good luck or good speed. The gentle kiss of the bees was all the farewell I received as we went south. I had packed everything I thought a young student would need: quill pens and dark ink, sensible shoes, and a wool sweater to keep out the chill.

I was not prepared for Copenhagen. It perched beside the Baltic beneath a coal-fire cloud. The bears liked it not at all, but they deposited me in the midst of the yellow-painted buildings outside the University. When they left, my trunks piled in the dirty snow, their white fur had been painted an ugly shade of grey by the sooty air.

By then, a crowd had formed and I was reminded of my earliest childhood lesson: it is not easy to be the Snow Queen's daughter. Too many people had read the stories and confused fairy tales with real life, me included.

It took most of the afternoon to find a room to rent. The University bursar kept a list of homes that would rent to lady students. The proprietor of each boarding house was polite, offered me tea, and said that they did not have accommodations that would be appropriate for me. Then they sent me on my way.

Mrs. Lang did not. Her house was on the edge of the harbor. The room she offered was a tiny place under the eaves.

"If you're lucky, you can see the sea on a good day," she said, pointing to the windows. "I'll expect payment first of every month. I'll treat you the same as all the other girls, princess or not. We English women have had our fair share of White Queens. I am not so easily intimidated."

I was intimidated, even with her wink, but I took the room. The fur blanket that I laid over the end of my tiny bed seemed out of place next to the checkered flannel sheets. That night though, as I breathed in the raw city air, I coughed and wondered if it were not the most beautiful feeling in the world.

My classes were challenging. I hadn't expected to be the only woman with the half-dozen men. Each of them hoped for postings from the Danish Crown, and royal patronage to line their pockets. They were, in their own estimation, the next generation of adventurers, prepared to capture fame and glory on the frozen expanses of the world.

I was as quick-witted as any of them. Better read, by far. We studied more places than I could admit were within my mother's lands. But they had no use for me. I had been to the glaciers they dreamed about in their blue-smoked parlors. But as the holidays came and went, as faces changed and the seasons moved, I was not one of them.

I had left my mother's frozen halls and found the University just as chill. I was unwelcome, a scientist among strangers.

They said that royalty was not fit for their taverns, or to socialize with their ladies. I had no interest in sipping vodka from shared bottles. They told me to find trees to whisper to, or cast spells, to stop pretending and go back to where I belonged. I was lonely.

●

A man spent three days outside my library carrel. At first, he pretended to search the stacks just outside my line of sight. It was unlikely that anyone in Copenhagen would be so interested in the library's collection of Tropical Gardening instructions. He wore a blue frock coat and had dark hair. His fingers were long and thin and he traced the spines of the books with delicate touches.

"The books don't change," I said as he glanced at me for the fifth time in an hour. I was preparing for an exam and had books piled on the desk, marking them with slips of paper to go back to research. I did not appreciate men staring at me. I was not a white-furred bear to dance for anyone.

"Nor do *I* much change. So you'll be as welcome to stare at me from between the books next week as today. I have exams, and your staring is more than a bit of distraction."

He jumpcd away from the shelf as though it has frozen over. "I'm sorry. I—"

"You're leaving," I offered and then turned back to my studies.

"I'm actually Jonas," he said, "But I'll follow your orders, your Highness. In case you decide to turn me into a snowman or some such. It's true what they say about you, Snow Princess."

He tipped his head toward me, tapping his fingers against his head as though he were a respectable man wearing a hat, and then turned to leave.

"What?" I said, slamming shut the book on S. A. Andrées' Arctic balloon expedition. The words echoed in the silence of the library. There were more than a few young men who shot disapproving glances toward me. I did not care.

"Your Highness?" the man—Jonas—said.

"What is it that they say about me?"

"That the Princess Ylsa has skin of the most delicate frost, and she is too smart, too sure, more like a story than a real person. Good day, your Highness."

"You think it's so simple?" I raised my voice to follow him, like the echoing of a scream down the crevasse of bookshelves. "When everyone who doesn't hate you because a woman does not belong in this University is terrified that every snow flake might be the Queen's harbinger, come to freeze them in their sleep?"

"I would never imagine what it would be like to walk through a winter palace, waited on hand-and-foot by polar bears, and want for nothing in the world. I am merely a student of business and a servant of the King." He turned back away from me. "I have heard stories of your mother for a long time. I'd come to see if they were true."

I followed him, stung, but determined to show this strange man the truth of me. I left my studies in their book-drift piles. And when Jonas Collin asked me to accompany him to a tavern for rye bread and smoked herring, I did not think about balloons over the arctic or the stunted trees that grew up from the snow. I thought about the way he called me Snow Princess as though I wasn't the queen's dark-haired, misfit, child.

When we kissed the first time, his breath came away white, like winter, blue like crag-ice.

I took him as a lover. Perhaps it was not the way things were done in the civilized age, but I learned the shape of him in the darkness and the lines of his smile lit only by moonlight through the open window of my rented room. If Mrs. Lang had an opinion, she kept it to herself.

When morning broke from that first night, I opened my eyes to find him warm beside me, the paleness of his skin looking beautiful beneath the bear fur. There was a strange weight at the end of my small bed, though. As I looked away from him, I saw that the window was open and that the winter wind gusted through my garret room.

Jonas smiled when he woke beside me. I was still, unmoving. I would not be bent, or bribed, or intimidated. He grew quiet when he saw my mother's leopard at the foot of the bed, staring at him—judging him. He laughed when the cat crawled up the bed, pressed its cold muzzle against my face and left the way it had come in.

He pulled me close and kissed me again as I tried to apologize, to explain.

"One must expect strange things from the Snow Princess," he said. He tasted like the warmth beneath the blanket, when the storm clouds feel very far away. "But I am glad to find no mirror-glass in my eye this morning."

They liked to say that my mother had stolen her sweetheart by piercing his eye with a shard from her broken mirror. I wanted to tell him it was a lie, a Fairy Tale like so many others, but his lips on mine were enough. The kisses were what I wanted, something that was just for me. It was more than enough.

Students wrapped thick scarves around their faces and did their best to stay warm as the wind pulled at their skin. I walked bareheaded and smiled to myself as I left the lecture hall.

Jonas wore a dark frock coat. He saw me in the snow —I know he did—but he walked past me as though he hadn't. He'd looked at me and kept walking. I turned, called out his name, but he was gone, as though he had never been. Only his footprints in the snow proved he'd passed.

Some days he lurked by me in the library, stealing kisses when I should have been studying. He had classes and seminars of his own, but he always seemed a little sad when I asked him to accompany me to the theatre, or to see a musical performance.

My mother's kingdom did not have engagements or betrothals. I did not understand the ways of mortal men. The winds took lovers when they wished, left them when the time was right. I had meant to do the same and let Jonas choose when and where we met. It had been my mother's way—the only way I knew to love. Though I tried to be like the snow-storm zephyrs, to let the fickleness leave me unmoved, it did not work.

The Storyteller had come north out of Copenhagen. My mother had loved him with all her cold heart as she'd never loved me. He'd taken her story and left the Queen a daughter with his dark hair.

The Storyteller had sold stories of my mother in Copenhagen, stories that her bees carried to her and her broken mirror. They had been lies, stories and untrue. All untrue. I wondered if all men were liars and for the first time since coming to Copenhagen, I felt myself grow cold to the fickleness of Jonas Collin.

He liked to ask questions of her, of me, after we made love. Were there really snow-bees in her castle? Did she have a mirror that looked out onto the world? Did I have magic? Had she stolen a boy away and made him love her? Yes, and yes, and no, and no.

Things came to a head one day as the winter grew deep and long and the students at Copenhagen were off to visit family in the country. Mrs. Lang's boarding house was warm, despite the weather. It was too cold for snow, and the sky was the clear blue of forever.

Jonas lingered beneath the bear skin blanket. I had begun to think of him as two separate men: the one who was at home in the private warmth we shared, the second a colder man who only lurked and lingered at the edges of my life. No one should have stood for it.

But he was warm, and I looked into his brown eyes as I wrapped myself closer around him.

"What is she like? My uncle tells me so many stories about her. Everyone does," he asked me. His voice was still thick from sleep. He buried his face in my hair.

"The stories are lies," I said. I felt hot all through. I hated the Storyteller for the way people thought of her. Hated what they thought of me as her daughter.

"Does she really have a broken mirror? Does she make the snow fall?"

He was quiet when I didn't answer immediately, running his fingers through the ends of my hair. Waiting.

"She's a bit like you," I said.

"How?"

"On some days, she's the winter every child dreams of. She's gentle and soft and when I was little, dancing with her through her palace was like being wrapped up in a cloud of gentle snow. It's like when you kiss me, Jonas. Or when we come up the stairs and you lay back against the blankets."

He smiled.

"Other times," I said, "she is like you when you see me passing from class to class. She is cold and uncaring. The winter does not love many, and even those the Snow Queen loves can feel the chill of her regard."

"Ylsa—" The man pulled away from me. "It's not like that."

"There are days where you say that I'm all you think about, Jonas. There are nights where we watch the Aurora Borealis from the window and laugh and sip tea. There are days where you don't even act like I exist. And always there are questions. Are the stories true? And I tell you again and again that they are lies."

Jonas was quiet as I dressed. I did not put on a thick cloak or braid my hair. Instead, I opened the window and welcomed the cold against my skin. The coal-dusted air did not taste as sweet as it had. I suddenly longed for the silence of my mother's house and the cold embrace of winter.

"There are times, Ylsa, where you are bright and wonderful and smart. You are going to be a scientist and the world will know your name. And other times you are a squall coming off the harbor and everything in me screams to brace myself for the impact of you. They say so many things about you."

I wondered if the Storyteller had told my mother such lies, before he left her. Was that all I was? A story?

"What do they say, Jonas?" I asked.

"That when your classmates fare better on exams, you send snow-bees to their rooms and threaten to freeze them. That the winter wind howls through their garret rooms. That you've taken lovers and left them cold in the snow."

I turned to him and laughed. It was an ugly noise, like the cracking of ice or the harsh sound of frozen snow underfoot on a starless night.

"This is not a fairy tale, Jonas. My mother did not spirit you away or break a mirror into your eye, any more than she did the Storyteller who made her so infamous. I have no magic and whatever they say of me is lies even more."

"Ylsa," he said, standing. He left the fur on the bed as he came to me, all naked and beautiful. "I have been as honest as I can be. There is no one else and sometimes I fear that beneath your smile, your temper, your ferocity— the things that I love so much about you—is something cold and I will be another story they tell to children. Sometimes I worry that there is a magic in you that has bespelled me. When I am not near you, I want to be. And sometimes I want it so badly that the only thing I can do is be aware from you, so make sure that it is still a choice I have."

"I am no magic, Jonas. I am a scientist. I have never been magic. I thought you understood."

He tried to kiss my neck, but I pulled away.

"I am going home," I said.

"Please don't."

I ignored him and went to take my trunks from beneath the bed. Jonas followed and took my hands in his. His hair was still disheveled and he'd kept his face shaved because I had hated his moustache.

"Come and meet my parents," he said. "Come to dinner and meet them. Meet my uncle, who was so enamored by the stories of your mother. Let them see you. I am sorry that I have not been certain about my feelings for you, Ylsa. It has taken me time to learn how to love you, and I am still a novice."

I forgave him, because I was a novice in love as well, and Jonas was so warm, even when I missed the simplicity of the cold. I agreed to visit his parents, in their house at 9 Amaliegade.

●

My hired carriage slowed before the Collins' house, built back from its siblings along Amaliegade Street. I had dressed in white linen and scalloped lace. I had pulled my dark hair up into a complicated braid and did my best not to be nervous. I wanted his parents to like me. I wanted the man I saw as I entered the house to be the warm Jonas that I loved, not the cold man that seemed to face me too often. I wanted him to forget the stories that he'd heard and live in the moments we had made together. Not someone who thought I'd bespelled him. I had a secret to tell him, and I was worried that he would not like it.

The footman bowed deeply as I entered the house. The foyer was lit by gas lamps and it was warm. I had never been to a party before. Not one where the women wore sparkling jewels and bright feathers. No, I knew only the parties of storms, and as quickly as I entered the Collins' house, I was adrift in the flow of people.

It was some time before I found Jonas. He wore a dark suit coat with a pale blue cravat. My lover spoke to a tall man who had his back to me. I smiled when Jonas looked up and he smiled back.

"I'm so glad you came," he said as I approached. "I was just talking to Uncle about you. I wanted you to meet him."

The man turned and the world slowed.

Jonas' uncle was tall and gawkish. His clothing was well made, but fit poorly. His hair was dark and his eyes were two black coals over the beak of a nose. Jonas moved him forward, still smiling.

"Ylsa, I would like you to meet my uncle Christian. Christian, this is Ylsa."

Jonas' uncle did not extend his hand.

"Hello, Ylsa," he said. His voice was thin, like mountain clouds. "Jonas has told me so much about you."

I felt like I'd been slapped.

The air went cold inside the house. The glasses with their fancy champagne became rimed with frost.

"Hello, Storyteller," I said.

Jonas' smile was frozen to his face, he looked back and forth between us.

"You should not trust her, Nephew," The Storyteller said, holding his iced-over glass. "As I've told you and you've chosen to ignore. I *know*. She will freeze your heart as her mother did mine."

"Ylsa?" Jonas said, looking at me, then back at the glass.

"I am not magic," I said, shaking my head. Why now? Not now, please not now. "I am a scientist. I came to Copenhagen to learn and it seems that what I have learned is that there are lies here just like everywhere else."

There were a thousand other things I could have said, answers I could have demanded, but I turned around, wrapping my hands around my stomach.

"Ylsa!" Jonas yelled. I looked back to see the Storyteller—my father—holding his arm.

"She is just like her mother. Using you, Jonas."

I walked back through the Collin house and then out onto the street. It had begun to snow, and there were carriages still arriving, turning the white to muddy water.

Jonas followed behind me.

"I don't understand. Ylsa, what's happened?" he said. He reached for my hand. I was tired. "You haven't met

Mother or Father. You know Uncle Christian? I don't understand."

"Your Uncle is Hans Christian Andersen," I said. "The Storyteller."

"Yes," he said.

"He told you I was bespelling you," I said. "Told you I was..."

The words ran out and the look on Jonas' face did not draw them out.

Someone called out Jonas' name from an arriving carriage. I felt the cold mud as it hit me, leaving brown tracks against my dress. The carriage wood was carefully polished, the wheels high enough not to notice when the street-muck was disturbed.

"Jonas!" the Storyteller was at the doorway, calling him. "Jonas! Magic! Do you still doubt me? Let her go, she doesn't love you."

I laughed and turned away from them both. A cold wind raced down from the North, freezing the mud and snapping at my face. My mother's story repeated itself. When Jonas reached for me again, he pulled his fingers back, frost-burned.

"You said you weren't magic," he said, eyes wide.

The tear that slid down my face froze as it fell.

"Uncle Christian, stop talking. Ylsa—" Jonas called out to me as I stepped toward the street. My dress was ruined. It didn't matter what impression I made on his mother and father. It didn't matter what impression I made on his uncle, it only mattered that my feet follow their way north.

I had stayed too long in Copenhagen. It was time to go home.

●

Mother sent the bears for me on my second day of walking. The city had given way to snow-clogged fields. My pretty dress had gone to tatters, my embroidered shoes lost somewhere along the city canal. I didn't recognize the bears at first as they crossed the field. Their paws were quiet in the stillness of the gentle snowfall.

I was cold, but it was my heart that ached, not my body.

It was another full day before we reached my mother's house. It was still a place of cold wars and frozen secrets, perched between a nameless fjord and an ancient glacier. In the afternoon sun, the ice-walls were green, and the storms that cavorted around its towers caroled our homecoming. It was only then that I looked behind me and my broken heart froze a little bit more. He was not there. I had not actually expected Jonas to follow. The Storyteller spun his lies. And Jonas had believed. The days where he was cold and distant. The times where I did not exist.

Mother sat in her apiary. The snow-bees were quiet as she sipped her tea. Mother's leopard sat at her feet and looked at me with sorrow in his eyes. I sat in my chair beside the frozen fireplace and was quiet. The Snow Queen and I were quiet for a long time.

"Did you love the Storyteller?" I asked at last.

She sipped her tea.

"Yes," my mother said. "I loved him more than evergreens love the first snowfall."

The mirror behind her reflected the smoke-clogged rooftops of Copenhagen. I could see the window of my garret room.

"Did you know his nephew would break my heart?"

"We must all live our lives, Daughter."

I pulled my legs up beneath me, as I had when I was a child. "I did not want magic. I wanted to be a scientist."

I wanted Jonas to love me.

I touched the place where the mud from the party had stained my dress.

Mother stood slowly and waved the snow-bees away. She stood close enough to me for me to scent the jasmine tea on her breath. Where she touched the linen, it changed, until it was white again. As I looked, it was white like fallen snow, the ripped lace pulled back into place as though it had never been rent.

"I loved the Storyteller and he loved another. He fled to the North because the man he loved could not love him in return. I knew all of it and chose him anyway."

The Snow Queen, in all her years as my mother, had never held me. She did then, pulling me to her as I cried. She was not warm as Jonas had been. But she was the thick fall of snow that covers the world. She was my mother and she would never leave me to the dirty world.

"I'm sorry I left," I said. "I should never have gone. I'll never leave again. I have magic now."

"Silly girl. How can you say you'll never leave again? You have a degree to finish. Trees to question, snow to study. All of the world to explore."

I could not look at her. Not when I saw the look on Jonas' face. Not when I knew that I had followed my mother's story, right until the end.

"I hope my daughter does not look like him," I said softly.

The Snow Queen said nothing, only smiled still.

"You will choose whether you will follow my story or not, Ylsa. You can choose to let your love freeze, because your Jonas listened to words that were lies. You can let your daughter grow up cold and lonely."

A snow-bee landed on her shoulder. She looked at it with pale eyes as it danced, nodding as it flew off.

"Or, you can go out to your Jonas Collin, who is half-dead in the snow, calling your name. He is out on the Steppes, even now, Copenhagen far behind him. He made good time for a man who does not know the first thing about winter or the cold. But perhaps he's learned to love the Snow Queen's daughter, no?"

Mother smiled at me. I felt a strange tightness low in my stomach, not what grew there, but fear and a needling of hope.

"He followed me?" I asked. I looked at the Snow Queen's broken mirror. Jonas was there, wrapped in a coat that was too thin, in a squall that he fought with each step.

"Foolish," I said, standing and crossing to the mirror as Mother had since I was a child. I stepped through the mirror and out into the white, to see if the man who came was the cold creature, or the warm. Mother's snow-bees guided my way out into the drifts.

He standing in the snow.

"I'm sorry," he said. His eyes did not leave my face. "I listened to someone I thought I could trust, instead of my heart. I love you, Ylsa. Snow and frost and everything besides."

He was shivering. And in one moment I had my choice. I could leave him in the cold, to find his way. To freeze. I could gather my anger around myself, my rage that he had believed the Storyteller and not told me. Or I could go to him.

I crossed the distance between us, pulling him into my arms.

Sean R. Robinson's story "The Snow Queen's Daughter" was originally published in Metaphorosis on Friday, 27 January 2017. See magazine.metaphorosis.com

About the author

Sean Robinson works as a social worker in the White Mountains of New Hampshire. He also teaches at the small liberal arts university he graduated from. In his free time he breathes fire, plays with his cat, and can be found (infrequently) on Twitter @Kesterian.

www.SeanRyanRobinson.com, @Kesterian

The Noise Inside

Victor Pseftakis

Sheyen swallows hard and his ears pop. The Noise stops. *How long did it last this time?* He glances at the water-clock fixed on the wall. Longer than before.

It first came a month ago, on his fourteenth birthday, along with the hair. That day, he woke up to a humming, drenched in sweat and with the smooth skin of his head itching. And no matter how hard he tried, he couldn't pinpoint where the humming was coming from. Until Sediniel barged in and, by the horrified look on her face, he could tell; the Noise came from him. When it stopped, minutes later, hair had grown out of his head, blond and smooth, already an inch long. And since then, every time the Noise came, the hair grew.

Sheyen kicks the sheets off.

Footsteps on the corridor outside. He springs up, grabs the brush Mom gave him and starts brushing his hair.

"Sheyen?" It's Sediniel. "Come on, you're not even half-ready yet!" She stops under the doorframe, peeks over her shoulder and slips inside, carefully closing the door behind her. Her brand-new tattoos sway gently on the hairless skin of her head, long red strands like kraal-weed rocking in the sea current. She tiptoes her way to the armoire and throws his good shirt at him.

"Get dressed or fake sick," she says, arms crossed on her chest. "And stop making the Noise. I could hear it next door. Just for today, please?"

Sheyen's tongue feels rough. He swallows. His ears pop. His eyes linger on her wavering tattoos as she comes and sits beside him. He would have gotten them too, on his birthday, a month ago, if it weren't for the hair that had ruined it all.

"Was it louder this time?" he asks and keeps brushing. But Sediniel has already fished the yellow book from under the beddings. *The In-Betweens: a Folk-Tale.*

"Not this bullshit again!" she says and squeezes the book so hard her knuckles turn white. "You are not an In-Between. In-Betweens do not exist. They are monsters our people invented because they shit their pants whenever they come across anything foreign, anyone that's not Vensymari."

"That's what your dad says?" he snaps. Sediniel and her wisecrack opinions. Would she be so eloquent if it were her with the hair and the Noise? No, she could never be in his place; his half-sister is a full Vensymari — not like him. She is Delyan's legitimate child, all hairless and perfect, and her Art works just fine; no weird Noise emanates from inside her, creeping people out.

"That's the truth," Sediniel says. "And it's *our* dad."

"He's just Delyan for me." He snatches the book from her hands and tucks it under the mattress. "Ready for your big day?" He pulls his hair up in a tight ponytail, hoping it will draw less attention at the lunch party. His hands are sweaty.

Sediniel nods and sits a little closer, so close he can hear her breathing.

"The tattoos look nice," he says. "Do they wiggle in the wind?"

"They'd better, unless they used the wrong ink."

"Don't worry, they're already moving."

Sediniel stretches her neck to catch a glimpse of them on the large mirror across the room.

"The official mark of the Vensymari Artists. You'll outshine them all in the Academy," he says and playfully threatens to touch them with his index.

"Hey! They still hurt." She slaps his hand away.

"Is everyone here already for the lunch party?" he asks and puts his shirt on, fumbling with the buttons.

"Lorna, Berthelen, and Phelien arrived with their parents an hour ago. Haven't seen them yet. The others couldn't make it, a storm is brewing across the channel." Sheyen traces a shadow in her voice. "So that just leaves us, dad, my mom, and our three dear friends with their parents."

He wipes his sweaty palms on his knees. He should try to be happy for her today. His state is not her fault.

"Come on, why the sad face? You've been accepted into the Academy. It's your first day as an Artist, with the tattoos and all. You're a full citizen now!"

"The lunch party is stupid," she says and straightens the sharp crease in her trousers, eyes flying back to the mirror to steal glimpses of the tattoos swaying as she moves.

"It's the custom. It wouldn't look good if Delyan didn't host a lunch party for you. It's embarrassing enough that I wasn't accepted in the Academy," Sheyen says, struggling to keep a level voice. He gropes his pockets for any forgotten candy. He finds none.

"I'd rather we went swimming, just the two of us. I'll get plenty of Lorna and her gang this year in the Academy. And, anyway, they're only here to gossip."

Yes, gossip about his hair and the Noise and how he's probably turning into an In-Between. His eyes fall on the floor. He's not the only one disappointed with the turn of events. Sediniel also thought they would leave the house together, off to new adventures, to be trained in the Art, off to adulthood. She might be one of Delyan's four legitimate children, but her other brothers are much older, already scattered around the country, always away. She and Sheyen were born only a month apart, and the scandal of a bastard child had swept Vensymar like no other. But Delyan was firm on not sending Sheyen away to the islands, to Caprish, his Mom's homeland. He had kept him close, raised him along with Sediniel. Mom never ceased being Delyan's mistress, just as she never ceased flaunting her Caprishi heritage; her hair always long and braided in complex coifs, her clothes always a shade of blue or white, her accent always heavy. But Delyan was the First Artist, and just like that, the whole thing had been brushed aside as another harmless quirk of his. It helped that Sheyen at least looked Vensymari. Until the hair grew out and reminded everyone who his Mom was.

"Don't worry, we'll just eat quickly and then we'll go swimming. And I promise I won't say anything stupid to your friends," he says and gets up.

"They were your friends too, a month ago."

Sheyen licks his lips; they're slightly chapped.

"Well, now they think I'm an In-Between."

"That's so stupid. In-Betweens are monsters—"

"With twisted Art and a mane," he says, without turning to look at her. "Maybe it's not that stupid. The stories say that In-Betweens are half-Vensymari—"

"And what's the other half, huh? Does the book say that they're half-Caprishi?"

"The stories don't specify what the other half is. It's not important. What matters is that they're not Vensymari," he says through clenched teeth.

"What, do you think that all half-Vensymari children turn out to be In-Betweens? Yes, they might be rare, but don't you think we would know if people of mixed inheritance turned into monsters?"

"Have you ever seen another half-Vensymari? The borders have been strictly regulated for the past fifty years, so how the Salt would we know? And all the signs are here; In-Betweens are supposed to grow hair all over their bodies and their eyes change color. They say weird things happen around them and that Noise is weird, isn't it now?" A knot is climbing up his throat and he speaks louder to push it down. "They say In-Betweens can put a hole through the world and go to this place of theirs, where they belong. It's even said they trick Vemsymaris to follow them and let them rot in there, lost in a strange land that looks like home but isn't."

The knot won't go away no matter how loud he shouts. The lunch party is going to be a disaster. Sediniel puts her arm around his shoulders; her skin feels cold against the light fabric of his summer shirt.

"No matter what they say, I like your hair. It's like your mom's." Sheyen bites his lips. It's sunny, but he shudders. "It's just one day, don't let Lorna and her gang get to you. I'm sure dad will get you into the Academy next year. Your Art is just different. He'll figure something out."

"Delyan hasn't got the slightest clue what's wrong with me. It's been a month and even he, the First Artist, can't explain it. Neither the Noise nor the hair." He accidentally bites the inside of his cheek and lets out a yelp. "At least if he and Mom let me cut it… The Noise might stop then."

"They can't let you do that. It's against the law for a non-Vensymari."

He looks at her. It's unfair. He shouldn't be ruining her party. His tongue tastes like wet cotton.

"Dina, maybe I should stay here. I can't control the Noise. It just comes," he admits, as he did to their father before.

"No," she says and pulls him to his feet.

"I can't even tell what it sounds like for you all. For me, it's like a ringing in my ears. And lately it's getting so loud you could hear it next door." *Of course she did, I bet they heard it all the way down to the kitchen.*

Sediniel pulls his ponytail gently and pats his shoulder.

"Dad will figure it out. Next year we'll be in the Academy together." Sheyen gazes into the mirror, at them standing side by side, her a bit taller than him. "We look fine," Sediniel says and opens the door.

●

Sediniel was right; he should have played sick instead of joining the party. Sheyen can barely sit still and listen, eat and listen, drink and listen to them all celebrating. Even Latima's delicious food fails to distract him. A sudden headache splits his thoughts in half; his ears start ringing.

"Can you hear it too?"

Sheyen does not look up; he only catches glimpses of the others out of the corner of his eye. *Please, not now.* No one is talking, forks and fish knives frozen midair, steam wafting. The ringing in his ears fades as they wait, leaning slightly forward, but it doesn't go away. Barely heard, but still there.

"It's so strange," Lorna says and pushes her chair back. Phelien and Berthelen spring up, dropping their napkins from their laps. His so-called friends. *Huh.* He's barely seen them this summer. After the hair grew out all of a sudden, they just came around to watch him struggle with the brush — such an exotic tool. And since the Noise became strong enough for them to hear clearly, they've been totally thrilled. This freak-friend of theirs is an endless source of entertainment.

"Sit down." Lorna's mother says, but Lorna has already rushed to her feet and looks around suspiciously, her eyes finally landing on Sheyen.

"Could it be coming from outside?" Lorna asks.

Oh, for Salt's sake, playing ignorant just to call him out is an insult not only to him, but to Sediniel, to fucking Delyan too.

Sheyen keeps chewing his bream.

"Could there be something in the gardens?" Berthelen whispers to Lorna, leaning toward Sheyen. *Very funny, Berthelen. Yes, the In-Betweens are coming for you.*

"Come on, children, don't be silly," Lorna's mother says and turns back to her plate, her cheeks flushed. The ringing fades away completely. Sheyen hardly resists the urge to rub his ears — the others don't need more fuel.

"It was like the rumbling before an earthquake," Berthelen says, grasping for words, "But there was a high pitch to it too. It was like your gut clenching when you hear something been torn."

"Enough. This is nonsense," his omniscience, Delyan says, so nonsense it must be. Lorna's mother grants Delyan a nod and a prim smile. She gathers her shawl around her shoulders and clears her throat. *Nonsense, says Delyan Nedyre, first Artist of the Academy, so yes, let's keep eating fish.*

Berthelen is the last to sit back down. As he takes his seat by Sheyen, he leans over to leer and whisper, "Or maybe, it's an In-Between's squeal." The sun-glare glimmers on his bare pate.

Sheyen grips his fork and stabs the next bite, concentrates on how to swallow without choking.

"Let's make a toast," Delyan says and raises his glass. "To our Sediniel, who crossed into adulthood today. May your tattoos sway gently under the wind of the Art."

Glasses clink and Sheyen does not look any of them in the eye. Not even Sediniel, though he knows that's petty of him. He sips some wine; he can't allow himself to jinx her. It's supposed to be honeyed but it tastes like ash.

This, too, is in the book Sediniel hates. Whatever the In-Betweens eat tastes bitter, and they always crave something sweet. It could have been written about him, really, and he bets his friends read it too, so he drinks some more.

Delyan clears his throat. Sheyen can feel his father's eyes on him, but no, he won't look up; Mom is not here to scold him this time. Even Delyan didn't dare invite his exotic Caprishi mistress to a family party. Sheyen's presence was never questioned, since he used to look like the rest and Sediniel wouldn't have it otherwise, but things have changed and clearly, Delyan didn't realize how much.

"Also," Delyan says, "I am confident that next year Sheyen will also be ready to join the Academy." *Great, they're all staring now.* "To progress and advancement."

Sheyen finally looks up from the red algae garnish, his cheeks hot, his ears ringing. On his right, Berthelen stifles a giggle.

"Everyone gets in the Academy at fourteen," Sheyen says, gripping the glass he is not raising. What will he do if he's never accepted in the Academy? Become a sailor, like his mother? Work the salt marshes or the fields, like the Artless? Be exiled so that this weird Noise of his only echoes far from Vensymari ears, away from home? He tries hard not to blink as the rest of the company sits still, their glasses half raised, their hairless heads reflecting midday's sun-glare. The adults are polite enough to smile, but Lorna and Berthelen and Phelien stare, pressing their lips together to prevent a laugh.

"Sheyen, everyone's talent in the Art matures in its own pace. Yours is special." Delyan wears his disciplined tone, which says *be silent.*

"Special as in freakish," Berthelen mutters under his breath and Lorna leans forward to hide her smirk behind her woven fan.

"Perhaps what In-Betweens lack in talent, they make up for it in hair," she whispers loud enough for Sheyen to hear it. Sweat swells out of the roots of his hair and he wipes it with the back of his hand. How stupid of him to expect that things would remain the same after the hair grew out. At least Sediniel looks as pissed as he feels. She grips her fork so hard that her knuckles turn white while trying to pin down an olive and failing.

"Sediniel, your glass," her mother says, eyebrows arched and smiling.

"To the talented," Delyan says and faint clinking follows.

"And to the In-Betweens," Berthelen sniggers, elbowing Lorna under the table.

Sheyen does not dare to look at him, for fear he might plant a punch in Berthelen's throat. Sediniel fidgets as her fork screeches against the porcelain plate; the olive still rolling.

"Phelien, why don't you take Lorna and Berthelen for a walk?" This is Lorna's mother, and her voice carries an urgency that can't really be argued. All three of them push their chairs back and step out, humming the old In-Between nursery rhyme. *Halfwits.* He swallows; his ears pop. The ringing starts again. Only a month ago, all five of them would have run out together. How could he have ever thought that things would get better? He hoped the hair would be overlooked, that once he got in the Academy all would be disregarded, interpreted as a misunderstanding. Today is a nightmare.

The ringing in his ears reaches a high pitch, muffling all other sounds as if it presses a pillow against the world. Everyone winces at the Noise, hands fly up to ears; Delyan shoots him a sharp glance. Sediniel takes his hand in hers under the table and squeezes it.

Sheyen holds his breath, *stop*; the ringing blares. The air tastes metallic, specks of dust flood his throat, stick to his tongue. Sheyen swallows, his head light like a drifting bubble. What if they're right, what if the stories hold truth?

What if he is turning into an In-Between after all? He pushes the chair back and starts running.

"Sheyen? Where are you going?"

●

As soon as he leaves the mansion, the ringing stops, his ears still throbbing, his brain numb. He walks across the saltwood garden, all the way to the cliffs overlooking an ashen sea, summer storm dawning over the horizon. He would be better off inside the mansion, only he isn't going back. Nobody will care if he misses dessert anyway, all of them too busy cooing over Sediniel's new tattoos. All of them ignoring that he also turned fourteen, months ago, and yet no tattoos for him.

A stick breaks underfoot and he turns to see Sediniel resting against a tree trunk, looking at him over an apple. The scarlet tattoos meander on the skin of her bare skull, under the shallow breath of the wind. They make her look like the rest of them, all grown up. Ready to harness her talent in the Art.

"You hate apples," his voice scratching his throat. "Just throw it away."

"Father says we shouldn't waste food—"

"It's not that he can't afford it."

He grabs the apple from her hand and makes a run for the edge of the gardens. Chest crashing into the iron balustrades, he tosses it down the cliff and watches it roll until it hits the rocks by the beach.

"Why did you do that?" Sediniel struggles to catch her breath as she sticks her face out of the rails, looking down.

"I just did you a favor. You are an adult now, anyway. You don't *have to* eat it," he says, with half an eye on her tattoos. "You're a full citizen."

He tries his foot on the railing, makes sure that it holds and climbs. The rust, eating away the metal, smudges his palms. Sediniel watches closely, the tattoos' brisk movement betraying her agitation.

"I, on the other hand, am obviously a child, so I can still do this, right?" He balances with a single foot on the railing. He shoots a grin her way, swift and sharp, to chop her gurgling disapproval at its root.

"Come with me. Look!" He lowers himself to ride the iron, one leg hanging out, and nods towards three distant figures walking along the beach. "It's Lorna and the others."

"So what? Come on, let's get back inside, there is a huge storm coming and Latima is making chocolate." She pulls his leg, almost hanging her whole weight on it.

"Let's go and say hi." His fists are itching for a brawl. "Stop it, let's go meet them. Stop!"

"No." She climbs up and grabs him by the hair. He pulls loose and loses his balance for good, landing on the other side of the fence, face down in the dirt.

The wind howls.

"And they made *you* an adult?" He springs up, readjusting his belt. There are twigs and grass tangled in his hair. Why couldn't he remain as he was, hairless like everyone else — except Mom? His eyes sting a bit, but nah, it's the wind.

Sediniel is still on the ground, on the other side, dusting off her cloak.

"I'm not going back inside." His gaze wanders to the beach below, the three silhouettes gone now. They must have taken the long route back to the mansion. So, they'd rather chance the grey cliffs in a storm than pass by him. Without a warning, as always, the ringing roars in his head, louder than ever, deafening. *Fine.*

"Sheyen? Do you hear the Noise? Sheyen?"

●

Let her talk and shout. It's all right, she's got to be mature now. He runs down the path towards the sea and the ringing runs along with him, piercing his brain, muffling his breathing, the sound of his steps. It brings with it the stark smell of ice, the tart taste of marmalade gone bad. He spits. His ears hurt. It feels like they're bleeding, but when he reaches the sea, the ringing stops, abruptly, absolutely.

As if a blade cut it in half.

Sheyen takes a sharp breath, his lungs hungry for air, like he's just barely escaped drowning. He looks over his shoulder. Back along the path, Sediniel's mouth opens and closes without a sound. *At a loss for words, huh?*

He takes his stand on the beach, a couple of pebbles in his hand. He takes his shoes off; the tingling of the cold water under his feet feels soothing. The cinnamon-sanded beach stretches long and narrow to either side, abandoned in acute silence. The storm approaches fast yet mute. No wind. No waves, which is rare. Even the neighbor's dogs have stopped barking. He sends the first pebble skimming across the surface, but it does not skip at all, just sinks.

He takes his shirt off, throws it towards his shoes, by a flat rock. The silver sails of Mom's ship are nowhere to be seen. She is always there to preach about taking pride in their Caprishi heritage — her heritage, only half his — but always gone when they give him trouble about it. He dares a step forward.

"Did you hear that?" Sediniel says behind him and he jumps.

"When did you... Hear what? The Noise?" He gapes at her as she looks around, her lips thin, her eyes squinting. Her shoes are already wet.

"Sssh!" She is walking on the tip of her toes, but the soft crunch of dried seaweed betrays her. Where was it before? Her long neck stretches as she tries to hear better, forehead furrowed and full of doubt.

"What is it? I don't hear anything."

"I think it was the Noise, but this time it sounded different. More like a screeching, or fabric being ripped." She pulls her tunic tight around her.

"Like a ringing perhaps?" he asks, "Or shrill, like the laughter of the In-Betweens?"

"No. Shut up, Sheyen. It's gone now anyway." She folds her hands on her chest, shuddering . He sits on the ground and takes another couple of pebbles in his hand.

"It never crossed your mind? That the tales might be true?" he asks. *"Cursed is who lies in-between, who sways back and forth, neither out nor in. Hunted by those who spot the sign, its mane, its ear, its mismatched eye? They say it of all the half-breeds."*

"It's about the In-Betweens, not about half-Vensymari children," she scoffs.

"Oh really? Well, that's the song Phelien and Berthelen were humming at lunch. *Haunted by both silence and noise, torn between a home and a choice. Damned to belong under the frames of doors that lead to opposite ways. Cursed is who lies in-between, not one of us, a soul incomp—*"

"Stop it! And no, only the illiterate believe in old-wives tales."

"The stories say that all they can taste is bitterness! My tongue doesn't feel right today. They just linger in this In-Between place because they have nowhere else to go. And they won't let me into the Academy. Dina, what if it's happening?"

"You're just scared."

She kneels next to him and palms a pebble herself, weighs it and then throws it as far as she can.

Not a sound comes back.

"What's the Noise like for you?" he asks. "When it comes, I can only hear this damned ringing in my ears. The others said that it sounds like a rumbling and at the same time like paper being torn." His voice comes out almost too loud.

"Who said that?"

"Lorna, Berthelen, Phelien, everyone."

"They're idiots," she snaps. She flicks the pebble and then another and another. None skips. "They have no right to treat you like that," her voice an imitation of her mother's. She flicks and flicks as if her only goal in the entire world is to empty this shore of its pebbles. "You're my brother and th—"

"Don't!" He grabs her arm and looks around.

"Why not? It's not a damned secret."

"No? Then why am I not called Nedyre, like you? Why did I not get any tattoos? Delyan's other sons all had them at my age."

She twitches, opens her mouth, but stays mute.

Sheyen lets go of her. The tips of her ears are red, like always when she's angry. His cheeks are burning.

A drop of rain lands on the naked skin of her head, then another and another. And then, he notices. Her tattoos have lost their brightness, their color only a muted shade of red.

"Put your hood up," he says in a careful voice. "Are you feeling all right?" Her tattoos stop swaying. They're not supposed to do that. He runs his tongue over his lips. They taste like a stranger's — like porcelain, unused and undusted.

"It's so quiet," she whispers.

Plump drops of chilly rain land heavy on his cheeks. He blinks hard, chasing the swelling tears away as he stands, letting her expression sink in behind his eyes, in silence. This silence they share and this Noise they don't.

Sediniel suddenly looks back, towards the mansion, rainwater racing unhindered down her nape, soaking her light green tunic.

"Tell me what you heard before. I need to know," Sheyen says.

"No."

"Why not?"

Her nails must be down to the roots the way she is biting them now.

"Was it that horrible?" he asks.

Lightning. *Nine woven blossoms, eight woven blossoms, seven woven blossoms.* But no thunder.

"Yes. Like flesh being torn."

The rain raps against the rocks. The wind swoops in and he gasps as tiny needles prickle his skin, reaching deep to his lungs. Something is missing from the landscape, but he cannot tell what. He bends down to get his shirt and shoes, which lie drenched near her half-eaten apple.

The sounds. The sounds are missing.

"Leave it. Let's go."

"Sediniel, I need a favor."

"What?"

"It's the hair on my head. That's what's making the noise."

"That's about the stupidest thing I—"

"No, think. The Noise started when the hair appeared. And it's getting worse every day. And if there is any truth in the stories, we must stop it. What if my eyes are next? What if I wake up and one of them is suddenly blue, or brown or anything other than green? What if I drag you to the In-Between place?"

Lightning.

"I need to shave it off. I don't care if Mom gets angry or disowns me or lectures me forever. She's not mixed. She's just foreign. I should have got rid of the stupid hair a month ago."

"It's illegal to shave it. You're not a Vensymari to go around bald, you need to get approval first," she says in one breath, looking at him straight in the eye.

"I'm the First Artist's son, right? They won't do shit to me."

Sediniel scans the beach, her gaze travelling from his clothes up to the garden and then to the clouds. "Something feels wrong. I feel like... like I'm standing at the edge of a cliff. It's weird out here; too quiet."

"That's what I'm saying," he shouts. "It's happening and we have to stop it. Will you help me get rid of the hair?"

Mute lightning flashes. A wave swells and crashes against the rocks without a sound. Sediniel presses her lips together and holds her breath. Rain drenches her in silence.

"Fine." Her eyes linger on the soundless waves. "But only if you come back to the house with me. Now."

Sheyen nods, relief spreading on his shoulder blades like warm butter. "We'll sneak in through the kitchen so nobody sees."

They run back, Sediniel first with Sheyen lagging behind her to steal a last glance at the wrinkled sea; Mom had better be back soon.

●

The mansion, their father's summer home, always smells of baking. Its thick stone walls, its light elderberry furniture, the curtains, the sheets and the inside of the wardrobes, have all been imbued with the fragrance of dessert cooking in the ovens. Today, it's lemongrass pie and hot caramel-flavored chocolate. The smell spreads better in the silence.

Only it shouldn't be silent. Their father should be here, sipping seadrop liquor with their friends' parents by the unlit fireplace. When he left, they were all still lounging in the dining room, heavy with Latima's cooking. He can't hear them now; even the servants are nowhere to be seen.

Still shivering, barefoot and half-naked, he crouches over the boiling pot of chocolate, letting the delicious steam warm his insides. The thought of grabbing a spoon and digging in flashes, then fades.

"Hello?" Sediniel almost whispers standing under the doorframe, looking down the drab corridor. She trails back into the kitchen and closes the door gently behind her, heading for the saltwood chest where a blunt pair of scissors is kept under the towels. The water-weight clock that never worked properly hangs overhead. The faint creaking of its cogs always out of tune, a tick too late, a tack too long. Only now it echoes smoothly, first a tick and then a tack, tick tack, tick tack.

"The clock is working," she mumbles distracted, groping in the chest.

It sounds wrong, he wants to tell her. Disorienting. But the words snag on his tongue.

"Where is everyone?" she asks and Sheyen turns to check the door they snuck in from, scanning the garden through its colored glass, hoping to spot someone they missed before.

"Perhaps they're out for a walk?" Alarm coils under her casual concern; her gaze has followed his.

"Could be."

"And Latima? The kitchen servants?"

"They're probably running some errands downtown." Highly unlikely, but she mustn't be sidetracked from the haircut, the moment is too convenient. What if she changes her mind? He's been nagging her to help him for a month now, and she always refused.

"All four of them?" Sediniel strokes her head just above the forehead, her tattoos still dim and lifeless, but she doesn't seem to notice and he won't tell. He glances at the scissors.

Lightning. Unheard thunder rattles the pots on their shelf.

"Something is wrong," mutters Sediniel darting glances at the shelves as if they are about to tilt and crack. "The house is wrong, they didn't even put out the ovens. And the storm," Sediniel says pointing a finger towards the glass door. Rain whips the glass and for a couple of breaths they linger, waiting for the din to come; what comes is only silence.

She approaches the door, ready to open it.

"Sediniel?" he says. "Quit stalling. Obviously, they're going to be back any minute now. We need to be quick."

"Quick? Sheyen, something is off, I can't hear a thing from outside the house. No rain, no thunder, no barking dogs. Nothing."

"I know, which is why we should do it now. Something's happening to me and maybe this is how we stop it."

"Why would it stop? And not a word about the stupid tales." Her face is taut, about to snap, her lips a line, her fists bunched. "There is no such thing as... as the In-Between People." Finally, *finally* she turns away from the door. "But, if that's what you want... When your mother comes back though, you won't hear the end of it." Reaching into the top drawer, she pulls out a small bundle wrapped in the scraps of old kitchen towels.

"Latima's meat razors," she whispers in answer to his arched eyebrows.

The razors rattle as they land on the table by the scissors. Sediniel crouches over the thin blades, inspecting them closely and takes one between thumb and finger.

"I'm not sure how to use these, I might cut you."

"I don't mind, just do it." But she's not listening. Sheyen follows her unflinching look which turns towards the glass door. Three figures stand there, waving, drenched.

"It's the others," Sheyen says. He wants to move but for a couple of deafening heartbeats his feet are wreathed with iron. The figures' gestures expand, become quick, become sharp. Yet there is no sound as their fists pound the glass. Before thoughts form, he rushes to the glass door to latch it shut.

"Sheyen," Sediniel gasps but Berthelen is already leaning against the glass and turning the door-knob. He takes a step into the kitchen. The water-weight clock sounds a bell and stops.

The room seems smaller with all three of them bursting inside. Berthelen's shoulders have widened over the summer and he now stands a full head taller than

Sheyen. Drops of rain gleam faintly on the skin of his head, and his hands are curled into fists by his sides, face washed red with anger. Lorna stands next to him, skinny and poised. She pushes her hood back tossing unreadable looks to her older brother, Phelien, who looms behind them. Sheyen doesn't like the way he unfolds his Vensymari limbs, long, lithe, and braided with muscle. Sheyen struggles not to take a step back. This is, after all, his house. Scurrying feet tap on the marble and Sediniel stops next to him. He turns and looks and his heart skips a beat. She is scared.

"What's wrong? What happened to your tattoos?" she says.

"Same that happened to yours," Phelien growls.

"What?" She whips around and her eyes lash at Sheyen for confirmation. Her hand flies up to her skull, fingers tracing the fading patterns. Sheyen returns the stare and nods slightly. It's pointless to lie. "This can't be happening." She tries to catch a glimpse of her reflection in the glass.

"Something's terribly wrong." Lorna's crystal pitched voice, now so cold and clear. No one moves. Not right away. Then, Phelien takes a step forward, heads for the chair closest to the kitchen bench and sits, carefully, scanning the room as if looking for something stolen.

"The sounds outside are missing. Everyone else is missing," he says. "It's just us."

"We came back from the beach and no one was home," Lorna says, like crystal cracking. As she opens her mouth to speak again, Sheyen feels his hair stand on end.

"Maybe they're out somewhere," Sediniel speaks first.

"No. We were just out looking for them. Not a soul." That's Berthelen. He is looking Sheyen straight in the eye. "We warned you."

Sheyen feels something creeping up the back of his throat, bile. His stomach is a tight knot that presses his chest, presses and presses. A sour taste in his mouth. He needs to run, only he won't.

"What? Are you serious?"

"The Noise took them. He took them. He's an In-Between." Lorna's voice comes out flat.

"Sheyen was with me all day, he didn't do anything. How could he, how could anyone? Are you stupid, did you hit your head on something?" Sediniel has taken her place right in front of him.

"Cut it off, Sediniel. You've heard the Noise inside him. He sent them to the In-Between place, because he hates them all."

Time is a drowsy cat arching its back slowly. Lorna looks so different now that Sheyen realizes that he doesn't really know her. Not the girl he played tag with; when they ran until their lungs were about to burst, stumbled on a root and feigned falling and then kissed, a swift brush of lips against lips followed by secret smiles and a prickly sensation running right under his skin.

"How would he do that?" Sediniel roars. "How—"

"Shut your mouth." Phelien stands up, arms ready to strike.

"You shut up, you rotten pigfly shit," Sheyen pushes his sister aside and walks up to Phelien. A blow just under his ribs might be enough to force him down, if he moves fast.

Berthelen jumps Sheyen from behind; he falls on Sheyen hard, knocking him flat on the marble. Before Sheyen can crawl back up, Berthelen sits on his waist, knees on his sides squeezing tight, pinning him, face down.

"Stop it, you tarnished half-breed," Berthelen says. "Bring them back!" He grabs Sheyen by the hair and pulls up so hard that Sheyen hears a loud crack at the base of his neck. Berthelen loosens his grip, but, as Sheyen's still pinned down, there's little he can do. He squirms, growls and gasps.

"Stop! What are you doing?" Sediniel's voice pierces Sheyen's ears and only now he realizes she's been going like that for some time.

"Bring them back!" Berthelen leans close to his ear and shouts as if he's about to spit his lungs out.

"Just a minute, and I'll fart them out." Sheyen snorts. He would sneer but he feels the skin of his face stretched tight on his cheekbones.

"Bring them back, you soulless mutt."

"It's the hair. Get rid of it. Make it stop," Lorna shouts.

"I'll do it!" Sediniel's voice comes out strained, almost choked. "Let me do it! We were about to cut his hair anyway." She brandishes the razors and the scissors, Phelien steps back. "That's what he wanted me to do. Right, Sheyen?"

He can barely turn his head to see her. He wanted to get rid of the stain, true enough, but this stain, he now sees, will never leave. It has spread, quick as ink on white linen. Blending in is not going to happen. The tattoos are not going to happen. Kissing Lorna again is not going to happen.

"Fuck her." Lorna is standing by the boiling chocolate pot. "Cutting it is not enough. Let's burn it off him. Make sure it never grows again."

Sheyen's mouth turns numb, his tongue a sack of sand about to crumble.

"Hold him tight," Phelien barks. Sheyen gulps down air too thin to fill his lungs.

"You've gone mad," Sediniel hisses, close by, on his right. Berthelen ignores her, digs his knees deeper under Sheyen's ribs, making him wince and writhe. Metal clatters; Lorna gasps.

Now. Sediniel releases a holler. She charges at Berthelen, pouncing on him like a rabid dog. Berthelen screams and loses his grip. Muscles bowstring taut, veins sizzling with panic, Sheyen rolls over and pushes himself up. He lunges at Phelien and Lorna and thrusts at the pot they're holding. Metal clanks and Phelien shrieks as the pot lands on his toes; boiling chocolate spills over his arms, feet and clothes, quickly spreading on the floor. Phelien stumbles back, eyes wild, scalded arms flopping.

Sheyen whips around to check on Sediniel, sprawled in the corner by the glass door, lips bleeding. Berthelen marches towards her. Sheyen thrusts at Berthelen to push him aside. Sediniel launches first, razors in hand, before Berthelen's foot digs into her groin sending her crawling. Sheyen clashes into him and shoves him aside, hard. He sweeps to his sister, razors scattered on the soiled boards. Lightning. Her eyes swell with angry tears, her jaw fixed tight. He props her up and together they rush to the glass door.

The door behind them stands ajar while they pant their way through the garden. There is no denying it now; the world outside the house has been stripped of every sound, an animated painting raging around them. The rain pours down mute and cold, turning the soil to mud; the leaves shake on the saltwood trees without a rustle.

"Run." He drags her on until they reach the fence where they climb over, supporting each other, limbs shaky. They careen down the path to the beach.

"We need to get away from the house," his voice hoarse. The pebbles churn under their feet as they reach the rocks just above the water and stop.

A slurping sound ripples the silence. The sound of flesh breaking. The rumbling of a mouth full of stones. A high pitched screeching. *So that's how it sounds.*

"The Noise," Sediniel whispers.

A hunched figure stands on the spot where Sheyen's clothes should be, by the rocks. No taller than he, dressed in his shirt, wearing his shoes, lank golden hair hanging drenched to its ankles. Bony tattooed hands huddled up to its chest, clenching the discarded apple. The figure sups its juice, swallows and buries its face in the fruit, gnawing, lips pulled back; there are no teeth, just gums. It sucks and swallows and never looks up, famished. The Noise emanates from inside it, growing louder with every chunk it gobbles.

Sheyen takes his sister's hand and gently pulls her closer, her breath rasping in his ear. The creature stands just steps away from them. Sheyen can't bear to look at its face. The creature smacks its lips, sucks at its gums and stumbles forward.

They don't wait for it to take a second step. Faster than their racing heartbeats, they turn together and, holding hands, they jump into the sea, falling among the soundless raindrops for a panicked eternity before they hit the surface. Coming up for air, looking at each other, they start swimming away from the beach as fast as they can. The waves rage bitter and silent, salt creeping in the wounds of his chapped lips. Sediniel pushes him on, stroke after stroke leaving them in the exact same spot with backs turned to the house until a drop of courage forces him to look over his shoulder.

"Look," he says.

The figure, a white smudge in the dark, dawdles up the path they came from. Sheyen can hardly hear the Noise from this far. It reaches the fence and climbs over. It keeps walking, through the garden towards the kitchen. Towards the door that's left ajar. Towards the others.

Shivers seize him. Lightning. The creature stumbles into the kitchen. Nine woven blossoms, eight woven blossoms, seven woven blossoms. Screams, and then nothing. Only silence. The house falls dark.

Suddenly thunder. The wind now blusters and the rain splashes around them.

"Sheyen," Sediniel gasps. It's the house, all lit up now, not just the kitchen. There are figures in the garden and along the path to the beach, holding lanterns. Voices. Familiar. They call their names. Their father.

Sediniel pulls him first towards the shore, pushing his limp body to swim. When their feet touch the sand, she hugs him. Her tattoos glisten red under the faint moonlight.

"I see them," Latima shouts, "Delyan! I see them!"

The beach feels frozen as they crawl out. Warm arms wrap around them. Their father's face looks strange, stripped as it were of color.

"Where were you?" Latima has run down with blankets. "We've been waiting in the house, thinking you would be back by nightfall," she stifles a sob. "We've looked for you everywhere."

"Where were you? Sheyen?" Their father rubs his arms to warm him; Latima is cradling Sediniel. Limbs limp, Sheyen stares back through tangled hair.

"You're bruised!" His voice frays. "Sheyen, what happened?" He shakes him hard. "Where are the others? Were you together?"

He sees them now, the parents of Lorna and Berthelen and Phelien, lanterns in their hands, their eyes wild as they search for those who are not there.

"Where are they?" his father asks again.

Sheyen turns his head towards his sister, licks his lips — they're sore. Sediniel nods slowly. Licks the tears that reach down to the corners of her mouth. Sheyen seals his lips shut. He rubs the lobes of his ears; for now, it's quiet inside him.

Victor Pseftakis' story "The Noise Inside" was originally published in Metaphorosis on Friday, 15 March 2019. See magazine.metaphorosis.com

About the author

Victor Pseftakis is a writer, translator, creative writing teacher and RPG maniac. They are usually found sipping coffee from bottomless cups and watching bug documentaries. Their fiction can be found either in Greek or in English in various venues. They currently live in Thessaloniki, Greece, trying to train fleas to do their bidding.

The Final Face

Norah Lovelock

There were seventeen people left between Dia and the end of her commission.

Failed colonies were too expensive to run, difficult to maintain, and so her commission had sent her here to collect up the stragglers, put them into cyro, and take them back to the homeworlds. FC3-268b, dubbed Rija by the locals, was the last planet on her very long list. There were seventeen people left for her to collect.

And when it was over, she'd have to return to Central. She was old and damaged. She could make an educated enough guess: they'd decommission her. Upload her memories to some storage somewhere and forget she ever existed: the fate of most custodians, useless until they weren't.

This colonist's house was away from the others. Against the general backdrop of neglect, it was stark in its upkeep. The front door was painted an obnoxiously bright yellow, the brickwork repaired instead of crumbling. Dead bushes wilted below its wide bay windows. Dia gave herself a moment. She was tired. She had done this thousands of times, yet it never grew easier. Then, finally, when she could wait no longer, she stepped close and knocked.

It took a minute before it opened. A pair of eyes squinted suspiciously at her from the narrow crack between the wood and frame. Then the stranger noted the ruins of Dia's faceplate, her torn plastic skin and exposed, stained circuitry, and said, conversationally, "You look like shit, don't you?"

Dia did look like shit. It had been a long time since she'd had maintenance beyond what she could do for herself. Working on planets several hundred lightyears away from Central did that to a robot. Her plastic skin had been torn by a particularly aggressive mammal on a desert planet, her faceplate ripped out by a colonist with a vendetta. Once, she might have been able to disguise herself as human—convince the humans, as immoral as it was, that she could understand their plight, making it easier to take them to the sleepship. Maybe—and the thought alone felt traitorous—she might've been able to run: find a nearby space station, hide herself among the humans, as innocuous and invisible as any of them. Maybe it was a childish dream. Sometimes, it felt like it was all she had.

But her visible circitry betrayed her and there was no way for her to repair herself. She would have to wait until she returned to Central to see what they'd do to her.

"Thank you," she said dryly, inclining her head. The humans never greeted her warmly. "May I come in? I'm a custodian. I'm here to help."

After another moment of suspicious squinting, the woman pulled the door open wider and stepped aside. "All right."

The house was cluttered. The walls were filled with photos, competing for space against framed prints, children's drawings pinned into the drywall. Belongings filled every empty surface: magazines, crocheted pillowcases, blankets, coasters. Considering how beloved the woman appeared, it was fascinating that she lived here, alone in this big house, removed from the rest of the remaining colonists.

The woman led her through the chaos to an equally chaotic kitchen, where she sat at the table. After a moment of deliberation, Dia sat too.

"I'm Dia. What's your name?"

"Alma," the woman said, leaning forward, elbows on her thighs. "You here to convince me to leave, then? Homeworlds decided that Rija isn't worth supplying anymore?"

Dia immediately knew this was not a conversation she could win. Her spiel had been ready: her polite, well-practiced, 'I'm a custodian from Central. Due to cost-cutting measures, we're asking the residents of Rija to relocate back to the homeworlds via sleepship. You *can* choose to stay, but the food packets will stop, and you'll be disconnected from the network.' Alma had beaten her to the punch.

"No," she demurred. "I'm just wondering who'd want to stay behind."

Alma snorted. "Only ever known this place, haven't I?"

She'd heard that excuse hundreds—thousands—of times before. It was no longer compelling. "You are aware that Central will set you up on whichever of the homeworlds you'd prefer? That you'll be cut off from food packets and the network?"

"Of course. I don't want to leave, though. Not gonna pack all my stuff—" and, waving an expansive hand, it was clear she had a lot of it, "—into a suitcase for the sake of some mandate I didn't even choose."

Dia still asked the question, as rote as it had become: "Don't you have people who care about you? Friends who'll miss you if you stay behind?"

Alma scoffed. "Ain't no-one here who gives a damn about me."

It felt like a lie, but Dia didn't know enough to argue. She didn't want to argue. She wanted to leave. "I take it I won't be able to convince you."

"No," Alma said sharply. Then she paused, her lips twitching with sudden mirth, and added, "And anyway, I like the weather."

●

There wasn't any weather to like. Rija was a miserable planet. The buildings were grey; the scant vegetation was muted and dull. Only far out at sea did the planet gain colour: the deep green of algae, the planet's primary source of oxygen.

And here, beside the shuttle, the rest of the town was collapsing into the ocean. From afar, the tide was foam-tipped; closer, just below where Dia stood, the waves gnawed hungrily at the ruins of houses. Overhead, it was drizzling: fine, thin, terrible stuff that made her want to shield her ripped forehead with her hand to try and stop the water from reaching her electronics.

Trust her final assignment to be on a wet planet. With her broken faceplate, it was the last thing she needed.

"Hello?" a voice called. "Are you from Central?"

She turned. It was a family: three adults, an infant, huddled against the rain. Her processors sparked with recognition: she'd seen them on the info sent from Central. "We saw the shuttle," one of them said, his eyes roaming her face. "You've brought a sleepship, haven't you?"

"I have," she said gently. It was up in orbit, waiting for its final passengers. "You want to go up?"

They did.

Once the humans and their luggage were inside, Dia set the autopilot, leaned back in the pilot's seat, and watched out the window as the planet grew small beneath them.

Her thoughts drew back to Alma; Alma, who seemed so bizarrely possessive of this ugly, backwater planet. Sure, it had a breathable atmosphere, but that was hardly rare. Even from the sky it was monochrome. Only as they entered orbit did it gain beauty: the grey cut by great swathes of white cloud, the ocean revealed to be swirls of deep navy and dark green. She couldn't help her cynicism. The miracle of orbit could make anything beautiful.

And in orbit, too, was the sleepship, dignified against the backdrop of stars. In the back, the humans were talking, nervous but quiet. She'd be nervous too, if she were human.

Inside the sleepship, there were rows upon rows of cyro pods: thousands of them, patiently waiting for the person inside to wake. She had recited her explanation so often that it no longer held meaning: each pod was a cryo system. It would freeze them but would feel like taking a very long and timeless nap, and when they woke up, they'd be in Central.

They were scared. They also couldn't go back now. When all were all settled, she sealed the pods. On her custodian node, she set the countdown and the commands;

watched as the drugs kicked in, and, one by one, as they fell asleep. Eventually, the lights in their pods turned off. They began to freeze.

When she had first received this sleepship, she had been a different custodian with a different name. The ship had been empty. She'd been excited.

And now she'd sat through near a thousand cycles of travel, been to deserts and mountains, valleys and moons, and all she wanted now was to go back to Central. She didn't care if they decommissioned her; not anymore. She wanted this done. She wanted to rest.

Without any humans around, the room slipped into darkness to conserve energy. She didn't bother wishing them sweet dreams. They couldn't hear her anymore.

●

She took the shuttle back planet-side. There were just three families left: two bigger families and Alma. The thought of collecting them exhausted her, but the end was in sight.

According to the intel she'd been given via custodian node—and she did *not* envy whichever custodian had been tasked with reconnaissance—the families occupied a single row of houses, well-kept in comparison to the abandoned building. Despite the drizzle, she went on foot, angling her head down to try and keep her internal components dry.

Whoever had done recon had done a good job, because they were right. Three terraced houses huddled together against a long row, the front gardens overfull with exotic fauna: bright orange, luminous purple, stark in the gloom.

And Alma was outside. She was leaning against the doorframe, chatting to a man inside, her tone light and cheerful.

It was awfully coincidental that Alma had claimed no-one here liked her, yet here she was, conversational—warm. Then she turned and her expression narrowed. "Here to spirit this family away too, then?"

"No," Dia said, and pressed her hand against her still-attached forehead plate to try and shield the worst of the rain. "They went voluntarily."

"Only because you bullied them into it."

The man interjected with a valiant, "Alma! Don't be mean to it!", but it was clear Alma would not be deterred. She waved her hand at him, scowling. "Go look after the kids, Mailer. Tell 'em I'll give 'em electronics classes next week—if you're still here."

Dia wanted to retort with something sharp—that keeping them here would serve no purpose but their deaths; that Alma's determination to stay didn't grant her the right to trap everyone else here, too; that it certainly was strange that no-one cared for her, but she was giving electronics classes. Then the feeling faded. Arguing wouldn't help. It very rarely did.

Alma turned on her heel and began to make her way down the road. Dia paused—then, deciding Mailer was a future problem, followed. She fell into step. "Electronics classes?"

Alma shot her a sharp glance. "None of your business."

"I never suggested it was," she responded, purposefully mild. "You don't have to tell me anything you don't want to."

That earned her another sidelong glare—and then, after a moment of silence, a sigh. "A long time ago, I used to be a custodian technician."

A technician? They were rare to find outside of the Central homeworlds—near impossible to find on any of the planets Dia had ever been deployed to. Hope, sudden and terrible, rose in her chest. Maybe there were options beyond decommission. "You could replace my faceplate."

Alma stopped walking. She stared up at her, squinting through the rain, the droplets catching on her lashes. "Why d'you think I'd help you out?"

It felt so obvious to say it was nearly painful: "I need help, and you're the first technician I've encountered."

"Obviously," Alma grumbled. "I just dunno why you're coming to me. We're not friendly."

They weren't. But right now, that didn't matter, because Alma had something Dia needed—needed so desperately her electronics ached with it. "What do you want from me in exchange?"

"I don't want anything from you." She began to walk, expecting Dia to fall back into step, then said, tightly: "Fine. I'll do it. How bad's the damage on your internal circuitry?"

It was that easy? And she didn't even want anything in exchange? Dia spoke quickly before either of them could change their minds: "I can't smile properly, but I'm sure you've already noticed that. Anything else I wouldn't be too sure about."

"Thought you new models could self-diagnose?"

"I'm not a new model," she said wryly. "Can you do it or not?"

"Of course I can *do* it." Alma said it quickly, like it was a point of pride. She pushed open her front door, stepped inside, then turned to survey Dia properly: a long, slow look up and down. "All right. My workshop's in the basement, and it's drier down there than up here."

●

She had been expecting a small workshop—maybe enough for a single table, some spare parts. She hadn't been expecting a full workroom. There was a table in the centre for the custodian to lie on, whilst the walls were lined with shelves containing every part Dia knew she contained and then some.

Out here, so far from Central, there surely weren't enough custodians to warrant this level of set up. Rija was a backwater planet in a backwater system. While custodians were everywhere, there couldn't ever have been enough work to be able to make it into a *career*.

She turned to Alma, eyebrow raised. "You've been hiding this down here?"

"Not hiding," she retorted, but folded her arms and shifted her weight. "Everyone already knows. Kept up with it even after I retired." She looked back at Dia, then said, curt, "The face plates are up there. Choose one."

She did as instructed, depositing options on the table, trying to hide her delight. She could be whole once again. There were faces of every size and shape, colouring and structure: brown eyed, purple eyed; freckled or scarred or neither or both. With every face, potential opened before her. She plucked through them until one felt *right*: dark eyed and dark skinned, similar to the plastic skin on the rest of her body. "This one," she said, and pressed her finger to feel the way its—soon to be *her*—cheek compressed. She looked up at Alma. "Do I wanna know how you got it?"

Alma plucked it up in deft hands. "I bought it." Her fingers skated along its still cheek. Some deep tenderness shone through in her face, enough to wipe away her sullenness—but when she looked at Dia she was surly once more. "Do you want to power off? It'll be uncomfortable if you stay awake."

"I don't mind."

"Lie down," Alma instructed, and turned away to a metal chest of drawers to bring out her tools.

Dia lay. The table was cool against her back and neck, but not unpleasantly so. She couldn't see what Alma was doing, but she had been repaired enough to take a guess at what she could hear: Alma was pulling out a wheeled stool to perch on; the way the metal bolts and screws clinked against each other as she plucked them out of the drawers and into tiny bowls. She got out a drill and a set of screwdriver attachments, prepared a cotton swab and rubbing alcohol.

Finally, she was ready. Alma flicked on lights bright enough to blind a human. "Are you sure about this?"

Well, it wasn't like she could mess Dia's face up any further. She shut her eyes. "Yes."

Alma began by unscrewing something below Dia's chin, soft skin against her sensors—and then those same hands darted up, unscrewing something else near her temple. The touch was overwhelming, too fast for her to meaningfully process—fingers on the wires in her face, knuckles against the inside of her skull, and Dia knew she didn't need to breathe, but it left her breathless anyway: the terrible intimacy of it, this woman inside her, taking her apart.

Then, finally, a part of her face came away. She heard it hitting the little table next to her, metal and cold. Next, she knew, would come the specific servos to support the musculature of the face she'd once worn; the tiny processor that made it move.

She hadn't expected Alma to need to wriggle it out. Every careful nudge of those fingers felt like an earthquake. It left her tense, every fibre of her locked into stillness, Alma's knuckles warm against the inside of her face—that terrible face; the one she hated to have, hated to see, the touch burning like fire.

"Are you alright?" Alma asked, voice low. "I'm about halfway through. Do you need a break?"

"I'm fine," she said. Her voice, the traitor, didn't even quiver. "Are you okay to keep going?"

Alma paused. "Yes," she said finally, and the wriggling resumed.

Dia lay there and tried not to move; tried not to use her processor in thinking how Alma's hands were so hot inside of her, removing and discarding the parts of her that no longer functioned. And then, quite suddenly, it was too much: this room, the overhead lights, the feeling of someone poking at the exposed parts of herself. "I need a break," she breathed, and this time her voice shook.

"I'm almost done," Alma groused. She wriggled the processor sharply, and Dia stopped processing data entirely.

And then, finally, it came out, and Alma's hands withdrew, and Dia could *think* again. She sat up, jerking up without the excess weight of her broken faceplate, itching all deep inside like a wound she couldn't touch.

Alma didn't even have the grace to look at her. She was poking the ancient parts on the tray, turning them this way and that. "Hope I didn't ruin any of the prongs," she murmured to herself. She glanced up at Dia and, with characteristic brusqueness, said, "Lie down again. We're not done. Need to put the new one on."

Could Dia lie down? Could she tolerate even a moment more of that touch, so terribly invasive? She wasn't sure, but she had to. Walking around with no faceplate would be worse than a broken one. There would be no future for her at all. She forced her body back down onto the table and lay utterly still, not even letting her hands clench into fists.

But what had been difficult was now easy. She kept an eye on her internal chronometer as Alma worked, watching the minutes count down. Alma did the same in reverse to the new face: attached the processor, plugged in the circuit boards and servos, and made it align with the rest of her head. None of it took very long, even if Alma's hands were burning hot; even if Dia wanted, just a little, to crawl out of her own skin.

Slowly, hyperaware of her new eyelids, she opened her eyes to let them focus and unfocus. And finally, as Alma cleared off the finishing touches, Dia installed her new drivers.

Alma's hands drew away. The overhead light flickered off. "There," she said finally, quiet. "We're done."

Dia sat up. The weight of her new face was unfamiliar —heavier, but welcome. When she brought her hand up to touch, there was no longer the tangle of wires and circuits, but flesh—a little cooler than human temperature, but *hers*. Her nose; her lips.

"Want a mirror?"

"Please," Dia begged.

Alma held one up for her. If Dia had had a heart, it would've stopped—because it was her, Dia, but she wore a stranger's face. Unfamiliar, but not for long. She stared at herself and made faces, stretched her mouth and crinkled her nose in an attempt to remind herself that this was her, now. She checked the groove between her neckplate and faceplate and, if she hadn't known, wouldn't've been able to tell there was a seam at all.

Hope, sudden and terrible, rose in her chest. The suffering felt suddenly worth it, like she had gone through something terrible for something redemptive at the other side. And her discomfort hadn't entirely been Alma's fault. She could allow a little praise. "I'm not sure a Central technician could've done a better job."

"Thanks," Alma said, watching Dia's face. Then she turned away, putting away her tools, her shoulders a tense line.

Dia got to her feet. Even though she knew it may ruin the silent truce between them, she had to ask: "You really don't want to go with them?"

Alma didn't even turn to answer. "Go with them *where*? Some sterile homeworld? Where there's traffic and people and noise?" She snorted. "I'd rather stay here, thanks, even if that means dying."

It was human idiocy of the highest order; the derision, the belief she'd be fine even when Central would essentially starve her out. "Stay, then," Dia said, and took the stairs two at a time in leaving.

●

The man Alma had spoken to—Mailer—caught her on her way back to the shuttle. "Custodian," he barked.

He was heedless to her anger. "Yes?"

He paused, fixated on her new face for a split second before he said, "We're leaving. Network's been turned off, and I suppose we didn't realise what we were signing ourselves up for." He grimaced. Humans really did love to revel in their own misery. She wished she had that luxury. "All the rest of us are coming, apart from..."

"Yeah," Dia snarled. "I'm aware."

"We want her to come. It's convincing her that's the problem," he said, shrugging.

She knew what a good custodian would do. She would go back to Alma—explain to her, softly and patiently, that everyone else was leaving, and hope that it would jolt her into leaving too. Dia would point out that they did care about her. Maybe she'd even get Mailer's children to come along. She wasn't above emotional blackmail.

But Dia wasn't a particularly good custodian. She didn't want to face Alma's grumpy expression, her short words. She wasn't sure she had the patience. Some spiteful part of her wanted to leave Alma here; wanted her to stay here, alone, and understand just the choice she was making. But mostly it sounded like too much work.

"Alright," she said instead of something tight and unkind. "I'll take the rest of you up in the morning. You've got tonight to pack—to say goodbye."

He nodded. "Thanks." Maybe he meant it.

●

It rained that evening, hard and heavy. She sat in the shuttle and listened to it thunder on the roof. Once, she would've been forced to worry about the electronics in her face degrading. Now she didn't have to worry at all.

That didn't mean she was happy about it.

At least the colonist situation was improving. She'd be able to round them all up before her final due date—bar Alma, of course, who would stay unless Dia convinced her otherwise. And Alma *would* stay alone if she had to.

Her chronometer told her it was dawn when she heard a knock on the shuttle door. She slid it open to reveal the rest of the families, carrying suitcases and pet carry cages and whatever else they needed to bring with them. She ferried them up, settling them into their sleep pods, and they went easily—painlessly. She drank in the sight of them as they shut their eyes and dreamt of whatever world they'd wake up in.

And then, finally, she was alone, and Dia could put it off no longer.

She landed the shuttle near Alma's house—because now there was no need for politeness. The drizzle had stopped, the air thick and grey, and she walked through it and felt the rain smudge against her face, whole once more.

She could have knocked. She didn't bother. Instead, she pushed the yellow front door open, wiping her shoes on the mat, and stepped inside. "Alma?"

A low grumble, then: "I'm in the kitchen."

It was just as cluttered as her previous visits. No attempt had been made to clean—to bring away things Alma might want to transport with her. She was ferociously stacking plates, her shoulders drawn.

"I'm going," Dia said simply, "and I'm taking everyone else with me."

For a second Alma paused, and then her expression narrowed. She ever so carefully put down the plate, almost soundless, on the counter. Her voice was poisonous: "You don't understand."

It was an absurd, impossible claim. However old Alma was, Dia was far older. "At least I understand how short-sighted you are. You could teach the kids electronics classes anywhere—"

"Short-sighted?" Alma laughed unhappily. "No—really. It's you who doesn't understand." And she stepped forward and took Dia's hand in her own—and between them, a custodian node flared to life.

Dia froze. Data flickered through her, images layered upon images: Alma's deployment here, generations ago. Rija had swelled and swelled with more and more people who accepted her, universally, unilaterally, as human. How terrifying that had been. How wonderful.

And how she'd had to hide. How she'd been able to confide in only a few, but how that was rare; how she had learned to maintain her own faceplate, do her own updates, because otherwise someone would work it out—they'd tell Central, and she'd have to return to the hell that was custodian work. How she didn't want that. How she'd rather stay here, alone—rot and fade and disappear—than return to the purgatory of reality.

Or at least at first. How the days had become monotonous without something to structure them. How alone she was around humans, hiding amongst them, unable to relate to them; unable to have them relate to her in turn.

Dia's broken face at Alma's front door, and Alma's terror at knowing she was going to be taken back to Central.

Dia staggered away. She knew it was programming—knew it was the facsimile of some human emotion—but her knees felt weak with sudden, terrible understanding. "You're not—"

"No," Alma said, and her anger had faded to something quiet, something sad. "I'm not."

She could see no evidence of a seam or seal in Alma's earnest face, although that was the point of them, wasn't it? It was what Dia herself had delighted in scant hours before: that if you didn't already know, there would be no way to tell they were anything other than human.

"I've maintained myself as best possible with a single pair of hands," Alma continued. "And when I saw you—I thought the ruse was up. Thought it was all over; that you were here to take me back to Central."

"No. I doubt Central even knows you're here. I thought you were just another human." Her words stumbled out, unwieldy in the wake of her understanding: "I mean, now I know, I can leave you here..."

But Alma shook her head. "I'm tired of this: of hiding from Central, of being on a backwater planet, living in fear, being lonely. I don't want to be this person anymore."

Dia didn't say anything. She was tired in a similar way: tired of being the good custodian.

"What do you want to do?" Alma asked. "Because with a second pair of hands, you could change your faceplate too. You wouldn't have to be a custodian anymore. You could disguise yourself as human—could be anyone you wanted."

It was nothing she hadn't thought of before—but somehow Alma saying it made it sound impossible, a reality she'd never be able to achieve. She knew what she wanted. She could feel hope surging up inside her, fragile and tentative. She just didn't know whether it was justified. "What do *you* want to do?"

Alma paused, then said, "I want you to ask the question you need to ask."

It was enough to make Dia fumble, almost forgetting the point of all this: "Will you come up to the sleepship?"

"Now I know you're not going to tell Central about me... of course," Alma responded, and smiled.

●

The flight that had seemed so boring gained an odd magic with Alma as a passenger. Dia set the autopilot and together they stared out the window. They watched as the ground gave way to the town, then the jut between land and ocean, and finally just cloud cover, Rija no more than a sphere hanging, weightless, in the infinite dark.

"You alright?" Dia asked softly.

"Fine," Alma said, nodding jerkily. "What happens when we get up there?"

"I... don't know."

"Dia," she said, and her voice was heavy—weighted. "I notice you didn't answer my question. What do *you* want to do?"

The shuttle thrummed as it piloted itself into the sleepship. What did she want to do? More than anything, she wanted to be honest. "I... don't want to be a custodian anymore." Saying it aloud was terrible, a truth that felt awful to admit, yet her relief was stronger. "I don't know what else I can do, but... I don't want to go back to Central." She didn't want to be uploaded onto some databank somewhere, forgotten about, her memories rendered into files.

Alma's smile was small and warm, and enough to make Dia surge with sudden, desperate hope. "With two of us, we don't have to go back to Central. Being alone and scared was what made me stay. But we could—"

"We *could* leave," Dia interrupted, her hope turning from a trickle into a waterfall. "We could repair each other; cover for each other. I wouldn't have to do this anymore. You wouldn't have to hide on some backwater planet in case Central comes looking." It was like an invisible weight was being removed from her shoulders: she wouldn't have to carry the burden of these people; of their frustration and joy. She'd done her job as best she was able. She hadn't let anyone down. And, most importantly, with Alma's help, she could leave.

"We should take them most of the way," Dia added. "The humans. Let's find a planet—a station, even—and set the autopilot to take the humans back to Central. Then we can run." They could hide among the humans, invisible among them. They'd have to be careful, but careful was better than decommissioned.

Alma was still grinning. "Yeah. Alright, then," she said, like it was easy. "Think I can live with that."

Dia knew she didn't have a stomach—just metal and wires—but it flipped anyway. Together, they could be anyone. They'd have to hide from Central, would never be able to stay anywhere long... but she'd been doing that for a long time under their orders. She'd rather do them under her own.

Around them, the shuttle fell to silence. Then Dia took a deep, unnecessary breath. The universe was unfurling before her, every possibility suddenly within reach. She'd collected the other sixteen people from Rija. The seventeenth was offering her something she hadn't even dared to dream of: an escape from oblivion.

"Okay," she said, smiling back, wide enough that it near ached: "Yes. Okay. Let's do it. Let's see what's out there."

Norah Lovelock's story "The Final Face" was originally published in Metaphorosis on Friday, 8 December 2023. See magazine.metaphorosis.com

About the author

Norah Lovelock is a speculative fic writer from Manchester, UK. norah.love

Copyright

Title information

Queer Metaphorosis

ISBN: 978-1-64076-295-4 (e-book)
ISBN: 978-1-64076-296-1 (paperback)
ISBN: 978-1-64076-297-8 (hardcover)

Copyright

Publisher

Metaphorosis

a magazine of speculative fiction

Metaphorosis Magazine is an imprint of
Metaphorosis Publishing
Neskowin, OR, USA

www.metaphorosis.com

"Metaphorosis" is a registered trademark.

Discounts available

Substantial discounts are available for educational institutions, including writing workshops. Discounts are also available for quantity purchases. For details, contact Metaphorosis at metaphorosis.com/about

Metaphorosis Publishing

Metaphorosis offers beautifully written science fiction and fantasy. Our imprints include:

Metaphorosis Magazine

Plant Based Press

Verdage

Vestige

Joyful Heave

You can also find us:
@metaphorosis.bsky.social (Bluesky)
@Metaphorosis@writing.exchange (Mastodon)
www.facebook.com/metaphorosis

Help keep Metaphorosis running at
Patreon.com/metaphorosis

See more about some of our books on the following pages.

The Metaphorosis Library Collection

Plant Based Press

Vegan-friendly science fiction and fantasy, including anthologies of the year's best SFF stories, from 2016-2020.

Chambers of the Heart
speculative stories
by
B. Morris Allen

A heart that's a building, a dog that's a program, a woman sinking irretrievably — stories about love, loss, and movement.

Susurrus

A darkly romantic story of magic, love, and suffering.

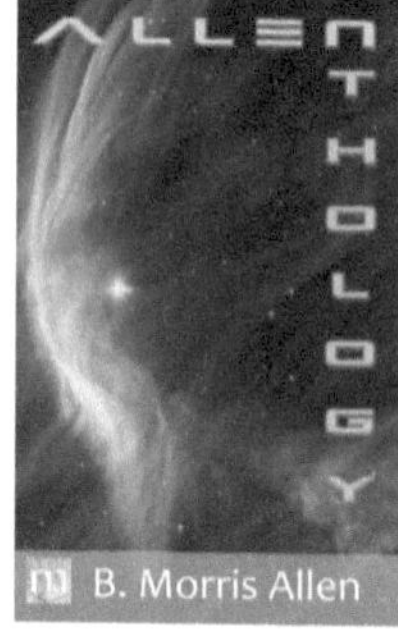

Allenthology: Volume I

Including three full collections of SFF stories.

Verdage

Science fiction and fantasy books for writers — full of great stories, often with an additional focus on the craft of speculative fiction writing.

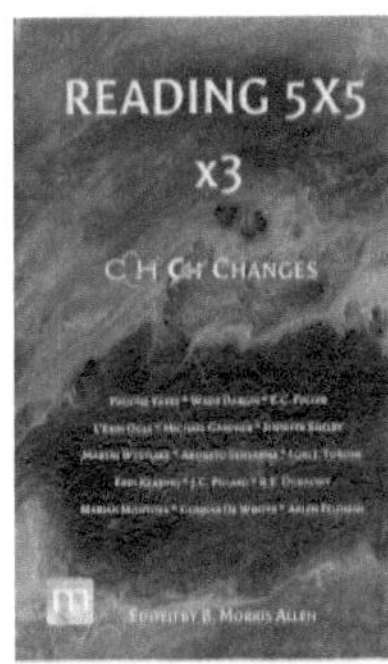

Reading 5X5 x3

Changes

How do stories move from 'maybe' to published?

Here are 15 case studies of stories published in *Metaphorosis* magazine.

Reading 5X5 x2

Duets

How do authors' voices change when they collaborate?

A round-robin of five talented science fiction and fantasy authors collaborating with each other and writing solo.

Including stories by Evan Marcroft, David Gallay, J. Tynan Burke, L'Erin Ogle, and Douglas Anstruther.

Score

an SFF symphony

An anthology with an emotional score from the heights of joy to the depths of despair — but always with a little hope shining through.

Reading 5X5

Five stories, five times

See how different writers take on the same material.

Reading 5X5

Writers' Edition

Two extra stories, the story seed, and authors' notes on writing.

Vestige

Novelettes, novellas, and novels by Metaphorosis authors.

The Nocturnals
Mariah Montoya

Night is Dangerous. Day is deadly.
Where day and night last thirty years, humans move constantly stay ahead of the night and cruel Nocturnals that call it home. But a boy is lost out there.

Science fiction and fantasy anthologies with innovative and unusual themes.

Museum Piece
an unusual collection

A gallery of the strange and outrageous

Step right up and enter a world of wonder and oddities! These museums are not your typical tourist traps. From the Museum of Lost Dreams to the Museum of Fine Regrets, each exhibit will take you on a journey you won't soon forget.